THE
RHODES
READER

THE
RHODES
READER

Stories of VIRGINS, VILLAINS,
and VARMINTS

by Eugene Manlove Rhodes

Selected by W. H. Hutchinson

NORMAN: UNIVERSITY OF OKLAHOMA PRESS

By W. H. Hutchinson

The Little World Waddies (editor) (Chico, California, 1946)

A Notebook of the Old West (Chico, California, 1947)

One Man's West (Chico, California, 1948)

Another Notebook of the Old West (Chico, California, 1954)

*A Bar Cross Man: The Life and Personal Writings of
Eugene Manlove Rhodes* (Norman, 1956)

The Rhodes Reader (editor) (Norman, 1957)

Oil, Land, and Politics: The California Career of Thomas Robert Bard
(2 vols., Norman, 1965)

Library of Congress Catalog Card Number: 57-11196

New edition copyright 1957 by the University of Oklahoma Press,
Publishing Division of the University.
First edition, November, 1957.
Second printing, December, 1960.
Third printing, June, 1966.
Manufactured in the U.S.A.

FOR F. BOURN HAYNE

in lieu of words

Virgins, Villains, and Varmints

W. H. Hutchinson

A MAN WHO HAD PUNCHED COWS in the Raft River country and then in the Sand Hills as a youth opened an essay in *Harper's* with this sentence: "A literary critic can discuss detective stories without being called before the board of governors, but the even more popular form of packaged fiction called the Western appears to be off limits." It is considered possible that Bernard DeVoto knew somewhat of what he wrote.[1] Behind his simple statement is the solid fact that the "western" has been dismissed by literary critics, sociologists, and certified historians of the American scene as an error of popular taste. No claim is made to any Brahmin caste-mark in what follows.

The basis for this venture is the same as the basis for a backraise on two small pair after the draw—personal opinion. This opinion has been formed over a lively lifetime as the writer has read "westerns," first as an avocation and for the last decade as vocational guidance. The difference is the same as that between keeping a mistress and being married.

[1] "Phaëthon on Gunsmoke Trail," December, 1954.

In the first instance, you read for the *what* of the story, thus helping the author to sustain the illusion of reality. In the second, you read for the *how* of the story, that you may learn what the author can teach you about "grabbing the reader by the throat and giving it to him while his eyes pop."[2] This may seem a peculiar exercise. It is essential if we are to comprehend one reason why the "western" has been the bar sinister on any American literary escutcheon for some years past.[3]

Hand in hand with this exercise goes a study of the title of this piece, the same title that was used to announce the seminar on which it is based.[4] It seems highly probable that the title, of itself, induced a larger attendance at that seminar than would have been the case had it been announced as a study of "Vulgar Caricatures of Hegelian World Historical Personalities in a Genre of American Popular Fiction."

The basic fact about the "western" has been overlooked consistently, perhaps deliberately, by those who overlook it. It was and is written for the same reason that all other popular fiction—Dickens, Stevenson, Conrad, Hemingway, and Faulkner not excepted—was and is written: to provide entertainment for the reader and economic well-being, or a facsimile thereof, for the writer. The "western" was and is a commercial product, a standard brand of merchandise for which the customers ask by name—Brand, Drago, Ernenwein, Fox, Foreman, Grey, Haycox, McDonald, Raine, Short. And when the customers—first editors, then readers—ask for a "western," what do they mean?

Depending upon the capillary attraction of the individual, the western-libel may encompass anything from John Ledyard's influence upon Thomas Jefferson down to the latest issue of *Powder-*

[2] Attributed to Jack Lait, New York *Daily Mirror.*

[3] The Western Writers of America have as their goal the improvement of the literary caliber of the "western" and its acceptance on the same plane as other forms of native writing.

[4] The first draft of this essay was an oral seminar by the author during his work in the Rhodes Collection at the Huntington Library. A prose version appeared in the Huntington Library *Quarterly*, August, 1953, and my thanks are due that inspiriting workplace and Dr. French Fogle, editor, for permission to revise, expand, and improve that version for inclusion here.

A certain vestigial honesty compels the admission that the title is not mine own creation. Mr. Thomas B. Clark used it first in *American Heritage*, Spring, 1952, for his article on Beadle's dime novels.

Other than this conveyance, the essay is mine own save where footnotes indicate my obligations.

smoke Yarns in the local newsstand. The Fur Trade, Gold Rushes, Overlanders, Indians, Cavalry, the whole complex of Bernard De-Voto's "theme of wonder" can be lumped as "westerns." For our purposes here, the epithet covers but one segment of this complex, the last one in time—the Cowboy–Free Range–Horseback era—told in fiction form in its primary colors of black-and-white and blood-on-the-saddle; "horse opera," the "oater" of Hollywood.

The parents of this stylized art form can be limned with broad strokes of an opinionated brush. Maternal genes and chromosomes came from the timeless womb that has produced the sun god for all ages and all peoples; a blood link to El Cid, Taras Bulba, Robin Hood, and, more recently, Davy Crockett, *redivivus*. The American line of descent can be traced from the writings and editings of Timothy Flint, specifically in the narrative of James Ohio Pattie, through the frontier-Gothic romances of Fenimore Cooper and Mayne Reid to the "yellowbacks"—Col. Prentiss Ingraham and Ned Buntline for ready references—that took over about the time of Fort Sumter and held the field until the turn of the century. This ancestral strain received an incestuous infusion from the buckskin extravaganzas of Buffalo Bill Cody, and this infusion is sustained today by innumerable arena performances by professional *road-eeo* cowboys who could not unroll their beds in an old-time cow camp and would not want to.

The paternity of the "western" may seem as obscure as the sire of a bastard calf on the open range, but such is not the case. Humor is the father of the "western" as we know it: the half-horse and half-alligator tall tales of the *Davy Crockett Almanacs* which the grotesqueries and conventions of Bret Harte fixed in our literary tapestry. Mark Twain, too, had a part in this, as did O. Henry, while Henry Wallace Phillips and Alfred Henry Lewis brought it to its full and fleeting peak.[5] The most recent manifestations of this unalloyed ancestral strain have been the "Painting Pistoleer" yarns by Walker Tompkins in *Zane Grey's Western Magazine*, recently deceased, and the "Buffalo Bend" stories by Michael Fessier [Foster] in *Saturday Evening Post*.[6]

[5] Take the word *which* in Harte's "Truthful James" and compare it with the same word usage in Lewis's *Wolfville* by his "Old Cattleman." Like finding a drowned cat in the cream jug.

[6] Michael Foster died while this was being written. S. Omar Barker is the only major writer in the field today who consistently uses humor in its olden application and its primeval style.

The offspring of these parents made its first faltering steps as a respectable member of the "outdoor-action" story that made a fair share of the contents of such magazines as *Munsey's*, *McClure's*, *Everybody's* and *Scribner's* during the late 1890's with writers like Jack London, Stewart Edward White, Joseph Conrad, Rex Emerson Beach, J. Olivier Curwood, and Will Levington Comfort.[7] The discernible "westerns" in this period, by Phillips, Owen Wister, White, and O. Henry, were not yet tinged with the tar brush. They were treated as just another face in the "outdoor-action" school, and, as such, they received a fair amount of both space and attention in the current literary journals and supplements. This meed of recognition, this inclusion in the fold of American letters, continued for the first decade of this century as the "western" began to take its final, fatal shape—*The Virginian*, 1902; *Chip of the Flying U*, 1905; *Whispering Smith*, 1906; *Bar-20*, 1907; *Hopalong Cassidy* and *Bucky O'Connor*, 1910.[8] For an opinion, the demarcation comes in 1912 with a book whose closing and most memorable phrase was "Roll the stone! . . . Lassiter I love you!"

Riders of the Purple Sage not only gave Zane Grey his first taste of success after four unremunerative novels, it ushered in the "western" as we know it. It should be pointed out that, in this book, Grey was ahead of himself, far ahead of the art form he did so much to implant in the consciousness of generations of readers, in the significance of his closing phrase above. When Lassiter did roll that rock, he and the beauteous heroine were sealed in a hidden valley, presumably for all time, with no clergyman in their past, present, or foreseeable future. This was a daring departure from the morals of the current "outdoor-action" school. It was made palatable by the dread alternative in the plot that the heroine otherwise would wind up as a Mormon plural. This, in itself, affords a striking comment on the polygamy propaganda residue in the national psyche, but as a literary convention it did not take. The basic ingredients that Grey borrowed bodily from *The Virginian*, rejecting Wister's still discernible humor, and beat to a froth in *Riders of the Purple Sage* have remained unchanged in essence ever since—virgins, villains, and varmints.

---

[7] Beach and Curwood are shown as their by-lines of that period.

[8] Wister, Bower, Spearman, Mulford, and Raine in order of titles. Harold Bell Wright probably belongs in here, but enough is enough.

Woman in the "western" was a sawdust doll, and the tags used to depict her character were obvious. If she wore calico or gingham, had hair to her waist when the braids "accidentally" came unwound, possessed a clear complection and lustrous eyes, she was *good*—lineal descendant of Ouida's idealized English maidens genteelly skirting the whirlpool of life—and the hero would get his just reward in the end by claiming her hand. If she wore tights, or spangles, and worked in a saloon, she was *bad* and was doomed to a miserable end—either as an accomplice of the villain or as a lone figure stumbling off into scorching sun or numbing blizzard, with only her thoughts of what might have been for protection. Occasionally, she was given the chance to lead a better life—Hereafter.

Women are not that simple, as any fool or fictioneer should know by experience. In a sense, however, there were only two classes of women in the free range days and everybody knew where they stood, which made for an unembarrassed social life all around. Women in the "western" were not typical of their sex at large any more than the libidinous neurotics or man-eating viragos who populate today's fiction are typical. Their appearances in the "western" made it easier for the reader to concentrate on the action-plot without getting petticoats in his mind and thus complicating the author's task.

If the "western" villain leered and drooled, he was a *heavy* villain, whose slavering approach to the heroine, or to the material crux of the plot, was easily predictable. His end was a matter of physical violence, honorable on the hero's part, generally fatal. If he dressed like a parson or gambler, he was a *sneaky* villain to be dealt with, after unmasking, even as the sidewinder who rattles not or if he does cannot be heard. Along with these two categories of Anglo-Saxon menace there was the Mexican or anyone with swarthy skin, flashing teeth, and silver-studded costume. These characters were *always* cast as villains, major or minor, until the rise of the Good Neighbor Policy, and even the hint of one such in a story line was an automatic signal for the reader to mark him well for justice. This type-casting of the *hombre del país* can be attributed to the Texas influence on the folk-ways of the free range, or it can be traced to a residual fear of the Spanish Armada and the Inquisition. In either case, *Westward Ho* presages the role the Spaniard and his New World descendants were foreordained to play in the "western" story.

As to the varmints in the "western," they were largely incidental props. Coyote, lion, bear, deer, antelope, snake, sheep, sheepherder, Indian, *cañon, malpaís, mesquite,* blizzard, drought, and desert were inserted as needed by the demands of the plot. Properly classed among these varmints, for an opinion, was the *hero.* No breed of men ever won the West or lifted a mortgage against such odds and to such little purpose. Not even Francis X. Aubry ever rode so far so fast without saddle boils or a played-out horse. They could fast like a *fakir,* water-out like a camel, win the *good* girl, spurn the *bad* girl, destroy the villain, absorb punishment like a Marine Corps legend, and do it all while overburdened with forty pounds of assorted hardware, mostly lethal. It would be nice to be like that—which is what the author intended you to feel.[9]

Despite the obvious literary defects of two-dimensional characters, of insistence on action-plot, of exaggerated use of horses, hardship, idiom, and costume, the "western" grabbed an audience from the start. *Riders of the Purple Sage* sold over one million copies; *When a Man's a Man* sold eight hundred thousand copies; during World War I, His Majesty's Government purchased half a million copies of William MacLeod Raine's novels for distribution to the troops. When that war ended, the rising tide of *chili con carnage* became a flood, even as the spate of so-called magazines for men, *Male, Saga, Mr. America, ad nauseam,* afflicts us today.

On the crest of this tidal wave were the pulp paper magazines—looked down upon by any and every right-thinking literary person, carrying little advertising and that of the truss-and-goitre type, but serving the reading needs of millions and requiring more original material at better rates than is the case today, unfortunately. This was the golden age for writers of "westerns"—*Argosy* was a weekly, consuming some six million words of new material a year, *Adventure* appeared thrice-monthly, needing four million words of fuel per annum, while *Short Story* and *Blue Book,* among others, were in this bracket. These *books* were balanced as to contents, but they used a goodly proportion of "westerns" both in their 60/90,000-word lead stories and in their shorts and fillers. Over and above these were the

---

[9] One further stylization is worth noting. The sheep *vs.* cattle animosity provides the plot for many a yarn. Yet, it is extremely hard to find an authentic portrayal of the sheer, animalistic brutality involved in a sheep slaughter. Such deeds do not sort with the *caballero's* way.

strictly "western story" magazines, apparently limited only by the press capacity of the nation and their editors' ability to find material.

Added to these predominantly masculine books in the mid-twenties was *Ranch Romances*, pioneer in the "western love" story where the formula "western" was told from the heroine's point of view to provide self-identification for women readers with the story line and plot. Additional demand for "westerns" swelled from Hollywood, where box-office float had been discovered with Broncho Billy Anderson and then traced to the mother lode with Fred Thompson, William S. Hart, Harry Carey, Tom Mix, Jack Hoxie, Hoot Gibson, *et al.*, *et seq.*

With demand established, supply came posthaste as in any commodity market. Using either the peak-and-valley technique or the steadily rising curve, depending on story length desired and the prospective editor's known foibles, using very basic plots with only the skill of the wordsmith to make dialog, character tags, costumes, and settings appear untarnished, the production of "westerns" became a lucrative business. William MacLeod Raine produced two novels a year for twenty-five years, besides short stories and articles. His popularity was so great that his English publishers bought his manuscripts sight unseen and, so Raine purportedly believed, did not bother to read them before printing. But Raine was a volumetric piker in the "western" game.

There were many men riding the typewriter range who could produce half a million to a million words a year, all salable. One of the best of them, nameless here because of friendship, had a blackboard in his office on which he kept four story outlines going simultaneously, using two secretaries and a dictating machine because he was conducting a successful advertising agency on the side. Harry Sinclair Drago used several aliases, "Bliss Lomax" and "Will Ermine," and it was not unusual for a writer to make the same issue of a magazine with two stories or more, by this judicious use of his aliases, which, also, came in handy to spread his output among several hard-cover publishers. For the classical example, there can be no better choice than the "Old Master of Thud and Blunder," the twentieth century's Sir Walter Scott, Frederick Schiller Faust, who wanted to be a quill-pen poet.[10] In his writing career, 1917–44, he produced over thirty million words under a baker's dozen of names, three of

---

[10] Faust was killed on the Italian front as a war correspondent in 1944.

which, at least, were reserved for his "western" output—"Evan Evans," "Peter Dawson," and "Max Brand." This productive tradition has not suffered. A current practitioner in the field is reputed by *Publishers' Weekly* to bypass conventional methods and compose his "westerns" directly for the press by means of a linotype.

This variant of automation is one of the few major changes in the "western" since *Riders of the Purple Sage*. This statement is made with full benefit of Seth M. Agnew's opinion (*Saturday Review*, March 14, 1953) that ". . . throughout the field, there is an undoubted trend away from the pattern. There is more attention paid to historical accuracy and mood. There is a realization, as one author put it, that the gun that could fire and does not has more suspense than a dozen corpses. The standard western, however, has not been abandoned entirely. But it has been upgraded." The major changes in the "western" since Grey poured the mould have concerned women. If this be upgrading, let us make the most of it.

One significant change was the rise in the pulp field of the "western love" magazines for which *Ranch Romances* showed the way and, thus, kept many a writer of "westerns" from direct starvation. These books made possible a story element which Alan Bosworth calls "Sally's Sweater." The story opening introduces the heroine galloping across the range, or swaying to the motion of a buckboard, with ample varbiage devoted to the inevitable movement of her second-skin sateen blouse. The story problem, setting, and characters are quickly introduced, and then back to Sally's Sweater. Whenever the action lags, this handy *divertissement* flogs it up again. By and large, it is as close as the formula "western" has come towards permitting raw sex to get in the way of action.

The other change has occurred in the slick-paper magazines, where, it should be noted, the writer can expect more help than in the pulps from both editors and readers in closing the gap between what he means when he writes and what they get when they read. Ernest Haycox pioneered this change and Luke Short is now its ablest exponent.[11] This departure from the norm involves the use of two women: one *good* but suspect of either evil or primitive passion, the other *bad* but so suspect of do-to-ride-the-river-with-

---

[11] Frederick D. Glidden uses the name "Luke Short"; another skillful exponent of this school, Jonathan Glidden, uses the old Faust pseudonym, "Peter Dawson."

virtues that the hero spends a lot of his time and the readers' time trying to suppress his hormones and get his sense of values back on the *good* standard. The use of the two-woman angle introduced something of the psychological suspense narrative into the "western" formula which, heretofore, depended upon simple issues and direct decisions with conclusive consequences—all stemming from direct action, generally physical, by the protagonist.

It is easy to dismiss the "western" as escape trash, and it has been dismissed in this wise ever since it engulfed literary people in the twenties. It is not so easy to dismiss the fact that for some forty-five years the "western" has held and enhanced the audience it grabbed. The Council of Books in Wartime published over 1,300 titles in Editions for the Armed Services; 160 of these, the largest identifiable bloc, were "westerns." The last count at my local newsstand showed thirty-odd exclusively "western" pulps together with five "western love" magazines. Cursory notes indicate that 200 "westerns" appeared in book form in 1951, 213 in 1952, and at least 114 original "westerns" in 1953. The "western" accounted for 16 per cent of all the varnish-covered paperback reprints in 1951, and a personal count of the nearest revolving wire-rack emporium will prove there has been no diminution. In point of fact, the paperback book, in both original and reprint editions, has been a massive shot in the arm for the "western."

Other evidence as to the sustained appeal of the "western" comes from a count of the "comic" books that are built around past or current heroes of the Hollywood "western." This leads logically to the number of "westerns" released, or re-released annually by Hollywood. It invites tabulation of the number of "western" radio scripts aired annually and leads, inevitably, to the ubiquitous presence of "Cheyenne," "Wyatt," "Wild Bill Hickok," "Hop-along," *et al.*, in the bat-cave called television.

Other evidence concerning the "western" comes from a highly improbable source. M. Jean Paul Sartre's existentialist monthly, *Les Temps Modernes*, has dubbed *Shane* ". . . that nostalgic outlaw of a Racine-like modesty." And a body of serious French appraisal of the "western" in film form apparently has equated it with *le jazz hot* as our finest native flowering. A Swedish critic, Harry Schein, writing in *The American Scholar*, has termed *High Noon* ". . . the most convincing and, likewise, certainly the most honest explanation of

American foreign policy." He says, too, "The pistol in westerns is by now accepted as a phallic symbol." *"Methinks yon Cassius,"* *etc.*, but if there be reason with this foreign accolade for the "western movie," some of it must rub off on the "western story" from which the horse-operas were and are derived. It is worth noting, too, that the "western" story long has been one of our most stable and staple exports, with foreign editions in tongues amounting to Babel.[12]

The popular appeal of the "western" seems destined to endure until the last fragmentary memory of our last, wholly-owned frontier, "the Cattle Kingdom" defined by Walter Prescott Webb, has been obliterated from our national consciousness. The question naturally arises as to what legacy of letters the "western" has caused to bloom amidst the piled compost of its millions of words. The question is not easy to answer.[13] Any arrogation of omnipotence brings to mind the advice given by an old-timer to a cow camp button: "Son, I wouldn't set that kerosene on the stove. It ain't judicious." Some of the best of it has been preserved by anthologists, which is another way of saying by personal opinion, the same criterion that has governed that which follows.

The surest craftsmanship, the most assimilable prose, has been achieved by men who did with words what Frederick Remington did for the western scene with another medium—capture it from the "outside-in." They combined a surpassing mastery of craft with extraordinarily detailed knowledge to produce "westerns" that are exercises in intellectual analysis rather than immediacies of human experience. Ernest Haycox, Luke Short, Peter Dawson the Latter, T. T. Flynn, L. L. Foreman, Les Savage, Jr., and Norman Fox, for examples, all unquestionably are fine craftsmen writing fine fiction —giving their readers the meat in the coconut without the labor of husking it. They know more about what their audience wants than that audience knows or wants to know about the same. If they did not know this, they would be wasting their time, their agents' time, and the time of many editors, which leads to an inconvenient short-

[12] German editions of Zane Grey are found in the Lenin Library, Moscow.

[13] Jeff C. Dykes tried it in *The Brand Book* (Chicago "Westerners," September, 1955), for the period 1902–52. He covered a great deal more of the Western scene than just the "western" of this opinionated piece. The longest attempt was made by Joe B. Frantz and Julian E. Choate, Jr., in *The American Cowboy* (Norman, 1955).

ness of tempers all around and brings the writer down with creeping poliomyelitis of the exchequer. In this knowledge of market wants, needs, or preconceptions, they are doing precisely what Bret Harte did when he wrote his stories amidst the urbanities of San Francisco for the Eastern readers of whom he had been one. That these men wrote, are still writing, "westerns" from the "outside-in" cannot cause their work to be dismissed—there comes to mind no *good* book about the North Pole written by an Eskimo. That some of these authors, like Haycox, disliked horses and most things Western, that others, like Max Brand, actively loathed them, cannot mitigate the fact that the "outside-inners" have written the best entertainment and employed the finest craftsmanship in the "western" field.

The truest legacies in the "western" field have been left by men who did with prose what Charles M. Russell did with another medium—capture the free range days from the "inside-out." Several of these men were outsiders who knew their craft before they absorbed the West by a process of mental and spiritual osmosis that vitally affected the stature of their work. Others were insiders-born who learned their trade and used it to give their birthright meaning.

Owen Wister, "a Pennsylvanian writing about a Virginian in Montana," seems to have made the first genuine contribution to American literature with *The Virginian*. It seems from here that Wister started out to write another story of humor in a Western setting and suffered a range-change that produced the strong, silent "When-you-call-me-that—smile!" hero. There are skeletal remains of the Johnson County War, which Wister learned about from first-hand participants, in this book, and the evolution of *The Virginian* from *Lin McLean* and *The Jimmy John Boss* may rest on this excavated evidence. It has been ably shown by DeVoto, J. Frank Dobie, and Walter Prescott Webb that Wister was the first to distill certain essential oils from the free range days and bottle them for market in fiction form. Coming off the presses in April, 1902, *The Virginian* went through six printings in six weeks, sixteen printings inside its first year. The stage version ran for ten years, in New York and on the road, and at least three versions have been perpetrated by Hollywood.[14]

14 It made money for its author, a new and wholly agreeable Wisterian experience, thus meeting the test of certain moderns that if your "westerns" don't make money, you ain't writing "westerns."

xvii

Andy Adams must be included on any list, although applying the term fiction to Adams's solid narratives seems pure courtesy. His books are constructed of the minutiae of daily working life on the range and up the trail, all artifacts and properties included, as meticulously as Luis Ortega braids *la reata* from strings that he has prepared himself. You have only to read *The Log of a Cowboy* in comparison with Emerson Hough's *North of 36* to taste the difference.

Stewart Edward White has certain short stories, most of them in *Arizona Nights* and the best of them involving Señor Buck Clark, that deserve to live in any critical appraisal of the "western."

W. C. Tuttle, a volumetric producer for many years, created three characters, Sad Sontag, Hashknife Hartley, and Sleepy Stephens, around whom he built some hundreds of yarns, the best of which are in the great tradition of salty humor and credible action. The radio series that Tuttle, himself, adapted from his stories afforded what one set of ears considers the finest audio or video "western" ever offered an undiscerning public.

George Patullo, who went up like a skyrocket in the "western" hierarchy and then exploded with inherited affluence, left some short stories to mark his passage and keep his name alive. His "Off the Trail" (*McClure's*, March 3, 1912) will grab your guts and twist them tight today, and his 1911 collection, *The Untamed*, has preserved "Corazón," which may well be the finest story about a horse ever written.

Eugene Cunningham, one of the finest literary mechanics to work the "western" field, has set down the West Texas–Mexican border country of his raising in novels that possess but one flaw—his lapidary skill at preparing a piece of merchandise for the market place. His latest, *Riding Gun*, appearing in 1956 after an absence from print of some fifteen years, can be used as a text for comparison with the contemporary school of the "western." The difference is that between a vigorous and genuine *ocotillo* and an equally vigorous but hybridized and cultivated flat-leaf succulent. It is quite probable, however, that the nuances and subtleties of shading in Cunningham's characterizations will be lost on a generation conditioned to having their characters ride the range as hag-ridden as was ever Hamlet.[15]

[15] Ernest Haycox has been credited with introducing the Hamlet strain into

Regardless of the merits of the foregoing selection, the contributions of the authors mentioned, excluding Wister and Adams, have been lumped with the rest of the "westerns," good, bad, and indifferent, that have made the genre. The same dismissal has been applied to the last name on my personal list, and in no case is the margin of error greater than in thus evaluating the writings of Eugene Manlove Rhodes.

Insofar as the public and the critics generally were concerned in his lifetime, Rhodes wrote "westerns." There was one exception to this critical dismissal and a most notable one, Bernard DeVoto, who had known the cowpuncher world as a youth and then had let his cultivated mind play upon that world, upon all the facets of the land he loved, with the genius of gusto given to but few. His regard for Rhodes, as man and man of letters, abided with him for many, many years. Since DeVoto possessed another rare quality—the capacity for rounded maturity—his published appraisals of Rhodes gain added weight.

In 1938, he termed Rhodes' stories: ". . . the only embodiment on the level of art of one segment of American experience. They are the only body of fiction devoted to the cattle kingdom which is both true to it and written by an artist in prose."[16]

In 1954, he said again: "Back in 1938 I pointed out that only Gene Rhodes had succeeded in making first-rate fiction out of the cattle business. The statement still stands but the argument would be tighter if Mr. Walter Van Tilburg Clark had not meanwhile published an excellent novel called *The Oxbow Incident.* . . . But Mr. Clark's subject is the mob spirit that leads to a lynching. So his scene might be almost anywhere and though he uses a few stage properties from horse opera, he uses none of its sentiments or traditions." In this same piece, he says of the "western": ". . . it was turned into the path that has led to its present solemnity by its one novelist, Rhodes, and by the fabulists Harold Bell Wright and Zane Grey."[17]

In 1955, in one of the last pieces turned out before his death,

---

the sun-god ancestry. In Mayne Reid's frontier-Gothic romances, you can find the Hamlet strain as pronounced as in anything by Haycox, Schafer, Short, *et al.;* specifically, *The Scalp Hunters,* where Reid made a wondrous switch of James Kirker's name and character.

[16] "The Novelist of the Cattle Kingdom," in *The Hired Man on Horseback* (Boston, 1938).

[17] "Phaëthon on Gunsmoke Trail," *Harper's* (December, 1955).

DeVoto devoted himself to a discussion of Owen Wister, his literary origins and the resultant birth of the "western." Speaking herein of *The Virginian*, he summed up his case for Gene Rhodes: "The cowboy story has seldom produced anything as good; apart from Gene Rhodes, it has not even tried to do anything different."[18]

It is comforting to have such a buttress as Bernard DeVoto for purely personal opinions, comforting because it is Rhodes as a precursor of, and practitioner concurrent with, the virgins-villains-varmints school who requires detailed examination.

In the women in his stories, and the best of them have no women whatsoever, Rhodes is at his worst, and that is worse than any other man of stature in the "western" field. If his women are young women, they are passionately and infrangibly virginal, and his heroes move like marionettes in their presence. It is extremely hard to find even the suspicion of a *bad* woman in all his writings; he had known them, *seguro que si!*, but they had no place in his fiction. Occasionally, an older woman appears fleetingly in his stories after years of frontier abrasion have made her road-weary. Only when this happens is Rhodes' feminine cast at all credible.

In portraying his villains, Rhodes veered wildly from the formula. *Imprimis*, he never cast his villains by the color of their skin. If he has the Hispanic New Mexican in a villainous role, it is because his prototype was that in life. Rhodes' Anglo villains are both *heavy* and *sneaky*, as heretofore defined, but they are that because they were that in life, and whatever category they fit makes but a part of Rhodes' villainous whole—the sons of Mary. His true villains are always those who did not work with their hands—bankers, merchants, lawyers, *políticos*—and who profited, grew swollen and fat, on the lives of those who did work with their hands for daily bread and conquered the frontier while doing it. It would have been easier by far to two-dimensionalize these characters, but Rhodes went to infinite pains in his story construction to show how these villains of his were parasites at the breasts of the country that had nurtured him. He did this because it was true to his experience, true to his country and his people. In doing it, he limned in fiction the salient truth about the west-that-was—a truth unrecognized, over-

[18] "Birth of an Art," *Harper's* (December, 1955). The first two chapters of DeVoto's unfinished book would have discussed the "western" probably beyond further need. This piece has benefited from an exchange of opinions with Mr. DeVoto on the subject before his death.

looked, and neglected for many years by the serious scholars—the truth that the West was the captive, exploited province of the financial, political, and industrial East.

It is only when Rhodes has his villain a proper Easterner that said villain becomes incredible. This is not due to the characterization or motivation of that villain but to the affected mannerisms given him and to his speech.

Indeed, it is the speech he gives to his characters from Western life—a speech far removed from the idiom of the "western"—that has led many critics, and not a few true Rhodesians, to feel that Gene Rhodes' fictional cowboys all talked like Gene Rhodes. There is some truth to this feeling. Rhodes recognized his tendency when he used pages 65–67 of *Bransford in Arcadia* to explain the availability of classical literature to his cow persons through the medium of Bull Durham coupons that were negotiable for volumes in Munro's Library of Popular Novels. Rhodes was a reader, an omnivorous reader, all of his life, devouring everything that came his way even unto *The Congressional Record*. The brave-talking heroes of Sir Walter Scott's fiction almost ruined him. He revered Shakespeare and Conrad, and he felt that Stevenson and Kipling had used the English language more skillfully than any others. So his cowboys' speech is pricked with allusions and larded with classical quotations. Yet, he had real-life examples in Bill Barbee, the Texan who revelled in *Richard III*, in Aloys Priesser, the Bavarian chemist of Engle, in Henri Touissant, the *Jornada* pioneer whose library contained the world's classics. There were others, but these three will do to point this premise: if T. S. Eliot in his plays has made his county, or country-bred, English families oversubtle in their appreciation of English literature, so much and no more can be charged against Gene Rhodes and his riders of the stars. He gave an idealized depiction, in fine prose, of men who had the language within themselves but who lacked the idiom of their readers to say it themselves, in life, in such wise.

When it comes to the varmints in his stories, Rhodes again veered wildly from the formula under discussion. You have only to compare the horses in his yarns—Wisenose, Brown Jug, Buck, Cry Baby, and Abou Ben Adam—with the horseflesh in other "westerns" to prove the point. The flora and fauna of his chosen country are integral parts of his fiction, as they were of the very lives of the characters he took from life. His people are what they are, do what they do, because of their country, its needs, demands, and conditionings.

It is the vasty land itself, shimmering in the heat or shrouded in infrequent mists, eroded, dusty, sun-drenched, as implacable and as compelling as the sea, that makes Rhodes' canvas for his portraits of the West-That-Was. Only Walter Van Tilburg Clark can equal the evocative richness of Rhodes' landscapes and both men share the inability to enrich certain of their human types.

It is these major differences, both of accomplishment and shortcoming, from the formula "western," past and present, that give Rhodes his place. There is a reason for these differences, for this place; reason quite apart from the mechanics of prose construction.

No other writer of "westerns," Andy Adams included, encompassed so much living in the trans-Mississippi West they all purported, still purport, to record as did Rhodes. He had had twelve years of prairie and sky in Nebraska and Kansas—wind, grass, drought, blizzards, cyclones, grasshoppers, and green buds swelling in the creek bottoms when spring came—before he came to New Mexico with his father in 1881, "the year that Billy the Kid was killed."

Thereafter, for twenty-five years, he was horse-wrangler, bronc rider, cowboy, miner, wagon freighter, school teacher, road-builder, dishwasher, homesteader, carpenter, water-mason, blacksmith, and rancher who went broke in the losing battle against drought, cow-country interest, and from an uneconomic passion for raising horses in a land where the feral bands were a nuisance.[19]

It is not necessary to live as did Rhodes to write stories about the West, or even "western" stories, as a number of currently prominent practitioners will be happy to tell anyone who cares to write them on the matter. It is the fact that Rhodes *did* live it, that the totality of the free range experience was summated in his personal life, that makes his writings come from the "inside-out," from a deep wellspring of personal experience that was the abiding strength of his life. There is yet another factor in Rhodes' writings that is

[19] It is interesting to note that Rhodes, like Frederic Remington, Charles M. Russell, and Ross Santee, was a horseman and not a cowman. No "cowman right" ever has touched the magic that these four have made. Others may wish to add Will James to this select circle.

lacking from those, like this, written wherever the typewriter is handy.

Rhodes wrote his stories, almost all of them that are worth while, far removed from the country and the life he loved; the country and the life he left because his personal code demanded it. His knowledge was sharpened by the expatriate's longing, deepened by distance, enhanced by the frustrations of his exile. His land and his people came out on paper as the remembered mellow haze of a coal-oil lamp seen shining through the cabin window when the man and his world were young. Yet upon what he wrote, you may, as an archaeologist, depend. The people and the land of six New Mexico counties, Socorro, Sierra, Doña Ana, Lincoln, Otero, and Grant, are preserved for all time in the clear amber of his joyous, dancing, illuminated prose.

If the "western" had not burgeoned as it did, only to wither literarily as the inevitable result of incest, Rhodes might have gained in his lifetime the stature which some now feel is his. Certainly, at the time he started his real career, the competition was tough. Stevenson, Kipling, Conrad, London, Stephen Crane, Rex Beach, Stewart Edward White, all were working the outdoor-action-adventure field on a higher level, of pay and merit, than the dime novel or the emergent forerunners of the pulps. Admittedly, these writers did not specialize in the so-called "western" for which Wister, Hough, Adams, Lewis, and Phillips had made the first rough castings. But, and this is the point to be remembered, everything they did write competed in the editorial market places with Rhodes' fiction. He hit his stride, with his own style and tone and pace, against such competition, and he maintained his place until both his productivity and his critical acclaim were inundated by the tidal wave of "westerns" that crested in the twenties behind Zane Grey's first breaking on the pleasant literary beach staked off by the cognoscenti as their own.

In the rise of "regional" writing in those same twenties, following the blazes of Turner and the steps of Paxson, Rhodes did not seem to qualify, even though New Mexico so claims him today. Certainly, his people, places, and incidents are regional to a degree of being provincial, often happily parochial, while being at the same time universal—meaning anywhere west of the one hundredth meridian and north of a given point. But they were accepted, typed, and dismissed as "westerns." A suitable example comes from the

New York Times Book Review, November 19, 1933, where *The Trusty Knaves* got mentioned under the section-heading, "Western Loot," while Kenneth Roberts' *Rabble in Arms* got the full treatment under a banner head, "An Epic Tale of the American Revolution." Not to disparage Kenneth Roberts, but to make a point, it can be said that *Rabble* contained no more valid history, no more authentic Americana, no more good writing and reading, than did *Knaves.* It did, however, possess one singular advantage. It was laid in a setting that had no built-in connotations to the critical mind.

There is another factor in Rhodes' critical dismissal. His work in the twenties and thirties ran exactly counter to the mainstream of literary acclaim. Implicit in everything Rhodes wrote are the best traditions, values, customs, and morals—the basic philosophy—of the American physical frontier. This sorted poorly with F. Scott Fitzgerald, Mencken, Nathan, Sherwood Anderson, *et al.,* and, most certainly, had little in common with *The Plastic Age, Little Caesar, Black Oxen, Three Soldiers, A Farewell to Arms,* or Judge Ben Lindsey's theories about companionating. For final and conclusive critical damnation, he wrote for the *Saturday Evening Post.*

Rhodes, himself, contributed to his own neglect. He was dismissed by the literati because he allegedly wrote "westerns," but, while his stories gave great satisfaction to *Satevepost* readers, the great reader market for "westerns" never cottoned to them as books. Rhodes was a poet-cowboy, not a cowboy-poet nor even a cowboy-writer, in his love of words and their uses. Only a writer for radio can appreciate exactly how Rhodes, remembering the tales he had heard in his youth, wrote to fire his readers' minds through their ears and not their eyes. He was a conscious and deliberate prose stylist, an anomaly in his genre, and his plots were incredibly intricate. The humor in his yarns subtly combined the humor of words with a scene sense of the comic situation he had learned from Henry Wallace Phillips. The "western" fan picking up a Rhodes story was apt to react like a pup with his first porcupine and to learn the lesson of abstention with but one experience.[20]

Rhodes' other and greatest contribution to his own neglect was his productivity. He was a slow worker by nature and a spasmodic one, writing not alone for his market but, also, taking inordinate pains that every word would stand up in the minds of those in New

---

[20] The sales of his books document this premise. His magazine popularity did not carry over into hard-cover sales.

Mexico who had known Gene Rhodes as well as Rhodes had known them and their joint country. In adding up the corpus of his life's work, he, himself, could arrive at but 1,200,000 words which is a mere bagatelle alongside the output of Grey, Mulford, Raine, Seltzer, Drago, Tuttle, Cunningham, or a score of others, past and present Lack of output, ordinarily, is an acceptable yardstick for critical acclaim, but it was not so with Rhodes. More important, practically speaking, is the fact that five-year gaps between books are worse than two-year gaps between major periodical appearances when it comes to keeping an author in his public's mind. And, certainly, such gaps give a book publisher no reason to waste time, money, and effort in promoting the sale of such infrequencies.

Despite Rhodes' lack of productivity, it is interesting to note that he did achieve a very high degree of utilization of what he did write. More interesting is the fact that his work continues to find a niche in the current market place—anthologies, reprints, television, and films—and this despite Frank Dobie's latest feeling that "His fiction becomes increasingly dated."[21]

What Don Pancho says, in part, is absolutely true. Rhodes' style, technique, and tone, all are hopelessly archaic in most of his stories. His very early stories are an emetic and, as has been noted, so are his characterizations of women and of Eastern society, people, and manners. But——

The best of his yarns about his own country and his own people retain the nourishing, essential juices of true literature. Coming upon them today, when the expanse of the "western-story" is a vast reach of sheer craftsmanship speckled with great cloud-patches of slipshod writing and escapist plots, Rhodes' stories have the startling impact of an antelope's rump seen shining across long, arid, sun-drenched leagues where no living thing was thought to be.[22]

There is only one obstacle in the way of those who would seek to read Rhodes today, to hone these opinions against the stone of personal experience. Barring one paperback reprint, *Sunset Land*, Eugene Manlove Rhodes is out of print.[23] His published books have

---

[21] *Guide to Life and Literature of the Southwest* (rev. ed., Dallas, 1952).

[22] No attempt has been made here, or hereafter, to select the best of Rhodes' output. As has been said, "One man's fish is another's *poisson*."

[23] Dell Publications scheduled another one for 1956 to contain more material from *The Best Novels . . . of Eugene Manlove Rhodes*. There is, however, many a slip between schedule and paperback.

been pursued for years by what DeVoto terms "a coterie as select and discriminating as any that ever boosted a tenth-rate English poet into a first-rate reputation." If his books, or his stories in frayed copies of old magazines, can be found today they will ring like a shod hoof on *malpaís* in the mind and heart of any purchaser who knows the West-That-Was. They will make, also, a severe dent in the purse.[24] It is this scarcity and price that give solid substance to the partisan literary summation of Gene Rhodes that first was made of De Maupassant: "He was almost irreproachable in a genre which was not."

[24] Henry Holt & Co. issued *Good Men and True* at $1.00 net; a good copy of the first edition has been quoted recently at $27.50.

Contents

THE
RHODES
READER

I. Loved I Not Honor More

This was Rhodes' sixth published piece of fiction, appearing in *Out West*, February, 1903. It shows the changes wrought by the gifted editor, Charles Fletcher Lummis, himself a New Mexican at heart, in the "locoed cowpuncher from Engle" since he first came under Lummis' tutelage. It has never been reprinted since its first appearance, save an excerpt in William A. Keleher's *The Fabulous Frontier* (Santa Fé, 1945).

The essential truths behind this story are as recorded, for Rhodes was "Wildcat" Thompson in the story. Rhodes was running horses in the San Andres mountains at the time of the Boer War. He was, literally, "hubbing Hell on a starveout spread." He was considering matrimony very seriously and he needed money as badly as he needed grass and water. He did have the chance to sell as many horses as he could gather to Her Majesty's Government, and he did refuse because his sympathies were with the Boers.

That he actually did fight the Britisher, as here recorded, has not been verified. That he would have done so had the occasion demanded it and the opportunity come to hand is beyond question.

Rhodes' own philosophy—master of no man and servant of none—is the dominant in this story. It made the pervading thread in everything he ever wrote.

O FAST IS HISTORY MADE THESE DAYS! For all this was only a little while ago.

When Emil James came around the bend in the cañon, to the opening where the ranch stood, he reined up his horse and whistled.

"O-Oh!" he said. "My stars alive! Didn't the water came! Spring, pipe-line, water-pen, troughs, corral, saddle-house—all washed away—*vamoosed!* Bet Wildcat rared up and fell over backwards!"

He rode up in front of the *jacal* house.

"*You* Wildcat!"

Wildcat came to the open door; "Hello Emil—get down. You're just in time for supper."

"You bet. Food is the biggest part of my diet. I see you've moved your ranch down the cañon, and I was afraid I'd find you down there hunting for the pieces. Think you'll like it any better down on the flat?"

"You unsaddle your horse, you old fool, and shut up! I'm pretty sore about this washout. I'm set back about two hundred dollars by it."

After supper was finished, Emil shoved back his plate, lit a cigarette, and said: "You got any likely young horses to sell?"

"Betcher neck. You know anybody that wants to buy."

"Yes, indeedy. McNew said to tell you Old Man Forest will pay twenty-five for all you had that would stand fourteen and a half hands, four year olds and up, sound and broken. Greys, roans, duns and pacers barred. He's going to take down a bunch, and said to tell you you'd better gather yours and drive with him. They're to be delivered at the Nations' pasture at El Paso the 20th. They'll take outlaws all right, but no broncos."

"When's Billy going to start?"

"He'll camp at Lava Gap the night of the 24th, he said."

"By George," said Wildcat, "this here'll be just like getting money from home, and express charges prepaid. I was sure needin' it, too, as the hobo said when he fell in the creek. I can put up about twenty-five head. I'll go over tomorrow and get one of the Morris boys to help me gather my little old ponies, and hit the road. Don't know what's going to happen. Why, last spring you couldn't *throw* a horse away, much less sell one."

4

"I tell you, old man," he confided to Show Me, his "top horse," the next day, as they climbed the winding trail to the Morris ranch, "we was cutting it pretty fine that time, for certain. Now, if I can pay old Forest five hundred on that mortgage, the old skeezicks will let me have a renewal for another year for the other half. Then I can sell my steers for enough to keep Buddie in school, and fix up the pipe-line and trough again, and next year I can sure win out. Then when my little bunch of cattle's paid for, I'll go and ask the gray-eyed girl a question. Every time I get the mail, I'm scared to death for fear I'll hear some feller has snapped her up. Tell you what, they can cuss the brown-tailed mares all they want to, but they've sure pulled me out of the hole, this time."

All the way down to El Paso, Wildcat was in fine feather. There were dust, heat, thirst and perverse horses; but they did not affect his cheerfulness. There were days of scant and withered grass, in spots the rain had missed; nights when they had failed of water for the horses, and these had to be herded all night to keep them from going back. Even when they struck the Felipe ranch, only to find the windmill broken, and were forced to run the heavy horsepower, tying a rope to the horn of the saddle and riding tediously around—Wildcat ran the power and diverted himself with hilarious song, as if he were enjoying himself to the full.

It was noon on the sixth day when they drew near Ft. Bliss, and saw a large band of horses rounded up and held near the Nations' pasture.

Wildcat and McNew stopped their bunch, and rode ahead to investigate. The first man they struck was Pat Garrett. Their greetings were cool, for McNew and Garrett were seriously at outs, and Wildcat was a partisan of McNew's.

"Hello, Garrett!" said Billy, "What's all this doings, here? Looks like all the horse men in the country had come down."

"Ye-es," said Garrett, "there's quite a crowd. Forest sent me a bid on my old sticks, and me and McCall come down here and found Frank and Tillman Wayne, Briscoe, Johnnie Woods, and Newberry—and now you fellows."

"Why, what on earth is Forest going to do with so many horses?" queried Wildcat.

"He's got a contract with the British Government for a thousand head. The big stiff in the buggy with him is the officer that's receiving them."

5

Garrett and McNew rode ahead to the crowd, but Wildcat turned and looked around at the grim, gray mountain which rose abruptly from the plain just west of them.

Unforeseen, unheralded, the crisis was upon him—the hour that was to be the supreme test of his manhood. Five hundred dollars— the price of a jewel, a gown, a night's play—the price of a soul. It was not the massive rock-ribbed mountain that he saw. It was a lonely, wind-swept street of low adobes, overhung with rushing clouds. A few stars peered out through one clear space overhead. Gusts of rain and hail smote his face, and the swaying cottonwoods moaned together. A door was thrown open, and a broad beam of warm light shot out across the storm. And, in the doorway, her eyes alight with love and welcome, a woman—a woman with gray eyes.

The light went out, and instead he saw the bold, black "scare-head" of a yellow journal:

PRESIDENT KRUEGER'S MESSAGE TO THE AMERICANS
"Tell Them They Are Helping To Murder Us."

It was over now, and the gray-eyed girl would never know. He turned his horse and rode toward the little knot of men by the buggy. There was nothing different, unless a little grey in the lean, hard, impassive face. He sat a little straighter in the saddle, with a slight lifting of his head; and there was a certain compression of the corners of his mouth—that was all. Many men had seen Wildcat's lips tighten so; and most of them had unpleasant recollections connected with it.

"Well, Wildcat," was Forest's greeting, as he drew near, "how many ponies have you got to sell?"

"I don't believe I'll sell," was the response.

"Won't *sell?*" demanded McNew, in astonishment. "Why, what's eating you?"

"I didn't know they were for the English," replied Wildcat. "I'm a Boer man—me. If I was to sell, feeling the way I do, I would always feel like it was blood-money, and I'd have to sneak round a corner in hell to dodge Judas Iscariot. I know the Boers 'll capture the horses all right, but—"

"Aw!" ejaculated the Englishman, in amazement, and brought a gold-rimmed monocle to bear.

"Why, you idiot," said Billy, "they'll get all the horses they want, of somebody. 'Taint like you was their only chance. And you'd just as well have the money."

"Just so," said Wildcat. "Now I'm claiming to be a friend of yours, ain't I? If you and Pat was to get on the warpath and go gunning for each other, would it be white for me to sell cartridges to Pat, if he run out, because I needed the money, and Garrett could get plenty somewhere else? Don't talk to me—it don't look to me like it was honor, nohow."

"You always *was* a crazy fool!" snarled Forest. "But just let me tell you one thing, young man. If you ain't right up to the scratch with that money you owe me, down goes your meathouse! 'Honor!' " he laughed derisively. "The honor of a cowboy!"

Wildcat swung his horse in beside the buggy, thrusting a dark face over the wheel. It was easy to see, now, how he came by his sobriquet.

" 'Honor' was the word I used, sir—the honor of a cowboy! You may be justified in swearing at it, but, except for your gray hairs, you are hardly wise. Our standard may be lower than most people's—anyhow, it's *different*. But when we do draw the line, we don't step over it. And you—By God, sir, there's nothing in the world you *wouldn't* do for money! You'd sell your grandmother's grave for ten cents! And you threaten me with your dirty old mortgage—you gray-headed old scoundrel!"

The Englishman climbed out of the buggy, scrupulously brushed the dirt from his coat where it had grazed the wheel, screwed the monocle in his eye, and said regarding Wildcat with a fixed and glassy stare,

"Ah—my good man—if you are such a friend to the Boers, why don't you go and help them?"

Wildcat wheeled upon him, "I'll tell you, me good man," he said, in confidential tones, "I was afraid I'd get hurt—you know!"

"Aw!" Then, after a moment of incredulous staring, "Will you be so good as to tell me exactly the difference between the Boer war and your Philippine war?"

Wildcat threw his leg over his saddle-horn, rested his elbow on his knee, and his chin on his hand. "With great pleasure," he said. "It's like this. The only way anyone can stand up for either war is to reckon the Boers and Filipinos are just cattle. So, just to oblige you, we'll consider 'em cattle. And even then there's a difference. Like this.

7

"Now, 'sposing I had a big farm, and was raisin' mighty valuable crops on it. 'Spose me and my brother had had cattle on it once and quarreled and jawed and lawed and fought about them, till we was most give out—and most broke, too. Then we makes it up and goes ahead and builds fences around our land to keep out any of our neighbor's cattle, and put our own in our poorest fields, and wish to God we could get rid of 'em somehow.

"Then if I was to go 'way off somewheres, and buy a lot more cattle, range delivery, from some one that I knew didn't own them, first whipping him for claiming to own 'em—wild cattle, scrubby some of 'em, all scattered in mountains and brush country—and go to work and pay out twenty or thirty times as much more as what they cost me, for hands and horses and chuck and corn; and after all that, never gathered anything but dead, and dogies and weak sisters—why that would be just like our war.

"And 'spose you had just dead oodles of cattle—fancy stock, and Herefords, and Polled Angus, and Durhams, and Chihuahuas and old long-horns—all kinds of cattle—more cattle than anybody—and a little old Dutchman was to be raising a little bunch of milk-pan cows; and you was to crowd him, and eat out his grass, and steal his calves, and make him move. 'Spose you made him move *twice*, and you got his ranch and improvements both times. And he went 'way out in the desert, and you was to follow him up and bother him again.

"Then 'spose he was to knock you down, and pull your hair, and pour sand in your eyes, and slap your face, and drag you with your own rope"—

A subdued titter ran around the circle.

"And if you was to call up all your cowboys, and all the men that had your stock on shares, and was to drive the Dutchman out in the brush, and shut up his wife and children to die of neglect and starvation and sickness"—he lowered his face to a level with the other's—"That would be like the Boer war."

He whirled and shook his fist at the crowd, his eyes ablaze. "You!" he cried. "You! How many of you would see one man starve one woman and child to death, and put up with it, much less help him? How does multiplying it by thousands help it? How many of you would let him have your horses to hunt down the Dutchman in the brush?"

8

The Englishman went very white. Garrett stretched a long arm, stroked his mustache slowly, and looked dreamily out across the plain. "You needn't rub it in no more, Thompson," he said. "I don't want to sell no horses, nohow."

McNew took off his sombrero, looked at it and scratched his head. "I hate to be on the same side with you, Pat," shaking his head gravely—"but I reckon you and me and Wildcat together are Public Opinion in this here neck of the woods. Come on, all you Boer men!" he added, with challenge in his voice, as he joined Garrett and Thompson.

McCall drove the spurs into his bronco. "Guess I'll just side you fellows. Don't have to sell my horses, anyway. My money don't cost me nothing—I work for it." And one by one the rest followed him.

Forest spluttered in impotent wrath, as he saw his prospective profits slipping away. He had exacted no forfeit from any of the vendors, horse men being usually only too glad to sell.

The Englishman walked up to Thompson. "I'm wishing you were a couple of stone heavier, my man," he said. "I should like uncommonly well to thrash you."

Flap! Wildcat was off his horse, and had thrown his gun into a soap weed. "I should like uncommonly well to have you try it," he said, in his sweetest tones. "But—aw—pawdon me, me man, if you were a couple of stone lighter, you would come a good deal nearer doing it." He threw off spurs and overshirt, took the silk kerchief from his neck and knotted it around his waist in lieu of a belt. The others crowded round, turning their saddle horses loose.

Forest danced in an agony of helpless rage. "You're never going to fight him, Major? This scum, this ruffian, this nobody?" he screamed.

"I am quite capable of judging for myself, thank you," replied the Briton, coldly. "This man is no ruffian." He methodically divested himself of coat, vest, collar, tie and cuffs, laid them carefully on the buggy seat, with the monocle on top, and came back.

"It is only fair to say that your man is hopelessly outclassed, you know," he said, addressing the crowd. "I was thought the best man with my hands in Cambridge, my last year there. So he needn't feel cut up, you know, if he gets worsted. As he says, I am not very fit; but even so, there is no disgrace in taking a whipping from me."

9

Newberry rubbed his nose—it was broken—in reminiscent fashion. "Some of us don't think it any disgrace to take one from Wildcat," he suggested.

"It's very decent of you to warn me," said Wildcat, eyeing his adversary with a respect he had not hitherto shown. "Still, I might sort of promise you'll know you've been in a fight."

Then was seen the singular spectacle of "Bertie" Vaughn, Major of a crack British regiment, a pet of Mayfair and Belgravia, standing up to do battle with an utter stranger.

In weight, reach and skill, the advantage was overwhelmingly with the Briton. Against him were arrayed youth, activity and toughness. The cowboy's wiry muscles, and the staying power due to long years of plain living and hard work, made him a dangerous opponent. Lithe and agile as his namesake, the wildcat, his natural quickness made up for much of his lack of science. Yet from the first it was evident that the soldier had made no idle boast. In the beginning Thompson went to work hammer and tongs; only to find his well-meant blows easily warded off, blocked and ducked by his burly antagonist, while a series of disconcerting, lightly delivered counters and short arm blows interfered sadly with the continuity of his onslaughts; and the Englishman wore a confident and easy smile which he found very exasperating. At the end of three or four minutes of this kind of work, the Briton was almost untouched, while divers bruises and little trickling streams of blood began to show on Wildcat's face, and into Wildcat's skull had percolated the certainty that if the battle was continued on these lines there could be but one result.

He sprang back and charged, striking with all his force, ricochetting like a billiard ball; circled swiftly round, rushed in again, chin well down, taking a blow on top of the head, and leaping nimbly aside. Round and round he went, darting in and out, giving his enemy no rest, and aiming terrible blows at Vaughn's body, which, for the most part, he succeeded in warding off or at least in breaking their force. In this process the cowboy was severely punished, being twice knocked down; but he didn't seem to mind a little thing like that.

Into the attack, Wildcat was putting three times the energy the Major was expending in the defense; but he was standing it better. For a long time he continued to hammer at Vaughn's trunk, willing to take two blows to give one; and succeeded in getting in a few good licks which distressed the gentleman greatly. The jaunty smile faded from his face, and he fought warily, devoting much more attention to diverting the American's vicious body blows than to offensive measures.

Suddenly Wildcat changed his target. In and back, landing fairly on the nose, receiving a blow in return that closed one eye and staggered him. Back again, a blow in the mouth, with a sharp counter from the Briton that fairly lifted him from his feet and sent him down again. Another rush, and he landed fairly on Vaughn's eye, ducked, drew back, and feinted for the face. The Englishman threw up his guard to protect his one serviceable eye. Crash! Thompson struck him fairly over the heart with every pound of strength in his wiry young body behind the blow, and the victim went down like a log. He rose slowly, weakly, gasping for breath. It looked as though youth and endurance were to win, after all.

Confident of victory, the cowboy rushed in again. But the other realized that if he were to win at all it must be done in the next sixty seconds. Instead of standing to take the charge, he met the American, struck him fairly on the forehead, and, calling up all his reserves, rushed in return. Wildcat jumped back, but the other was upon him, and a shower of merciless blows beat upon his face. Blinded, dazed, bewildered, he lunged fiercely at random, missed and clinched. Back and forward, heaving, trampling, struggling, straining—Vaughn almost exhausted, the other with both eyes closed, fighting desperately in the dark. And then—his left arm closed around the Briton's waist, his right wrist pushing savagely at his throat, a roar of voices thundered in his ears, the blood surged to his temples, to his stunned and dizzy brain the world seemed swaying, reeling. A last furious effort, calling up all his remaining strength, and he bent his foeman over backward. They struggled, tottered, fell; but as they went down Vaughn's right hand shot upward convulsively, catching the American under the chin.

"And the subsequent proceedings interested him no more."

They went down together, a confused sprawl of arms and legs, the cowboy on top. McCall and Briscoe untangled them and laid the vanquished Thompson, limp and helpless, on the ground. The victor's case was hardly less disastrous. He lay sobbing for breath—utterly unable to rise. Garrett and Johnnie Woods helped him sit up, and gave him water from a canteen. He had struck the back of his head on a rock when he fell, and was bleeding profusely.

"What a—ghastly—fluke!" he panted, as they ministered to him. "Couldn't—have struck—another blow, 'pon honor! Bellows—to mend—you know." He regarded the unconscious Thompson anxiously with his unbattered eye. "I hope he's—not hurt? Plucky beggar!"

"He'll be all right in a little," said McNew, who, with McCall, was laboring over the fallen champion. "We'll fetch him around."

"I say," continued the Major, "there's some—old Scotch in—my coat. Give him some—of that."

They poured the liquor down Wildcat's throat. He coughed, choked, and rolled his eyes.

"What a beastly—shame!" the Major began. Then an inspiration came to his gallant heart that would have done credit to Bayard himself. He winked jovially at Garrett. "I'm dead—licked—done for —you know!" he whispered. "Hit my—head on a rock!" And he fell over and relaxed into an inert mass of abject humanity, torn, disordered, plastered with blood and sweat.

Wildcat sat up with McCall's assistance, and propped open his best eye with a trembling and uncertain forefinger. His gaze wandered around till it fell upon the prostrate form of his Perfidious Foeman. He silently surveyed the battered ruins for a while with an air of vague interest, felt soberly for his own head, exactly as if he thought it might be there or thereabouts, but wasn't positive, and, as if he "wanted to count it" when he finally found it. Then he inquired languidly,

"What's the matter with *him?* Mule?"

"Knocked out—struck his head on a rock when you both fell," replied Garrett, bending over the shamming Briton and chafing his hands industriously.

"He's not hurt," snapped Forest, "He's just—"

Garrett took Forest by one arm and leg, McNew by the other. They jammed him into the buggy with appropriate language. Then they took the Major's apparel out and gave Forest some earnest advice as to his departure, which he took—advice and departure both. As he left, the Major groaned, rolled over, and gazed blankly around.

Wildcat looked very much ashamed. "Let's call it a draw,

Major," he said, crawling to the other's side and holding out his hand. "You caught me a sockdolager on the jaw as we fell, and I just this minute came to. You had me fairly licked, and it was just the old Happen-so that you struck your head."

"Don't mention it, my dear fellow," said the Major as they shook hands warmly. "Delighted to have met you, I'm sure!"

They got painfully to their feet, Thompson very wobbly as to his knees, the Major still scant of breath.

During the combat, Nations had ridden down from the slaughter-house, and had been a silent spectator of the proceedings. He now made the first observation that had escaped him since his arrival on the scene.

"Hoss-trade all off, I guess? Well—bring your horses down and put 'em in the pasture. There ain't much grass, but they won't starve. You two bruisers come on down and I'll dip you in the trough. We get dinner and then go down and take in El Paso."

There was a murmur of acquiescence, and the crowd started after the horse-herd which had grazed off. A hundred yards away, they halted, wheeled, and Garrett shouted as they all took off their sombreros:

"Three cheers for Major Vaughn!" And the response came with waving hats and revolver shots to accompany it.

"*Hip! Hip!* HOORAY!"

Thompson shook his head, "There'll be a hot time in the old town tonight!" he said, and they hobbled on their way.

II. Sticky Pierce, Diplomat

This is one of the very few early stories in Rhodes' frontier-Gothic period, appearing in *Out West*, October, 1906, to show the wit and humour he later developed so highly.

In it, albeit well disguised, is Rhodes' feeling of wrath for the ignorance of the East about their exploited, captive provinces in the West.

The titular hero is derived from Ed Pierce, who, in later years, told Ross Santee many anecdotes about the man who wrote the story.

THERE WAS NOT A CLOUD IN THE SKY when I awoke. The afternoon sun beat down in a pitiless glare upon the silent desert; the shade of the single lonely cedar where we slept had shifted till the blistering heat had wakened me, and Sticky's share of the shade was fast leaving him as well.

I rolled over and looked sleepily around. Our hobbled horses were contentedly cropping the tender grasses at the edge of the little pond, perhaps half an acre in extent, that we dignified by the name of "Cedar Lake." Behind us lay the Oscura range and Mocking Bird, through which we had passed in the cool gray of dawn. The San Andrés and Organs stretched away to where, a hundred and twenty miles to the south, El Paso huddled at the foot of Mr. Franklin; beyond, in Old Mexico, two ranges merged mistily into the turquoise sky. Around us on all sides lay the desert, vast and level and bare, a dazzling patch of white in the center reflecting the light like a mirror. This mirror was the "White Sands," forty miles square. Just beyond them the Jarilla hills hung between earth and heaven, like Mahomet's coffin, the eye looking calmly under them to the plain beyond—this being a common effect of mirage in the Southwest. Beyond them, rimming the eastern horizon, were flat-topped, pine-covered Sacramento; then the mighty stretch of the White Mountain directly east of us; sixty miles long, fourteen thousand feet high, its summit a spotless cone of purest white—six feet deep of dazzling snow under the sweltering July sun. We looked directly across the top of the Philip Hills to its base, and between us and the hills lay an irregular black ribbon—the "Mal Pais," or Bad Lands. This was a river of molten stone that had poured down the center of the valley centuries before and cooled off in all fantastic forms; seventy miles long from the crater to its southern extremity, from one to fifteen miles wide; its edges fringed with capes, promontories, islands, inlets, straits, and bays of weird and intricate design, where lava and desert mutually encroached upon each other, their fingers interlocking in an eternal clasp.

Farther north the White Mountain dwindled to the Nogal and Carizo, in whose foothills White Oaks nestled, ninety miles away. Due north the plain swept on till the eye saw nothing, till it was wearied with the strain; and resting, saw beyond that—nothing again.

This it is—these vast horizons, this absolute freedom that makes so much of the indescribable charm of life out-of-doors in this "land where it is always afternoon." Whoso has felt that fascination shall never quite escape it—though he has left behind the ashes of ten thousand camp fires, he shall forget not one.

"Sticky!" I cried. "You Sticky Pierce, wake up!"

He sat up and held out an habitual hand. "Le's curl one. Gimme the credentials."

I handed him tobacco and papers, and he was soon puffing

vigorously. As he caught sight of the Jarillas, apparently floating in mid-air, he paused, with a flourish of his cigarette hand.

"They ought to be arrested for having no visible means of support. Le's eat and drift. It'll be plenty cool by the time we shape up."

" 'Sta bueno. I'll rig up if you'll build the dinner."

Accordingly Sticky started a fire of mesquite roots and branches, opened our little chuck box with a clatter, baked bread, made coffee, pounded jerky, fried it with bacon and made gravy. Meanwhile I fed the horses in their nosebags, harnessed them as they ate, and filled the twenty-gallon keg which swung on the side of the wagon. For we were to make a dry camp that night thirty miles on, and the only water we would pass—the Malpais Spring—was bitter with alkali.

By four o'clock we were on our way. A welcome breeze was stirring now, and it was cool and pleasant. The ponies snorted cheerfully as they scampered down the road, whisking their tails in high spirits.

"I'm getting plenty weary of the cow-clerking," I grumbled. "I yearn for an income that comes in, in place of one that you have to go out and run down—chase it all day, and have it break out of the corral at sundown. The way I figure it, I've been working for Armour and Co. all these years for my board and clothes—doing without the clothes and stealing the grub myself—all but a little coffee and flour and salt. Cowman is just *peon* spelled polite. You do the work and dodge the taxes, while some one in Chicago sits in his office and makes the profit—earning his bread in the sweat of your brow. And horses is worse. You sell them for about half enough to pay for half breaking them, and folks come back and kick because they ain't gentle. I sure hope I get my paws on this city job. And I think I can turn the trick by putting up a blue front and using a little tact."

"Tact," remarked Sticky, "is my long suit—tact and strategy. Speaking of tact—and the little disconcertaincies of the cow business —and imperfectly fractured horses—'d I ever relate to you my diplomacies in the case of Archibald Campbell?"

"So far, your conduct has been above reproach," I replied.

Sticky rolled his eyes compassionately. "Now is the appointed hour," he said. He sat further down on his suspender buttons, leaning luxuriously against the "lazy back" of the seat, and began.

"It was—let me see—ten, eleven years ago that I ran into a streak of bad luck—end-ways. I had a ranch up in Mogollon county. First the shack burned down, and all our sticks with it. The wife took sick, babies next. Then a drought come along and I lost a hundred and twenty-two-or-three per cent of my cattle—and them not all paid for yet. 'Never mind, Sticky,' says the good wife. 'Sometimes things'll come like that for awhile, and then turn right around and get worse—so cheer up!'

"I was seriously considerin' the buyin' of a mask and another gun, and going into High Finance, when I got a letter from good old Jimmy Dodds. It stated would I come to oncet to Albuquerque, and he thought I could get a wagon to run for the Lazy H.

"That suited me right down to the ground—ninety silver-eagle-birds and a free hand. The old man didn't just use you as a speaking trumpet to give orders through, nor yet as a pair of springs to break the jolts in rough going. You got the work done and no questions asked—hired, fired, bought and sold as you sweetly well pleased. The best ponies in the country to work on and as adequate a set of punchers as ever throwed a loop.

"The old Rod had resigned because things didn't go to suit him. They stopped his pay and his chuck and then cut his mount from him—and he got mad and quit. Seems he had a private brand, and was dreadful absent-minded, and disregarded the unities a heap. His cows was raising twins of assorted ages till it had occasioned a good deal of comment among the neighbors. They shot him or was rude to him, or something.

"The old man was East, and the top hand was issuin' powders pro temporary. And Jimmy wanted me to be Johnny-on-the-spot when the old man should develop, his orbits and trajectories bein' some erratic and hard to foresee.

"Well, I assembles Mike Wolf, the same bein' my most important and only creditor, and assigns to him, his heirs and assigns forever, all my right, title and interest in an undivided sixty-or-seventy-millionth share of the public debt, lands and buildings, includin' the City of Washington and a lot of ornamental post-offices, some forts and a navy, and the hereditaments and appurtenances thereunto—the aforesaid bein' my total assets—as security for what was due him on my late neat cattle, until such time as I should be willin' and able to lift my debt by transfer of money current with the merchant. He was some remonstrative at this, but I explains that I had pawned my American citizenship to him, and wouldn't vote till I had redeemed it, addin' that the hardest thing in the way of sleight-of-hand I never learned was to put my hand in my pocket and pull out a dollar that wasn't there.

"Then I rides over to the burg, landing there with a net capital of no dollars and no cents, the savings of thirty-eight years. Jimmy wasn't more than twice as well hooked-up as I was, but he whacked up fair with me, and I starts in to play the slow game of set-down, there being two-and-a-half men per job per day in Albuquerque just then.

"Well, I got the wagon all right and one fine, large and sub-sequent day I pays Mr. Wolf in full, him sorrowfully but firmly declining to partake of any interest; which was pretty damn white of him, when you stop to consider the style of nose he wore, and shows what climate will do.

"Well, what I'm alluding at only concerns my trials and tribs whilst waiting for the old man to conclude his devistions in the effete East and return to the path of rectitude for the purpose of engaging my valuable services as the General Staff of the Lazy H.

"To make a short story long, Jimmy had just blowed in all his dough building a nest for his corn-fed bird down in Texas, and had rented it to said Archibald for twenty a month till mating time, reserving one room for himself. And he was grubbing away in a lumber yard, saving up his *dinero* to buy lining for the nest.

"Him and me camped in that room, cooking on a limited oil stove. I ain't never cared much for coal oil as seasoning since. Believe I like *chili* better anyhow.

"I had been there mebbe-so two-three weeks when along comes a letter from home, and the wife and one baby was sick again—the baby pretty bad. I walks up to the house, looking down my nose. I guess I was looking some *triste* and forlorn, for Mistress A., who was sewin' on the gallery, calls to me as I goes round the corner to my little old room, 'Oh, Mr. Pierce!' she says, 'is there anything wrong?'

"I thought that was real nice of her, so I camps on the steps and tells her all about it, from the Garden of Eden to the present day—staying there rising of an hour or two. I was used to having people help each other in trouble, so I didn't think nothing of it, 'cepting that the Mistress was just like folks.

"What do you dam well think? That night Archibald takes Jimmy out for a heart-to-heart talk, and tells him he'll be obliged to give notice! *Yes!*

" 'Mrs. Campbell feels that she has no privacy,' he says. 'Mr. Pierce sat out on the piazza all afternoon and several of our friends drove by and saw him there,' he says. 'She was *so* mortified.' 'D I tell you where Archibald came from?

"*Geddap, you Roman-nosed white-eyed shirking snails!* Earn your corn! You'd trot up and down in the shade of a tree all day! Goin' to camp here? Durn your hides! *Rattle yo' hocks!*

"Jimmy talked to him like a maiden aunt—told him to go and be damned, with trills and variations. Expounded his theories as to Archibald's derivation and—as far as he was concerned—his destination, enlargin' on the grief he felt at his belonging, in a manner, to the same species. He was very copious in his language when properly approached, was Jimmy.

"Naturally, he couldn't tell me about this little discrepancy, so he goes down town and confides in the first man he meets, the same being Sammy Clarkson.

"Now Sammy had a habit of getting drunk four times a month, each paroxysm lasting ten or twelve days; so the next time I sees him he ups and tells me all about it, first swearin' me never to name it to Jimmy or the Archibald. So there I was.

"I saddles my nag and disperses casually across the country toward Gran Quivera, searchin' for fresh air and room. I fetched up at Baldy Russell's needing water, and stayed there for three days, moderating. My problem was to dissuade Archie from abstractin' that twenty per from the vacuum in Jimmy's pocket, without ever mentioning it to him—or to Jimmy either. And 'twas my move.

"Sunday I started back, still perplexed in my intellects as to how and what the bally hell to do. It was forty miles back, so I acquires a big canteen and fills it, havin' no desire to onkwore the experience of the trip out.

"I was nearly half way when I lifted up my eyes and became aware of a buckboard careering and pirooting madly across the landscape in a hasty, unpremeditated manner. Presently they struck a big soap-weed, and turned over, omitting the driver and all the rig but the front wheels. This aroused my curiosity and I loped up. The team had started for San Francisco like they was in a hurry. Every few yards they'd straddle a soapweed, and them wheel's stick straight up over the horses' backs, givin' the outfit a highly indecorous expression.

"This roused the horses to greater enthusiasm and they faded tumultuously away beyond the Tropic of Capricorn. Long after the curve of the world swallowed them up, a meandering, billowy dust-cloud in the dim and silent distance marked their devastatin' course.

"The man was coming back to the road, so I slowed down to a jog; and when I got up close, behold you, it was Archibald!

"I greeted him cheerful and solicitous. He wasn't hurt, but some worried about his horses.

" 'Oh, they're all right!' I informs him. 'The boys'll get them in the spring round-up. Our play is to get back to our fire-side or oil-stove, as the case may be. We'll take turn-about riding my horse. Them there steeds of yours is lost to sight, to memory dear. Say, they take less time to pass a given point than ary team I ever saw.'

" 'I should say they was dear! That buckboard cost me sixty-five dollars, harness twenty-five, and the horses about fifty apiece. The man said they were perfectly gentle. Just listen to this—it sounds nice from this angle.' And he reads me part of a letter to his dad, statin' how he had just invested in a pair of broncos, perfectly beautiful, and him and the Missus was goin' projectin' all over the country. He was going out for a trial spin and would write more fully on his return. He had named them Alfred and Amigo—' Here I cut in.

" 'Which one was Amigo? I couldn't tell by the way they was comporting of themselves.'

"He turns red in the face. 'Not Amigo!' he explains—'O-mega.'

" 'Oh, I guess not!' I says, 'I been dwellin' with the *paisano* people all my life.'

" 'But this isn't *Amigo*. That's Spanish for friend—Omega is a Greek letter. See here!' And he holds the letter for me to look at it. But the first thing I beheld was the way he had spelled bronco—b-r-o-n-c-h-o.

" 'O that mine enemy would write a book!' is what I thinks. Out loud I says:

" 'I'm sorry—but I'm sure obligated to lick you. I've been trying to break folks of spelling bronco that-a-way for years, writing letters and arguing, and it does no good. Folks seem to think a bronco is a horse afflicted with bronchitis, or consumption, or puny some way. B-r-o-n-c-o—is a Spanish word signifyin' wild. The c has the sound of k—always. If it was spelled c-h-o—it would rhyme with *poncho* and wouldn't mean nothing at all. If you was guessin' now, would you say Alfred and Dago was afflicted with lung trouble, or just wild and dissipated?'

" 'Wild,' says Archie, laughing. 'Wild and debauched.'

" '*Very* well. All the writers spell it wrong, just the same as the magazine pictures always depict a man throwin' a rope in such a way that he's bound to snare his own horse and the horn of the saddle next whirl. Fame and undying gratitude await that man who can draw a cowboy throwin' his twine right-end-to, so's he can drop it over somethin' if the fancy struck him.'

" 'I have tried patiently to reform this light-hearted and disrespectful habit of spelling Spanish by the light of nature, and I promised myself that I'd wallop every one I found trying to disseminate the misleadin' idea that a bronco was a meek, dejected and spiritless invalid. So get yourself in shape, for it's a long ways to town, and we've got to be promenadin'.'

" 'You're joking,' says Archie.

" 'Never was more serious,' I says. 'This is a subject on which I feel deeply.' And I swatted him.

"He was a real nice little fellow and fought hard. He could box too, but of course he couldn't stand any hack with me. I was hard as nails, and in earnest, and knew what I wanted. More than all, I knew I was going to win—and he didn't. And Archie was too puzzled at my ways and means to do well.

"My plans and specifications didn't require that I should disfigure him much, so I worked on his body. I got skinned up some, but I got his wind after a while, and he collapsed.

" 'Now, you remember and correct any one that makes that error in the future,' says I. 'Take a drink and rest a little and we'll be going. You ride the horse first.'

"He swore he wouldn't go with me, but I argued and coaxed. Told him it would be real inhospitable of me not to help him. Told him that the Good Book says to give the broke a drink, and a lift to a man afoot. Assured him that it was a matter of principle with me, that there was nothing personal about it; pointin' with pride to my bloody face, which I dassn't wash 'cause water was so scarce. This last argument helped most. I jollied him up and we finally goes on in good humor, gassing cheerfully, changing every two mile or so. He had never heard of how to ride and tie, and I explained that to him. After a while he breaks out into a great laugh.

" 'The most ridiculous thing I ever heard of—fighting to impress your ideas of spellin' on a man!'

" 'Well, you remember it, don't you?' says I, tartly.

" 'I certain do,' says Archibald. 'The impression is quite distinct. Say, I have a friend who would enjoy you. He will be out here before long. Come up and dine with us and meet him. He is a novelist, and I'm sure you are a character.'

" 'Up where?' says I, pointedly. 'And it's not *my* idea of spelling, but the right way. The other is the device of the intellectually becalmed, who are too lazy to inquire and too self-sufficient to respect the rights of an ancient and honorable tongue. Up where?'

"Archie was decent enough to blush. 'er—why up to the Cisneros house, corner of Fresnal and Manzanares. We're going to move. Don't know just when my friend will arrive—we are looking for him any day.'

" 'Don't think I'll be able to come. I expect to go to work before then.' And we went on talking of other things.

"A few miles further on I offers to get off and let him ride again. He says:

" 'Oh no—I'll walk a while yet. I should think you'd hurt your feet awfully, walking in those high-heeled boots. I wonder that a man as intelligent as you would follow such a foolish fashion.'

"I climbed down. 'Fashion! Now you have hurt my tenderest feelin's. I want you to know that the cow business can't be carried on without high heels. If there wasn't one in the world, they would be invented in a thousand different places before night. There are two things that make them absolutely sinquanonymous. If you go to get on a horse that is rarin', plungin', pawin', kickin', and buckin' all to oncet, wearing them little dinky toothpick shoes like your'n, it wouldn't be no time before you'd stick your foot clean through the stirrup. The bronc' would drag you, tear your clothes and spill your money and brains all over the range.

" 'The other reason is nearly as important. You rope a half-broke horse in the *remuda*. If you've got high heels, you jab one of them into the free soil of North America, bend the other knee, and sit down on the rope. That braces you and you stop the horse. No one can hold them with low heels. They just slide and the horse drags you till you waste him. And boot-legs keep the thorns out of your bow legs if you're not wearing chaps, keep your pantalets from working up under your elbows when you ride, keep rattlers from biting you when you're down.' I took a big swig of water and set the canteen in the shade of a soap weed. 'Now I'm due to learn you something. Put up your fists!' says I. 'You've insulted me.'

" 'You double-damned idiot!'" says Archibald—and we had it. I tell you he was mad, and he was doing mighty well too. Finally I stepped on the canteen.

" 'King's X,' I cries, bein' willin' to encourage him. 'We can't afford to spill the water. Besides, I'm satisfied. You'd make a right smart man with a little practice.'

"Say, that lad was so vexed, he sat down and cried. Cussed me something awful. Wanted to fight it out to a finish. Dared me to. I said, No! I had sufficiently vindicated the good sense of me and my likes—that I hoped it was clear to him that high-heels was as necessary to a cow-servant as pedals to a wheel-fiend, or U. S. Senators to a Railroad. And after a time he got on and we started, him conversing real sarcastic.

"We hadn't gone a quarter of a mile before he drags in this writer friend of his again. This really did grate on me sure enough, for no one likes to be made a holy show of. Of course, I was just aputting on about the other things. But I didn't want to fire up about anything reasonable. I knowed if I kept taking offense at far-fetched things, he would get his thought-mill geared up and grindin' after a while.

" 'Really you *must* meet Burns,' he insists. 'He dotes on freaks, and if ever there was one, you're it. Come and give him your views on orthography and high-heeled boots—and any other subject you're insane about. He'll put them before more people in a week than you'd reach if you went on about belaboring your betters till you were older than Methuselah. You ought to ventilate your mind and get the cobwebs out of it. And he'll show you where you're as ignorant about most things as I was about your technicalities. He'll "learn" you something. Why, you unspeakable ass, don't you know that one person can't "learn" another anything? The teacher teaches, the pupil learns. And that ain't all—if you try any of your remarkable mnemonic systems on him, he'll lick you till you like it. I'll tell you what I'll do. You come and stay a week with us, and I'll not assassinate you, as I fully intended to do when the opportunity offered. "I met a fool i' the forest!" Lord, how Burns would revel in searching out the tortuous and intricate windings of your darkened mind!'

"I quite liked the creature when it spunked up this-a-way, but I didn't lose sight of the main issue. 'I'll see,' says I, trudging along. 'Where did you say you were going to live?'

" 'At the corner of Fresnal and Manzanares Avenue.'

" 'Hardly think I can come. That's such an aristocratic locality. I'd have to blow myself for clothes to match—and then my *valley* wouldn't know how to get me into them.'

" 'Goodness! don't think of dressing up. That would spoil it all. Come just as you are. You have no idea how interesting your mode of dress is. Especially the jaunty angle at which all of you wear your *sombreros*. You needn't tell me you don't know it is picturesque.'

" 'Picturesque!' I says sadly, sitting down. 'Picturesque! Really you dishearten me! I never saw a man with such a genius for smoothing my fur the wrong way. Perhaps you think we spend an hour or two every morning before a looking glass trying our hats on. You blind bat, do you see that sun? Do you know it shines, daytimes, three hundred days a year and more? Do you know that the kind of man that wears *sombreros* lives out of doors and on horseback? Did you ever see a man chasing a steer and holding a silk umbrella over him—say? When the sun shines on this side of my face I tilt my hat *so*—when it shines on the other side I tilt it *so*—and other times I tilt it any which way because I'm never used to having it on straight! Picturesque! Bah! Get down off the horse!'

"But Archie was too premature for me. He hit the pony and loped up.

"Have I committed another solecism? You are the most sensitive man I ever saw,' he said, putting his thumb to his nose and wiggling his fingers. 'I suppose you want to fight again to soothe your lacerated feelings? Yah! You pachyderm! You fragile little angel! You Spanish Noah Webster! Of course, you try to look picturesque.

You walk with a swagger and trot out your weird talk for the grand stand! You delicate, tender little hot-house plant! Now you make up your mind either to walk to town in your precious high-heeled boots or to come and meet my friend and then invite him—and me—to come out to the ranch where you're going to work and stay as long as we jolly well please! Do you hear, you longeared crank?'

" 'I hear. Where did you say to come to visit you?'

" 'Damn you, don't come anywhere! You stay right where you are at Jimmy Dodds' place, as I'm going to."

" 'I am sure,' said I, 'that I'll be delighted to meet your friend. What you have said of him makes me sure I shall like him.'

" 'Hold on!' says Archie. 'Stand still! How do you spell bronco?'

" 'B-r-o-w-n-c-h-o-u-g-h,' says I, standing at attention. 'Bronco; a horse with asthma or hay fever.'

" 'Correct. We've both learned something. Come along, old man. Motley's the only wear.'

"We had a real jolly time when they come out to the ranch. Gimme those utensils and drive while I twist a smoke."

III. The Numismatist

This, Rhodes' first appearance in the *Saturday Evening Post* (March 2, 1907), was a signed collaboration with Henry Wallace Phillips. It was reprinted in *Trolley Folly* (Indianapolis, 1909), a collection of Phillips' short stories, without any credit to Rhodes.

"The Numismatist's" election-bet strategy in this story is based on an actual occurrence in New Mexico during the Cleveland-Blaine presidential contest of 1884. The outcome of this election hinged upon the vote in New York State. The first wire received in Deming, New Mexico, gave the victory to Blaine. This news was sent out to all the surrounding camps, including the roaring burg of Silver City, to which the telegraph lines had not yet reached all the way. Shortly after this first wire had been received in Deming, another wire came to a prominent merchant there from a personal friend in New York which said, simply, "Bet your life!" Watt Wilkerson was despatched forthwith to Silver City with a satchel full of money. Posing as a miner come down from Georgetown, hungry for news and other creature comforts, Wilkerson made a cleaning, but the Silver City slickers were the ones who made the bets on the basis of that first information which the honest miner from the hills did not have.

Phillips' own western heritage, from his boyhood in the Dakotas and along the upper Missouri, shows clearly when the beaten "Frenchy" is described as looking ". . . like ration day at Rosebud." Only a man who had witnessed the beef issues to the starving Sioux could have described the effects of a pistol-whipping so succinctly.

ELECTION DAY, '96, was big medicine in Terrapin. Miners all down from the upper camps, shoutin' Free Silver, and morose about John Sherman. All the cow-boys from the immediate vicinity were in. The immediate vicinity of any point in the Northwest is a good big scope of country—say as far as two men can ride fast in as many days as it takes to get there.

In Brown's Bank there was a sound of deviltry by night. Them back from the bar couldn't get back. A damsel with a dulcimer was dispensin' sweet strains, and a minority of the convention thought they was singing to keep her from feeling conspicuous, each delegate voting for a different tune. The toot ongsom was calculated to make an escaped lunatic homesick.

In the middle of this dispensation I comes in, late. I endeavored to attract the attention of the bar creature by shouting and sign talk, for I wanted to do my duty. I know I yelled, for I could feel my jaw waggle, and my breath give out—but I couldn't hear nothin'. No one would take my money. Some one or two drinks were handed to me, however, a handful of cigars and six dollars change. Them Free Silver fellows shore believed what they said.

So I looked around in search of distraction. Five deep they stood around the faro and roulette layouts. Dealers looked like a Turkish bath from raking in money and shovin' over chips. One fellow at the faro table had more'n six bushels of checks and was betting with a shovel.

I made for the poker-rooms. Both locked. I hammers. "Shove your money under the door," yells some one inside, "and go away."

Here was a fine how-de-do. Six months' wages in my pocket and no action in sight. I went out in front to hear myself think. On the porch sat a man, unostentatious, hugging his knee, observing of the moon.

I shoved a cigar at him. He nods, sticks it in his face, and hands me up matches over his shoulder. I likes his looks.

And his sayin' nothing sounded good, too, for my ear-drums were jarred clear to my ankles. I found out later that he wasn't always silent. He was a sort of human layer-cake that way—big slabs of talk and thin streaks of keeping still.

He didn't look quite like a cow-boy. Cow-boys' eyes is all puckered up by sun and wind. Nor quite like a miner. His hands was white but they wasn't tin-horn's hands, not by no means. He wasn't drunk, and I couldn't understand him at all, so I felt around.

"Stranger?" says I. He nods.

"Miner?"

"Once."

"Cow-boy?"

"Once. Everything else—once. Just now I am a numismatist."

I set down by him to show that didn't make no difference to me. "Is it—very bad?" I says, kinder solemn and hushed-like.

"A collector of rare coins," he explains, laughing. His laugh was good, too.

"Oh—I see. Got any of them with you?"

"Just one. Be careful of it," he says, and hands it to me. I holds it up to the light. 'Twas a common old iron dollar.

"Broke?"

He straightened up indignantly. "Not on your life—that's no counterfeit!" he says.

I liked him. I felt friendly. My experience is that the difference between the friend that can help you but won't and the enemy that would hurt you but can't isn't worth notice. So I dug. When I gave his dollar back I slid five yellow twenties with it.

He looks 'em over carefully, feeling of them, edges and both sides, with his fingertips. "Very interesting," he says. "Very beautiful. How clear the letter is!" And he hands 'em back.

"They're yours, Stranger," says I. "For your collection."

He swells up. "Not much. I'd beg before I'd accept charity."

"You don't understand me," I says, sparring for time. "I meant as a sporting venture. I'm superstitious. Men with a wad always lose it. So why shouldn't a broke man win? Take it and win us a home."

"Oh, that's different," says Stranger. "I accept with pleasure—

the more so as I have an infallible system of winning at roulette, founded on long observation."

"Yes?" says I, beginning to feel sorry for my hundred.

"Yes. I have observed that, if you play enough, you always lose. You just mathematically must. The percentage is a scientific certain-t-y-ty. My system is to bet high, win, and quit before you begin to lose."

"How did you ever study it out?" says I, beginning to be glad about my investment again. "I never tried that way, but it sounds promising."

"Such being the case, I got a hunch," says Stranger. "Here goes for a gold chain or a wooden leg. Take my hand and watch me peer into the future."

We wiggled through to the table after a while. The dealer was a voluptuous swell, accentuated with solid gold log chains and ruby rings where convenient. I knew him. He wore a copyrighted smile losing, and a nasty sneer when he won. An overbearing man and opportune, Frenchy, addicted to killing his fellow-man in sheer self-defense, during the absence of his assailant's friends. Such was his unrefuted statement, the dead gentlemen having never given their testimony. He had been so fortunate in his protections that lots of folks rarely ever went out of their way to annoy him.

Stranger began hostilities by depositing a twenty on the black. Red ensued. Another twenty on black. Black comes. Frenchy shoved over a ten, and Stranger looked pained.

"I bet twenty dollars," he said, lifting of his brows.

"Ten dollars is the limit for any one bet," snaps Frenchy, rolling the ball again. "Don't delay the game. Bet or give up your place."

"But you took my twenty." He stopped the wheel. "No bets this whirl," says Stranger.

The crowd stopped talking and side-stepped for an alibi in case the gentleman should engage in self-defense.

Frenchy bares his teeth and snarls. "You lost. I got the mon. Why didn't you inquire? You orter understand a game before you buck it. This is my game and my rules goes. See?"

"I see," says Stranger quiet. "Give me tens for these twenties, please."

Snickers from the crowd. Frenchy had them buffaloed to a

standstill. All the same, they had no use for a fellow that let his rights be trampled on this way. And yet Stranger didn't look noways like a man of patient proclivities, given to turning the other cheek. Some wise ones cashed their chips when they remarked his easy smile.

When Frenchy began to roll again we had the table mostly to ourselves. I moves over by the wheel to watch the lookout, him having a game eye and a propensity to be sole witness for Frenchy when his life was attempted.

"I will now declare myself as for W. J. Bryan," says Stranger, dropping ten each on the squares marked 16, 2, 1.

"Twenty-seven, red, odd and McKinley," drones Frenchy, and scoops our thirty.

Stranger strings thirty more on 16, 2, 1.

"Nine, black, odd! Great Republican gains!"

Frenchy's singsong was plumb exasperating.

Stranger adorns his three numbers again with his last thirty, and, as an afterthought, put his rare old iron dollar on single o.

"Single green," chants Frenchy. "Populist, by jingo!" I says, as Frenchy rakes the three tens and pays 'em, with five more to the green.

Ten each on 16, 2, 1. Then he planks the six on double green. "I hate a piker!" he states. And oo came.

"Alfalfa," I yells. "Grangers for ever!"

Things was looking up now, but Stranger was noways concerned. "Six thirty-fives is two hundred and ten—six I had makes two sixteen. Hold on till I make a purty." He bets ten straight on 16, ten on each corner, ten on each side. Same play for 2, and a lone ten on the unit. I never seen a board look so plumb ridiculous.

"Hope springs infernal in the human breast. Let 'er go, Hanna!" he says. "A short life and a merry one!"

The ball spun nearly two weeks. "Sixteen, black and even," remarks Frenchy.

I takes a swift glance at the wheel then, to corroborate my ears. "And Bryan," suggests Stranger.

"Bryan! Bryan!" yells the crowd. Miners and cow-boys is Democrats *ex officio*, and Frenchy's surreptitious habit of defending himself was endearin' Stranger to 'em. Besides, he was winning. That helps with crowds.

Paying them bets was complex. We was over eleven hundred to the good on the turn. Other business was suspended, and the crowd lined up, leaving the gladiators the center of the stage, and a twenty-foot lane so they could have plenty of air.

"I will now avenge the crime of '73," remarks Stranger. "I'm getting it trained." He made the same layout. Strike me dead, if the ball didn't jump in a pocket—out—and back—and out again and deliberated between 2 and 35 while the wheel went around fourteen times. You could have heard the split-second hand on a stop watch in the next county while it balanced—and at last rope-walked down in two.

"Two, red, even," says Frenchy in a shocked voice, like he was seein' things at night.

No one could yell—they was a-catching of their breath. And we lays by twelve hundred and fifty more.

"Before proceeding further with my witchcraft," says Stranger, "I would ask you to set your valuation of layout, lookout, license and good-will. Because," he says, "any fool can see that the ball stops on the one this time. Science, poetry, logic, romance, sentiment and justice point to it, like spokes to a hub. And if you're going to bank with that chicken feed"—jerking his chin toward the shattered fragments of the bank roll—"you'll have to lower your limit . . . before I play. Oh, I'm learning fast."

Frenchy looks unhappy, but there wasn't nothing to say. His pile wasn't big enough to pay if Stranger's predictions was accurate. "Bring me my sack, Brown," he calls out. Brown opens his safe and lugs over the sack. Frenchy pours it out on the table—ten thousand dollars, bills of all sizes from five to a thousand, and a coffee-pot full of gold. "Shoot," he says. "You're faded."

Stranger eclipses the one spot with ten dollar bills: ten each on corners, the four sides and the middle. "It's a sure thing—we'd just as well have some side money," he says, betting ten each on black, odd, first column, first dozen and 1 to 18. "Mr. Brown," he says, "the gentleman who runs the game will hand you seventy dollars when the ball stops. Drinks for the crowd while it lasts," and drops ten each on 16 and 2, for luck.

Buz-z-z. The ball hums a cheerful ditty, like hot coffee on a cold day. Buz-z-z—Click.

Frenchy goes into a trance, chewing his mouth. He moistens his lips and makes an effort. "One, black, and odd!" His voice was cracked and horrified.

"What a pleasant dream!" I thinks. "It's a shame to wake up and wrangle horses, but it must be near day." I tries to open my eyes, but couldn't. 'Twas no dream of avarice. Stranger was just visible above a pyramid of deferred dividends.

"Great Democratic gains," he announces. "Gentlemen—in fact, all of you—what'll you have?"

"I guess that includes me, all right," states a big miner. "Strictly speaking, I don't want no drink now, but, if you'd just as soon tell me what color my old pack-mare's next colt'll be, I sh'd be obliged."

No one wanted a drink—nobody moved. More miracles was what they wanted. "What? No drinks?" says Stranger. "Prohibition landslide in Terrapin? Can I believe my ears—or my nose? Well, then, I will pursue my hellish purpose. I appeal to the calm judgment of this crowd, if they ever heard of an election without repeaters?" But he doesn't let his gaze wander to the crowd none whatever. He never taken both eyes off Frenchy to oncet, since the limit had been pulled on him.

He decorated the board just as it was the last time, and looks on with pleased expectancy while the ball spins. I hope I may be saved if it didn't come a repeater!

Stranger yawns as he pulls in thirteen hundred and twenty dollars. "Thanking you for your kind attention," he states, "the entertainment is now concluded. Will some one trust me for a sack?"

"Feet cold?" sneers Frenchy.

"Oh no, I'm quite comfortable. But I *might* lose if I kept on," Stranger explains. "Those numbers may not come again for ever so long. This is a piking game, anyhow. I like to bet my money in large chunks."

"You seem to be a sort of a Democrat," suggests Frenchy. "Why not back up your views? Here's seven thousand says McKinley's elected."

"Why, *that's* my game," says Stranger, beaming. "That's just what I wanted. Bryan's going to sweep the country from Dan to Milwaukee."

I gives him the nudge, for I sees our pile a-glimmering. I don't mind betting on cards or horses and such, but politics is tricky. But he prattles on, plumb carried away by the courage of his convictions.

Frenchy's nose dented. Why, I learned later, but I'll tell you now. Terrapin was sixty miles from a telegraph office and all right-minded citizens was here present. But this sure-thing sport, knowing we was all for Bryan, had posted a relay on the North trail to bring him news. It was now way past mid-night. He had known McKinley was in since about the time I was staking Stranger, and poor, innocent, confiding Stranger walks right into his trap.

"Even money?" asks Frenchy.

"I would shorely scorn to take such an advantage of you," says Stranger. "I'll give you a chance for your white alley. I will now proceed to divide my capital into five parts. The first part contains fifteen hundred dollars, which I bet you against five hundred dollars that Bryan is our next President. I will then bet you fifteen hundred even that Bryan carries thirty-six states, a list of which I will make out and seal. Third pile, two thousand dollars, gives you a chance to break even if you're lucky. Give me odds of five to one and I bet this two thousand that Bryan carries four other states, names of which will also be deposited under seal with stake-holder. Pile number four, five hundred dollars, goes even that I made a good bet. Number five, one hundred and sixty-six dollars, goes in my pocket for tobacco and postage stamps and other luxuries."

"You're delirious. Your money's a gift," says Frenchy. "Make out your agreements. It'll take more'n I got to cover that five to one bet, but I can borrow the Northern Pacific on that proposition." He takes Brown off for a confidential and comes back with the money by the time Stranger had the bet in writing and signed.

Frenchy reads it aloud. "You are all witnesses," he says, and slaps his fist to it. "Name your stake-holder."

"Put it in Mr. Brown's safe—money, agreement and my two lists of states. Decide tomorrow at five P. M. when the stage comes in."

They makes a bundle of it and locks it up. "And now," says Stranger to me, "my presentiments points for bed."

"Why couldn't you quit when I wanted you to, you ijit?" I says. "You made the worst break I ever see."

"You certainly surprise me. Haven't I raised you to a position of opulence by my acumen and foresight? Your ingratitude grieves me to my heart's core—and just when we stand to more than double our money, too."

"Acumen! Foresight!" I jeers. "'Twas blind, bulldog, damnfool luck. I furnished all the judgment used when I tried to stop you. I put up the money, and you had a right to harken to me."

"You're my partner," says he calmly. "Half this money is yours, and all, if you need it. But I lost *your* money. This here is the proceeds of my iron dollar. By to-morrow night we'll have eleven thousand, anyway, and here you're complaining. I do hate a quitter.

"And I hate a fool. You have a chance to win one bet, and that's all."

"You'll regret this hasty speech to-morrow night. Follow me, and you'll wear diamonds!"

"Yes—on the seat of my pants," I rejoins bitterly. And all them somewhat diverse prophecies came to pass.

When we woke, after noon, 'twas pretty well known how the election went, and we was guyed unmerciful.

But Stranger wasn' noways dejected. "Rumor—mere rumor. 'Out of the nettle danger we may pluck the flower safety,'" he spouts, waving his hands like a windmill. "I've been in worse emergencies, and always emerged."

I was considerable sore and was for not showing up to turn over the money, but he persuaded me.

"At the worst Frenchy owes me ten that I won fair on the second bet last night," he says. "If I have to collect that, I aim to charge him something for collectin'. I had that in mind last night if the green hadn't come when my dollar was on it."

I sees reason in this, and oils my guns.

Frenchy was waitin' with his lookout, gay and cheerful. "Did you bring your sack?" was his greeting.

"Why, no, I forgot. Hi! Bud!" Stranger gives a boy five dollars. "Bring an ore sack to the barkeep for me, and keep the change."

We gets Brown with the package of stake money and prognostications on our way through the crowd to a back room. Brown busts the package and begins the hollow mockery.

"Bet number one." He reads the specifications. "Bryan loses. Any objections?"

Stranger shakes his head sorrowful, and pushes over the two-thousand-dollar packet.

"Bet number two." Brown breaks the list of thirty-six states. "For Bryan," he reads: "Connecticut, New York, Indiana, Illinois,

Michigan, Minnesota—" His feelings overcome him and he laughs till the tears roll down his face. Frenchy leers, and the lookout rocks himself back and forward. And to cap it off comes a knock, and barkeep comes in with the sack Stranger ordered.

They howled. "I'll give you ten for your sack," gasps Frenchy.

"You needn't rub it in," says Stranger, injured. "I certain was mistook in them estimates. Pass on to the next."

"Third bet," wheezes Brown. He wipes his cheeks and tears open the list of four states. "Bryan will carry—" he begins. He turns pale, his tongue stuck to the roof of his mouth, and his eyes bugged out so you could hang your hat on 'em.

"TEXAS!" he screeches. "*Arkansas, Georgia,* SOUTH CARO-LINA!"

"*Then* I made a good bet!" observes Stranger, popping the rest of the money into the sack.

"What!" yells Frenchy. "You were to name four additional states —forty in all!"

"Oh, no. Four *others.* These four were not in my list of thirty-six. You lost and I've got the mon. Why didn't you inquire? You orter understand a game before you play it. This is my game, and my rules go. See?"

Stranger's gun was dangling on his right hip, but, as Frenchy drew, Stranger's right hand caught his'n, gun and all, and Stranger's left produced a .45 from nowhere at all and proceeds to bend it over Frenchy's head. The tin-horn couldn't get his right hand loose, so he reaches around with his left, jerks Stranger's gun from his hip. But he only wastes time snapping it, for that one wasn't loaded.

I thought maybe Brown and the lookout would double up on my pardner, but they didn't. They just shoved the two pits of their two stomachs up against the muzzles of my two guns, and looked foolish.

"Nuff!" screams Frenchy, letting go his gun. He looks like ration day at Rosebud. Me and Stranger walks out, sticking closer'n brothers, lockstepping, back to back.

"What I tell you?" says Stranger, turning in at a butcher shop. And there he asks may we use the scales, and pours our ill-gotten gains into both scoops till they balance. "Take your choice, pardner," he says. "You're short on faith, but you're hell on works!"

Next to a restaurant. Before our order comes, in steps Billy

Edwards. He was a deputy sheriff, but white. "Would you mind my asking your name? 'Cause Frenchy doesn't know. He's swearing out a warrant for you, alleging assault with intent to kill," says Billy politely. "They haven't give me the warrant yet. Course if they had I wouldn't tell you this, for you might get away before I found you."

I'd never thought to ask his name!

"Artemus G. Jones," says he, and he stuck his thumb in his vest. "Set down and take supper with us."

"Ar—ahem. Er—what does the G. stand for?"

Artie looks embarrassed. "Galatians," he sighs.

"What? Was you named after—"

"I was named," says Artie, "after a family scrap. Can't you suppress it? Artemus G. ought to identify me."

"I—I thought it might spell easier," says Billy.

After supper we walks over and gets the warrant. Billy arrests Artie and disarms him. "*You* know *your* business—I'll make any kind of bet on that," says Billy; "but in your place I should have been far away on a bounding bronco."

We went to be tried before Judge Eliot. Frenchy kept a jack-leg lawyer named Satterlee, and he was helping persecute.

"Have you legal advice, prisoner?" says his Honor.

"A little," says Artie softly.

"Proceed. Call the plaintiff."

Frenchy took the stand and told a horrible tale of wanton robbery and brutal, unprovoked violence. He had won an election bet from prisoner, and prisoner had taken the money by force. He showed his wounds. He shore looked like he'd been playing goat with a buzz-saw.

Brown and the lookout was good witnesses, but they let out, when the Judge questioned them, that Artie had the money in his sack before the trouble began and that Frenchy had a gun. And not a word about my presence of mind.

Artie allowed he wouldn't cross-examine them. His Honor was riled. "Will you take the stand, sir?" he says.

Artie stretches. "Oh, no—I guess it's not worth while to take up your time. Ugh—o—oaoh," he says, yawning.

Judge was furious. "Prisoner, if you've got any witnesses in your defense, call 'em. As the evidence stands—up you go!"

Artie placed himself on top of his feet. "Your Honor," he says, "call Billy Edwards."

Billy gives his name, sex, color, and other essentials. Then says Artie:

"You arrested me to-night?"

"Yes."

"Was my gun loaded?"

"One of them was empty. The other one had five cartridges in it," Edwards promptly asserts.

"Was the loaded one bloody?"

"Awful."

"That's all," says Artie with a gracious wave of his hand, dismissing the witness. "Your Honor, our friend the Gaul, alias Frenchy, is before you. I am refined by nature. One gentle pull on the trigger would have removed all doubt. He would have been dead dead. He isn't. I move that my client, Artemus G. Jones, me, I, myself, be discharged, and plaintiff reprimanded for frivolity in taking up the time of the court. Had I wished to kill this jigger I certainly would have shot him. The gun that was bloody was the gun of Artemus," and Artie paid the whole blamed court a compliment by the way he retired.

Frenchy's lawyer began to holler, but the judge cut him quick. "Sit down, Mr. Satterlee," says he. "Unless you can prove your client is dead, the court will pursue the course indicated by the learned counsel for defense."

"Selah!" says Satterlee. "I'm down. Set 'em up in the other alley."

IV. The Long Shift

Appearing first in *McClure's*, August, 1907, then making
pages 43–53 in *West Is West* (New York, 1917), this otherwise has not been published in book form.

Mines, mining, and miners were integral parts of Rhodes'
life in New Mexico. What he writes of here was what he had
known first-hand, including his unusual hero, Caradoc Hughes.

Hughes was dead when Rhodes wrote this story, killed for
his trait of camp-robbing while working for Rhodes' brother,
Clarence, in Old Mexico. This, then, may be construed as
Rhodes' tribute to a man who was beyond the pale but yet
had once fulfilled the frontier's criterion of a Man.

ECHOES OF THE EXPLOSION yet volleyed from cliff to cliff; a thin
cloud of smoke and dust hung heavily over the shaft mouth. They
huddled together on the dump—the four men of the night shift,
peacefully asleep a moment since; the young manager, still holding

a pen in his nerveless fingers; the blacksmith, the cook, and the Mexican water-carrier—all that were left of the Argonauts.

No one spoke; there was no need. The dynamite, stored in the eighty-foot cross-cut, had exploded; no one knew how or why. The shaft walls had heaved and crushed together; the dump had fallen in for yards; the very hillside had slipped and closed over the spot where the shaft of the Golden Fleece had been. The eight men of the day-shift were buried alive. Working in the further stopes and cross-cuts of the deeper levels, they could hardly have been killed outright. Remained for them the long, slow agony of suffocation—or the mercy of the fire. For there was scarcely room to hope that the explosion had not fired the timber work.

They knew this, these silent men at the pit mouth; knew there was no chance that they could clear away the shaft in time—not if they were eighty instead of eight. To tear away that tangle of shattered rock was a matter of weeks; the air supply in the living grave beneath was a matter of days or hours. They knew, too, that their comrades were even then speaking hopefully of "the boys"; that to the last the prisoners would hold unfaltering trust—in them! And one fell on his face and cried on the name of God—Van Atta, manager and half owner.

"No hope, no hope, no hope!" he sobbed. "We can't save 'em. Keough wanted me to put in a ventilator shaft. I wouldn't—and now I have murdered them! They will wait for us—wait—wait— O God! God! God!"

He was young, inexperienced, half-invalid yet, now brought for the first time face to face with sudden and violent death: small wonder if he broke down for a moment. A moment only—he sprang to his feet, his face new-lighted with hope and energy.

"The old Showdown tunnel! They will remember that—if they are alive they will expect us to break through from there! Keough intended to connect it with Gallery Four on the last level, to save hoisting. I surveyed it then—I know the bearings—we can tear out some kind of a hole.—Come on, men! Oh, my God, we'll do it yet!"

They clambered down the steep, boulder-strewn mountainside, bearing drills, hammers, "spoons," picks, shovels, powder, fuse, caps, water, candles—all needful to begin work.

Near the face, far back in the winding tunnel, Van Atta drove a gad into the hanging wall. "Start from here. Keep an angle of forty-five degrees from the course of the tunnel, and a twenty degree dip. It is twenty-four to twenty-five feet in, and seven feet below us."

"Go!" said Price, holding the starter in place. White began another hole above him.

Van Atta raised his voice to be heard above the beating hammers. "Jones will sharpen steel now and help you later. The work will fall on you five; Charlie and I are out of it. The Mexican boy could do more work than either of us. We three will rig up some sort of makeshift ventilator, move the forge and cook outfit down, muck away for you, cook your meals. Save yourselves for the drills. Tell us what you need, and we will get it. Jones will work our steel bars up into the longest possible set of drills. We'll shoot out till the longest drill will reach, and then drive a hole right through. We can pump in fresh air then, pour down water and coffee and soup, and break out the balance afterwards. If we only had more men! Had we better send some one to San Clemente for help? Or north to the ranches by Red Mesa?"

"Red Mesa is closer, but there may be no one there. It's forty-five mile to San Clemente," said Lone Miller. "The boy couldn't do it afoot—we can't spare a man. By the time they got back, it might be too late—and the man's work here might make all the difference." He swung his hammer savagely. "But there's two other men besides ourselves on Malibu Knob. Doc Hughes is only five miles from here," he blurted out at last. "He's at the Nymyer copper claim and another Welshman with him. We can do it with them. They just got out from town. I saw them when I was out hunting yesterday afternoon. Doc is a dirty mutt—a low-down camp-robber. I'll get him yet, the damned scoundrel! . . . Not now. He can break more rock than any man that walks. Send for him. Maybe he'll come," he sneered. "Tell him it's our only chance for help—that we can't break through in time. Tell him I said so—me, Lone Miller—that I asked him to come."

"That's a whiskey-bloat's job," said Charlie, the cook. "Keep your men for men's work." He was gone.

"The other monkey is good, too," said Miller. "Not so good as Caradoc Hughes, but a miner. Trust Cousin Jock for that."

Two of the night-shift were Welshmen. "Goeslong, moi son," said one, well pleased.

Swiftly the hammers fell, square and true; slipping so easily that the work seemed as effortless as driving tacks. But back and shoulders were in each blow—the tough ash handles bent, the drills sank steadily into the rock. No ordinary toil—their best, and better than their best.

Without, the blacksmith beat a brave tattoo on the glowing steel, sharpening set after set of drills. The starters were a foot long, each succeeding drill five or six inches longer than the preceding one, and slightly narrower at the bit, so that it would follow in the hole. Seven or eight drills made a set, the longest four or five feet. Carefully he wrought, and watched with anxious eye as he plunged the hissing points into the water and, holding them up, saw the temper draw steel-blue and white-specked to the edge.

Meantime the Mexican lad and the manager worked on their improvised ventilating rig—lengths of pipe laid down the tunnel, screwed together, and connected with an extra bellows set up on the dump. Before they were done, the first shots were fired. Leaving Clovis to finish tightening up the joints, Van Atta went into the tunnel. The candles smoldered faintly through the sickly smoke, where Miller and White worked on a new hole. Williams, on his hands and knees between striker and holder, threw the broken rock to Price, who carried it farther back.

"That's it—that's good!" said Van, screwing a length of hose on his pipe-line to carry the fresh air quite to the front. "Whew! This powder is rank! I'll have fresh air pumped down in a jiffy. You two boys go back to the air till it's your time to drill. I'll get a wheel-barrow and muck away. Don't make the mistake of cutting the drift so small you can't work to advantage—and don't waste time pounding dull steel."

From this time on Clovis or Van pumped in fresh air steadily. Van, at the bellows, in the gathering dusk, glimpsed two speeding forms black against the sky-line. "Oh, good work! Good work, Cooky!" he cried exultingly. "Ten miles, and over that trail! He must have run all the way over!"

A shout went up in the tunnel when Van told his news. "I was afraid something would happen," said Miller. "They might have been away—hunting, maybe. Sundown's the best time for deer."

A burly giant came puffing down the tunnel: Caradoc Hughes, huge, brutal, broad-chested, red-faced, red-haired, bull-necked, thick-lipped. He bellowed strange greetings and shouldered the striker aside. "Le's see, moi son! Taper off a bit!"

"Taake foive," said Davis, following more quietly, as he took the drill from the holder. Caradoc grinned villainously at Miller. "Halloo! Hast thy gun, lad? Spaare moi life a bit, wilt 'ee? Have no time for scrappin' now."

"You're more useful alive, Taffy—just now," replied Miller, without looking up. Doc, chuckling coarsely, polished the drill-head with wicked, smashing blows. "*Whoosh!*" he grunted, expelling his breath violently at each stroke, as he brought the hammer down with all his bulk behind it. "Whoosh!"

Far behind, the cook limped painfully in. Later he brought steaming coffee and great Dutch ovens full of beef and beans. The bellows worked unceasingly, the wheelbarrow carried the broken rock away. At the front they paired off, changing at frequent intervals, holding and striking alternately. They worked. . . . But the shots were frequent, the charges heavy; the giant-powder fumes—sluggish, stupefying, poisonous—hung in the air in spite of the ventilator, dragged on the men's energies, dulled the onset. Their heads ached relentlessly. As each relay came off, they hurried out to the blessed pure air; and, thinking of the prisoners, entombed and suffocating, stumbled back again to strike with all their manhood behind each blow.

Van, when they went out in the air, made them wrap up warmly, lest their tortured muscles should stiffen. Van sent Charlie to them with food and hot coffee. Van brought water. He was here, there, and everywhere, pumping at the bellows, mucking away, keeping the drift true. The little man of brains anticipated every need; brought powder or fuse already cut and capped; saving a minute here, half a minute there. He loaded and fired the holes, sparing his men so much of the labor and powder smoke. He praised them, cheered them on, kept their hearts up, voiced their pride; till each man nerved himself to utmost effort, thrilled to know that solid and stubborn granite were less enduring than his own unchanging will.

And, when he crept back to Charlie and Clovis, it was Van who despised himself, whose heartsick thought was that his feeble body unfitted him to do a man's work on the firing-line. . . . So the night wore on; and ever the hammers rang, the drills bit deep; slowly, steadily, inch by inch, foot by foot, they tore the prison wall away.

As he rested, Caradoc goaded his disdainful enemy with taunt and slur—"Little pot, soon hot"—and such ancestral wit. For the long time Miller made no answer to these rude sallies, but the insults festered. "You know the old saw, Doc," he said at last, with ominous quiet. "The Almighty made some men big and some small, but Colonel Colt evened things up. Best think it over."

After each shot the crews went to the drilling, leaving the muckers to work out rock loosened by previous shots with pick and gad, straightening the uneven walls and roof as best they could. Their desperate haste invited disaster. It came before dawn. White was holding for Williams, when a heavy rock jarred from the roof and fell on the striker's shoulder. The hammer, glancing from the drill head, crushed the holder's hand to mangled flesh. The work stopped. White rose unsteadily. "Keep a-hummin'—keep the hammers going," he said, as he started out, dizzy and sick. Williams, in scarce less distress for his unlucky blow, followed him.

"Bide a bit!" bellowed Caradoc. "Harken! I hear summat! God's love, hear that! There's salve for they hurrt, lad! They're alive, they're alive, I tell 'ee! Happen the heat's drivin' 'em down bottom by way o' the winze!"

Tap-tap-tap! Muffled and dull and hollow it sounded from the rock before them. Tap-tap-tap! Doc snatched his hammer and thundered on the drill head. "They livin'!" he roared. "Seven feet an' more we've made this night, and fair gettin' limbered up a bit!"

"I'll eat a bite and go to town after help," said White, as Van bandaged his hand. "I'm no good here, but I can walk. I tell you these men are fagged. I ought to know. If you get close enough to drill a hole through, 'twill be all. The strain will be over, and every mother's son'll drop in his tracks. I'll send enough men from town to tear out that last ten feet by the roots."

"You can't, man. You're tired out and suffering. There is at least one bone broken in your hand. You'll give out."

"I—I wasn't aiming to walk on my hands, you know. Run along now. I'm twenty-one past, and it is my job to walk across Malibu Flat this day. If you look across the desert to San Clemente about dark, there'll be a big light on Ghost Mountain to let you know I made it. So-long!" He filled a canteen and went to do his part: not the least where each did well.

The long weary day dragged as they toiled at their endless task. The Mexican lad loaded his patient burros with kegs and went to the spring for water. Before noon Van Atta was on the verge of collapse. The others forced him to quit his part in the mucking. "Else will us bind 'ee handfast," observed Caradoc. "Happen us'll need thy brains yet, lad. Will be there with t'brawn—do 'ee keep care o' the only head here that's worth owt." So Van, cursing and shamed, cleaned out the holes when "mud" clogged them, picked out the followers, loaded and fired the holes, and sometimes took a short spell at pumping; while Charlie and Clovis stacked up no more rock, for lack of time, but wheeled it far down the tunnel and dumped it.

The incessant clangor of steel on ringing steel—hammer and hold, hold and hammer—mud! Clean—change drills, hammer! Load, fire—clean away—room for the hammers! The air was hot, foul, and intolerable, from candles, steaming breath and dripping bodies, dust and powder fumes. Hour after hour they drove home the assault; stripped to the waist, soaked and streaked with sweat and dust; with fingers cramped from gripping on hammer and drill; with finger-joints that cracked and bled, wrists bruised and swollen from jarring blows. The rough and calloused hands were blistering now; eyes were red-rimmed and sunken, faces haggard and drawn; back, muscles and joints strained and sore; worse than all, the powder headache throbbed at their temples with torture intolerable. . . . But the brave music of clashing steel rang steadily, clear, unfaltering, where flesh and blood flung itself at the everlasting hill.

A muffled roar came from the heart of the rock. The prisoners were working toward them.

"That's bad," said Van. "They'll make the air worse with every shot—and they can't hit our drift short of a miracle. They are lessening their chances."

"I don't rightly know that," said Caradoc. "Was on the last shift in Gallery Foar, myself. Was a horse there, I moind, hard as the Gaates o' Hell. Happen they'll smash that up and save us mony the weary blow."

The terrible strain began to tell. But Caradoc and his indomitable foe kept the heartbreaking pace hour after hour. Price was deadly sick, bleeding from nose and mouth; Williams' hurt shoulder was stiffened till striking was out of the question for him. So these two held. The others kept on pluckily, but their strength was leaving them. Inexorable Nature was extorting punishment for her outraged laws: the end was near, of men or task. The shifts were timed no longer. Each man kept up the savage hammering till he felt his strength fail: and as he stepped back, breathless, a silent spectre behind him rose up and took his place.

From the steel bars Jones fashioned a set of twenty-four drills, with all his cunning and loving care on every point; a hair's breadth difference between the bits, the longest drill twelve feet, its bit barely wider than the octagonal steel; he welded rods of iron for spoons of suitable lengths. They made the last few feet of the drift wider and higher than the rest, to have ample room for double drilling. At sundown they set off the last shots. They had torn out fourteen feet; they must drill a hole through the eleven-foot wall that remained. They had scarcely started when Clovis came, pouring out a torrent of voluble Spanish. A fire blazed on Ghost Mountain; help was coming.

One thing was left to fear. Thrice they had heard the muffled shots from within. Since then there had been no sign. Were the prisoners dead, or had they seen the unwisdom of further exhaustion of the air?

"They'll be too far gone to work, hours before they actually suffocate," said Van. "We'll be in time, please God!"

They called up every reserve that pride or hope or fear could bring. Two men struck at once, the hammers following each other so swiftly that it seemed impossible for the holder to turn the drill between blows.

"Scant mercy on they beasties this night," said Price. "They'll coom to t'hill-foot in foar hours. Near two they'll need to win oop t'hill—'tis mortal steep, an' they beasties'll be jaded sore. Will be in season for t'Graveyard shift."

"Not so—coom midnight will be full moon. 'Tis a sandy desert and a weary hill by night."

"Be't midnight, then. Williams, moi son, canst hold t'drill alone? I be fair rested oop by now, and can pound a bit. Us'll burn no more powder, an' t'air will clear oop ere long."

45

"Good for you, Cousin Jock!" said Miller heartily. By tacit consent Miller and Caradoc worked together. It depended on them —and they knew it. Shoulder to shoulder, blow for blow, they set their faces grimly to such work as few are called to do.

Neither Charlie nor Van Atta could be trusted to hold—for them to strike would be simply loss of time. The hole must be driven absolutely true, or the drill would bind, and they would have to begin again. At intervals one of the others would hold, giving Williams a few minutes' respite to straighten his aching back and his cramped and stiffened fingers. Van Atta cleaned the hole and called the depth. Ten inches; twenty—thirty—fifty—"Sixty inches!" he called exultingly. "An inch every two minutes, after all these hours! The world can't beat it!"

The drill "jumped" with crash and jar; Miller's hammer just missed Williams' hand, and Doc's closely following, was checked in mid-air by a violent effort. The holder drew the drill and turned the point to the light. An inch was broken from the bit; any succeeding drill would batter and break at once; the hole was lost.

A despairing silence: Williams fell against the wall and hid his eyes. Doc's head dropped over on his hairy chest. Miller's face was ghastly. . . . Van Atta rose weakly, picked up the starter, sank on one knee, with his face to the breast; holding the drill in place beside the lost hole, just above his shoulder, his eyes on the bit, he waited. A second—and Miller's hammer crashed down. *Clang! Clang! Clang!*

"God's blood!" Red with shame, the giant sprang up and showered down blow on mighty blow. A murmur ran around the circle; the little band closed grimly to the final test. Jones shaped the broken drill again and hurried back to bear his part in the renewed attack. The two enemies were doing the work. The others worked gallantly—but the leaders were making five inches to their two. What matter, where each gave his best? Five inches—ten—thirty—forty!

At fifty inches Price gave way, totally unable to do more. When Caradoc and Miller stepped back, breathless, Jones and Davis tapped away doggedly, but there was no force to their blows.

The big Welshman had bitten his lip; blood trickled from his mouth as he grinned at his mate. " 'Tis oop to us now. A rare team we make—and good for them beyond!"

Miller nodded. There was no contempt in his glance now.

Truly, this was a man; fit to stand to a king's back, though he fought for his crown—strong of heart and arm—this man he had dared despise. Foot to foot, blow for blow, unyielding, unswerving, they stood up to the tremendous task. Sixty—seventy! Davis and Jones made a last desperate spurt and fell back, exhausted, utterly forspent. Seventy-five! *Miller and Hughes!*

They planted their feet firmly and looked into each other's eyes as they began again. Miller's hammer kept the appalling pace, gave no sign that his strength was failing—ebbing away with every blow. . . . Somewhere, out in the far-off world, there was music and light and laughter. Perhaps he, too, had known pleasure, running streams that laughed in the sunshine, the free winds of heaven—youth—love—rest. It might have been so—long, long since. He did not know. Life had dwindled to these narrowing, flinty walls, this dim-litten circle, with its wavering center of steel where they must strike—strike hard! He and Doc—good old Doc—brave Doc! . . . Something stirred in the shadows behind—far-off, meaningless voices reached him over the rising clangor of steel. . . . Men, perhaps. If they would go away. . . . They drew his reeling senses from the shining steel, that he must strike—strike hard! Eighty—eighty-five—ninety!

Without warning, Miller pitched over on his face, unconscious. Their best was down. What lay in the silence beyond that granite wall?

Caradoc leaned heavily against the wall while they bore his fallen foe away. "Look to him—'tis a man!" he said. There was no triumph in his tones. He staggered forward. "*Whoosh!*" he grunted, as he struck out. "*Whoosh!*"

His eyes were sunken in his head, his blotched and purple face was fallen in; his sobbing breath whistled between his clenched teeth, his breast heaved almost to bursting; but his mighty shoulders drove home the drill. Ninety-five inches—a hundred! And still that tireless hammer rose and fell!

"Easy—mud—mud!" yelled Price, at the drill. "It's done! We've struck their drift!"

A dozen light taps, and the drill leaped through. The incredible had happened. They had struck the side wall of the counter-drift made by the prisoners on pure guess. They pulled out the drill. A rush of foul, sickening air followed. Price shouted down the hole. A mumbled response came back. Van Atta thrust the nozzle of the hose onto the hole, stuffed his handkerchief around it to keep it tight, and ran down the tunnel. Halfway out he met Charlie.

"Run!" he gasped. "We're through—they're alive; all of 'em! Pump—pump hard!"

Any San Clemente man will tell you the rest. Except this:

"Miller," said Caradoc, "wast roight. I robbed thy camp. Will take nowt more o' thine—nor no man's if so be I can think betoimes. T'is an old habit wi' me. But 'tis a shameful thing to do—for him as stood in moi shoes this night. Lad . . . wilt shake hands wi' a thief?"

"You can't steal anything of mine, Doc. What's mine is yours. God! How you worked—and were good for more, when I fell over like a baby."

"Toosh! Goeslong, moi son! Didst thy part, little Hop-o'-moi-thumb. Pounded steel two hours afore e'er I began. Shoulds't ha' been a Welshman!"

V. The Enchanted Valley

Appearing first in *Redbook*, March, 1909, then making pages 274-86 in *West Is West*, this has not been published otherwise in book form.

A suitable subtitle for this recall of the olden days and ways might be "Before the Railroad Came." There were not many such spots as *Son Todos* in Rhodes' boyhood, if, indeed, there ever was an actual prototype for this community. But the remembered fragments—water from one, trees from another, the way of life between man and man from all of them—were here combined to make the ideal.

Clearly stated herein is the bondage of the West to the financial and industrial East. It is stated with great good humor, which possibly explains why no serious thinker ever regarded Rhodes as a social historian. Matters such as these, properly, are to be treated with abiding concern and great, massive accretions of unalloyed dismay. That the frontier forgot to be joyless was not considered by the serious thinkers, despite Mark Twain's testimony to the contrary.

Most of the characters herein use names from real life; Emil James, for example, being twice sheriff of Socorro County.

Reeling, the white wrack of stars fled down the west, save where a grim rear-guard, rock-stubborn in the rout, still held the dawn at bay.

In the Hueco stage, L. Orrin Sewall, cramped and stiffened from the long night ride, glanced enviously at his one fellow passenger, now sleeping peacefully on the impromptu berth—happily combined of seat, baggage, lap-robe, and mail sack—which Sewall had found impossible. Thereon, as to the manner born, Emil James curled luxuriously, oblivious of whip-crack, lurch and jolting wheel.

Weird, ghostly, the giant candelabra of the *saguarro* shaped forth from the shadows ahead, bore down upon them, slipped by and faded back to dimness in the rear.

As it grew lighter, Sewall saw that they were plunging against an enormous mass of mountain, blue-black, huge, forbidding. The black became gray—brown—pink—but Sewall looked vainly for gap or gateway in the frowning wall. He was about to question the silent driver, when Emil rolled over and sat up.

"Ugh-h! I dreamed I was asleep!" he said blinking and stretching. "Hello! here we are! Say, you'd hate to make that drive by daylight."

Sewall turned. The grouped windmills of La Mancha, the last stage-station, were already far below them, so clearly outlined as to seem almost at hand, yet shrunken to toy dimensions. Tiny but distinct, a meager feather of smoke curled lazily above the cookhouse.

The stage-road, white and straight, dimmed to a line, a speck—nothing. Beyond the overwhelming desert, Pinetop and La Fantasia loomed monstrous and unbelievable. The early camp-fire of San Clemente shone redly, palpitant, firefly sparks through the faint thin mists of dawn.

"There's where we started from—those fires yonder," said Emil, pointing. "Eighty consecutive miles from here, those fires are. Don't look it, do they?"

They wheeled swiftly up the steady slope of foot-hill, over a road of decomposed granite, yellow and red and golden warm, picked with white gleam of crystal and quartz, so beaten and packed that it was resonant under the scampering, rhythmical feet. Scurry of rabbit, whir of startled quail, perfume of blossomed mesquite;

the ranked *saguarro*, fluted and gray-green now to the clearer light. To right, to left, down the spinning brown isles of pungent tar brush, there was flaunting of riotous scarlet, flash of crimson flame—the flower of the cactus.

Snuffing cheerfully in the cool freshness, the four ponies swung gaily around the long sinuous curves, eluding ridge or *arroyo*, ever sacrificing distance to grade.

And now they were at the very base of the Hueco's mighty prodigious, buttressed bulk. The hazy crest formed a battlement frowning and sheer, with upshoot of granite needle and spur, already flushing to a delicate pink in the upper sunrise.

"So that's the Hoo-ee-co mountain, is it?" asked Sewall.

Emil sat up, a malicious light in his eye. All the long road from San Clemente to sleepy-time his companion had enlightened the aboriginal mind with precisely worded, cock-sure information—more especially crushing current political heresies under the weight of expert authority. In labeled pigeon-holes of Sewall's neat and orderly mind were filed phonographically accurate records of the wisdoms promulgated by Prof. J. Langdon Leighton, of Pharos University; endorsed by men whose names were synonyms of success, and full of sonorous words as blessed as Mesopotamia. Emil had been so entranced with some of the more poetical terms that he had privately added them to his own vocabulary; rolling them in silent anticipation as sweet morsels under his tongue. "Empiric," "demagogue," and "charlatan"—always delivered by Sewall in accents of virulent and scornful superiority—especially appealed to Emil as words useful to him in his vocation.

"Hoo-ee-co?" he echoed, "No siree! H-u-e-c-o. You pronounce it 'whaco,' and it means 'hollow' like a tree."

"Why do you call it that?" continued Sewall. "And where's the town?"

Emil looked puzzled. "Why—why, we call it that—well, partly because that's its name, partly because the mountain is a hollow mountain. And the town's in the hollow basin inside, like a saucer."

"Someway," said Sewall, disappointed, "I'd got the impression that the town—what's its name—Son Todos?—that Son Todos was quite a place."

"Oh, well—like a butter-bowl, then," said Emil, generously. "Saucer-shaped, I meant, not saucer-sized. Strictly speaking, there ain't no town. Just a four-story settlement, like. Farms in the valley, cows and horses on the hillsides, mines underground, and goats in the upper air. Son Todos, where we stop—stage-station, post-office, store, everything else—was the first ranch, and the valley took the name."

"But why Son Todos?"

"What d'ye want us to call it?" said Emil, petulantly. " 'South West New J. Q. Adamsburg?' 'New Canterbury?' 'Versailes Center?' 'Tyre and Sidon?' 'Son Todos' means 'That's all.' Because—well, just because that's all. You can't go no further."

"What queer names you have in this country," meditated Sewall.

"You from Schenectady, too?" queried Emil, tartly.

"Schenectady? Oh, no; I'm from Poughkeepsie," said Sewall in all simplicity.

The driver choked. "This here dust all the time is mighty bad for my throat," he explained his first and last contribution to the council.

A pipe-line, straddling on crazy stilts, rambled drunkenly down the tangled hillside to a string of watering troughs, where a few cattle were straggling in. In the overhanging, broken precipice ahead, Sewall now became aware of a shallow fissure set obliquely to the mountain's trend. Suddenly it became an appalling chasm, deep hewn by the stupendous chisels of fire and frost and flood. Into this they plunged blindly though it apparently ended in a hopeless "box" a little higher up.

"Surely there is some mistake!" ejaculated the Easterner. "We can never get up there!"

"Yes we can. There's an escalator. You'll see!" said Emil reassuringly.

At the last moment, rounding a turmoil of broken and splintered rock, they came to an angled cleft, narrow, portentous, dark; widening to a wild cañon, scarred and gashed and torn, its cliffs carven grotesquely to dragon and gnome and leering face, spiteful, haggard, importunate, sinister. Turning, twisting, by boulder and gully and scar and cairn, flood-torn wash, abrupt steeps, hog-back, with downward plunge and squeal of protesting brakes, they held their doubtful way. The solid rock opened magically before them; closed irrevocably behind.

"We call this Zig-Zag," volunteered Emil. "A—eh—a whim of ours," he added, diffidently.

Sewall actually smiled. "It *is* crooked," he admitted.

"Yes. Good thing, too. No snakes in the valley. Break their backs trying to get through."

Another turn, followed by a long steep pitch up a buttressed shoulder: a black lettered boulder flashed them ironical warning:

DANGER!
SLOW DOWN TO EIGHT MILES AN HOUR!

They came to the top in a breathless scramble, bursting through that unquiet gateway, that shuddering confusion of hobgoblin nightmare, into a waiting, waking, sunlit world beyond.

So beautiful it was, so peaceful and sheltered, so sharp the contrast with the savage grandeur of the Pass, that Sewall involuntarily broke into an exclamation of delight. He quoted under his breath:

"The island valley of Avilion;
Where falls not hail, or rain, or any snow,
Nor ever wind blows loudly."

The air was fragrant, balmy, aquiver with bird-song and questing bee. The saucer slopes, though boulder strewn, were smooth and symmetrical in contour, thin-parked with cedar and live oak and dotted with strange flowers. Cattle and horses grazed leisurely, raising their heads to regard the intruders with mild contemplation. Bands of snow-white Angora goats, escorted by knowing collies, were on their browsing way to the herbs and shrubs of the higher reaches. Above the winding road they could see the frequent scar of dump or tunnel and rock huts clinging to the hillsides.

The flat floor of the saucer was a sweeping field of shaded emerald, unbroken save for winding irrigating ditches and dividing fences, and twice grateful after the pale desert. There were no buildings on the floor; the level land, which alone could be cultivated to advantage, was too valuable.

On the lower hill, barely above the floor, the road circled around this farm land. Just above it, wherever a tiny rill ran sparkling down the mountain, were nestled homes of flat-roofed adobe or stone, deep set in orchards, vineyards and gardens. For this, the hill was terraced with much toil to a sort of giant stairway, blasted from a rocky slope. The lower side of each step was walled with the boulders, filled in behind with small rocks and debris, laboriously covered with soil and leveled for irrigation; always with a "tank" on the top for the hoarding of water.

"I have never seen a fairer spot," said Sewall, drawing a long breath. "But I suppose, like every other place, it has its drawbacks?"

"It has," assented Emil, decidedly. "Real things—beef, milk, eggs, grain, fruit—they have the best and to spare. The mines are good, too—but low grade ore and the long haul to the smelter—see? Even their beef-herds can't be driven across the desert in first class shape. Too far between water-holes. They get the highest market-price for what they use, but the surplus—well, freight and shrinkage wipes out the profit. You just merely get day wages for your trip. Then you blow in the day wages seeing El Paso. That about right."

"So there's no money. They're learning, though. They're raising their own pork now, which isn't considered a proper thing for a cowman to do. They make ropes out of colts' tails and rawhide, mold their own candles, and let the women wash with *amole* to save buying soap. But there's no ready money. Everything's bought on time. One week after steer-sale the money's all back in Kansas City. Exports: ore, cattle, mohair, and raw material for freshmen. Imports: everything else. But they'd be the happiest *gente* on earth only for one thing."

"What's that?" asked the tourist, much interested.

"Debt."

"Whom do they owe?"

"Each other," said Emil, with an explanatory wiggle of his fingers. "Always buying and trading—no cash. It spoils their peace of mind. And here we are."

Where the largest rivulet tinkled bell-like over mimic cascades to a natural shelf, stood a cottonwood grove. In its dense, impenetrable shade the stage drew up before the low rambling building of Son Todos—post-office, store, hotel, livery stable, blacksmith shop. Freight depot it was, too, judging from the evidence of the huge-wheeled wagons rigged with chains and stretchers for twenty-horse "jerk-line" teams; each with another wagon, smaller indeed, but still enormous, trailed behind. A chuck-box, in the trail wagons, replaced the usual end-gate; water barrels were swung on platforms built at either side, just forward of the rear wheels.

"You see," explained Emil, as they sat down to breakfast *al fresco*, with an orchestra of far-off mocking birds and the cheerful undertone of broken waters, "You see, it's no trouble to produce here, but it's a long ways to the consumer. If you do your own hauling—well, you likely ain't got more than one little muzzle-loading, four-horse rig. You go down full of freight, come back mebbe empty and mebbe full of booze. Got your choice of bad or worse. Whitly now, he's got five or six big freight outfits like them yonder. He does the freighting as cheap as the boys could do it themselves. But still he makes money on it, for he freights, as you may say, by the wholesale, and gets retail rates, d'ye see? And he gets his own stuff brought back for nothing. Keeps the teams on the road all the time. No loss for idle plant."

"He ought to get rich," said Sewall.

"Well, yes. He is doing well—buying some city property in El Paso. But as for actual cash—well, you see, he carries 'em all over and that takes a lot of money."

"Carries them over? I don't understand."

"He sells us everything we need—grub, clothes, barbed-wire, saddles, everything—on a year's time," explained Emil. "Sells them, I mean; I don't live here myself. Just come over once or twice in a while to get rested. So they bring their produce—ore, mohair, grain and baled alfalfa—and turn it in on account. He don't buy it, 'cause naturally, mail only coming in once a week, he can't keep track of prices. He just credits 'em with the quantity, sells it for them the best he can, and charges a fair freight. If there's anything over, he pays their taxes for 'em, or may-be-so sends money for their kids off at school, as the case might be.

"Yes—Whitly is well fixed, all right. They don't grudge it to him. He keeps a look-out for good things. If there's a boy that ought to go to college or a young woman of energy and enterprise wanting to try the city—why, Whitly finds 'em a chance. But as for cash, he spends it fixin' up things; improvements, you know—a little old flour mill here, a sorghum mill there—something to help 'em all. And he coughs up surreptitious for valley-folks out in the said sad world that's sick or in trouble. There ain't many of 'em."

Sewall nodded. "I can understand that," he said. "Prisoners of content."

"So while the old man handles a lot of coin, he don't keep it in stock," continued Emil. "Any margin that might be comin' to the valley he brings back in the shape of canned progress—the latest thing in sewing machines, phonographs, and the like. He's comfortable—same as the rest—and he saves them the trouble of thinking. But about all he gets out of it is the fun of being boss.

"Well, so long, I am going up to see a friend. Folks'll drop in bimeby after their mail. Be good!"

"No," said Emil, carelessly, an hour later, answering Cal Rucker's question as to the newcomer, "not a bad sort of fellow. He'll maybe want to measure the Huecos with his little foot-rule and reduce 'em to grains Troy—but there's no harm in him."

Here he was interrupted. George, brother to Cal, rode into the yard, coming directly to the "gallery" of Cal's bachelor home, and to the point.

"Hullo, Cal! Howdy, Mr. James. Say, Cal—you got any money?"

Cal turned his pockets wrong-side out, made hopeful search of his hat, and shook his head with decision.

"Too bad," said George. "I owe Tom Hendricks on them milk-cows, and he needs it. I allowed I could borrow it off Whitly, but he just blew his roll for a threshing-machine. Told me he hadn't cash to give Tom Garrett an advance for boring a well over the Divide. I've got a good lot comin' from Miss Hagan's boardin'-house at the Mormon mine for milk, butter, eggs, and garden truck. But 'course she can't pay till the boarders pay, and they can't pay till Jimmy Dodds gets returns from his last shipment.

"So Hendricks'll nicely have to wait," interrupted Cal, cheerfully dismissing the subject as trivial. "Come along, you two, and see my pigs."

They stirred up the sleeping beauties—one white and one spotted.

"Now, them's sure nice hawgs," said George admiringly. "Say, Cal, give you that gun you was wantin' for 'em."

"I'll give you one of 'em for it," was the counter offer.

"No, you won't. Tell you what I will do, though," George proposed. "You've got to be gone to the roundups. Let me fat 'em on shares. I got plenty of milk and corn and I stay to home steady."

"All right," said Cal, nothing loth. "Keep 'em till December first for half?"

"Help me start 'em!" said George.

After some jockeying, the pigs went merrily frisking on their way. Emil and his host were returning when George came back.

"Hey, buddie! 'Spose one of them hawgs die? How that? Do we whack on the other one?"

"Nary whack. I was always luckier than you was," returned Cal, confidently. "George's married!" he added in a commiserating aside to his guest. "White one's mine, spotted one's yours, for better or worse."

"That's fair. It's understood then—the white one's yourn, and Spot's mine?"

"Sure thing!" Cal agreed.

George rode a few steps and turned back again, struck with a sudden thought.

"Tell you what, Cal—I'll give you the gun for your white pig."

He held out the gun, tempting in its silver and pearl. Cal's eyes twinkled covetously.

"Belt and all?" he queried, shrewdly.

"Belt and all!"

"I'll go you once."

George promptly unbuckled the belt and handed it over. Then Emil spoke for the first time.

"Run along now, Callie boy, and shoot tin cans. I want to make a little talk with your brother."

When Cal was on his way, Emil twisted his hands in the saddle-strings and said diffidently:

"I didn't want to be too forward, Mr. Rucker—not knowing you very well, but—well, your brother's an old friend of mine, and this is no use to me just now. If it'll help you any, you're welcome. Been there myself." He held out a crumpled and wadded hundred dollar bill.

George spread it out, regarding him gravely.

"Why, this is right clever of you, Mr. James, if you're sure you can spare it?"

Emil waved his hand.

"All right, then, and thank you kindly. We'll go back and have Cal stand good for this, if you'd rather. Good old noodle, Cal," said George, with fraternal indulgence. "Lucky chap!"

Emil looked back.

Lucky Cal stood half-turned toward them, scratching his head, glancing alternately at his brother and at the six-shooter on his open palm, his whole attitude expressive of dawning distrust.

"I guess that won't be necessary," drawled Emil, tone and face of preternatural gravity. "I have a good deal of confidence in your commercial ability, Mr. Rucker."

"Thank you again, then. I'll do as much for some other fellow. See them blame pigs hike, will you? *Adios!*"

"Me for a nap," announced Emil, as he came up the path.

Cal sat on the gallery, a puzzled look on his face, regarding the six-shooter with marked disfavor.

"Good gun, Cal?" asked Emil, with lifted brows.

Cal half raised the gun and gazed solicitously after his departing brother.

"I've a blame good mind to see!" he said earnestly.

When Emil awoke in the late afternoon, his host was not visible. So Emil made his way to Son Todos, finding there a lively crowd of old acquaintances. But Sewall adroitly appropriated him and drew him apart. He had changed notably in twenty-four hours, his slightly patronizing attitude was abandoned for one of enthusiasm, informality, and eager inquiry.

"This is the greatest place I ever saw," he said. "I want you to explain a number of things to me. In the first place, how do you reconcile Mr. Whitly's paternal guidance with his saloon-keeping?"

"That's easy," returned Emil. "He does that to hold the boys down. He hates whisky some, but drunkenness a good deal more. So long as he keeps a saloon, d'ye see, no one else is going to—not in this valley. And when a man you like, a man that's done you favors, advises you to taper off—especially if you owe him a good deal of money and intend to owe him more—why you're apt to heed as well as hear. Besides that, you know he won't let you have another drop anyhow."

"That's clear enough," said Sewall. "But, see here," he added suspiciously, "you mustn't play any more tricks on travelers."

"Tricks?"

"Oh, you're innocent, aren't you? You told me these people have no money. Why, they've got it to burn! Buying, selling, paying debts, trading and giving boot, and always handing over the cash."

Emil recalled the solemn political and financial maxims laid down by his fellow traveler on the previous night, but refrained from comment.

"Oh, well!" he said with lightsome gesture, "I told you they had the real thing—land, stock, produce. If there's more money in circulation than there used to be, they're not really any better off than they were before—they just seem to be."

Sewall chuckled.

"Oh, you don't fool me any more with your whimsicalities. Your pretended opinions are only a part of the characteristic quiet fun that seems to prevail here—like the 'slow down' sign at the pass. Oh, I like it here! The people are the jolliest, friendliest, best-natured set I've ever met! No blues or hard-luck stories here.

"I don't mind telling you, in confidence, that I came here to look into Mr. James Dodd's coppermining proposition. I'll own that you fooled me with your humorous account of financial conditions, and that I had formed an unfavorable opinion of the business ability and energy of these people. But when I see them, everyone with elastic step, sparkling eye, high spirits—everyone, even Mr. Dodd's miners, with the confident assured air of men on the winning side— it's prepossessing, I tell you. Of course, one cannot allow such things to influence one's business judgment, but I must admit that their jaunty, care-free bearing has impressed me, and that I rather expect to find the mine a good thing."

"Oh, it's a good mine, all right, all right," murmured Emil.

"Be the mine what it may," declared the Easterner, bubbling with enthusiasm, "it's a great country! I intend to secure a holding here—shooting-box, summer-house, that sort of thing—and bring out my nervously prostrated friends to get back into tune with life."

"Let me make you acquainted with some of the boys," said Emil.

So presently they were the center of an animated group under the trees. Cal and George were among the number. When most of the male population were gathered to entertain Sewall, George edged Emil to one side. He was highly elated.

"There's been the blamedest goin's-on you ever heard of," he confided. "You see, that there bill of yours was about the first loose money around here for quite some time. Our credit's good; we all know each other. We'll pay all right, sometime. We'd rather owe a man always than go back on a debt. But somehow a good debt ain't the same thing as good coin. I reckon every fellow around here either owed debts he hated not payin', or else there was something he'd been a-wantin' bad for a long time. Cash made quick tradin'. You never saw such circulatin' since you was rolled down hill in a barrel, never."

"I tried to overtake a lie, once," suggested Emil, thoughtfully. "I think I understand."

"That's the way this was. I paid Hendricks. He handed it over to Nate Smith for four ponies he'd bought. Nate turned it in on his store bill. Whitly advanced it to Tommy Garrett on the well-borin'; and Tom paid it to his fireman. He's been lettin' Tom hold out his wages, 'count of Mis' Garret bein' sick."

"Well, Tom's man, he's sparkin' Miss Berenice. So he put the greenback up agin Squatty Robinson's new buggy and harness, first throw at dice. Squatty bought a stack of alfalfa from Lon—"

"—That tossed the dog, that worried the cat, that caught the rat, and so forth?" intimated Emil, politely.

"Anyway," George persevered, "along towards supper time the Foy boys that's driftin' on the Mormon paid it to Bill McCall for last winter's beef. Mac got four broncos from Nate for it—pick 'em anywhere on the range. Nate was now so plumb affluent that he loaned it to Jimmy Dodds. There bein' no change, Jimmy gave it to the four men on the night-shift. They put their heads together and handed it over to Mis' Hagan on their board bill. Mrs. Hagan's that tickled she puts Bobby on burro and surprises me with it—the same old bill with a red ink-blot on it—and I hereby returns the same to you with my compliments. Much obliged for the loan."

"Don't mention it," said Emil, pocketing the bill. "Whitly's lighting up. Guess the boys are going in."

The crowd was slowly sauntering by, deep in conversation.

"Really, I don't know," said Cal to Sewall as they passed, "George, he speaks pretty good Spanish. George, what does *'que tomas ustedes?'* mean?"

"What will you have?" translated the unsuspecting George.

The assembly, turning briskly to the saloon, answered in joyful chorus:

"Beer!"

And Cal squealed like a pig.

Alone that night, Emil stirred up the fire, took out the bill that had so prospered Son Todos, looked it over carefully, then sadly held it to the flame.

"Pity it's counterfeit!" he said. "I wonder, now, if all them debts is squared up honest?"

VI. The Trouble Man

This never has been published in book form nor otherwise reprinted since appearing in the *Saturday Evening Post*, November 20, 1909. This neglect may possibly be due to the fact that it is a sheep *vs.* cattle conflict with a difference.

The veritable incident on which the story is based occurred in the identical country where the yarn is laid—on the Bar W range around Carrizozo. The sheepman involved in the scrimmage was Dionisio Chavez. The late Frank M. King was a warrior in this affair and Rhodes, himself, rode for the Pete Johnson who appears in the story, as well as for Jim Nabours at about the time of the trouble.

i

BILLY BEEBE did not understand. There was no disguising the unpalatable fact: Rainbow treated him kindly. It galled him. Ballinger, his junior in Rainbow, was theme for ridicule and biting jest, target for contumely and abuse; while his own best efforts were met with grave, unfailing courtesy.

Yet the boys liked him; Billy was sure of that. And so far as the actual work was concerned, he was at least as good a roper and brand reader as Ballinger, quicker in action, a much better rider.

In irrelevant and extraneous matters—brains, principle, training, acquirements—Billy was conscious of unchallenged advantage. He was from Ohio, eligible to the Presidency, of family, rich, a college man; yet he had abandoned laudable moss-gathering, to become a rolling, bounding, riotous stone. He could not help feeling that it was rather noble of him. And then to be indulgently sheltered as an honored guest, how beloved soever! It hurt.

Not for himself alone was Billy grieved. Men paired on Rainbow. "One stick makes a poor fire"—so their word went. Billy sat at the feet of John Wesley Pringle—wrinkled, wind-brown Gamaliel. Ballinger was the disciple of Jeff Bransford, gay, willful, questionable man. Billy did not like him. His light banter, lapsing unexpectedly from broad Doric to irreproachable New English, carried in solution audacious, glancing disrespect of convention, established institutions, authorities, axioms, "accepted theories of irregular verbs"—too elusive for disproof, too intolerably subversive to be ignored. That Ballinger, his shadow, was accepted man of action, while Billy was still an outsider, was, in some sense, a reflection on Pringle. Vicarious jealousy was added to the pangs of wounded self-love.

Billy was having ample time for reflection now, riding with Pringle up the Long Range to the Block roundup. Through the slow, dreamy days they threaded the mazed ridges and cañons falling eastward to the Pecos from Guadalupe, Sacramento and White Mountain. They drove their string of thirteen horses each; tough circlers, wise cutting-horses, sedate night horses and patient old Steamboat, who, in the performance of pack duty, dropped his proper designation to be injuriously known as "the Wagon."

Their way lay through the heart of the Lincoln County War country—on winding trails, by glade and pine-clad mesa; by clear streams, bell-tinkling, beginning, with youth's eager haste, their journey to the far-off sea; by Seven Rivers, Bluewater, the Feliz, Penasco and Silver Spring.

Leisurely they rode, with shady halt at midday—leisurely, for an empire was to be worked. It would be months before they crossed the divide at Nogal, "threw in" with Bransford and Ballinger, now representing Rainbow with the Bar W, and drove home together down the west side.

While Billy pondered his problem Pringle sang or whistled tirelessly—old tunes of amazing variety, ranging from Nancy Lee and Auld Robin Gray to La Paloma Azul or the Nogal Waltz. But ever, by ranch house or brook or pass, he paused to tell of deeds there befallen in the years of old war, deeds violent and bloody, yet half redeemed by hardihood and unflinching courage.

Pringle's voice was low and unemphatic; his eyes were ever on the long horizon. Trojan nor Tyrian he favored, but as he told the Homeric tale of Buckshot Roberts, while they splashed through the broken waters of Ruidoso and held their winding way through the cutoff of Cedar Creek, Billy began dimly to understand.

Between him and Rainbow the difference was in kind, not in degree. The shadow of old names lay heavy on the land; these resolute ghosts yet shaped the acts of men. For Rainbow the Roman *virtus* was still the one virtue. Whenever these old names had been spoken, Billy remembered, men had listened. Horseshoers had listened at their shoeing; card-players had listened while the game went on; by campfires other speakers had ceased their talk to listen without comment. Not ill-doers, these listeners, but quiet men, kindly, generous; yet the tales to which they gave this tribute were too often of ill deeds. As if they asked not "Was this well done?" but rather "Was this done indeed—so that no man could have done more?" Were the deed good or evil, so it were done utterly it commanded admiration—therefore, imitation.

Something of all this he got into words. Pringle nodded gravely. "You've got it sized up, my son," he said. "Rainbow ain't strictly up to date and still holds to them elder ethics, like Norval on the Grampian Hills, William Dhu Tell, and the rest of them neck-or-nothing boys. This Mr. Rolando, that Eusebio sings about, give our sentiments to a T-Y—ty. He was some scrappy and always blowin' his own horn, but, by jings, he delivered the goods as per invoice and could take a major league lickin' with no whimperin'. This Rolando he don't hold forth about gate money or individual percentages. 'Get results for your team,' he says. 'Don't flinch, don't foul, hit the line hard, here goes nothing!'

"That's a purty fair code. And it's all the one we got. Pioneerin' is troublesome—pioneer is all the same word as pawn, and you throw away a pawn to gain a point. When we drive in a wild bunch, when we top off the boundin' bronco, it may look easy, but it's always a close thing. Even when we win we nearly lose; when we lose we nearly win. And that forms the stay-with-it-Bill-you're-doin'-well habit. See?

"So, we mostly size a fellow up by his abilities as a trouble man. Any kind of trouble—not necessarily the fightin' kind. If he goes the route, if he sets no limit, if he's enlisted for the war—why, you naturally depend on him.

"Now, take you and Jeff. Most ways you've got the edge on him. But you hold by rules and formulas and laws. There's things you must do or mustn't do—because somebody told you so. You go into a project with a mental reservation not to do anything indecorous or improper; also, to stop when you've taken a decent lickin'. But Jeff don't aim to stop while he can wiggle; and he makes up new rules as he goes along, to fit the situation. Naturally, when you get in a tight place you waste time rememberin' what the authorities prescribe as the neat thing. Now, Jeff consults only his own self, and he's mostly unanimous. Mebbe so you both do the same thing, mebbe not. But Jeff does it first. You're a good boy, Billy, but there's only one way to find out if you're a square peg or a round one."

"How's that?" demanded Billy, laughing, but half vexed.

"Get in the hole," said Pringle.

ii

"Aw, stay all night! What's the matter with you fellows? I haven't seen a soul for a week. Everybody's gone to the round-up."

Wes' shook his head: "Can't do it, Jimmy. Got to go out to good grass. You're all eat out here."

"I'll side you," said Jimmy decisively. "I got a lot of stored-up talk I've got to get out of my system. I know a bully place to make camp. Box cañon to hobble your horses in, good grass, and a little tank of water in the rocks for cookin'. Bring along your little old Wagon, and I'll tie on a hunk of venison to feed your faces with. Get there by dark."

"How come you didn't go to the work your black self?" asked Wes', as Beebe tossed his rope on the Wagon and led him up.

Jimmy's twinkling eyes lit up his beardless face. "They left me here to play shinny-on-your-own-side," he explained.

"Shinny?" echoed Billy.

"With the Three Rivers sheep," said Jimmy. "I'm to keep them from crossing the mountain."

"Oh, I see. You've got an agreement that the east side is for cattle and the west side for sheep."

Jimmy's face puckered. "Agreement? H'm yes, leastways, I'm agreed. I didn't ask them, but they've got the general idea. When I ketch 'em over here I drive them back. As I don't ever follow 'em beyond the summit they ought to savvy my the'ries by this time."

Pringle opened the gate. "Let's mosey along—they've got enough water. Which way, kid?"

"Left-hand trail," said Jimmy, falling in behind.

"But why don't you come to an understanding with them and fix on a dividing line?" insisted Beebe.

Jimmy lolled sidewise in his saddle, cocking an impish eye at his inquisitor. "Reckon ye don't have no sheep down Rainbow way? Thought not. Right there's the point exactly. They have a dividing line. They carry it with 'em wherever they go. For the cattle won't graze where sheep have been. Sheep pertects their own range, but we've got to look after ours or they'd drive us out. But the understanding's all right, all right. They don't speak no English, and I don't know no *paisano* talk, but I've fixed up a signal code they savvy as well's if they was all college aluminums."

"Oh, yes—sign talk," said Billy. "I've heard of that." Wes' turned his head aside.

"We-ell, not exactly. Sound talk'd be nearer. One shot means 'Git!' 'two means 'Hurry up!' and three—"

"But you've no right to do that," protested Billy warmly. "They've got just as much right here as your cattle, haven't they?"

"Surest thing they have—if they can make it stick," agreed Jimmy cordially. "And we've got just as much right to keep 'em off if we can. And we can. There ain't really no right to it. It's Uncle Sam's land we goth graze on, and Unkie is some busy with conversation on natural resources, and keepin' republics up in South America and down in Asia, and selectin' texts for coins and infernal revenue stamps, and upbuildin' Pittsburgh, and keepin' up the price of wool, and fightin' all the time to keep the laws from bein' better'n the Constitution, like a Bawston puncher trimmin' a growin' colt's foot down to fit last year's shoes. Shucks! *He* ain't got no time to look after us. We just got to do our own regulatin' or git out."

"How would you like it yourself?" demanded Billy.

Jimmy's eyes flashed. "If my brain was to leak out and I subsequent took to sheep-herdin', I'd like to see any dern puncher drive me out," he declared belligerently.

"Then you can't complain if—"

"He don't," interrupted Pringle. "None of us complain—nary a murmur. If the sheep men want to go they go, an' a little shootin' up the contagious vicinity don't hurt 'em none. It's all over oncet the noise stops. Besides, I think they mostly sorter enjoy it. Sheep-herdin' is mighty dull business, and a little excitement is mighty welcome. It gives 'em something to look forward to. But if they feel hostile they always get the first shot for keeps. That's a mighty big percentage in their favor, and the reports on file with the War Department shows that they generally get the best of it. Don't you worry none, my son. This ain't no new thing. It's been goin' on ever since Abraham's outfit and the L O T boys got to scrappin' on the Jordan range, and then some before that. After Abraham took to the hill country, I remember, somebody jumped one of his wells and two of Isaac's. It's been like that, in the shortgrass countries ever since. Human nature's not changed much. By jings! There they be now!"

Through the twilight the winding trail climbed the side of a long ridge. To their left was a deep, impassable cañon; beyond that a parallel ridge; and from beyond that ridge came the throbbing, drumming clamor of a sheep herd.

"The son of a gun!" said Jimmy. "He means to camp in our box cañon. I'll show him!" He spurred by the grazing horses and clattered on in the lead, striking fire from the stony trail.

On the shoulder of the further ridge heaved a gray fog, spreading, rolling slowly down the hillside. The bleating, the sound of myriad trampling feet, the multiplication of bewildering echoes, swelled to a steady, unchanging, ubiquitous tumult. A dog suddenly topped the ridge; another; then a Mexican herder bearing a long rifle. With one glance at Jimmy beyond the blackshadowed gulf he began turning the herd back, shouting to the dogs. They ran in obedient haste to aid, sending the stragglers scurrying after the main bunch.

Jimmy reined up, black and gigantic against the skyline. He drew his gun. Once, twice, thrice, he shot. The fire streamed out against the growing dark. The bullets, striking the rocks, whined spitefully. The echoes took up the sound and sent it crashing to and fro. The sheep rushed huddling together, panic-stricken. Herder and dogs urged them on. The herder threw up a hand and shouted.

"That boy's shootin' mighty close to that *paisano*," muttered Pringle. "He orter quit now. Reckon he's showin' off a leetle." He raised his voice in warning. "Hi! you Jimmy!" he called. "He's a-goin'! Let him be!"

"*Vamos! Hi-i!*" shrilled Jimmy gayly. He fired again. The Mexican clapped hand to his leg with an angry scream. With the one movement he sank to his knees, his long rifle fell to a level, cuddled to his shoulder, spitting fire. Jimmy's hand flew up; his gun dropped; he clutched at the saddle-horn, missed it, fell heavily to the ground. The Mexican dropped out of sight behind the ridge. It had been but a scant minute since he first appeared. The dogs followed with the remaining sheep. The ridge was bare. The dark fell fast.

Jimmy lay on his face. Pringle turned him over and opened his shirt.

He was quite dead.

iii

From Malagra to Willow Spring, the next available water, is the longest jump on the Bar W range. Working the "Long Lane" fenced by Malpais and White Mountain is easy enough. But after cutting out and branding there was the long wait for the slow day herd, the tedious holding to water from insufficient troughs. It was late when the day's "cut" was thrown in with the herd, sunset when the bobtail had caught their night horses and relieved the weary day herders.

The bobtail moves the herd to the bed ground—some distance from camp, to avoid mutual annoyance and alarm—and holds it while night horses are caught and supper eaten. A thankless job, missing the nightly joking and banter over the day's work. Then the first guard comes on and the bobtail goes, famished, to supper. It breakfasts by starlight, relieves the last guard, and holds cattle while breakfast is eaten, beds rolled and horses caught, turning them over to the day herders at sunup.

Bransford and Ballinger were two of the five bobtailers, hungry, tired, dusty and cross. With persuasive, soothing song they trotted around the restless cattle, with hasty, envious glances for the merry groups around the chuck wagon. The horse herd was coming in; four of the boys were butchering a yearling; beds were being dragged out and unrolled. Shouts of laughter arose; they were baiting the victim of some mishap by making public an exaggerated version of his discomfiture.

Turning his back on the camp, Jeff Bransford became aware of a man riding a big white horse down the old military road from Nogal way. The horse was trotting, but wearily; passing the herd he whinnied greeting, again wearily.

The cattle were slow to settle down. Jeff made several circlings before he had time for another campward glance. The horse herd was grazing off, and the boys were saddling and staking their night horses; but the stranger's horse, still saddled, was tied to a soapweed.

Jeff sniffed. "Oh, Solomon was sapient and Solomon was wise!" he crooned, keeping time with old Summersault's steady fox-trot. "And Solomon was marvelously wide between the eyes!" He sniffed again, his nose wrinkled, one eyebrow arched, one corner of his mouth pulled down; he twisted his mustache and looked sharply down his nose for consultation, pursing his lips. "H'm! That's funny!" he said aloud. "That horse is some tired. Why don't he turn him loose? Bransford, you old fool, sit up and take notice! 'Eternal vigilance is the price of liberty.' "

He had been a tired and a hungry man. He put his weariness by as a garment, keyed up the slackened strings, and rode on with every faculty on the alert. It is to be feared that Jeff's conscience was not altogether void of offense toward his fellows.

A yearling pushed tentatively from the herd. Jeff let her go, fell in after her and circled her back to the bunch behind Clay Cooper. Not by chance. Clay was from beyond the divide.

"Know the new man, Clay?" Jeff asked casually, as he fell back to preserve the proper interval.

Clay turned his head. "Sure. Clem Littlefield, Bonita man."

When the first guard came at last Jeff was on the farther side and so the last to go in. A dim horseman overtook him and waved a sweeping arm in dismissal.

"We've got 'em! Light a rag, you hungry man!"

Jeff turned back slowly, so meeting all the relieving guard and noting that Squatty Robinson, of the V V, was not of them, Ollie Jackson taking his place.

He rode thoughtfully into camp. Staking his horse in the starlight he observed a significant fact. Squatty had not staked his regular night horse, but Alizan, his favorite. He made a swift investigation and found that not a man from the east side had caught his usual night horse. Clay Cooper's horse was not staked, but tied short to a mesquit, with the bridle still on.

Pete Johnson, the foreman, was just leaving the fire for bed. Beyond the fire the east-side men were gathered, speaking in subdued voices. Ballinger, with loaded plate, sat down near them. The talking ceased. It started again at once. This time their voices rose clear and distinct in customary badinage.

"Why, this is face up," thought Jeff. "Trouble. Trouble from beyond the divide. They're going to hike shortly. They've told Pete that much, anyhow. Serious trouble—for they've kept it from the rest of them. Is it to my address? Likely. Old Wes' and Beebe are over there somewhere. If I had three guesses the first two'd be that them Rainbow chasers was in a tight."

He stumbled into the firelight, carrying his bridle, which he dropped by the wagon wheel. "This day's sure flown by like a week," he grumbled, fumbling around for cup and plate. "My stomach was just askin' was my throat cut."

As he bent over to spear a steak the tail of his eye took in the group beyond and intercepted a warning glance from Squatty to the stranger. There was an almost imperceptible thrusting motion of Squatty's chin and lips; a motion which included Jeff and the unconscious Ballinger. It was enough. Surmise, suspicion flamed to certainty. "My third guess," reflected Jeff sagely, "is just like the other two. Mr. John Wesley Pringle has been doing a running high jump or some such stunt, and has plumb neglected to come down."

He seated himself cross-legged and fell upon his supper vigorously, bandying quips and quirks with the bobtail as they ate. At last he jumped up, dropped his dishes clattering in the dishpan, and drew a long breath.

"I don't feel a bit hungry," he announced plaintively. "Gee! I'm glad I don't have to stand guard. I do hate to work between meals."

He shouldered his roll of bedding. "Good-by, old world—I'm going home!" he said, and melted into the darkness. Leo following, they unrolled their bed. But as Leo began pulling off his boots Jeff stopped him.

"Close that aperture in your face and keep it that way," he admonished guardedly. "You and me has got to do a ghost dance. Project around and help me find them Three Rivers men."

The Three Rivers men, Crosby and Os Hyde, were sound asleep. Awakened, they were disposed to peevish remonstrance.

"Keep quiet!" said Jeff, "Al, you slip on your boots and go tell Pete you and Os is goin' to Carrizo and that you'll be back in time to stand your guard. Tell him out loud. Then you come back here and you and Os crawl into our bed. I'll show him where it is while you're gone. You use our night horses. Me and Leo want to take yours."

"If there's anything else don't stand on ceremony," said Crosby. "Don't you want my tooth-brush?"

"You hurry up," responded Jeff. "D'ye think I'm doin' this for fun? We're It. We got to prove an alibi."

"Oh!" said Al.

A few minutes later, the Three Rivers men disappeared under the tarp of the Rainbow bed, while the Rainbow men, on Three Rivers horses, rode silently out of camp, avoiding the firelit circle.

Once over the ridge, well out of sight and hearing from camp, Jeff turned up the draw to the right and circled back toward the Nogal road on a long trot.

"Beautiful night," observed Leo after an interval. "I just love to ride. How far is it to the asylum?"

"Leo," said Jeff, "you're a good boy—a mighty good boy. But I don't believe you'd notice it if the sun didn't go down till after dark." He explained the situation. "Now, I'm going to leave you to hold the horses just this side of the Nogal road, while I go on afoot and eavesdrop. Them fellows'll be makin' big medicine when they come along here. I'll lay down by the road and get a line on their play. Don't you let them horses nicker."

Leo waited an interminable time before he heard the eastside men coming from camp. They passed by, talking, as Jeff had prophesied. After another small eternity Jeff joined him.

"I didn't get all the details," he reported. "But it seems that the Parsons City people has got it framed up to hang a sheepman some. Wes' is dead set against it—I didn't make out why. So there's a deadlock and we've got the casting vote. Call up your reserves, old man. We're due to ride around Nogal and beat that bunch to the divide."

It was midnight by the clock in the sky when they stood on Nogal divide. The air was chill. Clouds gathered blackly around Capitan, Nogal Peak and White Mountain. There was steady, low muttering of thunder; the far lightnings flashed pale and green and rose.

"Hustle along to Lincoln, Leo," commanded Jeff, "and tell the sheriff they state, positive, that the hangin' takes place prompt after breakfast. Tell him to bring a big posse—and a couple of battleships if he's got 'em handy. Meantime, I'll go over and try what the gentle art of persuasion can do. So long! If I don't come back the mule's yours."

He turned up the right-hand road.

iv

"Well?" said Pringle.

"Light up!" said Uncle Pete. "Nobody's goin' to shoot at ye from the dark. We don't do business that way. When we come we'll come in daylight, down the big middle of the road. Light up. I ain't got no gun. I come over for one last try to make you see reason. I knowed thar weren't use talkin' to you when you was fightin' mad. That's why I got the boys to put it off till mawnin'. And I wanted to send to Angus and Salado and the Bar W for Jimmy's friends. He ain't got no kinnery here. They've come. They all see it the same way. Chavez killed Jimmy, and they're goin' to hang him. And, since they've come, there's too many of us for you to fight."

Wes' lit the candle. "Set down. Talk all you want, but talk low and don't wake Billy," he said as the flame flared up.

That he did not want Billy waked up, that there was not even a passing glance to verify Uncle Pete's statement as to being un-armed, was, considering Uncle Pete's errand and his own position, a complete and voluminous commentary on the men and ethics of that time and place.

Pete Burleson carefully arranged his frame on a bench, and glanced around.

On his cot Billy tossed and moaned. His fevered sleep was tortured by a phantasmagoria of broken and hurried dreams, repeating with monstrous exaggeration the crowded hours of the past day. The brain-stunning shock and horror of sudden, bloody death, the rude litter, the night-long journey with their awful burden, the doubtful aisles of pine with star galazies wheeling beyond, the gaunt, bare hill above, the steep zigzag to the sleeping town, the flaming wrath of violent men—in his dream they came and went. Again, hasty messengers flashed across the haggard dawn; again, he shared the pursuit and capture of the sheep-herder. Sudden clash of unyielding wills; black anger; wild voices for swift death, quickly backed by wild, strong hands; Pringle's cool and steady defiance; his own hot, resolute protest; the prisoner's unflinching fatalism; the hard-won respite—all these and more—the lights, the swaying crowd, fierce faces black and bitter with inarticulate wrath—jumbled confusedly in shifting, unsequenced combinations leading ever to some incredible, unguessed catastrophe.

Beside him, peacefully asleep, lay the manslayer, so lately snatched from death, unconscious of the chain that bound him, oblivious of the menace of the coming day.

"He takes it pretty hard," observed Uncle Pete, nodding at Billy.

"Yes. He's never seen any sorrow. But he don't weaken one mite. I tried every way I could think of to get him out of here. Told him to sidle off down to Lincoln after the sheriff. But he was dead on to me."

"Yes? Well, he wouldn't 'a' got far, anyway," said Uncle Pete dryly. "We're watching every move. Still, it's a pity he didn't try. We'd 'a' got him without hurtin' him, and he'd 'a' been out o' this."

Wes' made no answer. Uncle Pete stroked his grizzled beard reflectively. He filled his pipe with cut plug and puffed deliberately.

"Now, look here," he said slowly: "Mr. Procopio Chavez killed Jimmy, and Mr. Procopio Chavez is going to hang. It wa'n't no weakenin' or doubt on my part that made me call the boys off yisterday evenin'. He's got to hang. I just wanted to keep you fellers from gettin' killed. There might 'a' been some sense in your fighting then, but there ain't now. There's too many of us."

"Me and Billy see the whole thing," said Wes', unmoved. "It was too bad Jimmy got killed, but he was certainly mighty brash.

73

The sheep-herder was goin' peaceable, but Jimmy kept shootin', and shootin' close. When that splinter of rock hit the Mexican man he thought he was shot, and he turned loose. Reckon it hurt him like sin. There's a black-and-blue spot on his leg big as the palm of your hand. You'd 'a' done just the same as he did.

"I ain't much enthusiastic about sheep-herders. In fact, I jerked my gun at the time; but I was way down the trail and he was out o' sight before I could shoot. Thinkin' it over careful, I don't see where this Mexican's got any hangin' comin'. You know, just as well as I do, no court's goin' to hang him on the testimony me and Billy's got to give in."

"I do," said Uncle Pete. "That's exactly why we're goin' to hang him ourselves. If we let him go it's just encouragin' the *pastores* to kill up some more of the boys. So we'll just stretch his neck. This is the last friendly warnin', my son. If you stick your fingers between the anvil and the hammer you'll get 'em pinched. 'Tain't any of your business, anyway. This ain't Rainbow. This is the White Mountain and we're strictly home rulers. And, moresoever, that war talk you made yesterday made the boys plumb sore."

"That war talk goes as she lays," said Pringle steadily. "No hangin' till after the shootin'. That goes."

"Now, now—what's the use?" remonstrated Uncle Pete. "Ye'll just get yourself hurted and 'twon't do the greaser any good. You might mebbe so stand us off in a good, thick 'dobe house, but not in this old shanty. If you want to swell up and be stubborn about it, it just means a grave apiece for you all and likely for some few of us."

"It don't make no difference to me," said Pringle, "if it means diggin' a grave in a hole in the cellar under the bottomless pit. I'm goin' to make my word good and do what I think's right."

"So am I, by Jupiter! Mr. Also Ran Pringle, it is a privilege to have known you!" Billy, half awake, covered Uncle Pete with a gun held in a steady hand. "Let's keep him here for a hostage and shoot him if they attempt to carry our their lynching," he suggested.

"We can't, Billy. Put it down," said Pringle mildly. "He's here under flag of truce."

"I was tryin' to save your derned fool hides," said Uncle Pete benignantly.

"Well—'tain't no use. We're just talkin' round and round in a circle, Uncle Pete. Turn your wolf loose when you get ready. As I said before, I don't noways dote on sheepmen, but I seen this, and I've got to see that this poor devil gets a square deal. I got to!"

Uncle Pete sighed. "It's a pity!" he said; "a great pity! Well, we're comin' quiet and peaceful. If there's any shootin' done you all have got to fire the first shot. We'll have the last one."

"Did you ever stop to think that the Rainbow men may not like this?" inquired Pringle. "If they're anyways dissatisfied they're liable to come up here and scratch your eyes out one by one."

"Jesso. That's why you're goin' to fire the first shot," explained Uncle Pete patiently. "Only for that—and likewise because it would be a sorter mean trick to do—we could get up on the hill and smoke you out with rifles at long range, out o' reach of your six-shooters. You all might get away, but the sheepherder's chained fast and we could shoot him to kingdom come, shack and all, in five minutes. But you've had fair warnin' and you'll get an even break. If you want to begin trouble it's your own lookout. That squares us with Rainbow."

"And you expect them to believe you?" demanded Billy.

"Believe us? Sure! Why shouldn't they?" said Uncle Pete simply. "Of course they'll believe us. It'll be so." He stood up and regarded them wistfully. "There don't seem to be any use o' sayin' any more, so I'll go. I hope there ain't no hard feelin's?"

"Not a bit!" said Pringle; but Billy threw his head back and laughed angrily. "Come, I like that! By Jove, if that isn't nerve for you! To wake a man up and announce that you're coming presently to kill him, and then expect to part the best of friends!"

"Ain't I doin' the friendly part?" demanded Uncle Pete stiffly. He was both nettled and hurt. "If I hadn't thought well of you fellers and done all I could for you, you'd 'a' been dead and done forgot about it by now. I give you all credit for doin' what you think is right, and you might do as much for me."

"Great Caesar's ghost! Do you want us to wish you good luck?" said Billy, exasperated almost to tears. "Have it your own way, by all means—you gentle-hearted old assassin! For my part, I'm going to do my level best to shoot you right between the eyes, but there won't be any hard feeling about it. I'll just be doing what I think is right—a duty I owe to the world. Say! I should think a gentleman of your sportsmanlike instincts would send over a gun for our prisoner. Twenty to one is big odds."

"Twenty to one is a purty good reason why you could surrender without no disgrace," rejoined Uncle Pete earnestly. "You can't make nothin' by fightin', cause you lose your point, anyway. And then, a majority of twenty to one—ain't that a good proof that you're wrong?"

"Now, Billy, you can't get around that. That's your own argument," cried Pringle, delighted. "You've stuck to it right along that you Republicans was dead right because you always get seven votes to our six. *Nux vomica*, you know."

Uncle Pete rose with some haste. "Here's where I go. I never could talk politics without gettin' mad," he said.

"Billy, you're certainly making good. You're a square peg. All the same, I wish," said Wes' Pringle plaintively, as Uncle Pete crunched heavily through the gravel, "that I could hear my favorite tune now."

Billy stared at him. "Does your mind hurt your head?" he asked solicitously.

"No, no—I'm not joking. It would do me good if I could only hear him sing it."

"Hear who sing what?"

"Why, hear Jeff Bransford sing The Little Eohippus—right now. Jeff's got the knack of doing the wrong thing at the right time. Hark! What's that?"

It was a firm footstep at the door, a serene voice low chanting:

"There was once a little animal
No bigger than a fox,
And on five toes he scampered—"

"Good Lord!" said Billy. "It's the man himself."

Questionable Bransford stepped through the half-open door, closed it and set his back to it.

"That's my cue! Who was it said eavesdroppers never heard good of themselves?"

v

He was smiling, his step was light, his tones were cheerful, ringing. His eyes had looked on evil and terrible things. In this desperate pass they wrinkled to pleasant, sunny warmth. He was unhurried, collected, confident. Billy found himself wondering how he had found this man loud, arbitrary, distasteful.

Welcome, question, answer; daybreak paled the ineffectual candle. The Mexican still slept.

"I crawled around the opposition camp like a snake in the grass," said Jeff. "There's two things I observed there that's mightily in our favor. The first thing is, there's no whisky goin'. And the reason for that is the second thing—and our one best big chance. Mister Burleson won't let 'em. Fact! Pretty much the entire population of the Pecos and tributary streams had arrived. Them that I know are mostly bad actors, and the ones I don't know looked real horrid to me; but your Uncle Pete is the bell mare. 'No booze!' he says, liftin' one finger; and that settled it. I reckon that when Uncle Simon Peter says 'Thumbs up!' those digits'll be elevated accordingly. If I can get him to see the gate the rest will only need a little gentle persuasion."

"I see you persuading them now," said Billy. "This is a plain case of the irresistible force and the immovable body."

"You will," said Jeff confidently. "You don't know what a jollier I am when I get down to it. Watch me! I'll show you a regular triumph of mind over matter."

"They're coming now," announced Wes' placidly. "Two by two, like the animals out o' the ark. I'm glad of it. I never was good at waitin'. Mr. Bransford will now oblige with his monologue entitled 'Givin' a bull the stop signal with a red flag.' Ladies will kindly remove their hats."

It was a grim and silent cavalcade. Uncle Pete rode at the head. As they turned the corner Jeff walked briskly down the path, hopped lightly on the fence, seated himself on the gatepost and waved an amiable hand.

"Stop, look and listen!" said this cheerful apparition.

The procession stopped. A murmur, originating from the Bar W contingent, ran down the ranks. Uncle Pete reined up and demanded of him with marked disfavor: "Who in merry hell are you?"

Jeff's teeth flashed white under his brown mustache. "I'm Ali Baba," he said, and paused expectantly. But the allusion was wasted on Uncle Pete. Seeing that no introduction was forthcoming, Jeff went on:

"I've been laboring with my friends inside, and I've got a proposition to make. As I told Pringle just now, I don't see any sense of us gettin' killed, and killin' a lot of you won't bring us alive again.

We'd put up a pretty fight—a very pretty fight. But you'd lay us out sooner or later. So what's the use?"

"I'm mighty glad to see some one with a leetle old horse-sense," said Uncle Pete. "Your friends is dead game sports all right, but they got mighty little judgment. If they'd only been a few of us I wouldn't 'a' blamed 'em a mite for not givin' up. But we got too much odds of 'em."

"This conversation is taking an unexpected turn," said Jeff, making his eyes round. "I ain't named giving up that I remember of. What I want to do is to rig up a compromise."

"If there's any halfway place between a hung Mexican and a live one," said Uncle Pete, "mebbe we can. And if not, not. This ain't no time for triflin', young fellow."

"Oh, shucks! I can think of half a dozen compromises," said Jeff blandly. "We might play seven-up and not count any turned-up jacks. But I was thinking of something different. I realize that you outnumber us, so I'll meet you a good deal more than half way. First, I want to show you something about my gun. Don't anybody shoot, 'cause I ain't going to. Hope I may die if I do!"

"You will if you do. Don't worry about that," said Uncle Pete. "And maybe so, anyhow. You're delayin' the game."

Jeff took this for permission. "Everybody please watch and see there is no deception."

Holding the gun, muzzle up, so all could see, he deliberately extracted all the cartridges but one. The audience exchanged puzzled looks.

Jeff twirled the cylinder and returned the gun to its scabbard. "Now!" he said, sparkling with enthusiasm. "You all see that I've only got one cartridge. I'm in no position to fight. If there's any fighting I'm already dead. What happens to me has no bearing on the discussion. I'm out of it.

"I realize that there's no use trying to intimidate you fellows. Any of you would take a big chance with odds against you, and here the odds is for you. So, as far as I'm concerned, I substitute a certainty for chance. I don't want to kill up a lot of rank strangers—or friends, either. There's nothing in it.

"Neither can I go back on old Wes' and Billy. So I take a half-way course. Just to manifest my entire disapproval, if any one makes a move to go through that gate I'll use my one shot—and it won't be on the man goin' through the gate, either. Nor yet on you, Uncle Pete. You're the leader. So if you want to give the word, go it! I'm not goin' to shoot you. Nor I ain't goin' to shoot any of the Bar W push. They're free to start the ball rolling."

Uncle Pete, thus deprived of the initiatory power, looked helplessly around the Bar W push for confirmation. They nodded in concert. "He'll do whatever he says," said Clay Cooper.

"Thanks," said Jeff pleasantly, "for this unsolicited testimonial. Now, boys, there's no dare about this. Just cause and effect. All of you are plumb safe to make a break—but one. To show you that there's nothing personal about it, no dislike or anything like that, I'll tell you how I picked that one. I started at some place near both ends or the middle and counted backward, or forward, sayin' to myself, 'Intra, mintra, cutra, corn, apple seed and brier thorn,' and when I got to 'thorn' that man was stuck. That's all. Them's the rules."

That part of Uncle Pete's face visible between beard and hat was purple through the brown. He glared at Jeff, opened his mouth, shut it tightly, and breathed heavily through his nose. He looked at his horse's ears, he looked at the low sun, he looked at the distant hills; his gaze wandered disconsolately back to the twinkling indomitable eyes of the man on the gatepost. Uncle Pete sighed deeply.

"That's good! I'll just about make the wagon by noon," he remarked gently. He took his quirt from his saddle-horn. "Young man," he said gravely, flicking his horse's flank, "any time you're out of a job come over and see me." He waved his hand, nodded, and was gone.

Clay Cooper spurred up and took his place, his black eyes snapping. "I like a damned fool," he hissed; "but you suit me too well!"

The forty followed; some pausing for quip or jest, some in frowning silence. But each, as he passed that bright, audacious figure, touched his hat in salute to a gallant foe.

Squatty Robinson was the last. He rode close up and whispered confidentially:

"I want you should do me a favor, Jeff. Just throw down on me and take my gun away. I don't want to go back to camp with any such tale as this."

"You see, Billy," explained Jeff, "you mustn't dare the denizens —never! They dare. They're uncultured; their lives ain't noways valuable to society and they know it. If you notice, I took pains not to dare anybody. Quite otherhow. I merely stated annoyin' consequences to some other fellow, attractive as I could, but impersonal. Just like I'd tell you: 'Billy, I wouldn't set the oil can on the fire—it might boil over.'

"Now, if I'd said: 'Uncle Pete, if anybody makes a break I'll shoot your eye out, anyhow,' there'd 'a' been only one dignified course open to him. Him and me would now be dear Alphonsing each other about payin' the ferryman.

"Spose I'd made oration to shoot the first man through the gate. Every man Jack would have come 'a-snuffin'—each one tryin' to be first. The way I put it up to 'em, to be first wasn't no graceful act— playin' safe at some one else's expense—and then they seen that some one else wouldn't be gettin' an equitable vibration. That's all there was to it. If there wasn't any first there couldn't conveniently be any second, so they went home. B-r-r-! I'm sleepy. Let's go by-by. Wake that dern lazy Mexican up and make him keep watch till the sheriff comes!"

VII. A Number of Things

This, appearing in the *Saturday Evening Post*, April 8, 1911, makes a veritable Baedeker to the life, times, and politics of Socorro, New Mexico, around 1900. Almost all of the characters appear in their rightful positions under their lawful names or with but a thin disguise, such as "Bruten" for Bruton. The railroad, too, gets the prominence it deserves in the story as it was reflected from life. That the Harvey Houses are mentioned favorably is a personal delight to him who writes this note, for the Harvey House at Kingman, Arizona, played much the same role in his life as other Harvey Houses did in Rhodes' career. They brought manna to the wasteland of a man's own cooking.

The story, itself, requires no comment.

STAGE DIRECTIONS: Enter, l.u.e., First Walking Gentleman. Enter, r.u.e., Second Walking—That will never do. They were both cowmen and, therefore, emphatically always riding gentlemen. Also, the stage and setting are worthy of notice. Socorro County was the stage. There are counties and counties. The waters of Socorro drain to Atlantic and Pacific. It consistently measures one hundred and seventy-four consecutive miles from east to west, or the reverse. The pole-to-equator dimension varies from seventy-eight to one hundred and twenty miles. The diagonals connecting both pairs of opposite corners are each one hundred and ninety-eight miles—just about the air line from Washington to New York. Area, sixteen thousand square miles plus—or more than that of Massachusetts and New Jersey combined.

To put it another way, the compact portion of the county, neglecting irregularities, is considerably larger than Maryland and Delaware together. In addition, there is a little bump or swelling, exactly the size of Rhode Island, projecting from the southwestern corner; a similar excrescence, a third larger, on the southeastern corner.

Mesa, mountain and forest, valley and desert and rolling upland —silence and the mellow sunlight over all. Consider now that from every favorable height you may not only view all this vast expanse— save when a great range walls your vision—but your kindling eye may look far out, beyond these man-made boundaries, to White Mountain in the sunrise, northward to Jemez Hill beyond Bernalillo, west to the Arizonan Mogollon, down between the long parallel ranges to Old Mexico.

A land of mighty mountains, far seen, gloriously tinted, misty opal, purple, blue and amethyst; a land of enchantment and mystery. Those same opalescent hills, seen closer, are decked with barbaric colors—reds, yellows or pinks, brown or green or gray; but, from afar, shapes and colors ebb and flow, altered daily, hourly, by subtle sorcery of atmosphere, distance and angle; deepening, fading, combining into new and fantastic forms and hues—to melt again as swiftly into others yet more bewildering.

An empire for size; but the inhabitants are not numerically dense. The population of the county is fifteen thousand, mostly Republicans. It is of record, however, that a Democrat was once laughed into the sheriff's office—because of what you are now to hear.

There's the stage: Río Grande near footlights. Also the railroad, with a thirty-mile spur to Magdalena, eighteen miles west and one up. Continental Divide beyond; other scattered ranges r. and l. Gulf of California in background.

Warm sunlight. Enter, l.u.e., First Riding Gentleman. Enter, r.u.e., Second Riding Gentleman. Creepy music.

i

On a golden-bright October day, John Wesley Pringle, F.R.G., crossed the Arizona line, heading for Socorro town, the county seat. He rode a sorrel horse and the sorrel horse was weary.

That same day and hour, Bally Russell, S.R.G., toiled through Lava Gap, in the far southeastern corner. He drove a team of mules—brown, blithe and buxom—to a wagon topheavy with hides. He, too, was for Socorro town.

Observe, now, that neither of these men had ever seen the other, or heard of the other; neither had ever been to the county seat. Bally was going to sell his hides; Pringle to catch a train. Why Pringle was leaving Arizona is—I don't care if Kipling did say it. It is another story. And it is high time for that The Other Stories book. We are growing old.

In general appearance the two men were rather alike. Both wore high-heeled boots, blue overalls, flannel shirts and gray hats; both were lean, hard, vigorous, brown and bald. Bally was a little the taller, balder, grayer, and older of the two; but Pringle was shorter and had more hair, by weight or count. Looking closely, you saw that Pringle's hair was grizzled where Bally's was only gray, and gray where Bally's was gone. And Bally had a roan mustache, while Pringle's was a frosty brindle.

It was fifteen years since; John Wesley was years younger than he is now, but he didn't look it then and he doesn't yet. You would at once have said that he was from fifty-seven to thirty-six or thereabout. Bally, on the other hand, looked to be anywhere from forty-five up.

There the resemblance ceased. Bally had the conventional number of fingers, especially thumbs, on each hand. He was married, hasty, smouldering, subdued, silent and iron-stubborn; while Pringle was swift, deliberate, and happy. A deep, quiet twinkle lurked in the back of his eye; he sang songs joyously as he rode, and most of his right thumb was in California, where they use long ropes.

At Magdalena, Pringle was lucky enough to find an old-time friend, Bill Sanders, eloquently running for sheriff on the Democratic ticket, with his foot on a brass rail. A joyful man was Sanders;

he introduced Pringle to all present, including McMillan, the district judge, and Elfego Baca, the prosecuting attorney. Next, he offered to give Pringle a wagon—which is to say, in English, he offered him the position of wagon-boss, rod, or foreman. Pringle said he must be going, though Sanders assured him that his, Sanders', opponent, the present sheriff, would undoubtedly be re-elected. But Pringle was firm. He sold the leg-weary horse and his saddle to Sanders, untied his coat from the cantle, and took the Elevator for Socorro.

The Elevator made one round trip daily, taking up eight cars and bringing down sixteen, together with the express-mail-baggage-passenger combination coach each way.

Judge and district attorney were fellow passengers. From them Pringle learned that the next train out from Socorro, on the main line, was the southbound express, half an hour after the Elevator's arrival.

So, as the bus clattered by uptown, Wes' seated himself on the baggage truck, with an admiring eye for the high crest of Socorro Mountain, looming high above the town—all rose and golddust under the low sun. The Elevator was shunted to its own little sidetrack. The engine, switch engine *ex officio* of the Socorro yards, bustled up and down and in and out the shining rails, puffing cheerfully, bunting, pulling, pushing the cars, shuffling them hither and yon.

A wagon loaded with hides and drawn by two merry brown mules crossed the track and halted by the station. A tall, grizzly-gray man climbed stiffly down and went to the office window.

The agent was deep in waybill and voucher. The grayish man waited patiently; he waited impatiently; he tipped his hat back and Wes' saw that he was bald. The bus came back from town; the passengers grumbled bitterly, for that "Five" was late again.

The muledriver cleared his throat and tapped on the sill. "Say, mister, can't you spare me a minute? I'm looking for Sperling Brothers' warehouse. Got a load of hides."

The agent finished his waybill. "Other side o' the track," he snapped, without looking up.

Number 817 was pushing back a long string of cars. The muledriver climbed to his seat and whipped up to beat the cars to the crossing. He was just too late and pulled up with his wagon across the main track and the mules' noses almost touching the cars, which had now stopped. The driver lighted a pipe and settled back to wait. Wes' rolled a cigarette.

Joyce, the brakeman, came briskly by. "Hi, you!" said the driver. "Can't you open up for me? Like to unload and chow. Sun'll be down along to'ard night."

Joyce grinned. He was a fine big man, and not bad-looking when he did not grin. "Engineer's gone to the eathouse for a cup of coffee," he said, and passed over to the Elevator, where, through the wide side door of the express car, conductor Pat Savage was visible, busy with his reports.

The driver looked at his watch and settled back. Wes', interested and happy, lit another cigarette. The engineer came back and pottered by the wheels with wrench and oil can. The muledriver lifted up his plaintive voice; "Hi, mister! Wish you'd pull up and let me by."

The engineer straightened up, turned and took a good, long, incredulous look. "Aw, go and take a long running jump at yourself!" he said, and bent to his work again.

A burst of loud and mocking laughter greeted this stroke of wit; Joyce trudged over from the Elevator. "Back off, you old fool!" he said. "Passenger train's coming."

The old fool regarded him without visible resentment.

"Can't back. Them mules ain't got no britchin'. You ain't got no right to keep the crossing blocked so long, I don't think."

"You don't tell me!" drawled Joyce. A titter from the waiting passengers encouraged him. "Back off—or I'll break every bone in your mizzable old carcass!"

"Oh, don't—don't do that!" said the driver pleadingly. "I'll come down." He came down with incredible swiftness, as if the spring seat had been a catapult and had hurled him away; he hit the ground on the balls of his feet and bounded forward; his heavy blacksnake whip licked forward as he came, the lash writhed over the brakeman's shoulder and bit through shirt and skin. Joyce threw up his hands to protect his eyes; the old fool's left hand snapped wickedly up under the brakeman's guard. A quick man might have counted one, two. It was all over; the brakeman was down in a huddle. The old fool climbed back to his seat; Wes' nursed his knees and smiled a pleasant smile.

85

A plume of black smoke rose above the northward curve: the passenger train swung into the tangent. Some of the passengers started to run out, followed by a wrathful agent. The man on the wagon held up his hand and checked them.

"Them mules," he stated simply, "can't back. There ain't no britchin.' "

Joyce rolled over, gasped, sat up dizzily and sighed. His legs were spread out to steady him. He rubbed his chin gingerly; his other hand stole over between his broad shoulders. It came back with a smear of blood on the finger. He stared hard and reproachfully at his assailant and shook the accusing bloody finger at him. "Look what you done! Five dollars fine for drawing blood on a fool! Aren't you 'shamed to pick on a poor boy like me?"

The finable one regarded his victim cheerfully.

"You're all right, bub," he grinned. The victim grinned back.

"Sure I am. But, say, daddy, you'd better back up now, sure enough. The Choochoo'll get you if you don't watch out."

"My mules," said daddy, leaning forward to explain, "can't back. There ain't no britchin'."

The train was in the yards, the whistle bellowed and screamed. Men were shouting, waving their hands. The driver sat unmoved. On his truck, Wes' murmured happily to himself his own delight.

The whistle delivered a final blasphemous imprecation; there was grinding of brakes and shriek of tortured steel; the train shivered to the reverse, slid in a shower of sparks and stopped, panting indignation, not twenty feet away. Not till then did the driver look up.

Wes' rose and sauntered to the wagon. Engineer and fireman swung down, vociferous; conductor and brakeman ran down beside the train; curious passengers boiled out and followed.

The trainmen came up with a rush.

The teamster reached under the seat and fished out a rusty double-barrelled shotgun. He swung it around with fine carelessness, cocking the hammers. "Don't now!" he said. They didn't.

The station agent was behind the wagon, bawling his wrongs. "Have him jailed! Arrest him for assault with deadly weapons—and for stopping the United States Mail!" he shrieked.

The wagoner turned his gun that way. "Sonny, you talk too much," he said reprovingly. "Show me that warehouse," he demanded of the station agent.

The agent pointed. "Over the-ere!" he chattered.

"Go and uncouple that train," said the man behind the gun.

The agent did this.

"Now give 'em the high ball."

The agent waved his hands and the freight cars drew apart. The wagon went through and turned the corner to the warehouse. Number five pulled up to the station; passengers and trainmen buzzed out like swarming bees.

Wes' mingled with the throng, listening. They were taking the offender's description; they were going to arrest him. Wes' pulled his hat over his eyes and thrust his right hand into his pocket; he had an idea. Standing close behind the conductor of the passenger, he said casually:

"I bet that man was a bad actor. I see his right thumb was off—shot off, likely."

The seed was sown on fertile ground. Other trainmen promptly remarked upon the missing member; the engineer interrupted as the agent was telephoning the sheriff: "And his right thumb was cut off. Notice that, Jim?"

"Course I did," said the agent testily. "Think I'm blind? I saw it when he first come. Hello, sheriff! That man's thumb was cut off—his right thumb. He asked for Sperling's warehouse. Mebbe Sperling can tell you who he is. Yes, I'll swear out the warrant. And he made a brutal and unprovoked assault on George Joyce."

"Hold on there," said Joyce. "Let me tell that. Hello, sheriff! This is me—Joyce. Say, that feller didn't make no assault on me. Hey? Mule kicked me. Yes; a mule. No complaint. Perfectly satisfied. Goodby."

ii

Unobserved, Wes' melted away and slipped over to the warehouse. The wagon stood on the scales. Seeing Wes', the mule man picked up his shotgun. "Sheriff, I reckon?"

"Not I," said Wes'. "But, say, old man, they're after you, they're after you. You're the individual they require. You acquainted in this town?"

"Know just one man—if you call that bein' acquainted—Jim Bruten. That's his house over yonder about a quarter, betweenst them two trees."

87

"Bruten—Bruten?" said Wes' musingly. "Cowman?"

"Best that ever throwed a loop."

Pringle handed his pocketbook to the other, first taking out a five-dollar bill. Next came his papers, followed by his gun and spurs. "Run along—I'll be the goat. I'll wiggle out after you make a getaway. Leave your team here and I'll send 'em to Bruten's. You tell Bruten to keep my stuff till I call for it. My name's in my notebook."

"Huh? Oh, yes! I see! Why, that's right friendly of you. You'll do to take along." The teamster grinned comprehension. "You do favor me a little. You're a little the shortest at one end, though. Do as much for you sometime."

"I'll look more like you when they come for me. I'll scowl. Go! Git! Vamos! You got to hurry!"

Springtime Morgan was elderly, sprightly, big, chunky, jolly, easy-going and—generally—wildly unexcitable. He jogged easily up to the warehouse and reined up. Wes' leaned back against the platform, resting his weight on his two elbows, and caroled blithesome:

> *"Standin' on the corner; didn't mean no harm—Mah Baby!*
> *Standin' on the corner; didn't mean no harm.*
> *Po-lice come along and grabs me by the arm—Mah Baby!"*

The sheriff looked down at John Wesley, twinkling, "Fine day, sir!"

"Beautiful," said John Wesley.

"Your name's Bally Russell, isn't it?"

"Why—er—no. Not precisely, that is. Why?"

The Sheriff laughed. "We just asked Sperling who you was," he explained. "Guess you'll have to come along with me."

"Is what's-his-name—Sperling—sure of it?"

"That's what he said. Anyhow, you're the man, whatever your name is."

Pringle dug up a stump of pencil and a scrap of paper and wrote laboriously. "How many l's?" he asked.

"Eh? How many what?"

"One l or two—in that name—Russell?"

The sheriff regarded him doubtfully. "Say, you come along! What do you want done with your mules? You goin' to try to get bail?"

"Bail?" Wes' echoed. "Oh! You're the sheriff?"

"You're a splendid guesser," said the sheriff. "What do you want to do with them two mules?"

Wes' looked the team over carefully. "Are these my mules?"

"Guess there's no doubt about it, Mr. Russell," said the sheriff patiently.

"Well–if you're sure," said Pringle hesitatingly–"perfectly sure–you might get some one to unload the hides and take the outfit over to Jim Bruten's. Tell Sperling to pay Bruten for the hides."

The sheriff took Wes' to the corner restaurant, sent for the station agent, and, pending his arrival, made arrangements for disposal of hides and mules according to Pringle's directions.

"This your man, Jim?" he asked, when the station agent came.

The station agent looked at Pringle, who was placidly devouring a pie; he looked at Pringle's right hand.

"That's him," he said.

Pringle bade fair to become a star boarder. He waived examination and didn't want bail; he would await the action of the grand jury, which was to meet in two weeks. He would not see a lawyer; he would not see his friend Bruten; he declined to discuss the affair or feigned ignorance of it. One irritating habit he had: he paid no attention when any one called him Russell. But he answered to Bally.

He was a model prisoner–neat, pleasant, and cheerful. The sheriff found him a decided acquisition; the guests of the Hotel Morgan were mostly preoccupied and somber. He whistled and sang; he made a rawhide quirt for Bob Lewis, the big, jolly deputy, young but good-natured; he started on another for the sheriff, which remained unfinished because the sheriff found out that Pringle could play chess. Springtime played passionately with his deputy, but beat him with monotonous regularity. When Pringle won the first game the sheriff implored him to plead guilty. "For then they'll not be apt to give you more'n a year and you'll stay here for any time under that. We'll have a bully time; but you plead not guilty and they'll cinch you to the limit and send you to Santa Fé."

He moved Wes' to the cell next the front door, whence he could keep an eye on the office. The table was pushed against the bars. Springtime sat in the corridor and Wes' in the cell. Springtime stood the cigars and the game went merrily on.

Here, too, sat Springtime and Deputy Lewis while they played, while their new friend might watch the game. That was why Wes' didn't stay. He had intended to stay, in all good faith; but chance brought his good intent to naught. When, late on the fourth night, Morgan and Lewis were interrupted in their game by a call for the latter's services, Wes' was tempted and fell; for the sheriff's coat lay on the floor and the keys were in the pocket. There were possibilities. He declined to finish the game for Lewis or to begin another. He said he was tired and would go to bed. The sheriff, waiting for his deputy's return, went to sleep in his chair. Pringle bent a pin, fastened it to a rawhide thong from the projected quirt, and fished patiently for the coat. He got it at last. He removed the pin from the thong and trimmed the hole from the thong with his knife. He gently unlocked the cell door. It fastened with a spring lock. He closed it with considerate softness and stood in the corridor regarding his dreaming captor. Then a luminous smile lit up his face.

He tiptoed to the front door and examined the lock. This was also a spring lock; his smile grew more beatific than ever. Very softly he unlocked it and went out.

A block away, he entered a little candy store and purchased much chewing gum. He went back to the jail, masticating systematically. At the window where the light shone through he looked in. The sheriff was sleeping soundly. He laid two wads of gum on the window sill, kneaded them swiftly into compactness and took careful impressions of the cell key and the great key of the outer door. He rubbed clean the wards of the keys. He went to the front door of the jail, opened it noiselessly, entered with a velvet foot, replaced the keys in the coat, left the coat exactly as it was, went out and closed the door with infinite caution until the lock-bolt snapped behind him. Then he returned to the windowsills, retrieved his precious chewing-gum moulds and set out for Bruten's house.

Bruten was aroused; after whispered colloquy, they stole to the kitchen. Bruten pulled down the curtain, stirred up the fire and found a large iron spoon in the pantry. Then he went upstairs and brought Pringle's belongings.

Meantime Pringle melted bullets in the iron spoon and poured the lead carefully into his improvised molds.

"There!" he said gleefully. "I can make keys from that model all right. That gum melted and sizzed away a little. File'em down a little smaller to allow for mistakes."

So saying, he bade his obliging host farewell and went out into the hilarious night.

Two hours later he crawled down from a freight train at San Marcial. Before he bought his ticket he went into the Harvey House to buy a cup of coffee. Miss Annie was on duty and poor Pringle forgot to buy his ticket.

iii

"Just this one—and one more—and then we'll all go home," said Little Dick. "Me, anyhow. At nine p.m. I hit the hay—me. You fellows can sleep and snooze and snore all day tomorrow; but Little Dick, he's got to fire the pusher up Lava Hill at daylight. Such a fool! Here I am, hoarse with prattlin' 'That's good! That's good! all night, like a biscuit-eatin', red-eyed, pea-green parrot—payday three weeks off and me due to get the grand and gloomy bounce unless I win out enough to square the call-boy. But I don't care!" Little Dick pushed his cap back coquettishly. "I guess I'm the wickedest man in this town!"

"I pass," said Pringle.

Little Dick looked at his cards. "I pass."

"Pass," said Thurgood.

"Pass," echoed Peterson. Cliff Hamerick, the dealer, tossed in a chip. "Ante up, everybody."

That rite performed, Pringle gathered up the cards. There was a tapping at the door. Entered Fred Richards, proprietor, and handed a small handbill to Pringle. "I don't want to delay the game, but I thought maybe you'd like to see this."

Pringle looked it over indifferently. "Why, no," he said, "this don't interest me. I don't want no reward." He tossed it over to 'Gene Thurgood. "Read it aloud, will you? I—I got a splinter in my thumb."

So Thurgood read:

FIVE HUNDRED DOLLARS REWARD !

For the apprehension of one Bally Russell, who broke jail at Socorro on the night of October 13. Russell is about five feet ten; pleasing manners, slightly bald, gray hair, grizzled mustache, blue eyes. First joint of thumb on right hand cut off.

"H'm!" said Cliff Hamerick. "That fits you pretty well."

"But my name isn't Russell," protested Pringle. "My name is— What did I say my name was?"

"Clark," said Little Dick.

"Smith," scoffed Peterson, the engineer. "John Smith—or Riley, maybe."

"Naw, it wasn't. Oh yes—Sperling! Frank—no—Fred Sperling," said Wes'. "But, gentlemen"—he assumed an air of injured innocence—"you grieve me! Do you s'pose, if I had broken jail in Socorro a week ago, I would be in San Marcial now, only twenty miles away—and not only that, but associating with vicious characters in a notorious den, where the sheriff would be sure to look the first thing? You—you hurt me—indeed you do! And if I was the man, do you s'pose I'd get up and leave a jackpot that I've been sweetenin' an hour—and my next deal? Not much!"

"But, dear man," said Little Dick encouragingly, "what do we care if you are or aren't? Your money's what we're after. What have you been adoin', anyhow?"

"Me? I don't know," said Pringle.

"Robbed a train or something," said Richards. "Read the rest, 'Gene."

"Oh, the rest is just about the mule's he's supposed to be driving; and the reward will be paid jointly by the sheriff and the Santa Fé, and so on," said Thurgood. "He didn't rob the train. He just stopped the train. I may as well tell you fellows now that this isn't Bally Russell. I know Bally Russell well, and I saw him day before yesterday, out toward Lava Gap, driving these same brown mules. He went right home from jail; but he didn't have no—"

"No what?" interrupted Pringle. He caught Thurgood's eye. Thurgood stole a swift glance at the stump of Pringle's thumb.

"No pleasant manners," said Thurgood. "And that isn't all. I met Bob Lewis, the deputy, as I come in, going out after him. Deal up, Sperling."

Wes' was looking at the handbill, "Oh!—me?" he said, startled, and began shuffling. "All right!"

Thurgood passed. Little Dick opened liberally. Peterson raised.

Hamerick stayed. Pringle picked up his hand. It was a small straight—the six, seven, eight and nine of clubs and the ten of hearts. He was a steady player. This hand would be good—barring improbable fours—if no one stood pat or drew and filled. It was not policy to allow the others a chance to fill. He shoved in his pile.

Little Dick spoke eloquently, but called. Peterson called for all the checks he had. Hamerick dropped out.

"That's a noble pile," said Pringle. "Dick, you and me have got about ten or twelve dollars side money."

"Fix it, Gene," said Little Dick. "Gimme two cards."

"Cards to you?" said Pringle to the engineer.

"Help yourself," said Peterson.

Pringle considered briefly. Peterson would not stand pat unless he really had a pat hand when his money was all in. Any full hand, any flush, or any straight, with Jack or higher at the head, would beat Pringle's little straight. Sighing softly, he slipped the ten of hearts under a stack of chips, face down, and drew one card to his four-flush.

Dick looked at his draw. "Oh, well, I'm beat, of course," he said in disgust, showing three aces and two unmatched cards. "I never help a hand. 'Gene—he can draw to a shoestring and catch a tannery; but not Little Dick."

"And here's all I got," said Peterson. "I might stand on ceremony, seeing as how I called you; but I won't. Beat it and take the money." He spread out a mixed straight, ten-spot high.

Pringle looked at his draw and sighed again. He meditatively inspected Peterson's five cards; he made a delicate adjustment of spacing and alignment. He looked at them in critical silence. Very softly he transferred a card from one end of the line to the other and surveyed the result dreamily.

"That's excellent!" he said, and pushed the tall chipstack gently with the back of his hand. They toppled over to Peterson in party-colored confusion. "Boys," he said, rising, "I think gambling is wrong."

"How about this side money," said Little Dick. "Did you really split?"

"You keep the side money, kid," said Pringle. "Square the callboy with it. I plumb hate to show this hand."

A chorus of protests arose at this.

"Oh, very well, then!" said Pringle. He drew out his pocket-book and turned it wrong side out. It contained two new, brightly filed keys and a ten-dollar bill. He threw the bill on the pile of chips and replaced the keys. "Only you've got to take that money, too, if you see these cards," he said, addressing Peterson. "I was afraid you had me beat. So I took a chance and split. I discarded this"—he turned up the ten of hearts— "and drew to these four clubs." He flipped over the four clubs.

Peterson's eyes bugged out. "Why—why, we were tied!"

"We were tied," agreed Pringle. "But I drew—this." He sadly turned over the five of spades. "Gambling is wrong. You keep the side bet, Dick. Goodby, boys."

"Here, you old fool; come back and get your ten dollars," Peterson called affectionately as Pringle gained the door. Pringle reached over the engineer's shoulder, took the bill and with it all the assorted chips his fingers could clutch. Dribbling some on the floor, he thrust them into his coat pocket and went out, whistling.

He betook himself to the railroad eating house. The chain of such eating houses along that particular route are each and all under the same management. It is the most systematically conducted business in America. The man at the head of it or his understudy can tell you, at any hour, exactly how many sirloin steaks are in the Bagdad refrigerator or the number of mince pies consumed at La Junta; how many dozen eggs are requisitioned at Dodge City or what was the laundry list at Bakersfield.

Railroad, express and telegraph service is his, gratis. In consideration, employees of those obliging corporations get meals at the slightest margin over cost and can usually be found when needed. Transients supply the dividends.

The eating house meals are not half-bad and cheap at half the price, which is what railroaders pay for them, as just stated. And the girls who serve in them are all good-looking. That is the one indispensable requisite. Miss Annie was the best looker in the service. She had the "graveyard shift" at San Marcial—from eleven at night to six in the morning.

Pringle took his seat on a tall stool and waited patiently. Miss Annie flitted back and forth, unseeing, serving a group of railroaders, hungry but merry; she chatted with them vivaciously. When their last order had been brought she paused at the eating counter opposite Pringle and looked non-committally over his head at the door. Pringle looked over her shoulder at the piled fruit. "Tick-tock," said the clock—"Tick-tock; tick-tock; tick-tock—"

Miss Annie felt a smile struggling at the corners of her scornful mouth, strive as she might. "Order?" she snapped.

John Wesley turned his eyes slowly upon her and gave a little startled jump. "Oh, good evening, Miss Annie." He brushed a lock of hair carefully over his bald spot.

"Order?" repeated Miss Annie sternly.

"You may bring me—er—grapefruit with brown gravy—asparagus—two cups of coffee, piping hot—cracked ice—a bottle of meat-sauce—maple syrup—and half a dozen mock-turtles on the half shell."

Miss Annie slid the cardboard menu along the counter to him. "When you're ready to give your order call me," she said, and flounced away to bear pie and cake and more coffee to the voracious railroaders.

The last and hungriest departed at length. Miss Annie sat beyond the cake tables and hummed a cheerful little tune. After a long wait John Wesley coughed gently. "Are you—busy?" he said.

Miss Annie came swiftly over and leaned her elbows on the counter. Her face was flushed; she looked as if she might give way to tears.

"Oh, Mr. Sperling, how can you act so? What makes you do it? Why don't you go away? Did you know there was a reward out for you?"

"Me?" said Pringle, astonished. An avaricious note came into his voice. "How much?"

"Don't tell me!" she said. "I saw you here the very night you broke jail. Why didn't you go on?"

"I liked the—the grub," said Wes'. "But I didn't do nothin', really, 'cept to break jail. I mean, they couldn't cinch me for interfering with the mail—'cause it wasn't me."

"They can send you up for breaking jail anyway," said Miss Annie. "And the way you live—a worthless gambler! Why don't you go to work?"

"You get changed to the day shift and I will," said Pringle; "but I can't sit around all night doing nothing."

"Do you think any girl is going to—"

"Yes?" said Pringle encouragingly. "Goin' to—"

"—put up with your wild ways—gambling and acting the fool, and breaking jail—" She paused—the door opened behind Wes'.

"—and coffee," said Pringle, without looking around. "Do you serve bread and cheese? And—"

"Coffee and cheese sandwich? Anything else?" said Miss Annie briskly.

"Not now," Pringle answered sadly. The newcomer took his seat at the corner with a ferocious scowl at Pringle. John Dewey he was, foreman of the bridge gang and, prior to Pringle's appearance, recipient of the major part of Miss Annie's smiles. He still got the smiles, for that matter; but he was dissatisfied that Pringle got so many of her frowns. A fine, big, upstanding, two-handed man was Dewey; but just now he was in a suspicious and irritable mood—a moody mood, so to speak.

Miss Annie brought the coffee and the sandwich and put them down with marked vigor, pointedly omitting the cream.

"Er—some meat-sauce, please," said Pringle.

Miss Annie pounced on a bottle of the desired condiment, slapped it down before Pringle with a jerk and tripped over for Dewey's order. As she turned away, John Wesley took the bottle up and poured a liberal portion into his coffee. Miss Annie's black eyes snapped with anger. Dewey's scowl grew surlier than ever.

After a prolonged but inaudible conversation with Dewey, Miss Annie came by again. "How much?" said John Wesley timidly. He passed over his ten-dollar bill.

Miss Annie swept it up, rang the cash register viciously, and tossed Pringle a five-dollar bill. He smoothed it out and looked at the cash register in mild surprise. The reading matter on it was brief—$5.

"Coffee with meat-sauce is five dollars here," Miss Annie sniffed.

"Ah, yes," said Wes'. He flipped the bill languidly across the counter. "Another cup, please."

Miss Annie brought it. Tears of rage stood in her eyes as Pringle emptied the bottle into the cup.

The black veins stood out on Dewey's face, but Wes' was blandly unconscious. He thrust his hand into his coat pocket and laid a pile of red, white and blue poker chips on the counter. Some rolled clattering to the floor on either side. "Some cream, please," said Pringle pleasantly.

Dewey rose, almost choking. The floor rocked under his heavy tread as he strode over to Pringle. His fists were clenched.

"This has gone far enough!" he thundered. "I like a gay lad, but you suit me too quick! When you offer poker chips to a lady—"

"Good as gold," murmured Pringle. "Fred Richards' monogram on every chip. Cream, please."

Dewey brought his ponderous fist down on the counter with a violent blow that made the dishes jump and spilt half the coffee. "I won't have it—d'ye hear?" he roared. "For two cents I'd whale you within an inch of your life!"

Wes' looked round over his shoulder with a wide-eyed and innocent smile. "You just orter see my big brother!" he said sweetly. "You wouldn't talk to him like this. You know I'm old and stiff-jointed. And Miss Annie, she took all my money; but if you'll take a poker chip—"

Dewey struck the proffered chip from Pringle's hand. "Playin' the baby act, are you? Old and stove-up? I'd shame to lay a hand on you. Bah! Annie, give this thing back his money. It won't come in here botherin' you again. And you—you got to behave different. It's half your fault. I been watchin' you eggin' him on to these smart-Aleck monkey-shines." He leaned across the counter. That leaning was his undoing. Pringle pressed the cold, round mouth of the empty sauce bottle to the back of Dewey's neck—and Dewey turned to stone.

Pringle slipped from his stool so that he stood behind the big foreman. "Never mind the cream, Annie," he said in his cheerfullest tones. "John, take a cup of coffee on me."

The unhappy foreman complied, choking with the double compulsion of his fiery wrath and the fiery sauce. Annie took one look at the bottle, buried her face in her hands, and shook with the violence of her emotion. Pringle slid most of the poker chips into his pocket. "Good night, Miss Annie," he said. "John and me must be going now."

"Night," sobbed Miss Annie.

"You go out ahead, John," suggested Pringle, and John went out ahead; but at the door Pringle paused.

"Oh, I got to go back a minute! Good night, John."

There was no sound except Dewey's labored breathing.

97

"Good night, John," said Pringle more distinctly; and he thrust the bottle mouth into John's ear.

"Good night," gurgled John. As his retreating form turned the corner, Pringle put the bottle in his pocket, took a leisurely glance at the frowning black crater beyond the river and re-entered the eating room.

Miss Annie's hands were on the counter and her head was in her hands, so exposing a plump and tender cheek.

"Good night, Miss Annie."

No answer.

"Goodby, Miss Annie."

"If you would stop your foolishness" said Miss Annie in a muffled voice—"if you would act like a man and not like a great overgrown boy—some girl—not me—but some girl—"

"That's so too," said Wes' reflectively. "I hadn't thought of that. There's compensations in most things, I guess."

Miss Annie raised her head for an indignant flashing glance and resumed her former position, leaving her cheek, if possible, more unguarded than before. A second later she was on her feet, rubbing her cheek vigorously—and Pringle was holding his hand to his ear.

"You don't intend to keep that up after we're married, I hope—"

"Married? Why, you old idiot, I wouldn't marry you if you were the last man on earth!"

"Madam!" said John Wesley, with stately dignity, "you pain me inexpressibly; but I respect your judgment more than ever. And let me tell you, madam, that if you were the last woman on earth and I was the last man on earth the human race would then become extinct." His hand was on the door. "Goodby, Miss Annie!" he said wistfully.

"Oh, goodby, with all my heart, if you're sure it's goodby!" said Miss Annie. With feminine inconsistency she added "And good luck to ye!" when the door had closed, and blew a kiss after him from her slender fingertips.

John Wesley strolled back toward the Richards place in high good humor. But in the broad lamplight before Armstrong's saloon stood a big black horse that he knew—the Bob Lewis horse. He wore a fancy silver-mounted saddle and a fancy plaited bridle; he pawed and jerked his head, from which a long hair rope led in through the open door. John Wesley paused reflectively. At the bar stood

Bob Lewis, holding the jerking rope. A crowd was lined up with him; others stood by the door and without, listening.

"Put up your horse, Bob," said Horsethief. "Isn't he hungry?"

"Naw," said Bob. "I left him at Anderson's Ranch, and got another to go on with. Just rode him in from there since dark. He ain't tired. I'm goin' on up to Socorro presently. But I was telling you about this Bally Russell. It's a mighty mysterious layout. I found Bally Russell all right, but he wasn't the man at all, though he kind of answered the description. But he had two good thumbs—"

Pringle waited to hear no more. He put hand to his pocket, produced a bunch of poker chips and tapped a listener on the shoulder. "Why, that's old Bob!" he said in a tone of pleased surprise. "Say, you help and we'll have the drinks on him. You get these chips out of it and I'll get a bushel of fun. I'll cut the rope and hide the horse—and you stay here and jerk the rope just like the horse does till Bob comes out."

The crowd near the door sniggered approval. Pringle cut the rope, led the horse around the corner and waited. "Jail is the safest place for me," he said—"to say nothing about that reward," he added gleefully. At the next corner he turned up the road for Socorro. He felt the keys in his pocket happily. "All the same, that's a right nice little girl," he said. "My big friend John is one lucky man."

At Socorro, he left the horse at Henry's livery stable, telling the sleepy Mexican that Bob Lewis would call for it. At four a.m. he routed out the long-suffering Bruten. They went to the jail. Wes' unlocked the front door and his old cell, which he found unoccupied, and gave the keys to Bruten, who closed the outer door. When his friend was safely away, Pringle shaded a match with his hand, found the chess table in the corridor, opened the drawer gently, put in his poker chips and the empty meat-sauce bottle, and closed the drawer. He entered his cell and slid the door till it snapped softly. There was no bedding, so he rolled up his coat for a pillow and fell peacefully asleep on the narrow iron bed.

iv

Springtime Morgan was helping his jailer serve breakfast to his prisoners when he was startled by a cry, and an overlapping crash.

Melquiadez the jailer, had dropped his tray and was edging away from the cell nearest the door at a ten-second clip.

The sheriff looked and pinched himself furtively. He propped his lower jaw back to normal with his free hand, breathing hard. Very carefully he put down his own tray and stared. His face grew redder and redder. He unlocked the cell and shook the sleeper roughly.

Pringle opened his eyes and smiled sleepily. "Doanwaneat nothing. Mush 'bliged. After while," he mumbled and rolled over with his face to the wall. Springtime collared him, jerked him out with a bump and shook him violently; desisting, he saw that his passive victim's melancholy face wore a look of patient, philosophical dignity verging upon the wooden.

"What d'ye mean?" the sheriff hissed in a furious whisper. "What d'ye mean by breaking in and out of my jail like this? Didn't I always treat you kindly? Don't you know that I'm running for re-election? Do you want to make me the laughingstock of the county and election less'n two weeks off? You get out of here!"

Pringle sat on the floor. He turned his eyes up to the sheriff trustingly. "But I want that reward," he said.

The sheriff clutched at his own hair.

"Reward! You say reward to me again and I'll murder you! How'd you get in here? Melquiadez! Melquiadez! Come here—quick! Never mind the breakfast. This fellow must have some keys. Let the breakfast wait."

They searched him to the bone, but found no key. There was no window in the cell from which keys could be thrown; no crevice or cranny in which they could be hidden. The sheriff sat heavily on the bunk and eyed his prisoner; the prisoner dusted himself, sat sociably beside him and yawned with unmistakable sincerity. From the other cells the prisoners clamored for breakfast.

"It's funny how they'll put a fellow in jail just for breaking out of jail, even if he's proved innocent of the charge they first put him in for," observed Pringle kindly, as one who makes talk to break an awkward silence. "Seems as if, with cells and bolts and bars and sheriffs to keep him in, he ought to be allowed to get out if he could. Now if they just put him in and left the doors open, and then he went away, that'd be different. That wouldn't be right."

This speculation was ignored.

"See here!" said Springtime. "You've got me into a devil of a muss. What d'ye say if we frame it up that I caught you? You won't get over six months for breaking jail if I pull for you; and I'll hand over the reward to you when you get out—honest Injun! Yes, and more with it. I can't afford to have this told on me."

"But—you didn't capture me!" said Pringle virtuously.

The sheriff gazed longingly at Pringle's neck and his fingers quivered. "I'll use all the pull I got to lighten your sentence if you stand for it. What spite have you got against me? Be a good fellow and help me out. You won't lose nothing. But, of course, I can't help you on your other fool break—holding up the train. You'll have to take what you get on that."

"I didn't hold up the train," said Wes' carelessly. "I didn't have anything to do with it and I can prove it. I told you all the time I wasn't the man. Don't you remember?"

He spoke with a confident certainty that troubled the sheriff's already bewildered mind. "Then, what in blazes did you break jail for?" he demanded.

"I didn't break jail," said Wes', yawning again.

"You didn't break—How did you get out?"

"You let me out," said Wes', "and in again. You walk in your sleep, sheriff."

The sheriff chewed his mouth, but no words came. He had not lost his temper before for years, but he restored the average now. His face was splotched with purple spots; his breath came in apoplectic wheezings. He groped for the door, opened it, slid it shut and went to the front door, gasping for air. He came back and clutched at the cell-railing.

"You tell that on me and I'll swear you into the pen myself," he said in low, guarded tones. "You just dare! You try it on! Why, damm your eyes, I've got a good mind to kick you out of here right now!"

"But the reward?" hinted John Wesley. "I'm broke."

Springtime tottered over and brought a chair. He put it down before the cell. He sat down, trembling, and mopped his brow.

"I'll take you down to the river and drown you," he said in a strangling voice.

"How about Melquiadez, then?" suggested Wes'.

"I wish Bob was here," groaned the unhappy sheriff. "Look here, Bally Russell—"

"But I'm not Bally Russell," said Pringle mildly. "I always said so. You ask your judge and district attorney if I am." The sheriff glared at him. "They know me. Ask 'em. Look here, sheriff; if I show you how to save your face—"

"If you can you'll save more than my face," interrupted the sheriff meaningly. "I was just figurin' on shootin' you and swearin' you were tryin' to get away!"

Pringle smiled. "Easy as ace-in-the-hole! You found out I was the wrong man and you hid me away, givin' out that I had escaped and offerin' a reward for a man of my description, so's to throw the right man off his guard. For, of course, the right man knew I was the wrong man; and so long as I was in jail the truth would be sure to come out at my trial. But if he was sure you was still after me he'd be careless—see? You just let on it was all a piece of head-work on your own account. Then, as I haven't broken jail, I don't have no trouble about that."

"No trouble about the reward either?" said Springtime. "But you won't have to buy no coffin, maybe—so that evens it up."

"Reward? Sure not. I been in jail all this time," said Pringle logically enough. "The reward was just a blind."

"I don't really believe you've been here all the time," said Springtime doubtfully. "But I'll try it. I'd try anything to get out of this. And you'd better stand hitched. If you doublecross me again I'll fix you good, election or no election. See if I don't!"

"But it's all true!" said Pringle earnestly. "If the judge and district attorney don't clear me of any possible share in the mixup down at the station I don't ask you to try it. If they clear me, you stick to that story and so'll I. It's true anyway. It must be true if you didn't walk in your sleep—and you say you didn't."

The sheriff rose and kicked the chair. "I'll go fetch Baca and the judge," he said. "Everything goes on this card. If it isn't ace-in-the-hole it's Santa Fé for yours."

Half an hour later he came back with Judge MacMillan and Elfego Baca.

"Be seated, gentlemen. I owe you an explanation, I reckon," said the sheriff lightly as they entered the jail corridor. "You know the man Bally Russell, who bucked up against the Santa Fe railroad a week or two back?"

"Who escaped?" queried the judge. "Yes—I confess that the

affair has worried me a great deal. Sanders has many friends and they are making capital of the escape as electioneering material. They allege—ahem! that you connived at it. Sanders may beat you yet." The sheriff gurgled inarticulately.

"Of course we know you didn't," supplied Baca hastily. "He must have had help from outside. Jim Bruten, probably. He's liable to do anything. You must remember that the man's offense was not heinous—only technically a crime, in fact. And he had serious provocation. A clever lawyer could make out a pretty case for him, for the freight-train crew were violating the law after they kept the track blocked over five minutes. Much sympathy was expressed for this man Russell and some sympathizer has not stopped at words— Bruten or another. Bruten is a Sanders man. All the same, Morgan, it's a bad thing for you—and me. There is no use of shutting your eyes to that. The railroaders are mad about it and the cattlemen all vote the Democratic ticket anyway. The Mexican vote is for us, solid; but this Russell business may beat you anyhow. It's a great pity he got away."

The time had come for the coup—win or lose.

"He didn't get away," said the sheriff blandly. "There he is."

"Good morning, gentlemen," said Pringle politely as the officials wheeled toward him.

"Why, that isn't the man at all!" said the judge, starting to his feet. "I know this man. Sanders introduced him to us at Magdalena. Pringle—John Wesley Pringle—odd name. Bless my soul! He came down from Magdalena with us the very day that the trouble occurred at the depot; and Frank Sperling told me that the man Russell was at his store two hours before he went down to the warehouse—that is to say, while we were still in Magdalena. You remember, Baca?"

"Perfectly," said Baca. "No possibility of mistake. This isn't the guilty party."

The sheriff threw a grateful glance at his troublesome prisoner. "Exactly so!" he said triumphantly. "Prisoners don't escape from my jail! This is the way of it: I soon found out we had the wrong man. Made some quiet inquiries that substantiated his statements— never mind the details. It occurred to me that if we turned him loose, or if we kept him in jail, the real offender would know I'd be after him next. Well this—er—Pringle—is a good natured fellow. Just to do me a good turn, he consented to stay in jail; 'cause I knew that Sanders bunch would get funny about the supposed jail-breaking. I put him in an out-of-the-way place—in my own room most of the time—and he kept still as a mice. Then I give it out that he had escaped and offered a reward to throw the real Bally Russell off his guard. In fact, my deputy is now after him. I got a tip that he lived out Lava Gap way and I am expecting Bob back with him most any day. Do you understand now?"

The judge wrung his hand. "That was a masterly bit of strategy, Morgan! I congratulate you. You have turned the tables on Sanders beautifully."

"Oh, that's nothing," said the sheriff modestly. "We got to fight the devil with fire sometimes. But I guess it's one on Sanders, all right. Now let's get down to cases. I told you all this now, instead of waitin' till Bob came, because we really ought to let Mr. Pringle go this mornin'. He's got business to 'tend to. He's lost a heap o' time, and he wants to go. I'm mighty obliged to you, Mr. Pringle."

"Not at all—not at all," said Pringle. "Always glad to help law and order along. But, say, Mr. Sheriff, if you really want to make your calling and election sure you ought to bring in some six or half a dozen prominent men of the opposition and explain things to them. They may not take your word for it. Let 'em see that I'm really here. Then you can go through the necessary formalities and let me go."

The sheriff was inclined to think this unnecessary, but was overruled. Accordingly it was done. Judge McMillan held the briefest special session "in chambers" on record and Pringle came forth a free man with a stainless reputation. Meanwhile the sheriff had breakfast for four brought in from a nearby restaurant and served it in the court-house hall to celebrate the joke on Sanders.

They were interrupted. Would the three officers kindly step to the door for a moment? They did—to meet there three men: Mr. 'Gene Thurgood, the Socorro agent of the Santa Fe and an unknown, whom Mr. Thurgood proceeded to introduce.

"Gentlemen," said Mr. Thurgood gravely, "this is my friend and neighbor, Mr. Bally Russell. Some one using his name got into some sort of disturbance up here and Mr. Agent swore out a warrant for him, giving the name of Bally Russell. I don't know why." His eyes roved to Pringle, but no flicker of recognition was in them. "Deputy came out after him and saw there'd been a mistake. But he told Bally about it. Naturally Bally wants to clear it up. He got me to drive up from San Marcial this morning and stand sponsor for him." He hustled his friend and neighbor to the front. "Mr. Agent, will you kindly tell the judge and these other gentlemen if he is the man you swore out a warrant for?"

"Of course he's not," said the agent. "He sort of looks like him as to general build, but the other man was bigger and his right thumb was cut off."

Bally held up his right thumb. The sheriff scratched his head and covertly scrutinized the unconscious Pringle, who was eating with the good appetite said to wait on an untroubled conscience.

"That certainly lets you out, Mr. Russell," smiled the district attorney.

"Thank you, sir," said Bally, looking with blank eyes over Pringle's head. "I want it all fixed so there couldn't be no mistake. I got a family."

"Can I go now?" asked the agent anxiously. "Lots of work to do and the night man is furious for being kept out of bed."

"Oh, yes, you can go," said the judge. "But won't you other gentlemen come in?"

"No, thank you," said Bally. "We got to go, too."

That breakfast was doomed to interruption. While they were discussing the latest development of the "Russell mystery," Bob Lewis entered with a forbidding scowl on his usually smiling face. He did not at first observe John Wesley, having eyes only for the sheriff.

"Sit down, Bob," said the sheriff hastily. "I was just telling Baca and the judge how we pretended his man got away while you went after the real Bally Russell." The sheriff leaned his forehead on his cupped hand and from this friendly shelter telegraphed a warning glance at his deputy.

Bob looked at the sheriff; he looked at Pringle; his feelings overcame him; he sank dejectedly into a chair and passed a hand wearily over his brow. But the warning had not been wasted. He swallowed a lump in his throat and "played up" to his chief's lead loyally and blindly. He nodded, being for the time incapable of speech.

"What's the matter with you?" Springtime continued. "Cheer up! It can't possibly be true! Hey, Melquiadez! Fetch in another breakfast for Bob."

"Make it two," said Bob. "I got a friend out here on the court-house steps. I'll go get him. Oh, sheriff, I've had an awful trip! I found Bally Russell—and he wasn't the man at all—"

"We know about that. It wasn't your fault," said Morgan.

"Then, last night, at San Marcial, somebody stole my horse and saddle." Here the deputy strangled, meeting Pringle's eye.

"Aw, never mind!" said the sheriff, anxious now to avert explanations until McMillan and Baca were away. "You've been a good deputy—I'll stand the loss. Anything else?"

"And somebody held my friend Dewey up with a gun." He avoided Pringle's earnest and attentive gaze. "Some of you know him. Say, he's bridge foreman at San Marcial, remember. He's got a vote and he's got a lot of men under him. Here—I'll bring him in and let him tell you. I'm not well."

It appeared that his friend was not well either. He showed the same alarming symptoms that Lewis had exhibited before, but worse, if anything. Lewis helped him to a chair and gave him a glass of water.

"There—there's Sperling now," said Dewey thickly, glaring at his foe. "That's the man who pulled the gun on me!"

Pringle rolled a wondering eye from Dewey to the others and arched his brows solicitously. The sheriff's mouth was set and stern; he tugged nervously at his belt.

"Why—the man's crazy!" exclaimed Baca. "This man couldn't hold you up. He has been right here in jail for the last ten or twelve days."

"You're surely mistaken, Mr. Dewey," said the judge more suavely, mindful of the coming election and the foreman's influence. "Probably your assailant looked like this gentleman. Mr. Pringle—Mr. Dewey." Pringle's bow and smile of acknowledgement were ill received. "But I assure you that he has not been out of this building since the tenth. Ask the sheriff."

"I've played chess with him every day," said the sheriff cheerfully, "and slept with him most every night. Case of mistaken identity."

Poor Dewey turned his questioning eyes on the unhappy Bob—and Bob nodded!

Dewey's face was all colors; the veins on neck and forehead

stood out, throbbing; he glowered at Pringle in black, dumb wrath. "I think you must be the devil!" he burst out at length.

Pringle shook his head sadly. "Really, I must get away from here," he said; and the words were music to the sheriff's ears. "There's some one around that looks most mighty like me; and if I wasn't plumb lucky he might 'a' got me in trouble. This is no good place for little me."

"Is Mister Bob Lewis here?"

They turned. In the doorway stood a ragged urchin.

"I'm Bob Lewis. What is it?"

"Telegram for Mister John Dewey, with Mister Bob Lewis."

Dewey tore it open, read it and turned his face to the wall. He threw the boy a quarter. "No answer," he said, and read the yellow slip again:

Socorro, New Mexico.

Mr. John Dewey:

Hear you have gone to Socorro to arrest that man. Please don't do it for you own sake. I can't explain here. If you do arrest him you will not find me here when you come back.

Annie

Dewey pulled himself together and came back to the table. He was really much of a man and he made an impressive figure as he stood there, not without somewhat of the dangerous and the terrible.

"You, whatever your name is," he said in a slow and quiet voice, "you was mighty brave last night when you had a gun and the drop on me! That's nothing—that's all right—if that was all; but the rest of you—! You're the judge and you're the sheriff and you're the district attorney—and you all back up this man's shameless lies to make a fool of me. Heaven knows what kind of conspiracy you're up to!" Judge MacMillan and Baca exchanged mystified glances. Dewey pointed his finger at Pringle. " 'Very well, John,' says I to myself, 'You're up against a frameup.' " But I'll get a gun now and when Mr. Fly-by-night steps out o' here we'll see how about it. That's what I thought; and now this comes"—the yellow paper fluttered over to Pringle—"and so I can't even do that! But let me tell you this: If you're not good to her you'll answer to me, man to man! If you make her happy, well and good. If you don't I'll break you with these two hands."

Pringle read the telegram; when he looked up he was entirely serious for once in his life. "Gentlemen," he said, "this is a personal matter of a very delicate nature. I have not behaved well to Mr. Dewey, but he is quite mistaken as to what I have really done. If Mr. Dewey will come with me for one minute I will convince him and make full amends."

"No violence, mind!" said the Sheriff.

"Let him try it if he dares!" gritted John Dewey.

Wes' led the way to the chess table in the corridor.

"Take one end of this table," he said, "and we'll carry it where the prisoners can't see—or the other fellows either."

They carried it back to the courthouse hall and into the judge's chambers, followed by wondering glances from Morgan, McMillan and Company. Pringle closed the door.

"I am waiting," said Dewey, ominously calm. "Don't feed me lies; my stomach's not good. I'm not a patient man. Try none of your tricks on me or I might forget myself."

"Look in the drawer," said Wes. "Notice what you find there and read your telegram again."

Dewey looked in. He took out the poker chips. They bore the familiar Richards monogram. He took out the meat-sauce bottle— and simultaneously experienced a rush of brains to the head. He held it up and looked at it; he held it to the back of his neck. The feel of it was hard and round and cold. He blushed.

"Ye blamed omadhoun, is that the gun that you nearly scared me out of my five wits with?"

"That's the gun."

"Then—then—" stammered Dewey, "Then the girl was not wanting to save ye from the jail, where ye well deserve to rot—but"

"To save you from being laughed out of the country. Exactly!" said Pringle.

"But why did she not tell me?" demanded Dewey, holding up the bottle.

"I am thinking," said Pringle, "that your future wife has a spice of the devil in her—or maybe she didn't want me killed just there. Keep the bottle, John; cash the chips and buy her a wedding present for me. For, truly, this is no place for me; I am going— going—gone!"

"Going? But you're in jail!"

Pringle shook his head. "I am free and innocent. The judge built me an alibi."

"Man!" said Dewey, "but you're past me! How come you to get them gowks to lie for you—and them in office? They should take shame to themselves."

"They're not lying—much—some of them. They're not only telling what they think to be the truth but what they know to be the truth. I can't just explain."

Dewey drew a long breath. "It's no great matter—so long as you really leave. Let's go er—a—Sperling! Hark here! If you ever decide just what your name is let me know, will you? And if hapchance I should have need to name a boy I'll remember you."

They came out into the hall.

"Gentlemen all," said Dewey, flushed and sparkling with recovered happiness, "I have done a great wrong to this bald-headed man, whose name I do not exactly remember; but doubtless ye know some of them. I take much pleasure in telling you—and 'tis the white naked truth—that I was misled of the devil and that this man did not hold me up with a gun last night or any other night; and that, moreover, he has but now done me great kindness, for the which I am much beholden to him. And ye will please forget any harsh words used to him or to your own selves, perhaps."

"Well—I'm all foot-loose, I guess?" said Wes'.

"Sure thing!" said the sheriff heartily.

"But, sheriff—er—" Wes' hesitated. "Wasn't there something else?" The sheriff braced himself, but a haunted expression crept grayly over his face. "My money—that you put in the safe?" explained Pringle.

"Oh, yes!" The sheriff gave him a look of grudging admiration not unmingled with relief. "Dear me! How did I forget?"

"I wouldn't a' mentioned it now," said Wes' diffidently, "only I've just barely got time to catch the Magdalena train."

"Huh?" said the sheriff, open-mouthed. "Magdalena?" Beads of sweat started on his brow.

"Bill Sanders said he'd give me a wagon," said Wes'.

Morgan looked helplessly at the judge.

"Sanders said he was an old friend," said the judge in a lifeless voice.

The sheriff got heavily to his feet, pulled a roll of bills from his pocket and dropped them, uncounted, into a hat. "Gentlemen," he said, "we all love Mr. Pringle dearly. If he goes to work for Bill Sanders that double of his will be getting him measured for a wooden overcoat. Let us all help him get away soon as far as possible."

"But I left a daisy good horse and saddle with Sanders," John Wesley protested.

"As I said to Bob just now," said the sheriff as the officeholders, mystified but obedient, made a silent contribution, "what's a horse more or less? I'll pay for any horse and saddle that you pick out on condition that you cross the river, ride east, ride hard and never come back. Bob'll go down town with you and pay for 'em. I'm like Bob was. I'm not well."

"Let me in on this," said Dewey eagerly.

Morgan stuffed the collection into Pringle's pocket. "Accept this slight token of our regard," he said with enthusiasm. "Goodby; oh, goodby!"

"So long, then!" said Wes. "Come on, Bob; we'll go down to Henry's stable and pick out a horse."

Meantime Joyce was busy making up the train for Magdalena. The station agent looked through the window. A string of cars was across the street. As Joyce trotted up to the head end to cut off the engine, a humble voice accosted him:

"Excuse me, sir; but would you be so kind as to move up the cars so I can cross over?"

Joyce looked up. He saw a pair of brown mules hitched to an empty wagon. The driver was an oldish man. He took off his hat and held it in his right hand, the thumb on top. "That is, if it's not too much trouble," he said politely. His hair was gray and he was partly bald.

Joyce swept off his cap with a ready and graceful curtsy.

"No trouble at all, sir," he said as he uncoupled. "Always happy to oblige." He backed out and waved his hands frantically to the engineer. "Pull up, Billy! Pull up—quick!" he said. The agent shut the window with a bang.

High on the eastern mesa jogged John Wesley Pringle, smiling pleasantly. He rode a high-stepping black horse, with a silver-mounted saddle, a plaited bridle and a hair hackamore. His rope, however, was a new manila; the hair leading rope of the hackamore had been freshly cut. John Wesley's spurs jingled musically to the steady rhythm of hoofbeats; and, to the same strong cadence, John Wesley chanted a grateful little song:

"The world is so full of a number of things,
I'm sure we should all be as happy at kings."

"That is, if Bruten and Bally and Thurgood don't talk," amended John Wesley thoughtfully. "Only for that, the sheriff's idea of sendin' me away was bully." He came to where the road split into four forks; he stopped and rubbed the side of his nose. "Now, Bob said one of the roads went to White Oaks, one to Rainbow, one to Lava Gap and one to Moongate—but I've plumb forgot which goes where. However, it makes no odds where a single man goes to. I'll let Springtime take his choice."

Feeling the reins loosed on his neck, Springtime tossed his head and followed the Rainbow trail. "All the same," said John Wesley Pringle, musing, "that was one right nice little girl."

VIII. The Barred Door

As originally submitted, Rhodes' title for this piece was "Stung!" The *Satevepost* changed it to a less blunt instrument for publication. It has not been published in any form since its first appearance in the *Saturday Evening Post*, May 6, 1911.

This piece had its genesis at the Alvarado Hotel, Albuquerque, New Mexico, on October 15, 1909, during a banquet in honor of President William Howard Taft, then making a tour of the country. The banquet, it was hoped, would be the medium of winning Taftian support for statehood for New Mexico. The speakers to present the territory's case had been chosen with great care—Holm O. Bursum, O. N. Marron, Thomas Benton Catron, and Albert Bacon Fall. The first three did their tasks well—mingling judicious pleas for New Mexico with judicious praise of President Taft. Fall, the final speaker, took his flamboyant courtroom manner in hand and ripped into Taft, the Republican party, and all those assorted politicians and promises that had led New Mexico down the garden path since 1846 by dangling the hope of statehood before her eyes. Rhodes, then living in Apalachin, New York, read about the incident in the papers and almost at once started work on this article which seems timely today in view of Alaska's and Hawaii's pleas for statehood.

SWINGING ROUND THE CIRCLE has become a fixed Presidential habit. It is an innocent and harmless amusement—strikingly like the merry-go-round of blessed memory, both as to motive and result. The children have a good time and the cost is trifling. As a slight drawback a merrymaker sometimes gets dizzy; but that is not serious—quite the contrary.

In October, 1909, President Taft, swinging round the circle, paused for refreshments at Albuquerque, New Mexico. There was the inevitable sound of revelry by night: New Mexico's capital had gathered there—also her voluptuous swells and some few rough-riders—and bright the electric lights shone over the usual thing. Among the inevitable speakers was the only A. B. Fall. Ever hear of Fall—Fall of New Mexico—cowboy, miner, lawyer, judge, gunfighter, able editor, rough-rider, farmer, private chevalier and brevet-captain of industry? Well, you will; in fact, you shall.

Fall is unique in one respect. He can, with equal ease and nonchalance, carry a safe Republican county for the Democrats or a safe Democratic county for the Republicans. And then do it all over again. From this you will infer that he is not a bigoted partisan. You win. He is simultaneously a Roosevelt-Democrat and a Fall-Republican. He has no acquaintances. Every New Mexican is either his steadfast friend or his bitter enemy; and they are all his admirers. Perhaps his best claim to distinction, however, is that he is the only rough-rider who has never been garnished with the decoration of the double cross for conspicuous carnage on the field of battle.

Pardon this digression and we will go back to our banquet, where all went merry as a marriage bell until Fall rose to say his little speech. Then there was—or were, when the construction calls for *were*—hurrying to and fro, and gathering tears, and tremblings of distress, and cheeks all pale which but an hour ago blushed at the praise of their own loveliness; for Fall wandered from his welcome to our fair city and tactlessly referred to the late passionate promise of immediate statehood for New Mexico. "Perhaps," said Mr. Fall, "this time the promise will be kept." Whereupon, says the associated press dispatch of that date, Mr. Taft "rebuked him."

An Invitation with a String to It

Time has shown that the rebuke was richly merited. That prom-

113

ise has not been kept. Mr. Fall should have known better. There was no excuse for such credulity.

In 1888, 1892, and 1896 the Republican national conventions adopted indefinite resolutions favoring statehood for the remaining territories in a vague, fish-eyed manner.

The Democrats took stronger ground, mentioning New Mexico by name in 1888 and condemning the course of the Republican party in refusing statehood. In 1892 they included Arizona in their plans and specifications, adding Oklahoma in 1896.

In 1910 and 1904 the Republicans favored home rule and "early" admission for these three territories. The Democrats came out for "immediate" admission in 1900; and, from mere condemnation of the party in power for failure to carry out its pledge to grant statehood, they "denounced"—which was a step in the right direction. The Democratic zeal may require explanation. They were viewing with alarm, you see, and this was a favorable spot for that kind of view. In 1904, joint statehood having become an issue, the Democrats declared for the immediate admission of Arizona and New Mexico as separate states.

Finally, in 1908, both political parties unequivocally declared for the immediate admission of Arizona and New Mexico as separate states.

It is quite fair to point out that there have been few years since 1888 in which, voting solidly together—voting as they "resolved"—the Republicans and Democrats might not have admitted these territories; as is shown by the fact that the enabling act of 1910 passed both houses unanimously. "Come in," they said; "the water's fine!"

Yet, as you know, the Senate, at the fatal psychological moment, voted to reject the states they had so unanimously invited to come in. Evidently the majority looked upon that invitation and the solemn pledges of 1908 as given in merely a Pickwickian sense.

No blame attaches to President Taft, who has acted throughout in entire good faith. I hereby cheerfully quote, as just praise of Mr. Taft's attitude, the following paragraph, written—not since March 4, 1911—by ex-Governor Prince, of New Mexico:

"President Taft has taken the highest ground as to the obligations of a party and its official representatives to carry into effect the pledges of its declaration of principles. Finding in the Chicago platform this unequivocal statement regarding 'immediate admission,' he insisted that a Republican Congress was bound to carry it into effect. Without this conscientious construction of party honor and party duty on the part of the President it is more than doubtful whether the statehood bill of 1910 would have been passed. Without this clear-cut plank he would not have felt obliged to insist on its fulfillment; so that, though so many platform declarations above recorded have been without effect, the very important influence of the last one adds new dignity and respect to the solemnly adopted pledges of great parties."

However, there is still a certain distinction between a political promise and a certified check.

Let me interrupt the graceful continuity of my strange story here to reassure you, O reader, mild or turbulent in your disposition, as the case may be. I know what you think. You think I am going to make a plea for New Mexico and show cause why she should be admitted. I am not going to do anything of the sort, for the sufficient reasons that you shall have in a moment. I am going to plead for something essentially and radically different—something that concerns you directly and personally; but first, let us get together, we two, and arrange for a few verbal short cuts.

Will you allow me to say "New Mexico" rather than "the territories of Arizona and New Mexico"? Arizona and New Mexico are indeed in the same sad case, but the phrase is cumbrous and awkward. Also, Arizona was part of a New Mexican county until 1863.

For similar economical motives, admitted—or admission—will be better than "admitted"—or "admission"—"to the glorious sisterhood of free and sovereign states."

In lieu of "citizens of the territories of Arizona and New Mexico" I shall say "denizens"—not only because it saves time and because it will be easier for you, as unambiguously representing your thought of us, but also because it is more accurate. We have never been citizens. When you call us that, smile. We are aliens in the land of our birth.

Such minor abbreviations as "p.m." for "psychological moment" are self-explanatory.

You may also note that I speak of "we" and "us" as one having a signed and sealed commission to speak for the New Mexicans. This is not thus. I speak for only one New Mexican—that excellent man, myself.

Some people say "we" for that an excruciating modesty forbids them to say "I"; but the motive that impels me to say "we" is that which actuated Mrs. Cobb's cook.

"Was the grocer's boy impudent to you again when you telephoned your order this morning?" said Mrs. Cobb.

"Yis, Mrs. Cobb, he was that; but I fixed him this time. I sez: 'Who the hell do you think you're talking to? This is Mrs. Cobb!'"

A Gray-Beard in Skirts

Having cleared the deck for action I will explain why I do not plead for New Mexico's admission. I am pained and grieved that New Mexico was not admitted. The small boy's benefit in the change from skirts to knickerbockers is less from the actual and potential service of the new garment than from his own pride and pleasure; but to keep a boy in skirts for sixty-three years has a tendency to make him conspicuous. If you see a gray-bearded boy in skirts you surmise that all is not normal beneath the gray hair; you infer and say, in the classic phrase of Ambrose Bierce, that there are flitter-mice in his campanile. It does not command your confidence. You do not hasten to enter into business relations with such a one.

My grief is not all for New Mexico, however. Some of it is for you; just as I should have grieved for you had you straitly promised that you would not grant admission to New Mexico—and nevertheless falsely admitted her.

Again, I do not plead for New Mexico's admission because you are but slightly interested in that subject or I am the more mistaken; whereas the point that I do deeply purpose to make is of vital concern to you, or should be. Moreover, there is absolutely no reason why New Mexico should desire statehood other than those reasons for which all the other states have desired statehood. And I have no reason to believe that if New Mexico were admitted her people would be any better citizens than the people of your own state—or any worse.

I do not plead for admission, because I am not seeking controversy, but striving to avoid controversy. I would fain persuade, convince, and not argue and exasperate. I hope to put forward in this paper no proposition to which you will not readily yield assent.

Last—and stronger than any of the preceding reasons—I do not plead for admission, because I think—no, deem, deem by all means—

because I deem it unmanly to plead as a suppliant for what we may justly demand as a right; for, though the reasons for which we desire statehood are precisely those for which other states have desired statehood, there are reasons why we should have statehood, why we have a right to statehood, such as no other territory has had. I refer to the specific promises made to the people of New Mexico at the time of the acquisition of that territory—made by General Kearny, confirmed by the treaty of Guadalupe Hidalgo.

The other states were admitted because of inherent, undenied and self-evident right. We have not only that same inherent and self-evident right—albeit oft denied; we have the word of this nation —not from the plausible tongues of politicians but the solemn pledge of this nation as a nation, signed and sealed, that we should not be discriminated against, but should be admitted to statehood under the terms of the constitution of the United States, on like terms with those accorded to other states, and on no meaner terms.

These are not the exact words of the treaty made with Mexico in 1848, when the United States acquired New Mexico; or of the treaty arranging the Gadsden Purchase; or yet of the business contract with the state of Texas, whereby Texas gave a quitclaim deed to what she had never owned: but that is the exact and unmistakable meaning of them. Therefore I scorn, in my haughtiest manner, to beg for what I may justly demand. "If reasons were as plentiful as blackberries I would give no man a reason on compulsion."

What I do plead for is that you shall stop, quit and cease to promise admission to us. Isn't that reasonable? Is it too much to ask? Remember, we do not ask you to tell the truth. Opinions vary as to the advisability of indiscriminate truth-telling; and, as I said before, I am striving to avoid moot points. Besides, to tell the truth in this case is quite unnecessary. What you think of us may be surmised any day, by any good surmiser, surmising only at odd moments. We merely ask you to quit lying to us. Consider that should you, in your state convention or even in your national convention, set forth these views, such a course may be attacked as novel or revolutionary; but no one is likely to point out the inherent impropriety of not lying.

Tribulations in Return for Contributions

You have made us three promises; you have not made these

promises good. Remains to consider why these promises were not kept; and why the promises were ever made—made, not given; the lairds of convention got value received—no, more than that—they got something in the line of concession or support for each promise made.

Kearny at Santa Fe, like Otis at Manila, promised more than he could deliver. The tale of Sinbad the Sailor is not more curious or more interesting than this of Kearny's: but we have no space for it here. In his formal proclamation of August 22, 1846, he said—claiming authority from the President: "It is the wish and intention of the United States to provide for New Mexico a free government, with the least possible delay, similar to those in the United States." He was an optimist. Pass we on.

In his message to Congress, January 23, 1850, President Taylor said:

"I did not hesitate to express to the people of these territories—California and New Mexico—my desire that each territory should . . . form a plan of a state constitution and submit the same to Congress, with a prayer for admission into the Union."

Thus we were bidden to the feast—to be turned back at the door. Why? I quote once more from Mr. [Bradford] Prince's valuable and accurate work, *The Struggle for Statehood*. He is speaking of the constitution of 1850:

"Besides the section of the constitution forever prohibiting slavery in New Mexico, there was a strong paragraph on that subject in the accompanying address, showing that slavery had always been the curse of the communities in which it existed.

"It is an evidence of the courage and high principle of the convention which formulated the constitution that, at that time, when the debate on slavery was raging in Congress—when they knew that the slave power was determined to have a new slave state to balance California and that if they declared for slavery they would be admitted in a moment—they sacrificed their prospects of immediate admission to the higher duty of protecting their cherished land from the incubus and wrong of human bondage. It should never be forgotten that this first constitutional convention in New Mexico, in which native New Mexicans composed over ninety per cent of the membership, took this high ground and maintained it courageously, although by so doing they were placing in jeopardy their own right to self-government."

The slaveowners were wise. Where mountains are there will you find freemen. There will be no Homestead tragedies in New Mexico.

This constitution was adopted. In all that wide stretch of country—tush!—in all that vast expanse, in all that mighty empire, only thirty-nine votes were cast against it. Accordingly the Compromise of 1850 admitted California as a free state and rejected New Mexico because she sought admission as a free state, and for no other reason.

You say you do not admit us because you think we are inferior. Nothing can be further from the truth. You think we are inferior because you have not admitted us. As you have just seen, you at first refused to admit us not because we were inferior or even because you thought we were inferior but because we were not time-servers.

Do not misunderstand me. We are not pained to find that you consider us your inferiors; because we know that it is not true. We are pained because, for that fond belief, you withhold from us self-government and citizenship. We realize that your feeling of superiority is a natural feeling and we are not surprised at it. We frequently have that feeling ourselves.

Nor did the New Mexicans confine their antislavery expressions to words. Let their deeds speak for them. During the Civil War, New Mexico supplied more volunteers to the Union cause, in proportion to population, than any state in the Union—sending 6,561 out of a total population of ninety-three thousand. Oregon, Nevada, Washington, Montana, Idaho, Wyoming, Nebraska and the two Dakotas, taken all together, sent just 7,261. Colorado, it is true, sent 4,093, or nearly two-thirds as many as New Mexico; but it should be remembered that most of the Colorado volunteers were of that same Spanish blood which now so disqualifies for citizenship.

When we consider that to a large extent the New Mexican volunteers paid themselves and supplied their own food, arms and equipment; and also that they delivered a rather neat article of plain, unfrilled fighting giving to the invading column of very adequate Texans a licking just a trifle more thorough than any other recorded in history—counting all this, I think we may safely decide that the views expressed by them in 1850 were sincere.

To skip weariful dates and details, fifty-four New Mexican statehood bills have been introduced in Congress since 1850, and seventeen have passed either Senate or House—always to perish of criminal negligence in the other chamber for reasons based on quantity, quality, latitude, longitude, altitude, attitude and platitude. Since 1890 no statehood bill has been defeated by a direct vote in either branch of Congress, until the Senate of the Sixty-first Congress welshed in 1911.

I have before me all those omitted details and dates, the House and Senate numbers of the bills, dates of introduction, amendments, votes taken; in some cases the hour and minute of the roll call. I spare you. They are confusing, amazing, incredible. They would make you long for despotism. To give them would serve no purpose save to display the profundity of my scholarship and the diligence of my research—both of which, if you will take it from me, are admirable, indeed, but uninteresting.

Nevertheless, if you don't know how your own Senator has voted, if you will let me know—always inclosing a two-cent stamp—you shall be informed, in the hope that some Chautauqua and other engagements will be prejudiced thereby. They say "hell has no fury like a woman scorned." This case is along those lines. If these Senators think they can leave us waiting at the church and get off with it—no, no; I mean to say, if they think they can slight our charms with impunity they are entitled to hazard another conjecture.

We sent up our cards with California in 1850. California was admitted, but we got "not at home" for ours. We knocked at the door with Colorado in 1874. Two years later, Colorado made it possible for seven resolute gentlemen to insert Mr. Hayes in the President's chair, but the door was slammed in New Mexico's face. We tripped up the steps with Washington, Montana and the Dakotas. The bouncer assisted us back down the steps, though the doors slipped ajar for the others. Thence arose the saying: "When is a door not ajar?"

A Tale of Two Territories

We came up—Arizona also this time and henceforth—with Idaho and Wyoming. The welcome on the mat was not for us. The other territories got in. We tried again, with Utah and Oklahoma. One of the candidates got a spotless robe and learned a new song. That was Utah.

All this reminds me of a story: A man went to the ball up above

Smith's store. The hall was filled too. They threw him out presently and he rolled downstairs; but he was not hurt and he was of a hopeful nature. He went back. This time they kicked him downstairs. Nothing daunted, he went up again and forced himself in. They dropped him out of the window. He sat in the street and looked long and earnestly at the North Star. His eyes filled with tears. Said he:

"I unnerstan' thish. Can't fool me! They don' wan' me at that danch!"

We tried to get in the dance again in more recent days, with Oklahoma. Oklahoma was admitted. Arizona and New Mexico were promised admission if they were willing to come in as one state.

Now it may have escaped your attention—as it has escaped the attention of many able journals that really could know such things if it were deemed expedient to know them—that New Mexico is Republican by a very large majority, while Arizona is Democratic by a very small majority; hence, that both together, as one state, would be Republican by a medium-sized majority. You may be sure that it did not escape Congress. That was not the only reason or the chief reason why Arizona and New Mexico did not desire joint statehood. Nor—nay, by no means—was that the reason, or any one of the reasons, alleged for trying to force joint statehood upon us. It is merely true.

The feeling against joint statehood was very strong, but was not due to any ill feeling between the territories. It was due to many small reasons all pulling the same way, which reasons you would not understand unless you were familiar with local conditions; and for one large reason, which you will fully understand, being the same reason for which we do not precisely marry the girl picked out for us by mamma as the one whom we must marry under threat of disinheritance—namely, because we do not wish to marry her, although she is a fine girl and one whom we can cheerfully recommend to our friends.

That was the way with us. New Mexico ardently desired, and desires, to marry El Paso County, Texas, to whom we have given many substantial pledges of affection—first mortgages and the like—and the passion was, and is, returned. This is said with all neighborly respect to Arizona. I think that most of the New Mexicans share my own belief that, on the average, the Arizona folks have a shade the best of us in the matter of good denizenship. And the Arizona people feel the same way about it.

Since, if these two should be one, New Mexico would be the one, and also since, if Arizona voted against joint statehood and New Mexico for it, New Mexico would so have the better chance for separate statehood, it is not surprising that New Mexico voted for the wedding reluctantly—but trusting Arizona to decline. In this disingenuous way, New Mexico could hope to escape both disinheritance and the girl. Arizona responded nobly. Her "No" was almost unanimous. I have a great admiration for Arizona.

The Amazing Paradox

That brings us down to the late futile enabling act of 1910. Let us again resort to shorthand. When we have occasion to speak of the joker in this act—providing that, before admission, the constitutions adopted by Arizona and New Mexico must be cordially approved by the President, the Senate, the House of Representatives, the National Baseball Commission and the Gridiron Club—let us agree to call it "the paradox"; for to deny self-government to a people by the terms of an act ostensibly granting self-government to that people is a contradiction in good set terms.

The paradox has been termed "a final expression of distrust," but this characterization cannot be successfully maintained. It is and was meant to be insulting and humiliating. No other state has ever been subjected to such terms. It was also absurd, because, if we cared to do things that way, we might meekly comply with all objections to get admitted. Once a state, we could amend our constitution to what shape we pleased, with none to molest or make us afraid—snapping scornful fingers at President and Congress. Not so absurd, however, if perchance no constitution of Democratic Arizona's framing could have been approved by the dwindling Republican majority in the Senate—preposterous, unless it were purposed and planned that no constitution should please.

Be that as it may, the paradox proposition cannot now justly be called the final expression of distrust. The final expression of distrust was when the Senate, at the last possible p.m., voted to refuse admission to us.

We understand this. You cannot fool us any longer. You do not want us at that dance.

It were easy to account for the inveterate hostility shown to us by imputing to you unworthy motives, which you would doubtless indignantly deny. Let us have no strife. This hostility is partly accounted for by such obvious and incontrovertible causes as prejudice, vainglory, provincialism, ignorance, presumption, bigotry, partisanship, conservatism and inertia.

This blind, unreasoning hatred, however, is also based upon something narrower than even the most zealous loving-kindness—baser than mere partisan advantage. It is based upon fear—a fear dating from three centuries back, when Spain and England grappled for world-mastery: from the day when the Invincible Armada went forth to benevolently assimilate the islanders.

Providence and Sir Francis Drake co-operated to defeat that philanthropic design, Providence contributing several ample little storms and Drake a desperate valor befitting the good English blood; but England has never quite recovered from the scare. And the English-speaking races have inherited it. It is part of their early training and education.

When a Spaniard appears in an English novel he is the villain *ex officio*, bent upon dark and hellish designs, in the accomplishment of which he is ever thwarted by a blond beast with a Gibson face. When, at the play, a swarthy man with strong white teeth and flashing black eyes comes down C., garbed in gay velvet, mystic, wonderful—some sort of a bias basque, all shirrs, gores, darts, jabots and things, pieces-of-eight sewn on his panties, and a nobby silk sash amidships—you hiss instinctively. Don't you, now? For you know, without waiting for further developments, that he is Spanish, execrable and doomed to misfortune.

It is pretty hard to pass on without any briefest reply to the legion-voiced, scurrilous attacks upon the Spanish-speaking natives of New Mexico. The historians of early California speak of the native Californians as frugal, hardy, temperate, liberty-loving, proud, unindustrious, credulous, uninventive, hospitable, generous and brave; but then the early historians of California had the advantage of knowing the Californians. The wholesale detractor of New Mexico has generally been a car-window expert with a foolish license. I lived among the New Mexicans twenty-five years and found them startlingly like folks, running all the way from pretty bad to middling good—unlike the people of another section, where I was once snowed in for a few years, of whom I earnestly say that "when they were bad they were very, very bad; and when they were good they were horrid."

When such evergreen hostility has been shown to these territories all down the road, why were all these promises made? It could not have been policy, since the denizens had no votes. Was it sheer wantonness? Was it love of lying for its own sake or simply for practice?

Not so, my masters. Every little movement has a meaning all its own. This puzzling problem is consistently controlled by the steadfast principles of barter. There is one place, and only one, where the denizens have had voice and vote. That is in the national conventions. These votes were needed for candidates or for measures— to point with pride or to view with alarm. At the p.m. the territorial delegates made their little bargain. Then they pointed or viewed— and in return got the conventional statehood plank.

A Myth for a Vacuum

Let us take a modern instance: Suppose you were manager of a Presidential candidate selected some months before the convention. You are erecting a platform. A political platform is not a declaration of principles; it is a device to catch votes. Suppose, in your carpentering, you were confronted with this cruel situation: that a labor plank was vociferously urged upon you, of such a sort that it would please laborers and infuriate capital; that a substitute plank should be frowningly urged upon you, of such differing import as to please and thaw capital, indeed, but to infuriate the laborers. What would a fellow do, then, poor thing?

Obviously a poor fellow would straddle and trim. He would endeavor to get a third plank, a just-as-good plank, of no meaning whatever—sound and fury, signifying nothing; which, pleasing no one, should at least anger no one. If, counting noses, the poor fellow found that the vote would be close, it follows as the night the day that there would then be a statehood plank for the territories—with a mental reservation.

And this, if you please—in stealthy secrecy, with toil and anxiety, pain and precaution, solemnly to exchange a nothing for a delusion, a myth for a vacuum, a mirage for a chimera—this is statesmanship! Surely, who does such ghostly and narrowless deeds has lost contact with reality.

This is a hypothetical case, but not too hypothetical. If you should inquire in the proper quarter concerning the labor plank of the last Republican national convention I venture to say that you will get no information. The proper quarter to make such queries is of the Postmaster-General. The accepted custom of our time is that the successful candidate for President shall appoint his campaign manager to be Postmaster-General. This may be because the qualities that go to make the manager of a successful campaign are precisely those that make a good Postmaster-General; but malignant folks say that such appointments are made in order that, as Postmaster-General, the appointee may be in a position suitably to reward special merit, he having met so many meritorious persons while yet but a campaign manager, and being also more thoroughly aware of what each meritable one would like as a suitable reward for his particular degree of merit than any other person whatever.

Mr. Hitchcock is the present Postmaster-General.

Do not think this mention of Mr. Hitchcock is malicious, invidious or superfluous. Mr. Hitchcock is just now "It" in New Mexico. A paper on New Mexico which did not mention Mr. Hitchcock would be that Hamlet thing. Mr. Hitchcock is the third, and, to my notion, the most satisfactory of the volunteer guardians of New Mexico. Mr. Quay and Mr. Beveridge were the others.

My objection to Mr. Beveridge as a guardian was not that Mr. Beveridge might not make an excellent guardian but that we did not really need a guardian—or if we needed one we nevertheless warmly did not want one. And we are growing no younger fast.

Mr. Hitchcock, as guardian, gives close attention to details. On some of these details I do not agree with Mr. Hitchcock—notably as to conditional candidates for our United States Senators. My own choice for United States Senator is that same A. B. Fall, so justly rebuked for credulity by Mr. Taft, as explained above. This is not because Mr. Fall is of my political party; I have no political party. And I seldom know what party is Mr. Fall's. It is simply because Mr. Fall is by far the most suitable man for the place—one to whom New Mexicans may justly point with pride, or whom they may view with alarm, according to their several bents.

Those Pleasant Practices of Politics

However, I did not make Judge Fall my first choice because he has already seen forty-some-odd years and will doubtless be Osler-ized before New Mexico chooses her first Senator. My first choice, therefore, fell upon my little son, now nine years of age, who will probably be in the prime of life when he assumes his toga.

Mr. Hitchcock has not seen fit to support either of my candidates. Now, though I have no very deep-seated objection to a dictator, I have the deepest possible objection to a dictator who will not do exactly as I wish. Such are the grounds of my opposition to Mr. Hitchcock.

Perhaps, however, the next Congress will admit us? Cut it out, now—stop your kiddin'! Ours is the incredulous attitude of that Western correspondent of a certain magazine man, set forth as thus:

P.S. Sam, are you on the water-wagon yet? Neither am I.

Congress has always "played politics" in the admission of territories—peanut politics. This does not imply that the senatorial objection to the recall was not conscientious. The storied wolf, you remember, cudgeled his poor head for a satisfactory excuse before he ate the lamb—satisfactory to his conscience, I mean; not to the lamb. Who am I to deny to a Senator as much conscience as a wolf? I make no doubt but that they squared it with conscience long ago. Ever since the Republican party lost so many senatorial seats in last fall's election it has been a foregone conclusion that Arizona's constitution would be defective or excessive. It was foreordained that Arizona should muddy the water supply.

The Democrats have long professed warm friendship for our territories—possibly from remorse for having defeated the statehood bill of 1875, because of their hasty, unwarranted and illogical assumption that Mr. Elkins, of New Mexico, was sincere in his cordial admiration for Mr. Burrows, of Michigan. The latter, you remember, had just made a "bloody shirt" speech, which Mr. Elkins had not heard; but, finding Mr. Burrows holding a levee for the purpose of receiving congratulations, Mr. Elkins warmly added his mite out of sheer neighborliness and guff. The nimble Democrats jumped to the conclusion that Mr. Elkins' action was the outward manifestation of Mr. Elkins' thought; and, therefore, they refused to let us play in their yard. Later they repented; and—ever since they have been out of power—they have warmly advocated statehood.

Far be it from me to say that the Democratic determination that Arizona and New Mexico must come in both at once, or not at all, was not due to disinterested devotion to the principle of the recall. I only say that, being in power in the House, having every prospect of electing the next President, and with a slender, wan and pale majority against them in the Senate, their action would not have been different had it been prompted by "practical politics" and not by devotion to principle. Doubtless they favor the recall; but, even if they did not favor the recall, they would not have consented to prolong a Republican majority by letting in two Republican Senators from New Mexico without as many Arizona Democrats to offset them. Such is not the practice.

Senator Bailey, however, is, as is well known, an idealist. No practical politics for him. So repugnant to him was the recall, that to defeat it he was willing to forego party advantage. He has been willing to do that for some time. So wroth was he when his Democratic colleagues voted to let Arizona manage her own concerns that he resigned—so, in a manner, reverting to type; for this was practical politics of the highest order. He recalled his resignation, however, as you know, and, greatly peeved, went his lone, wild way to the wild, wet woods.

I have never wished to be President. Like O. Henry Clay, or whoever it was, "I would rather write than be President"; but there has been a time when I should have loved dearly to be governor of Texas.

The Need of Every Knee

The objection to that luckless constitution was to the provision for judicial recall, as I understand it, and not to the recall of other officials. Personally I am not fierce and forward for that feature of the recall. I merely think it important that Arizona should have self-government. Neither do I believe in the peculiar sanctity of judges. I note that the men who become judges do wrong before they become judges and do wrong after they return to private life; if they indeed become mysteriously infallible, the attack being coterminous with their stay in office, it is a startling coincidence. I am not disappointed or indignant, however, that judges retain humanity during their term of office; I expected no less.

I do not believe that any judge not flagrantly and flamingly corrupt would be removed under the recall, any more than I believe that we would impeach our Presidents for amusement. Though it would be a grievous thing to recall a just judge, it would be a worse thing that a judge notoriously unjust could not be recalled. It is also a very silly thing to agree that we cannot in the future do what we may then be agreed to do because we have agreed that we could never agree to do that thing; as if a man were firmly to tie his own hands behind his own back with his own unassisted hands—which would be both foolish and difficult.

In J. G. Holland's novel, *The Bay Path*, is a parallel case: "She noticed that Mary Pynchon turned out her toes and moved her feet with a peculiar grace," he says. The statement caught my attention because the theory was new to me. My toes won't turn out. I have ridden the bounding bronco too long; whereon, if your toes turn out your spurs turn in, with lamentable results. Nor do I move with peculiar grace. For the same stern reason, my poor knees are stiff.

Yet I cannot imagine myself denying to any one the right to turn out his toes or the belief that to turn out the toes will result in peculiar grace of movement—any more than I would deny to others the right of either turning in their toes or keeping their feet pointing straight ahead, as pleased their fancy. To my mind, if Virginia and Wisconsin prefer to turn out their toes and not to have the recall, that is their business and not mine or Arizona's. In like manner, if Arizona wishes to have her feet parallel rather than at right angles and to have the recall, that is not my business, or Virginia's, or Wisconsin's. Every knee has its own needs.

What I think about the recall is of no importance. What is of importance is that Arizona thinks about the recall very much as I do, only more so; and, therefore, will not abandon the recall; the more, that Arizona thinks that the objection to the recall was but a pretext; that if she abandoned the recall and turned out her toes another pretext would be found, about Heaven knows what and she fears to guess. The late Senator Dolliver objected to us because we were not muddy enough. He was accustomed to seeing a "break up" every spring. Arizona holds that silent influences are at work to keep her out because she is considered radical—and because, in the coming struggle over the income tax, no more radical states are desired by leading incomists.

Now!

(1) If Arizona doesn't jellyfish on the recall—bless the dear girl! she won't—the Republican Senate will not let Arizona in.

(2) If the Republican Senate will not let Democratic Arizona in, the Democratic House will be severely blamed if it lets Republican New Mexico in.

(3) Arizona and New Mexico will get in—not yet, but not soon. If we are ever admitted it will not be for the justice of our cause or for our importunity, but because some party or faction needs our votes. If that time ever comes, and if, at that time, Mr. Taft shall have made his home in New Mexico or Arizona, we shall give him a hearty welcome as a neighbor; and we shall be pleased to have his aid and advice in framing our constitutions. The same is true of many members of the late Congress. However, if these gentlemen are not citizens of Arizona or of New Mexico, it will be, civilly speaking, strictly, literally and indubitably none of their business, so long as we provide for a "republican form of government," as prescribed by the Constitution of the United States.

Let me, this once, depart from my own rule and put forward a proposition to which you possibly may not agree. By Article IX of the treaty of Guadalupe Hidalgo it is provided that the people of the territory annexed to the United States under that treaty "shall be incorporated into the Union of the United States, and be admitted at the proper time—to be judged of by the Congress of the United States—to the enjoyment of all the rights of citizens of the United States according to the principles of the Constitution."

Better Than Promises

When the Congress of the United States passed the enabling act, by the unanimous vote of both your plagued houses, it may fairly be taken that they thereby pronounced judgment that the "proper time" had come; but, was it proposed in that enabling act to admit us "according to the principles of the Constitution"?

I think not. Certainly no such interpretation of the principles of the Constitution was used in fixing the terms of admission to other states. So far as I know, no one has ever denied that the requirement of that "amazing paradox," allowing the other states to frame our state constitutions, was extraconstitutional, undemanded by the United States Constitution. I charge that it is a direct violation of the guaranty to grant us admission "according to the principles of the Constitution"—said United States Constitution having provided for impeachment proceedings in nowise differing in principle from the recall—as well as an unwarranted insolence to us.

Addenda

I cannot close without calling upon you to share the admiration which I cannot withhold from my own moderation. "The hardest test of a gentleman," says Robert Louis, the well-beloved, "is to bear with fortitude the unspoken slights of the unworthy." There is a harder thing: to bear with fortitude the unspoken slights of the worthy.

Nor have I been mealy-mouthed.

And I trust you will not charge me with any tactful effort to ingratiate myself with you. Such endeavor was not needful to the accomplishment of my purpose, which was, if you remember, not to enlist your sympathies for New Mexican statehood but to enlist your aid in protecting us from any further promises. Will you do that? No—don't promise to make no promises. Just don't make them.

IX. The Fool's Heart

With Rhodes' permission, this story, appearing in the
Saturday Evening Post, May 11, 1915, was adapted into a two-
act play by Charles Milton Newcomb and produced by him
at Ohio Wesleyan University, 1919, with his students providing the cast. It was reprinted in *Suspense Stories* (Dellbook
No. 367, New York, 1950). It was adapted for television by
Ruth Woodman and performed on the CBS network program, "Suspense," January 16, 1951.

This is the tightest plotting Rhodes ever did. Overlong
by modern short-story standards, there is no room for de-
letions. It is that rarity among "westerns," a suspense story
that is true to the psychology of the people concerned. In it,
there is nothing of the current practice in psychological suspense stories laid in the West that have hero, heroine, villain,
and assorted bearers of the Winchester wandering through
their parts while racked by ill-digested hunks of other men's
wisdom.

CHARLEY ELLIS did not know where he was; he did not know where he was going; he was not even cheered by any hope of damnation. His worldly goods were the clothes he wore, the six-shooter on his thigh, the horse between his legs, and his saddle, bridle and spurs. He had no money; no friends closer than five hundred miles. Therefore, he whistled and sang; he sat jauntily; his wide hat took on the cant joyous; he cocked a bright eye appreciatively at a pleasant world—a lonesome world just now, but great fun.

By years, few-and-twenty; by size, of the great upper-middle class; blond, tanned, down-cheeked. Add a shock of tow-colored hair, a pug nose of engaging impudence—and you have the inventory.

All day he had ridden slowly across a dreary land of rolling hills, northward and ever northward; a steepest, interminable gray ridge of limestone on his right, knife-sharp, bleak and bare; the vast black bulk of San Mateo on the west; and all the long day the rider had seen no house, or road, or any man.

One thing troubled him a little: his big roan horse was road-weary and had lost his aforetime pleasing plumpness. He had also lost a shoe to-day and was intending to be very tenderfooted at once.

Charley was pleased, then, topping a hill, to observe that somebody had chopped a deep notch into the stubborn limestone ridge; and to see, framed in that tremendous notch, a low square of ranch buildings on a high tableland beyond. A dark and crooked chasm lay between—Ellis could see only the upper walls of it, but the steep angle of the sides gave the depth.

A deep and broad basin fell away before his feet. Westward it broke into misty branches between ridges blue-black with pine. Plainly the waters of these many valleys drained away through the deep-notched chasm.

It was late. The valley was dark with shadow. Beyond, the lonely ranch loomed high and mysterious in a blaze of the dying sunlight. Ellis felt his blood stir and thrill to watch it higher and higher above him as he followed down a plunging ridge. Higher and higher it rose; another downward step and it was gone.

Ellis led his horse now, to favor the unshod foot on the stony way. He came to a road in the valley; the road took him to a swift and noisy stream, brawling, foaming-white and narrow.

They drank; they splashed across.

A juniper stood beside the road. To it was nailed a signboard, with the rudely painted direction:

BOX O RANCH, FIVE MILES

Below was a penciled injunction:

Don't Try the Box Canon. It's Fenced.
Too rough Anyway. Keep to the Road.

"Vinegaroan, you old skeesicks," said Charley, "I'm goin' to leave you here and hoof it in. Good grass here and you're right tired. Besides that foot of yours'll be ruined with a little more of these rocks. I'll rustle a shoe and tack it on in the morning." He hung the saddle high in the juniper—for range cattle prefer a good sixty-dollar saddle to other feed. Tents and bedding are nutritious but dry. A line of washing has its points for delicate appetites; boots make dainty tidbits; harness is excellent—harness is the good old stand-by—harness is worthy of high praise, though buckle-y; but for all-round merit, wholesome, substantial, piquant, the saddle has no equal. Bridle and blankets are the customary relishes for the saddle, but the best cattle often omit them.

Charley hobbled old Vinegaroan and set out smartly, hobbling himself in his high-heeled boots. As the dim road wound into the falling dusk he regaled himself with the immortal saga of Sam Bass:

"Sam Bass he came from Indiana—it was his native state;
He came out here to Texas, and here he met his fate.
Sam always drank good liquor and spent his money free,
And a kinder-hearted fellow you'd seldom ever see!"

ii

The Box O Ranch stands on a bone-dry mesa, two miles from living water. It is a hollow square of adobe; within is a mighty cistern, large enough to store the filtered rain water from all the roofs. The site was chosen for shelter in Indian times; there is neither hill nor ridge within gunshot. One lonely cedar fronts the house, and no other tree is in sight; for that one tree the ranch was built there and not in another place. A mile away you come to the brink of Nogales Cañon, narrow and deep and dark; a thousand feet below the sunless waters carve their way to the far-off river. The ranch buildings and corrals now mark one corner of a fenced pasture, three miles square; the farther cliffs of Nogales Cañon make the southern fence.

The great mesas pyramid against the west, step on step; on that heaven-high pedestal San Mateo Peak basks in the sun, a sleeping lion. But the wonder and beauty of San Mateo are unprized. San Mateo is in America.

Two men came to the Box O in the glare of afternoon—a tall man, great of bone and coarse of face, hawk-nosed; a shorter man and younger, dark, thin-lipped, with little restless eyes, grey and shifting. He had broad eyebrows and a sharp thin nose.

A heavy revolver swung at the tall man's thigh—the short man had an automatic; each had a rifle under his knee. They were weary and thirst-parched; the horses stumbled as they walked—they were streaked and splashed with the white salt of sweat, caked with a mire of dust and lather, dried now by the last slow miles, so that no man might know their color.

The unlocked house lay silent and empty; the stove was cold; the dust of days lay on the table. "Good enough!" croaked the shorter man. "Luck's with us."

He led the way to the cistern. They drank eagerly, prudently; they sluiced the stinging dust from face and neck and hair.

"Ain't it good?" said the short man.

"Huh! That wasn't such a much. Wait till you're good and dry once—till your lips crack to the quick and your tongue swells black."

"Never for mine! I'm for getting out of this. I'm hunting the rainiest country I can find; and I stay there."

"If we get away! What if we don't find fresh horses in the pasture? There's none in sight."

"Reed's always got horses in the pasture. They're down in the cañon, where the sun hasn't dried up the grass. Oh, we'll get away, all right!

"They've got to track us, Laxon—and we've left a mighty crooked trail. They can't follow our trail at night and the Angel Gabriel couldn't guess where we are headed for."

"You don't allow much for chance? Or for—anything else? We sure don't deserve to get away," said Laxon.

He led his horse in, took off the bridle and pumped up a bucket of water. The poor beast drank greedily and his eyes begged for more.

"Not now, Bill. Another in ten minutes," he said in answer to a feeble nickering. He unsaddled; he sighed at the scalded back. "I'll douse a few bucketfuls on you quick as your pard gets his."

He turned his head. The younger man leaned sullenly against the wall. He had not moved. Laxon's face hardened. It was an ugly and brutal face at best—the uglier that he was slightly cross-eyed. Now it was the face of a devil.

"You worthless cur, get your horse! I thought you was yellow when you killed poor Mims last night—and now I know it! No need of it—not a bit. We could 'a' got his gun and his box of money without. Sink me to hell if I've not half a mind to give you up! If I was sure they'd hang you first I'd do it!"

"Don't let's quarrel, Jess. I'll get the horse, of course," said Moss wearily. "I'm just about all in—that's all. I could sleep a week!"

"Guess your horse ain't tired, you swine! I ought to kick you through the gate! Quarrel? You! Wish you'd try it. Wish you'd just raise your voice at me! Sleep, says he! Sleep, when somebody may drop in on us any time! All the sleep you get is the next hour. We ride to-night and sleep all day to-morrow in some hollow of the deep hills over beyond the Divide. No more daylight for us till we strike the Gila."

Moss made no answer. Laxon hobbled stiffly into the house and brought back canned tomatoes, corned beef and a butcher knife. They wolfed their food in silence.

"Sleep now, baby!" said Laxon. "I'll stand watch."

He spread the heavy saddle blankets in the sun; he gave the horses water, a little at a time, until they had their fill; with a gunny sack and pail he washed them carefully. Their sides were raw with spurring; there were ridges and welts where a doubled rope had lashed.

A cruel day to the northward two other horses lay stark and cold by Bluewater Corral; a cruel night beyond Bluewater the paymaster of the Harqua Hala Mine lay by the broken box of his trust, with a bullet in his heart.

Laxon found a can of baking powder and sprinkled it on the scalded backs.

"Pretty hard lines, Bill," he said, with a pat for the drooping neck. "All that heft of coin heaped up behind the cantle—that made it bad. Never mind! You'll come out all right—both of you."

His thoughts went back to those other horses at Bluewater. He had shot them at sunrise. He could not turn them loose to drink the icy water and die in agony; he could not stay; he could not shut them in the corral to endure the agony of thirst until the pursuit came up—a pursuit that so easily might lose the trail in the rock country and never come to Bluewater. It had been a bitter choice.

He built a fire and investigated the chuck room; he put on the coffee pot, took a careful look across the mesa and came back to Moss. The hour was up.

Moss slept heavily; his arms sprawled wide, his fingers jerking; he moaned and muttered in his sleep; his eyes were sunken and on his cheek the skin was stretched skulltight. The watcher was in less evil case; his reserves of stored-up vitality were scarcely touched as yet. Conscious of this, his anger for the outworn man gave way to rough compassion; the hour had stretched to nearly two before he shook the sleeper's shoulder.

"Come, Moss! You're rested a little and so's your horse. I've got some good hot coffee ready for you. Get a cup of that into your belly and you'll be as good as new. Then you go drive all the horses up out of the pasture—just about time before dark. While you're gone I'll cook a hot supper, bake up a few pones of bread for us to take along, and pack up enough other truck to do us. I'd go, but you're fifty pounds lighter'n me. Besides, you know the pasture."

"Oh, I'll go," said Moss as he drank his coffee. "There's a little corral down in the bottom. Guess I can ease a bunch in there and get me a new mount. The rest'll be easy."

"We'll pick out the likeliest, turn the others out and throw a scare into 'em," said Laxon. "We don't want to leave any fresh horses for them fellows, if they come. And, of course, they'll come."

"Yes, and they'll have a time finding out which is our tracks. I'll just leave this money here, and the rifle," said Moss in the corral. "That'll be so much weight off, anyway." He untied a slicker from behind the saddle. Unrolling it he took out an ore sack and tossed it over beside Laxon's saddle; it fell with a heavy clink of coins. "Say, Jess! Look over my doin' the baby act a while ago, will you? I should have taken care of my horse, of course—poor devil; but I was all in—so tired I hardly knew what I was about." He hesitated. "And—honest, Jess—I thought Mims was going after his gun."

"Guess I didn't sense how tired you was," said Jess, and there was relief in his voice. "Let it all slide. We're in bad and we got to stick together—us two."

At sundown Moss drove back twelve head of saddle stock. He had caught a big range sorrel at the horse pen in the cañon.

"This one'll do for me," he announced as he swung down.

"I'll take the big black," said Laxon. "Trot along now and eat your supper. I'll be ready by the time you're done. I've got our stuff all packed—and two canteens. Say, Moss, I've got two bed blankets. I'm goin' to carry my share of grub behind my saddle. My sack of money I'll wad up in my blanket and sling it across in front of me, see? We don't want any more sore-backed horses. You'd better do the same."

"All right!" said Moss. "You fix it up while I eat."

Laxon roped and saddled the black, and tied one of the grub sacks behind the cantle; he made a neat roll of his own sack of money and the blanket and tied it across behind the horn. Then he fixed his partner's money sack and grub sack the same way and thrust the rifle into the scabbard. He opened the outer gate of the corral and let the loose horses out on the eastern mesa.

"Hike, you! We'll fall in behind you in a pair of minutes and make you burn the breeze! . . . Now for Bill, the very tired horse, and we'll be all ready to hit the trail."

Bill was lying down in a corner. Laxon stirred him up and led him by the foretop out through the pasture gate. The saddle-house door opened noiselessly; Moss steadied his automatic against the doorframe and waited.

"You go hunt up your pardner, old Bill. You and him orter be good pals from now on. So long! Good luck!" said Laxon. He closed the gate.

Moss shot him between the shoulder blades. Laxon whirled and fell on his face; the swift automatic cracked. Laxon rose to his elbow, riddled and torn; bullet after bullet crashed through his body. He shot the sorrel horse between the eyes; the black reared up and broke his rope. As he fell backward a ball from Laxon's forty-five pierced his breast; falling, another shot broke his neck. Then Laxon laughed—and died.

iii

White, frantic, cursing, the trapped murderer staggered out from his ambush. Shaking horribly he made sure that Laxon was dead. "The squint-eyed devil!" he screamed.

He ran to the outer gate. The band of freed horses was close by and unalarmed, but twilight was deepening fast. What was to be done must be done quickly.

He set the outer gate open. He bridled old Bill and leaped on, barebacked; with infinite caution he made a wide circle beyond the little bunch of horses and worked them slowly toward the gate.

They came readily enough and, at first, it seemed that there would be no trouble; but at the gate they stopped, sniffed, saw those dim, mysterious forms stretched out at the further side, huddled, recoiled and broke away in a little, slow trot.

Moss could not stop them. Poor old Bill could only shuffle. The trot became a walk; they nibbled at the young grass.

Once he turned them back, but before they reached the gate they edged away uneasily. Twilight was done. Twice he turned them back. All the stars were out and blazing clear; a cool night breeze sprang up. Nearing the gate the horsese sniffed the air; they snorted, wheeled and broke away; the trot became a gallop, the gallop a run.

Moss slipped the bridle off and walked back to the corral. His whole body was shaking in a passion of rage and fear.

He drank deeply at the cistern; he reloaded the automatic; he went to the dead horses. Whatever came, he would not abandon that money. After all, there was a chance. He would keep the notes with him; he would hide the gold somewhere in the rocky cliffs of the cañon; he would climb out over the cliffs, where he would leave no track to follow; he would keep in the impassable hills, hiding by day; he would carry food and water; he would take the rifle and first time he saw a horseman alone he would have a horse.

Eagerly he untied the two treasure sacks and emptied one into the other. He started for the house. Then his heart stopped beating. It was a voice, faint and far away:

"Rabbit! Rabbit! Tail mighty white!
Yes, good Lord—he'll take it out o' sight!

In a frenzy of fear the murderer dropped his treasure and snatched up the rifle. He ran to the gate and crouched in the shadow. His hair stood up; his heart pounded at his ribs; his knees knocked together.

> *"Rabbit! Rabbit! Ears mighty long!*
> *Yes, good Lord—you set 'em on wrong!*
> *Set 'em on wrong!"*

It was a gay young voice, coming from the westward, nearer and nearer. Slinking in the shadows, Moss came to the corner. In the starlight he saw a man very near now, coming down the road afoot, singing as he came:

> *"Sam Bass he came from Indiana—it was his native state."*

From the west? His pursuers would be coming from the north along his track—they would not be singing, and there would be more than one. Why was this man afoot? With a desperate effort of the will Moss pulled himself together. He slipped back into the kitchen and lit the lamp. He threw dry sticks on the glowing coals— they broke into a crackling flame; the pleasant tingling incense of cedar filled the room. He dabbed at his burning face with a wet towel; he smoothed his hair hastily. Drawn, pale and haggard, the face in the glass gave him his cue—he was an invalid.

Would the man never come? He felt the mounting impulse to struggle no longer—to shriek out all the ghastly truth; to give up— anything, so he might sleep and die and rest. But he had no choice; he must fight on. Someway he must use this newcomer for his need. But why afoot? Why could not the man have a horse? Then his way would have been so easy. His throat and mouth were dust-dry— he drank deep of the cool water and felt new life steal along his veins.

Then—because he must busy himself to bridge the dreadful interval—he forced his hands to steadiness; he filled and lit a pipe.

"Hello, the house!"

Moss threw open the door; the dancing light leaped out against the dark. Along that golden pathway a man came, smiling.

"Hello yourself, and see how you like it! You're late. Turn your horse in the corral while I warm up supper for you."

iv

"I left my horse back up the road. I just love to walk," said

Charley. At the door he held up a warning hand. "Before I come in, let's have a clear understanding. No canned corn goes with me. I don't want anybody even to mention canned corn."

"Never heard of it," said Moss. "Sit ye down. How'd fried spuds, with onions and bacon, suit you?"

"Fine and dandy! Anything but ensilage." Ellis limped to a box by the fire and painfully removed a boot. "Cracky! Some blisters!"

Moss bent over the fire.

"You're not from round these parts, are you?" he asked. He raked out coal for the coffeepot and put the potatoes to warm.

"Nope. From Arizona—lookin' for work. What's the show to hook up with this outfit?"

"None. Everybody gone to the round-up. Oh, I don't live here myself. I'm just a-stayin' round for my health." . . . If I could only get to this man's horse—if I could leave this man in the trap! The pursuit must be here by to-morrow. Steady! I must feel my way. . . .

"Horse played out?"

"No; but he's right tired and he lost the shoe off his nigh forefoot to-day. Stake me to a new shoe, of course?"

"Sure!" . . . But this man will tell his story. I can never get away on a tired horse—they will overtake me; they will be here tomorrow. Shall I make it seem that Laxon and this man have killed each other? No; there will still be his tracks where he came—mine where I leave. How then? . . . "Sorry I can't let you have a horse to get yours. Just set myself afoot about sunset. Had all the saddle horses in the corral—saw a coyote—ran out to shoot at him—did you hear me, mister: I didn't get your name. Mine's Moss."

"Ellis—Charley Ellis. No; I was 'way over behind that hill at sundown. You're sure looking peaked and pale, Mr. Moss."

"It's nothing—weak heart," said Moss. The heavy brows made a black bar across his white face. . . . How then? I will stay here. I will be the dupe, the scapegoat—this man shall take my place, shall escape, shall be killed resisting arrest. . . . "Just a little twinge. I'm used to it. Where was I? Oh, yes—the horses. Well, I didn't shut the gate good. It blew open and away went my horses to the wild bunch. Idiotic, wasn't it? And I was planning to make a start to-night, ten mile or so, on a little hunting trip. That reminds me—I got a lot of bread baked up and it's out in my pack. You wash up and I'll go get it. There's the pan." . . . This man Ellis was the murderer! I left my horse. Ellis stole away while I was asleep. He tried to escape on my horse. He can't get far; the horse is about played out. When I woke and missed Ellis I found the dead man in the corral!

The black thought shaped and grew. He hugged it to his heart as he took bread from the pack sacks; he bettered it as he hid the sack of money. He struck a match and picked out a sheaf of five-dollar bills; he tore them partway across, near one corner, perhaps an inch. Then he took one bill from the torn package, crumpled it up and wadded it in his pocket, putting the others back in the sack.

Next, he found the empty ore sack, the one that had carried Laxon's half of the plunder. With a corner of it he pressed lightly over the dead man's back, so that a tiny smear of drying blood showed on the sack.

Then he took the bread and hurried to the house, dropping the ore sack outside the door. It was swiftly done. Ellis was just combing his hair when his host returned.

"There! Coffee's hot and potatoes will be in a jiffy. Sit up. Where'd you say you left your horse?"

"Where the wagon road crosses the creek west of the Box Cañon—where there's a sign nailed to a tree."

"Which sign? There's several—different places."

" 'Five miles to the Box O Ranch,' it says."

"Hobbled your horse, I reckon?"

"Yep. Wasn't really no need of hobbling, either—he won't go far. Some gaunted up, he is. He'll be glad when I get a job. And I'll say this for old Vinegaroan—he's a son-of-a-gun to pitch; but he don't put on. When he shows tired he's tired for fair. Only for his wild fool ways, he'd be the best horse I ever owned. But, then, if it hadn't been for them wild fool ways the V R wouldn't never 'a' let me got my clutches on him. They never raised a better horse, but he was spoiled in breaking. He thinks you want him to buck. Don't mean no harm by it."

"I see! Roan horse, branded 'V R' and some devilish; you might say he named himself."

"That's it."

"What is he—red roan?"

"Naw—blue roan. Mighty fine looker when he's fat—the old scoundrel!"

"Old horse? Or is that just a love name?"

Charley laughed.

"Just a love name. He's seven years old."

Moss poured the coffee and dished up the potatoes.

"There! She's ready—pitch in! I'll take a cup of coffee with you. Big horse?"

"Fifteen hands. Say, this slumgullion tastes mighty ample after —you know—fodder. Last night I stayed in a little log shack south of the peak."

Moss interrupted.

"How many rooms? So I can know whose house it was."

"Two rooms—'HG' burned on the door. 'Chas. J. Graham, Cañada Alamosa,' stenciled on the boxes. No one at home but canned corn and flour and coffee. Night before at the Anchor X Ranch. No one at home. Note sayin' they'd gone to ship steers at Magdalena. Didn't say nothing about goin' after chuck—but I know. There wasn't one cussed thing to eat except canned corn—not even coffee. Blest if I've seen a man for three days. Before that I laid up a couple of days with an old Mexican, right on the tiptop of the Black Range— hunting, and resting up my horse."

"I knowed a V R brand once, up North," said Moss reflectively. "On the hip for mares, it was; thigh for geldings; side for cattle."

"That one's on the Gila—Old Man Hearn—shoulder for horses; hip for cattle."

"Let me fill your cup," said Moss. "Now I'll tell you what—I wish you could lay up with me. I'd be glad to have you. But if you want work bad, and your horse can make eighteen or twenty miles by noon to-morrow, I think you can catch onto a job. They're meetin' at Rosedale to-morrow to start for the north round-up. This country here has done been worked. They'll light out after dinner and make camp about twenty-five miles north. You follow back the road you came here for about a mile. When the road bends to come here, at the head of the draw, you bear off to the left across the mesa, northwestlike. In six or eight miles you'll hit a plain road from the river, running west, up into the mountains. That'll take you straight to Rosedale."

"Well! I'll have to be up and doin', then, and catch'em before they move. Much obliged to you! Think I'm pretty sure of a job?"

"It's a cinch. Them V Cross T cattle are a snaky lot, and they never have enough men."

"Look here! Stake me to a number-one shoe and some nails, will you? Loan me a rasp and a hammer? I'll stick the tools up in the tree where the sign is. Clap a shoe on at daylight and shack along while it's cool. I'll make it by ten o'clock or later."

"But you'll stay all night?"

"No—we might oversleep. I'll chin with you a while and then hike along back and sleep on my saddle blankets. Then I'll be stirrin' soon in the mawnin'."

"Well, I'm sorry to see you go; but you know your own business. No more? Smoke up, then?" He tossed papers and tobacco across. "Say, I want you to send a Mex boy down here with a horse, so I can drive my runaways in off the flat. Don't forget!"

"I'll not. May I have a bucket and wash up these blistered feet of mine before I hike?"

"Sure you can! Sit still; I'll get the water. I'll rustle round and see if some of the boys ain't left some clean socks too; and I'll wrap you up a parcel of breakfast."

"Well, this is luck!" declared Charley a little later, soaking his feet luxuriantly and blowing smoke rings while his host busied himself packing a lunch. "A job, horseshoe, socks, supper and breakfast—and no canned corn! I'll do somebody else a good turn sometime—see if I don't! I wasn't looking for much like this a spell back, either. About an hour by sun, I was countin' on maybe makin' supper on a cigarette and a few verses of The Boston Burglar—unless I could shoot me a cottontail at sundown—most always you can find a rabbit at sundown. Then I sighted this dizzy old ranch peekin' through the gap at me. Bing! Just look at me now! Nobody's got nothin' on me! Right quaint, ain't it? What a difference a few hours'll make—the things that's waiting for a fellow and him not knowin' about it!"

Moss laughed.

"Well, I got to be steppin'," said Charley.

"Hold on! I'm not done with you yet. That's a good pair of boots you've got there—but they'll be just hell on those blistered feet. How'd you like to swap for my old ones? Sevens, mine are."

"So's mine. Why, I'll swap with you. Yours'll be a sight easier on me. I'm no great shakes on walking, me."

"Why, man, did you think I meant to swap even? Your boots are worth ten dollars—almost new—and mine just hang together.

I wouldn't take a mean advantage of you like that. Come! I'll make you an offer: Give me your boots and your forty-five, with the belt and scabbard, for my automatic, with its rigging and five dollars, and I'll throw in my boots."

"Shucks! You're cheating yourself! Trade boots and guns even —that'll be fair enough." Charley unbuckled his spurs.

"Don't be silly! Take the money. It's a long time till pay day. I've been all along that long road, my boy. If you're broke—I'm just guessing that, because I've been broke myself—why, you don't want to ask for an advance the first thing."

"I'll tell you what, then—swap spurs too. That'll make about an even break."

"Nonsense! Keep your spurs. You don't want these old pet-makers of mine. They'd be a hoodoo to a cowboy. Take the money, son. I wish it was more. I've got plenty enough, but not here. If you feel that way about it, call it a loan and pay it back when you're flush. Better still, pass it on to somebody else that needs it."

Charley surrendered.

"I'll take it, then—that way. You're all right, Mr. Moss! Try on your new boots and see how they fit."

"Fine as silk! Couldn't be better if they was made to order," said Moss. "Good boots. That's always the way with you young fellows. Every cent goes for a fancy outfit. Bet you've got a fire-new saddle—and you without a copper cent in your pocket."

"Well, purty nigh it," admitted Charley, grinning. "Set me back fifty-four pesos less'n a year ago. But she's a daisy."

"Swell fork?"

Charley snorted.

"Swell fork nothin'! No, sir; I don't need no roll. I ride'em slick—take off my spurs and grease my heels! I been throwed, of course—everybody has—but I never clawed leather yet and I don't need no swell fork!"

Moss smiled indulgently.

"Well, I must right you out for horseshoein'. You stay here and rest up. Number one shoe, I think you said?"

He came back with the horseshoe and tools, bringing also the discarded ore sack, now bulging with a liberal feed of corn.

"For Vinegaroan, with my love!" he said, laughing, and clapping Ellis on the shoulder.

A lump came into Charley's throat.

"I reckon you're a real-for-certain white man, Mr. Moss. If old Vinegaroan could talk he'd sure thank you. I'm going now and let you go to bed. You don't look so clean beat out as you did, but you look right tired. *Adiós!* And I hope to meet up with you again."

"Oh, you'll see me again! Good-by!"

They shook hands. Charley shouldered his pack and limped sturdily along the starlit road, turning once for a shouted "Good-by!" Moss waved a hand from the lighted doorway; a gay song floated back to him:

> *Ada! Ada! Open that do',*
> *Ada!*
> *Ada! Ada! Open that do',*
> *This mawnin'.*
> *Ada! Ada! Open that do',*
> *Or I'll open it with a fohty-fo'*
> *This mawnin'!"*

"Oh, yes! you'll see me again!" said Moss, smiling evilly. Then he closed the door. "Tired?" he said. "Tired? I've got to sleep if I swing for it."

v

BOX O RANCH, August fifth.
Statement of Elmer Moss

My name is Elmer Moss. I left Florence, Arizona, three weeks ago looking for work. I did not find a place and drifted on to this ranch. I stayed here a week or two, six years ago, when George Sligh worked here.

Last night my horse was pretty well give out and had lost a shoe; so I left him at the crossing of Nogales Creek, west of the pasture fence, and walked in.

I got in soon after dark and found a man who said his name was Charley Ellis, and that he was working here. He was a young fellow, with rather a pleasant face. He was about my size, with light hair and blue eyes and a pug nose. He made me welcome. Said he couldn't say about work, but for me to stay here till the boss came back. We talked quite late.

I woke up early in the morning. Ellis was not in his bed. I

supposed he had gone to wrangle horses out of the pasture and I went back to sleep, for I was very tired from riding a slow horse. I woke again after a while and got up. Ellis was not back yet. I went out into the corral. And there I found a dead man. He was shot all to pieces—I don't know how many times. There were two dead horses, both shot and both saddled.

I found the boot tracks where Ellis had gone back the way I came. He is trying to get away on my horse and leave me with a murdered man on my hands to explain.

I was so scared I didn't know what to do. I went out in the pasture to the rim, where I could see all over the cañon. If I could have got a horse I would have run away. There wasn't a horse in sight except one. That one was close up under the rimrock. He had been ridden almost to death. He wouldn't have carried me five miles. After I came back I found another one, in worse shape than the first, outside the corral gates. I let him in and gave him water and hay. There were horsetracks of all sizes round the corral.

I don't know what to do. I don't know what has happened here. It may be a week before anybody comes. If anyone comes today, or while the tracks are fresh that I made coming and that Ellis made going away, I'm all right. The story is all there, plain as print. My boots are new and his was all worn out. There's no chance for mistake. And my horse has lost a shoe from his left forefoot; so he will be easy tracked. And he's badly jaded—he can't go fast. If anybody comes to-day they can trail him up and catch him easy. If no one comes to-day I'm a goner.

I just now went and spread a tarp over the dead man. He was laughing when he died. He's laughing yet—and his eyes are wide open. It's horrible! Left everything else just as it was. Am writing this now, and taking my time at it, to get everything straight while there's no one to get me rattled and all mixed up. And in case I go out of my head. Or get hold of a horse somehow and try to get away. No, I won't try to run away. If I did it would be just the same as confessing that I was the murderer. If they caught me I'd hang sure.

Nothing can save me except the straight truth. And that won't help me none unless somebody comes along to-day. This man Ellis was about my size—but I told you that before. He wore blue overalls, pretty badly faded, and a gray flannel shirt. I didn't notice his hat; he didn't have it on much. I saw a revolver belt under his pillow and it's gone now; but I didn't see the gun.

That made me think. I went back and looked round everywhere to see where Ellis had reloaded his gun. I found fresh shells—nine of them, thirty-twos, automatic shells, smokeless, rimless—scattered over the floor of the saddle room just as an automatic would throw them. He killed his man from ambush. I went back and looked at the dead man. He was shot in the back—twice anyway. Hit six times in all, as near as I could see. I couldn't bear to touch him. He looked terrible, laughing that way—and I'm about to break down. There was a hole in his neck about the size a thirty-two would make.

There was a six-shooter in the sand near his hand with three empty shells in it. Them shells was what killed the horses—after the dead man was first shot, I reckon. I covered him up again. I see now that I shouldn't have gone near him. I see now—too late—that I never should have made one single foot-track in that corral. If I had only known—if I had only thought in time—the tracks in there would have cleared me. All I had to do was to stay out. But how could I think of that?

Later: There is a tree in front of the house and I have started a grave there. If no one comes by sundown I'll bury the poor fellow. I will rig up some sort of a sled and put the body on it and make the give-out pony drag it out to the grave.

The work of digging has done me good and steadied my nerves. I am half done and now I am able to set a little. I will go back and finish it now.

Later—ten o'clock: Thank God! When the grave was done and I climbed out I saw a big dust off in the north coming this way. I am saved! They are closer now and coming very fast—ten or twelve men on horseback. I have looked over this statement carefully and don't think I have forgotten anything. This is the truth and nothing but the truth, so help me God.

I want to make one thing straight: Moss is not my right name. I have used that name for nine years. I was of good family and had my chance in life; but I was wild. Whatever happens I will bring no more disgrace to the name. I shall stick to Elmer Moss. If it had rained and washed the tracks out—if the wind had covered them with sand—what a shape I would be in now! They are quite close. I am leaving my gun on these sheets of paper. I am going out to meet them.

"That's all," said Tom Hall.

No one answered. Every man drew a long, deep breath—almost a sigh. There was a shuffling of feet.

The dark looks that had been bent on Moss, where he sat leaning heavily on the table, were turned long since to pity and rough friendliness. A dozen stern-faced men were crowded in the kitchen—a little white and sick, some of them from what they had seen in the corral.

Each man looked at the others. Young Broyles let his hand rest lightly on Moss' shoulder. Then Old Man Teagardner frowned into his beard and spoke:

"Your story sounds like the truth, Mr. Moss," he said. "The boot-tracks going away from here are the same tracks we found in Bluewater Pens, and these two played-out horses came from Bluewater. If you're telling the truth you've been up against it hard. Still, you must be held as a prisoner—for the present, at least, till we find your man. And we'll want you to answer a few questions. What kind of a horse did you have?"

"A blue roan, V R brand, thin, fifteen hands high, no shoe on left forefoot, seven or eight years old. Saddle nearly new," answered Moss dully.

Then he raised his head and his voice swelled to sudden anger:

"You can ask me questions any time—you got me. Why don't you go after Ellis? That's your business! He's getting farther away every minute. Of course you'll keep me prisoner. What do you take me for—a fool? S'pose I'd think you'd find a man in the shape I'm in and let him go foot-loose as soon as he said: 'Please, mister, I didn't do it'? Send some of your gang after Ellis and I'll answer all the fool questions you can think up."

"Son," said Teagardner evenly, "your party won't get away. We've sent men or messages all over the country and everybody's forwarded it on. Every man not accounted for will be held on suspicion. Some of the boys will go in a little while; but, ten to one, your man Ellis is caught now—or killed. Say, boys, let's get out where we can get a breath of air."

"He won't fight, I tell you!" urged Moss as he followed his questioners outdoors. "He'll be as innocent as a lamb. If he don't ooze away without bein' seen his play is to saw it off onto me."

"All the more reason, then, why you should answer our questions."

148

"Questions!" cried Moss bitterly. "I wish somebody'd answer me a few. Who was that dead man? What did Ellis kill him for? Who was your gang lookin' for?"

"We don't know the dead man's name. None of us ever seen him before," said Cook. "We've followed them for two days. Robbery and murder. Now one has killed the other for his share of the stolen money."

"Then you didn't know the man you was after? But," said Moss, "this man may have got killed himself for reasons of his own. He may have nothing to do with your bank robbers. There was all sorts of shod horse-tracks leading away from the gate—I saw 'em this morning. Maybe that was the outfit you're after."

Teagardner stroked his long white beard and motioned the others to silence. Said he:

"Some of us'll follow 'em up, to be sure—but them was only saddle horses that they turned out, I judge—so us fellows couldn't get 'em. As I figure it out, that's how come your Ellis man to be in the fix he was. He shot his pardner and his pardner set him afoot before he died. So, when you come, Ellis left you to hold the sack. . . . Well! Cal, you and Hall pick out two other men to suit yourselves, and follow Ellis up. Watch close for any sign of him hiding out the money. He dassent keep it with him. We'll look for it here. Made your choice?"

"These two sticks'll do us, Uncle Ben."

"All right, then; get a mouthful to eat first and take something with you. I'll see you before you start. Broyles, you and Dick take the trail of that bunch of saddle horses after dinner. Bring 'em back— or see where they went to. It's just barely possible that there's been two separate gangs on the warpath here; but I judge not. I judge them's just saddle horses. Sam, you and Spike cook dinner. You other chaps make some sort of a coffin. Keep Moss with you. After while we'll all turn to and see if Ellis hid the money here."

"Now, whatever happens, you fellows get that man alive—*sabe?* No shooting. I ain't quite satisfied. Moss, he tells a straight-enough story and everything seems to back him up so far; but this man Ellis —where does he get off? If he comes along peaceful and unsuspicious —why, he's guilty and playin' foxy, layin' it all onto Moss. If he's scared it hangs him; if he keeps his upper lip right he's brazening it out, and we hang him for that. If he fights you he's guilty; if he hides out that proves he's guilty. If he gets clean away that's absolute proof. Any game where a man hasn't got one chance to win don't look just right."

Young Broyles burst into the room.

"See what I found! It was out in the corral, in the sand. I kicked at that ore sack layin' there by the dead horses—and I kicked up this! Nineteen five-dollar bills, done up like a pack of envelopes."

"They're all torn—see? and they're usually put up in hundred-dollar bunches, aren't they?" said Hall. "There's one gone—maybe."

"Yes," said Cal eagerly; "and that ore sack—there was two of 'em likely, and after the murder Ellis put all the stuff into one and dropped this bundle doin' it! Say! We ought to call Moss."

"I'll tell him," said Teagardner.

"But how'd them bills get torn? And where's the other one?" demanded Cal.

Hall shrugged his shoulders. "How'd I know? Come on, fellows—let's hike!"

Dinner was eaten; Broyles and Dick departed on their search; the coffin was made; and the dead man was laid in it.

"Shall you bury him now?" asked Moss.

"I hope so!" said Spike with a shudder.

"Me, too," echoed Sam. "I can't stand that awful laugh on his face. Let's get him out of sight, Uncle Ben."

"No. We want Ellis to see him, for one thing. Then again the sheriff may come and he may want to take charge. Besides, I think maybe we'll bury the murderer here and take this one to San Marcial."

Moss licked his lips.

"Put them both in one grave—why not? It's deep enough," suggested Cook. "They killed old Mims—let them talk it over together."

"Only one man shot Mims," said Teagardner. "This poor fellow may not have been the one. The man that killed him—his own pardner—the man that shot him in the back from behind a 'dobe wall, and then left an innocent man to stand for it—that's the man killed Mims. I don't think we've any right to force such company on this dead man. Come on! Let's get to work."

They dragged the dead horses far out on the plain; they piled sand where the blood pools had been; roof and wall and floor, they ransacked the house, outbuildings and the stables for the stolen money.

"You're forgetting one thing," said Moss. "As I am still your prisoner I am naturally still under suspicion. I may be the murderer after all and Ellis may be the victim—as, of course, he'll claim to be. Somebody ought to follow my track where I walked out to the rim this morning."

Teagardner eyed him, with mild reproach.

"Set your mind at rest, Mr. Moss. We're taking all bets. We did exactly that while you were resting just before dinner. You didn't take a step that isn't accounted for. You didn't ride one of the give-out horses down in the cañon and hide it there, either. And it will be the same with Ellis. That money will be found. We need it—as evidence."

"Well, if you've done looking I'd like to rest—to go to sleep if I can. I'm done!"

"Yes—you look fagged out. No wonder—you've been under a strain. It's blistering hot—we'll all go out to the grave, under that tree. It's the only cool place round here. Bring some water, you boys."

"Nice pleasant place for a sleep," suggested Sam, with a nervous giggle, at the grave side. "What's the matter with the shady side of the house?"

"No air," said Moss. "This suits me."

Teagardner sat on a stone and gazed long into the grave, smoking placidly. He was a very old man—tough and sturdy and straight and tall for all that. Long and long ago, Teagardner had been an oldtimer here. Half a lifetime since—at an age when most are content to become spectators—he had fared forth to new ventures; after a quarter century in Australia and the Far East—Hong-Kong last— he had come back to the land of his youth—to die.

If Napoleon, at eighty, had come back from St. Helena, some such position might have been his as was Uncle Ben's. Legend and myth had grown about his name, wild tales of the wild old days— the days when he had not been the Old Man, or everybody's Uncle Ben, but strong among the strongest. The chase had passed his way that morning and he had taken horse, despite his seven-and-seventy years, with none to say him nay.

"It is a deep grave—and the soil is tough," he said, raising his eyes at last. "You have been a miner, Mr. Moss?"

"After a fashion—yes."

"You must have worked hard digging this."

"I did. It seemed to do me good. I was nervous and excited. Shucks! I was scared—that's the kind of nervous I was."

"You say you rode across from Arizona. Where did you stay night before last?"

"In a two-room log house under San Mateo Peak, to the south; H. G. Ranch—or it has been once, for them letters are branded on the door. No one was there."

Spike nodded. "Charley Graham's. Charley, he's at the round-up."

"Well, I'm right sorry he wasn't there, as things turned out; but if you'll send a man over to-morrow he'll find the corn cans I opened—and some flour and coffee, and nothing else—only my horse's tracks and the shoe he lost somewhere on the road. That'll prove my alibi, all right—at least, as far as your bank robbery's concerned. The greenbacks you found seem to hook these two other gentlemen up with that."

"We'll send a man there all right, if needed. And it wasn't a bank that was robbed—it was a mine—a paymaster," said Uncle Ben.

"Well, you didn't tell me."

"No; I didn't tell you. And the night before that?"

"I stayed at the Anchor X Ranch. No one there, either. If your man goes that far he'll get canned corn straight—not even coffee to go with it. And he'll find a note to the effect that the outfit has gone to ship a bunch of steers at Magdalena."

Again Teagardner's quiet eye went round the circle and again the prisoner's story was confirmed.

"That's right. They load up to-day. Aw, let the man sleep, Uncle Ben. He's giving it to you straight."

But Uncle Ben persisted.

"And before that? You must have seen some man, somewhere, sometime."

Moss shook his head impatiently.

"For nearly a week before that I camped with an old Mexican hunter, on the divide south of Chloride, letting my horse rest up and hunting deer. Leastwise he hunted and I went along for company. I didn't have any rifle and he wouldn't lend me his. His name was Delfin Something-or-Other, and he lived in Springerville, he said. Say, old man, you make me tired! Am I to blame because no one lives in this accursed country? By George! If I could have taken a long look ahead I'd have hired me a witness and carried him with me."

"If we could take a long look ahead—or a short one—we'd be greatly surprised, some of us," Teagardner answered, without heat. "There—go to sleep, all of you. I slept last night. I'll call you when it's time."

He changed his seat to a softer one on the fresh mound of earth; he twisted his long gray beard and looked down into the grave. Moss watched him through narrowed lids. Then fatigue claimed him, stronger than horror or hate or fear, and he fell asleep.

vi

"You chuckle-headed idiots!" gasped Charley Ellis.

"Oh, that's all right too," said Tom Hall. "Some folks is too smart for their own good. You keep still."

Three men held Charley, one by each arm and one by the collar. His eyes were flashing; he was red with anger and considerably the worse for wear, having just made a sincere and conscientious attempt to break the neck of Mr. Moss—an almost successful attempt. It had taken more than three men to pull him off. Moss, white and smiling, mopped his bruised face beyond the coffin and the open grave; the sun setting between the clouds threw a red, angry light over all.

"Quiet having been resumed," observed Teagardner patiently, "let us pass on to unfinished business. Tom, we've been so all-fired busy explainin' the situation to Mr. Ellis that we haven't got your report yet. Spit it out!"

"Uncle Ben, this Ellis is the man we want," said Tom Hall. "We found where he'd tacked a shoe on the horse—of course Moss couldn't know that. We tracked him a ways towards Rosedale and then we met these three Rosedale men coming back with him. They told him they was holdin' everybody and gathered him in. He made no objection—handed over his gun without a word. It was an automatic thirty-two. Horse and saddle just as Moss described 'em, all right—and this ore sack tied on the saddle besides."

Uncle Ben shook his head.

"It won't do, Tom. Everything is as Moss told it—but everything is just as Ellis tells it, too. So far as I can see they've got only one horse, one saddle and one interestin' past between them."

"You blithering, blistering, gibbering, fat-headed fools!" said Charley pleasantly. "If you'd told me about what Moss said I would 'a' told you to leave my horse and let Moss try his hand at describin' him. He's got one white hoof; he's been cut with barbed wire; and my saddle's been sewed up with buckskin where the linin's ripped. Moss couldn't have told you that. Did you give me a fair chance for my life? No, sir; you come blunderin' in and let Moss look 'em all over—pretendin' to be petting old Vinegaroan. I wasn't mistrustin' anything like this. They said there'd been trouble and they was makin' all strangers account for themselves. That seemed reasonable enough and I wasn't worrying."

"We've got only your word for that," sneered Sam. "I reckon Moss could have told us all about it if we had asked him."

"And maybe again he couldn't—Ellis is right," said Hall soberly. "He didn't get an even break. I'm sorry."

"What about the ore sack?"

"Boys," said Uncle Ben, "you're going at this all wrong. Mr. Ellis says he took feed in that sack—that's reasonable. And that he kept the sack by him counts in his favor, I think."

"So do I," said Cal. "And I'll swear that if he had any money in it he must 'a' eat the bills and flung the coins away, one piece at a time. He never hid it after he left this house—that's sure. I know every inch of ground he's been over and my eyes is pretty near out from reading sign. I even went on, to make sure, after we met the Rosedale men, clear to where he met them and loped all the way back to catch up with 'em."

"How about this then?" cried Spike triumphantly. He was one of those who held Ellis. "I just took it out of his pocket."

It was a new five-dollar bill, and it was torn. Teagardner produced the package of bills. The tears matched exactly.

A horrible snarl burst from a dozen throats. They crowded and jostled, Moss with the rest; hands reached out to clutch at the prisoner.

"Hang him! Hang him!"

"Stand back! Stand back, you blind fools! I'll shoot the next man that touches him!" shouted Teagardner. "Stand back."

"You'll hang nobody, you howling dogs!" said Ellis coolly. "We stand just where we did before—my word against Moss'."

"Exactly!" said Uncle Ben. "Have a little sense, can't ye? Cook, if you was this man, and guilty, how would you say you got this bill?"

"I'd say Moss gave it to me, of course."

"And you, Spike, if you knew positively that Ellis was innocent—then how did he get this bill?"

"He must have got it from Moss," said Spike reluctantly.

Charley laughed. "Well, that's where I got it—when we traded boots and guns, like I was tellin' you."

"You're a damned liar!"

No one was holding Charley's foot. It now caught Moss squarely in the breast and hurled him over the mound of earth and almost into the grave.

"Old gentleman—Uncle Ben, as they call you"—said Charley then, "you seem to have charge here, and you're old enough to have a real idea once in a while. There's just as much against Moss as against me, and no more—isn't there?"

"Precisely—up to date."

"Well, then, why aren't we treated the same? Why am I held this way while he goes free?"

"That's right!" said Cal.

"Hold Moss, a couple of you," said Uncle Ben. "Now, Mr. Ellis, look here!" He pushed aside the unnailed coffin lid to show the dead man's face. "Do you know this man?"

"Hell, he's laughing! No; I never saw him before. What's he laughing at? What's the joke?"

"He is laughing at his murderer."

"Well, I know who that is," said Charley. "And that's more than the rest of you do."

Teagardner replaced the lid.

"All we know—yet—is that he is either laughing at you or laughing at Moss. Your stories exactly offset each other. What are we going to do next? Understand me—there'll be nobody hanged till he's proved guilty."

"Keep us!" said Charley. "Watch us night and day! Chain us together with every chain on the ranch. One of us is a liar. Send some of your men along the back track till you find where the liar's story don't fit with the certain truth. I can describe every little trifling thing at the ranches where I stayed; I can tell what my old Mexican hunter looks like, if you can find him. Can Moss?"

"Son," said Teagardner, "you've got the right idea, and your plan would work—if we had to do it; but we don't have to do it. You've overlooked one thing. There's two ends to every lie—and one end of this lie is on this side of the murder. If we find the money where you hid it after you left here—you swing, Ellis. If we find it here at the ranch—why, either of you may have hid it. Everything that's happened at the ranch may have been done by either of you two men—everything but one."

He turned a slow eye on Moss, who stood by the coffin, white and trembling, with a man at each arm. His voice rang—measured, stern and hard.

"Everything but one," he repeated. "Ellis had nothing to do with one thing. . . . Moss dug the grave. And the grave is too deep. I always thought the grave was too deep. Jump into the grave, Sam, and see why Moss made it so deep!"

Moss dropped to his knees; his guards held him up; they forced him forward to the edge of the grave. A shudder ran through the crowd; they swayed forward; the last ray of the sun fell on them in a golden shaft. Sam leaped into the grave.

"Moss dug his grave too deep—because he was afraid somebody might want to make it a little deeper," said Teagardner. "Ground solid there? Try the other end."

Sam found loose earth at the other end. He shoveled furiously; he came to a package wrapped in slickers. He threw it up. They slashed the cords; they unrolled the slickers; at the grave's edge they poured the blood-bought money at the murderer's feet.

X. Cheerful Land

Written especially for *West Is West* (New York, 1917), this made one of the tenuous threads by which Rhodes connected previously published short stories into a book-bulk whole. It has not seen print otherwise.
Here is a country, a people, a way of life and the code it lived by—New Mexico of the 1890's—set down in one of the finest evocative passages ever written about the West-That-Was.

Mr. EMIL JAMES rode down the main street of San Clemente in the bright mid-morning sun. From open doors a flourish of friendly hands kept pace with him. Emil waved gay return. Tippy-toes, absurd but admirable horse, cocked ears to left or right at each open door and tossed his forelock in cheerful salutation of his own.

Mr. Emil James, the bright sun, the street of open doors—these deserve separate consideration. Emil was a tall man with a long, serious face, only prevented from large mirth by reasons of state. His eyes were tranquil, wide, deep-blue and steady; he wore a grizzly-gray mustache and a long, thin, straight nose. The first was trimmed and disciplined, a mustache that knew its place; and Mr. James kept on intimate terms with the second. It was his habit, in perplexity or deliberation, to look down his nose for counsel. He did not squint, he merely glanced: a feat possible only because his eyes were so wide apart and his nose so very long. For the rest, he was a youngerly man who looked, and may have been, from thirty to forty or fifty.

He rode loose-reined and gently swaying, irresistibly giving the effect of one who sits at cheerful ease upon a shaded porch with luxurious feet upon a railing; relaxing, after stirring hurly-burly, to a little well-earned repose.

The blue eyes of Mr. James, twinkling deep beneath a shady hat-brim, made inevitable the porch-thought, just as his loose-limbed comfort suggested the oldest and best-beloved of easy-chairs. The gait was a walk, but it was a swinging walk, roguish, jaunty and whimsical; a walk which was apparently on the point of breaking into a jig; a knowing walk, cheerful and alert, plainly expecting some brisk adventure at any turn and confident of a creditable part in such joyous hazards as might arise.

Quite spontaneously and of his own motion, the Tippytoes horse has crowded into the story with Mr. James; which is as it should be. For this was a land of a strong white sun and cloudless skies, therefore of scant water and vast distances; where a horse and his rider are one.

No bully's horse ever met the world with such friendly eyes as Tippytoes; no bigot's horse would dare such rakish impudence of bearing; no weakling's horse could ever manage that joyous swagger. With every careless, confident line and motion, Tippytoes proclaimed his assurance that he carried a man.

That bright sun vouched for Emil's broad hatbrim and made it credible. The great mountains made soft that hat-brim, that it might be turned back when he rode in their cool and friendly shelter; just as the long dun reaches of Malibu Flat made soft that hat-brim, that it might bend to the strong winds which inhabit such dim immensities.

Wherever the eye might turn it fell on great mountains, even when you woke in the starlit night: crimson-edged against the rising sun or black against the dawn; gray, brown or blueblack of morning hours, dwindled and dim in the blaze of noon, neutral and smudged.

They were colors and shapes that changed and flowed with every change of angle or distance. Those work-day grays or browns melted with the miles to strong and nameless hues—rich, warm, crude, barbaric. But if you looked westward in the late afternoon to those raw and gaudy hills, the cool, deep shadows were trembling lilac, edged with rose and sparkled with golddust; the far-seen hills were purple or misty blue; they flamed in the magic sunset to iridescent opal and all the sea-shell splendor of dreams: they rose high in the iron twilight, mighty and magnificent, serene with promise and comfort and refuge.—"I lift up mine eyes unto the hills, from whence cometh my help."

On Emil's right hand, the silent levels of Malibu Flat lay spectral and somber, rising from northern nothingness and haze, stretching on and on across the world, fading again to nothing in the south.

Across the desert, dim and far, the Continental Divide rimmed out of the west—a long wall, uneven and unbroken, range after bristling range in a linked and welded chain: the purple island-cones of Datil, the nearer Hueco, the low red blaze of Red Mesa, the blue Malibu, Copa de Oro. This particular vertebra in the backbone of the Continent was known locally as Malibu Range, taking its name from the Malibu proper. Jointed and socketed with it, the Black Range made a lavender line along the south.

Straight across, where the Malibu was blue beyond the desert, thin, tenuous silhouettes of palest amethyst peered dim and ghostly over the Malibu wall—the double peaks of San Quentin, a long day further in the western deeps.

Near by, at Emil's back, the foursquare bulk of Pinetop Mountain gloomed above the north and the east; so near, the pine trees on the crest showed plain against the sky-line, inch-long and feather-slight.

Nearer, the high sharp cone of San Clemente Peak towered at his left: San Clemente Gap was notched deep beneath it. And from that Gap, San Clemente Draw made a steep semicircle southward around the base of Ghost Mountain, where tunnels gophered and mine dumps sprawled, where trail and road zigzagged doubtfully to derrick and dump.

Close beyond Ghost Mountain and high above it, up-leaping from illimitable chasms between, the magic crest of Fantasia Range swung across the sky with rush and onsweep, dominating day and night and dream.

There were those who found these vast horizons depressing and desolate, who took no healing of the hills, who miscalled that bright-cheering sun as a glaring sun, a flaming sun in a copper sky: so dull and gray their wonted skies, so leaden, sullen and unkind.

Not San Clemente. San Clemente found in these great spaces the lure of hope, new ventures, unguessed delights; knew that kindly sun as the giver of life, oppressor of gloom and despair, the underwriter of joy.

It might be admitted by San Clemente, without prejudice, that the sun was warmish, perhaps around midday or thereabouts. Nothing more.

First, the cowmen. They worked like demons of the pit at roundup time, cool spring or cool fall. But cattle could not be worked in summer. It was too hot—for the cattle. Nor in winter, which was too cold—for the cattle. These seasons were therefore set apart by all cattlemen as a half-life of gentle divertissement.

Ten-mule teams, twenty-mule teams, hauled ore through the Gap and across the eastern desert, variously known as Magdalena Valley or Magdalena Plain. Ridgepole, terminus of a railroad of sorts, branch of a jerkwater branch, was their journey's end. They brought back supplies and machinery on the return trip.

These freighters—Mexican all—drove by night, as a matter of course. The round trip took six days. Monday morning, load with ore and pull up to San Clemente ranch, the water nearest the Gap: across the Gap at twilight, then a long night drive, nooning from eight to five in the middle of Magdalena Plains on Tuesday, Ridgepole at Wednesday breakfast time, ore in the cars Wednesday night, load up return freight on Thursday morning, unload at San Clemente Saturday night; Sunday for *monte* and other delights of home. Freighters thought of the sun largely as a reliable sedative and aid to sleep.

The miners worked underground. This statement might be classed as a truism; but so many of us are unfamiliar with that underworld, that the story hopes it may be pardoned for emphasizing so obvious a fact. The sun concerned miners chiefly as something which made shade pleasant.

The miners were Cornishmen, Welshmen and a few Irish—even a few Americans. San Clemente, it will be seen, was cosmopolitan. They worked in three shifts, from seven in the morning to three in the afternoon, from three to eleven, from eleven at night till seven in the morning; eight hours for work, eight hours to sleep, eight hours for their very own, to be squandered or banked. Every two weeks they changed shifts in rotation.

Business San Clemente transacted that busy-ness within doors. The leisure of San Clemente, the getting on people, up-and-coming people, the eastern contingent—capitalists, promoters, pleasure-seekers and health-seekers—dwelt magnificently in "Chautaqua," braced and morally uplifted by straight streets. The story believes that the Chautaquans themselves referred to their rightangular suburb as "the North Side." Needless to state, the Chautaquans were independent alike of exertion and of the sun. As a whole, San Clemente was nocturnal of habit and swore by the sun.

Ridgepole stage-drivers were exceptions. The stage arrived at Ridgepole, and left that gateway town, to suit the convenience of a mixed train which frequently made connections at Saragossa with north-bound and south-bound passenger trains, which in turn were timed for close connection with the haughty Fliers on the main lines at Albuquerque or El Paso. Because of this arbitrary and thrice-removed fixing of hours, the Ridgepole stage went through by daylight. Hueco and Datil stages, running respectively west and northwest from San Clemente, were night lines.

The street of open doors was a long street, a leisurely street, a straggling street; above all, a tolerant street. The old wagon road followed closely the semicircle of San Clemente Draw around the foot of Ghost Mountain; the new and tolerant street made the same wide circling. Why not? Why be needlessly precise and prim and rectilinear? The road was a fine old road, its history such as the street delighted to honor. Besides, it was a shallow dig to water, near the draw; why go higher to dig deeper? Again, Sundown Ridge—low, rolling and broken—paralleled at once the winding draw, the old road, and the flowing lines of Ghost Mountain. A curving street made harmony with such environment; a straight street would be a jarring discord; and the street had no mind to make itself unpleasant, thank you. The very name of it was Roundabout: with such a name, how could a street be built straight?

That the doors of this tolerant street were open was not altogether due to the warmth of the climate. The story hopes that so much will have been guessed: that this tolerant and whimsical street was also a highly allegorical street: that the open doors were in some part a symbol and a sign of friendliness and welcome. If it has not been guessed, it is here expressly stated.

But if Roundabout Street was friendly, it had its own reticence; each house was set well back from the road. Superficial folk said this was because of the dust. But each house kept at a generous distance from its neighbors and the cause of that was not dust. It was a large desire for independence, privacy and elbow room.

At the upper end of the street, nearest the gateway to the eastern desert, stood the immemorial San Clemente Ranch, hidden and fenced by deep and impenetrable shade of ancient cottonwoods. The long row of one-storied rooms, the long, low stables and the corrals, were built in one continuous wall, forming a great quadrangle of massive adobe. All windows and doors faced on the enclosed courtyards. The outer walls, house, stable, and corrals, were two feet thick, pierced near the top by loopholes. The two-foot bench made within by an offset was for riflemen to stand upon in war. In peace it made a desirable shelf, that took near to four hundred yards to complete the square.

This had been a Gibraltar among ranches in the old Apache days, a virgin fortress famed by interminable songs of liquid, feminine, soft-syllabled Spanish.

On the western side once swung a mighty gate of double valves, bullet-proof, framed of hewn logs from Pinetop. Entering, in those old days, you turned at a right angle and rode down a titanic corridor, between walls ten feet high; to where, beyond the reach of any slantwise bullet through the outer gate, a second gateway turned through the inner wall.

The old ranch had long since been made base and headquarters for the freight teams, and was now named anew as "Chihuahua." Opposite the old outer portal, the inner wall was pierced for a straight road and now crumpled to unrepaired decay: the massive war-doors were long discarded for light-swinging peaceful gates that a child might open.

Through freighters, too, for whom San Clemente was a way station, made this a camping place and half-way house. Their schedules were semi-occasional: their westwise roads radiated fan-like from San Clemente Gap; they brought from the long Malibu Range what ore was rich enough to stand the long haul; in clipping-time, great bags of mohair from Son Todos, wool from Fuentes.

Above the song-haunted cottonwoods rose the high bell-tower of San Clemente Church—old, but younger than the ranch by a near century. "The groves were God's first temples"; mass and marriage and solemn service for the dead had been held under those old trees for generations before ever the church was built.

On Roundabout Street, on the Plaza of Business-town, on the low hills of compact Chautaqua, the comparative age of any building was accurately recorded by the size of its tributary cottonwood trees; swiftest of growth of all shade trees, dearest to the desert dweller.

Because men outnumbered the women by about three or thirteen to one, San Clemente ran largely to boarding houses. For the same reason, the town supported a surprisingly good hotel, the Ugly Duckling, which took up nearly all the south side of the Plaza.

The proprietor of the Duckling was a sentimental Dane; hence the name, a compliment at once to his greatest compatriot and to his own skill as purveyor of comfort. Thirty years back, half of San Clemente was persistent to know the young Dane as Andy Anderson; the other half clung stubbornly to Ole Oleson. They had compromised on Oleander. The young Dane had grown to be an old American now; as Oleander he was pillar and landmark in San Clemente; but his own name was a forgotten thing.

The Duckling was built of adobe. It was one story high and one room wide: nobody knew exactly how long it was. Upended, it would have made a notable skyscraper. Besides the hotel, the building housed the Post Office, the Telephone Exchange, three Stage-lines and sundry offices of mining companies, and the like. Even so, the Duckling bedrooms had never all been filled at once.

The long shady veranda of the Duckling was, *ex officio*, the San Clemente Club. Even at this early hour a dozen men utilized that shady comfort; half as many saddled horses, with dangling reins, visited together under the Duckling cottonwoods. Tippytoes slanted his eager ears that way.

Emil folded his hands on the saddle-horn and regarded the veranda benevolently.

"This is a fine bunch," he said.

The bunch gave vigorous and varied assent to this proposition; except Keough, who dented his nose in sneering silence, and old man Gibson, who snorted. It was a representative gathering, miners and freighters aside. First were young Billy Armstrong and "Pretty Pierre" Hines of Chautaqua. For the cattle interests were Owen Quinliven, half owner of the Double Dee brand, a huge brindled, freckle-faced ex-miner; Steve Thompson, smooth-faced and bright eyed, who gave the Hook-and-Ladder; and burly, surly Gibson— Old Man Gibson of the Berenda. The townsmen were represented by Cox, editor of *The Inland Empire;* black-browed Keough of the telephone exchange; Baker, manager of the three stage lines; Max Goldenburg of the New York Store; serious, flaxen-bearded, square-faced Oleander himself; and the quiet professional gentleman known as "Monte." The twelfth chair-warmer was Ed Dowlin, unclassified; lumberman, cattleman, mine owner and Free Lance.

"I hear," said Emil, addressing Keough, "that you had a right smart doings over on the Malibu last week. Got out of it lucky, didn't you?"

"You may think so," said Keough bitterly. "I fail to see it."

Emil took counsel with his nose.

"Why, you got 'em all out alive and unhurt, didn't you?"

"Including the fool that set off the powder." Keough's white and bloodless face flamed to sudden red. Emil exchanged a glance with Dowlin. Dowlin arched an eyebrow.

"He makes me sick, Keough does. All he thinks of is the money lost." Quinliven spat the words from his mouth; he had been trapped in mines himself.

"Get down and look at your saddle," suggested Billy. "Maybe somebody'll buy a cigar. Ed, you do it."

Emil shook his head. "Just now I'm looking for that new N 8 person. Anybody know where he is?"

Oleander jerked a thumb over his shoulder. "Out in the corral, getting Pat to show him how to throw a diamond hitch."

"Some boy," said Steve approvingly. "Yesterday he pestered Spencer into taking him all through the Torpedo and had him explain all about minin', from A to Izzard. Day before that he borrowed that little Redlegs outlaw hawse of mine and started in to learn how to stay topside, and how about it. Perseverin' cuss! I'd be ashamed to say how many times that little roan devil piled him. I took 'em over in a sandy draw, so there wasn't much chance for the kid to get hurt, and he stuck to it till he could ride him slick. The old scoundrel was pitchin' right peart, too. John Sayles, he got skinned up some, but he sure was enjoyin' himself a heap. He'll make a hand."

"He came also to me for a leetle eenstruction," said Monte diffidently. "He ees ver' deeligent escholar."

"Well, now, this is very gratifying," said Emil, "and goes to show that you never can tell. Why, when he climbed out of the stage in them dizzy duds, I didn't nowise pick him for a live one. Very next day I found him up on the wagon road learnin' how to hold a drill. My mistake. I'll go get him."

He raised his bridle hand and rode into the corral. There, flushed and perspiring, John Sayles Watterson, Jr., late of Princeton University, was engaged in packing empty boxes upon a patient and sleepy gray burro. In this design he was aided and abetted by old Pat Nunn.

"'Lo, Pat! Howdy, young man!'"

"Oh, good-day! Mr. James, isn't it?"

"Hello, yourself! Anything wanted?" said old Pat.

"A few words with the middle-aged one, *poco tiempo*. No hurry; go through with your lesson."

"There! That's solid! Good hitch for heavy stuff, the diamond is," said old Pat, a little later. "But it takes two men to throw it. You get Emil to show you the Lost Cowboy. And a plain N-hitch is good enough for just a roll of bedding and such. Here's your man, Emil. Go to him. I'll drag it."

"Nothing confidential, Pat—stick around. Now then, young man, I understand you're going to make a visit to the N 8 ranch, and are waiting for a chance to get out there. Is that right?"

"Right as rain."

"All aboard, then. I am now organizing a little expedition for the pursuit of happiness, and you are hereby invited to make one of two. I'm the other one."

"Done with you. How do we go? Horseback? When do we start?"

"We go in the slickest little covered spring wagon you ever rolled your eagle eye over," said Emil, "and we start from my place soon this evenin'—about half-past four. Horseback across Malibu Flat is too long a trip for a new beginner."

"Yours truly, and thank you kindly," said John Sayles. "I'll hire a rig from the hotel to take me and my traps to your ranch."

"Hire a pig with three long tusks!" said Emil. "Borrow yourself a horse from some one. Pat will lend you a horse—any one will. Stick your shiny new saddle on him, wrap a change of clothes in a slicker and tie it behind, strap your rifle under your leg and come along. You leave your other plunder here at the hotel and Oleander will send it out the next time the ranch wagon comes for supplies."

"But how will I get Mr. Nunn's horse to him?"

"Shucks! You turn him loose and he'll come straight home. Then you hurl your saddle in my wagon. Sometime tomorrow night I'll set you down at Fuentes. You get another horse there and ride him to the N 8 ranch. It's only twenty miles, and plain landmarks to ride for. Then you can turn that horse loose, too. Come along. You have got fifteen minutes to organize yourself. We'll shack along over to the Square and Compass, sleep while it's hot, and start this evening."

"Where are you going to, your own self, Emil?" asked old Pat.

"Over on the Malibu—just rammin' around."

At the upper end of Roundabout, young Watterson reined in and turned for a last look at the straggling town and the headlong hills beyond. The bells of San Clemente shook *terce* from the old church tower.

"Yes," said Emil, "horses are sure intelligent."

"How so? I don't get you."

"Son, you're going to try ranchin' one small spell, you tell me. Listen now; when they send you out to hunt saddle horses, you ride straight to the likeliest and the finest-looking glade you know. You'll find 'em there, if there's any grass there at all. Horses *like* beautiful places. They appreciate them. Humans is just the same way. San Clemente, now; it imagines it is here because of the mines. All bosh; people found the mines just as an excuse for staying here. Even finer country on the east side, though, where all our ranches are. I'll build a town there some day, when the railroad comes. Yes,

I will—you'll see! In the meantime old San Clemente is the most beautiful town I know."

"Take Ridgepole now—she's our rival. She's got richer mines and more of 'em, mines that have proved their stayin' qualities. She's got a railroad; we're handicapped by forty-five mile of blisterin' hell-roarin' desert. But San Clemente has double the people. 'Cause why? They don't know bless your heart—the San Clemente folks don't know. But I'll tell you; it's the pull of the big old mountain yonder, and little Ghost Mountain and the little parks of cedar and live oak and the sleepy curves or the draw.

"Mighty nice people, too—most of 'em is. A few mean ones, like the white-faced fiend Keough—stewin' about a little dirty money when men's lives were at stake. That's how you can pick the bad ones, kid—by the value they set on money. You'll find some several swine in San Clemente, if you keep your eye on the hog trough. Let's go!"

"Water," said Emil James, slowly and seriously, counting his fingers by way of tally—"matches, coffee, coffee-pot, sugar, tincow, tin cups and spoons—that's coffee." As he spoke he carefully packed the objects named on the shelves of the chuck-box, misses' and children's size, of "the slickest little spring wagon."

That spring wagon was the especial pride and comfort of Emil's heart. When you learn that he kept it painted and sheltered you will know—if you are a frontiersman—just where that little wagon stood in Emil's affections.

It was wrought by the best skill under Emil's jealous supervision: built to be both light and strong. Six woods went to the making of it—hickory, oak, tough hornbeam, black birch, whitewood—clear stock, straight grained—with gnarled Bois d'Arc for the hubs; all seasoned for seven years, and kiln dried to stand up in the dry air of the desert. The highest quality of iron and steel went to the fittings, the toughest and easiest of springs. The wagon bed, framed and panelled for lightness, had no nail or screw in it; cunningly joined by mortise, tenon, dowel and dovetail and housed joints; all locked to place by long and slender bolts at the four corners. A touch on the strong footbrake locked the wheels and there was a step in front of the front wheel.

Where the tail-gate might have been, the chuck box was "built in" to avoid superfluous weight, floor and sides of the wagon box being also floor and sides of the chuckbox. Between chuckbox and the only seat, the wagon box flared over the wheels, after the fashion of a hay rigging, just long enough and wide enough to accommodate a light set of bed springs. The deep space beneath it was for promiscuous cargo. Under the lazyback spring seat was a low oaken water-tank, also "built in"; doing away with the customary water-kegs, usually slung at the sides of such a wagon by iron straps.

The whole was surmounted by a ribbed top, braced and firm, leather covered. There were light racks and straps at the top for clothing or small effects; there were leather side curtains, with pockets in them, marvelous because they would go up and stay up, or come down and stay down; there was also that rarest of luxuries, a lantern that would give light.

"Bacon, frying-pan, knives, forks and plates—that's bacon. Flour, water, salt, baking powder, lard, dutchoven—that's bread. Beans, canned truck, spuds, pepper,—that's extrys."

"Don't forget the water for potatoes. Or are you doing that little ditty to exercise your lungs?"

"Son, if this is delayin' you any," said Emil benignly, "try to put up with it, will you? I'm considerable old maidish and set in my ways. And I can tell you something useful."

"Go as far as you like."

"All right! John Sayles Watterson, Junior; I have twice heard you strongly voice opinion that most men in this country do things well. It is true. We admit it. And now I am to tell you why. It is because a man in this country is always trying for two things; to be his own foreman, who says what now and next to do, and to be his own inspector, to see that before he quits he makes a good job of it. I'm inspecting; and I don't want my attention distracted. You keep still! . . . Shot gun and shells—that's quail and rabbits. Rifle and cartridges—that's venison. Blankets—that's bed. Your saddle and truck—that's under the bedsprings. Canteens, water-buckets, hobbles, ropes, nosebags—that's sundries. Corn for horses—that's good. Water —that's life. That's all. Let's go!—There! I near forgot the axle-grease!"

Pinto was a red horse, broad-belted with white. He wore a white shirt-front and white stockings, out-size, carelessly gartered.

He was also slashed and spangled and harlequin-checked with white as to head, neck, shoulders, side, flank and hip.

Paint was white, splashed with red; and afterward splattered with shakings from the brush. Moreover, to avoid monotony, he was freckled with little brown spots, and a long, narrow, irregular splotch of jet black criss-crossed down his off hip and thigh. Long curly tail, long curly mane were delicate cream. Just for a surprise, both ears were one color, a modest red. Then, while you were off your guard, one eye was black and the other a startling blue. John Sayles jumped when he came upon that blue eye unawares.

They made a sprightly team, worthy of the wondrous wagon. Emil had matched them with loving care, picking from his *caballada* of six hundred head. Their gaits were frisk, scamper and scurry; for town work they could saunter and strut.

They now wore an expression singularly carefree; they exchanged a knowing glance which said so plainly that they tolerated the harness only because of some private designs of their own, that John Sayles, intercepting that message by chance, felt like an eavesdropper.

There was a preliminary egg-dance; they scrambled back through the Gap, they turned sharply to the right on a faint and little-used road and scudded down the gentle slope of a long winding ridge, carpeted with a turf of short yellow grass, neighbored by a thousand yellow ridges precisely like it. Then John Sayles began to see how the desert had fooled him. Malibu Flat was not flat at all.

Seen from town, through the low gaps between the hillocks of Sundown Ridge, the plain had appeared to be absolutely level and either brown or of a dull slate color. John Sayles saw now that it was a wrinkled slope of gentle ridges for rather more than halfway across, all keeping the same long easy grade down to a narrow and insignificant gray strip near the middle, after which it immediately began to rise toward the other side in a shorter and steeper slope—a dark brown slope.

John Sayles dismissed Malibu Flat from his attention, rather disappointed, and turned to ask a few questions about the little bunches of cattle they passed, whose were they and where did they water—when, all at once, under their very feet the ridge broke away to yawning deeps. Below them stretched a red maze of foothills, heaped and tumbled; unseen before because the highest top of them was lower than the smooth ridge country.

The wagon road plunged and dived down the ridge-end, rope-walked a hog-back, twisted and squirmed through the red hills to a deep, winding cañon. And presently the cañon walls grew lower; another sharp bend and they came out upon a broad sea of plain, treeless, gray with scattered bunch grass, dotted with cattle and bands of horses; a plain that filled the horizon; that far-off brown slope was now a brown ribbon at the base of the Malibu.

After a little, their faint and grass-grown track joined a big, plain road, which bore quartering across the flat to the northwest.

"This is the Hueco-Datil road," said Emil. "We follow it as far as the third stage-station, so we can water the horses at midnight. Then we turn straight across."

The sun was low above the Malibu; the cool night wind began to rise. The horses snorted cheerfully and settled to a brisk jog. Far ahead—wherever the wagon topped a ground swell—a little green streak of low brush showed in a thin line of fuzz.

"The first station is behind us, way back where the stage road left the hills, maybe five mile before we come to it," added Emil. "We're making right good time."

John Sayles looked back and marvelled. The huddled red foothills were an insignificant splash, blazing low in the level light of sunset. Above, that easy slope of smooth ridges was unbelievably steep, merging indistinguishable with the mountain mass to which it made plinth and pedestal; Ghost Mountain was only a thin wraith-outline; beyond, Fantasia Range soared to incredible heights against the turquoise sky. Fascinated, the boy watched the shadow of the world creep over the plain and up the steeps, saw sunset hide in the crags and linger on the flame-tipped crest. The swift twilight came on with a rush.

John Sayles sighed and came back to the front seat. The thin line of brush met them halfway. They drove into it; without warning, all the world was a bush-dotted wilderness of white chalk-hills, rippling in low waves. The broad plain was gone. Nothing was left but the far mountains and the endless sink and swell of billowing chalk. The short twilight passed in breath; the stars blazed out.

Clouds of white dust lifted with the wheels: they gritted in the chalk-ruts, they lurched in the chuck-holes: the team slowed to a plodding walk. The black bulk of Pinetop shouldered into the desert and crowded the stage road further out. They came to a mile-wide sunken valley, lush with thick grass. This was the Sinks of the Percha; the lights of the second stage station twinkled across its deeps. They passed it, they climbed out of the sink and came to a good footing and a rolling country; they see-sawed up and down or wound between the little hills. It was near midnight when they watered at the third stage station. They left the stage-road here, turning sharply to the left. John Sayles, at Emil's urging, stretched out on the spring bed. The last he heard was the wheels crunching through the sand.

Emil stopped the wagon at two in the morning, to make camp for three vital hours, from two to five, when strength of horse and man is at lowest ebb. John Sayles roused up, helped to unharness and hobble, and crawled sleepily back to bed. At the first streak of dawn they pushed on again through endless undulations of sandhills, horse-high with gray-green and spicy sagebrush.

The swift daylight grew; and John Sayles was something disconcerted to find that La Fantasia was no further away than at sunset, while the Malibu was no nearer. There was only one proof of progress; that thin gray streak was wider now, dead ahead and clear-seen in the cool light of morning. Red sunrise brought them to it; a dead lowland of crumbling and rotten soil, starved and poisoned, leprous, blotched with alkali, without grass, without vegetation save for a morbid, fleshy and hateful jelly-growth known as Dead Man's Hand: leafless, flowerless, without even thorn or spine to the gnarled and crippled fingers.

They crossed a dry lake-bed crusted inch-deep with sparkling crystals of salt; they crossed the resonant and resilient bed of a dry soda-lake, spirit-level smooth; they climbed a sudden bench and came out on a fair and wholesome plain checkered with green patches of tall, thrifty salt grass and broad levels of bare ground, white and sun-glazed. This was good going; unbidden, the ponies took up their brisk jog-trot; nine brought them to a soapweed country and black grama. They were now on the upgrade and climbing toward Malibu. They made camp for nooning at the first clump of soapweeds big enough to afford a slender shade for the ponies.

Water from the oaken tank for the eager horses, a thankful roll, corn in the nosebags, then hobbles and a close cropped swath of black-grama; fire and a marvelous breakfast in the shade of the wagon; silence and sleep.

XI. The Bird in the Bush

Since magazine appearance in *Redbook*, April, 1917, this story has appeared but once and that in the limited edition collection, *The Little World Waddies* (El Paso, 1946).

Rhodes, in later years, called this story "ultra-whimsical," for what an authorial opinion may be worth. In essence, it combines three ingredients that distinguish Rhodes' work: a sense of situation comedy, an evocative description of the land, a sun-god with a difference. The result, for what an editorial opinion may be worth, is one of the most readable yarns Rhodes ever wrote.

The hero, Andrew Jackson Aforesaid Bates, is a combination of at least two real life figures. One of these, Hiram Yoast, had been implicated around Tombstone, Arizona, in the Earp-Clanton days before coming to New Mexico where he played an avuncular role in the practical education of the much younger Rhodes. The other was Tom Tucker, veteran of the Pleasant Valley (Tonto Basin) trouble who was right-bower to Oliver Milton Lee during the latter's trouble with Pat Garrett and after.

I LIKED the Big Sandy, and I liked the people. But I saw what was coming. Good rains—high grass—double your herds every washday—everything lovely! Then along comes old Mr. Drought. *Bing!* There you are, busted. It's like playing double or quits; if you don't pinch your bets, you're going home talking to yourself. It's got to be that way. So I sold out.

Then I went off alone and tried to establish communication with myself. "Look here, Andy," says I, "are you going to be a dern fool all your whole life? You're getting old, and you're getting bald, and those that know you best, they love you most—but they put up quarantine signs against you. It's time to quit your wild, fool ways and settle down.

"But, still, yet," I rejoins, "you can't never be satisfied in town, planted in rows, or packed in cans or stacked on shelves. And you'll never be anything more than a bald-headed boy so long as you stay on the free range. With that rep' you got, people wouldn't let you behave if you wanted to. Your poor old dad tried to hammer some farmin' into your head," says I. "Why not try that?"

"But, again, then," says I, "you got to jar loose from the cow-business gradual. A little bunch of bossies fenced safe from the depredations of unprincipled men—that's what you want, to tide you over till you get the hang of farming."

Good scheme, wasn't it? I thought so. I'd held onto some of my wisest cow-ponies. So now I picked out two and sold the rest. Deacon was experienced and observing and level-headed; Quaker didn't have near such good judgment, but he was Deacon's pardner. I fixed me up a pack, and we went projecting off, still-huntin' a home for our declining years.

We skipped Prescott. Prescott had forgiven me, all right, allowing I was as much sinned against as sinning; but they was likewise strong of the opinion that if I ever came back, they'd sin against me some more. They was mighty explicit about that.

We shunned Tonto Basin too, where cattle- and sheep-men was enjoyin' a war. I wasn't in any hurry. I reckon we put in three or four months on that search. But I hadn't found nothing quite to fit me.

I'd been climbing uphill two or three days,—hadn't seen a man since I left Salt River, and mighty few sheep-herders,—just a steady up, up, up, through a crooked, winding, wavy, hazy, cold, blue-black piny-woods country, and at last I came out on the big top. Oh, man!

The mountain dropped off in fifteen minutes all I'd climbed up in three days. Right under me was a mesa of low, red foothills; then came a great, round, gray-greenish-yellow basin, thirty or fifty miles across any which way, saucer-shaped, heaped high with sunshine. There was big mountains all around it; where I sat, on the south, they made a level black wall with one gate-way off to my left. The eastern curve was piny-black too, broken hills, round, rolling and low. Across in the southwest, maybe forty mile away, was a stretch of bare gray cliffs, straight upandicular, ending in a limestone elephant with one eye and a granite trunk six miles long. He looked mighty curious. He kept that one eye on me, and I felt little cold shivers playing up and down my backbone.

Running catawampus across the basin, like a crack in the saucer, was a cañon. It headed in a gap in the northeast and slipped off to the Pacific through a fold in the cliffs this side of that elephant. He had a mean eye.

It was wide and deep and crooked, that cañon. My side of the basin was wavy; north of the cañon-crack it rose in benches; and 'way beyond and above the last bench was a half-circle of misty, pinky granite knobs and spikes and spires, notched and jagged, domes and turrets and things. They took my eye. Seems like the nicest places to live are where you find that worn-down granite for soil. It's so clean and cheerful.

Down under us I saw a big white road striking across to the front gate at my left. Only for the road, I'd 'a' thought I was the first man on the job.

I'd been pursuing around at random, and there wasn't rightly any way to get down from where I was. But we made it sliding, somehow. It took us half a day. Down in the red feethills we found mines and things, all nailed up and abandoned. We found a little spring and made camp.

Soon in the morning we was out on the plain. Prettiest rolling mesa you ever see—black grama and crowfoot; plenty slick fat cattle, mostly branded J. B.; antelope, and too many bands of wild horses. Presently we hit an old wagon-track, rutted deep but grown up with grass. More old roads comes anglin' in, and at last we come to the big white road I'd seen from the summit.

It had been traveled a heap once, but not lately. It was ruler-straight across the mesa, till we pitched off into the breaks of a draw that led down to the main big cañon, getting deeper and deeper. Directly we come to the jump-off place, and the wagon-road took to the side-hill. It was dug out two or three thousand years ago and hadn't been repaired since—ribbed and gullied—rubble, with the soil all washed away. We twisted down and down and down some more, till at last we come out on the cañon-floor to orchards and ditches and a white town asleep in the sun.

Yessir! Every man I see was asleep, under the trees or on the porches; and they was all old, old men. I followed along between vineyards and open doors and alfalfa and cottonwood trees to a shady plaza with a 'cequia tinklin' down beside, mighty pleasant. I let the horses drink. There was a 'dobe store squandering around under the oldest cottonwood in the world, and in front sets an old jasper with a long, gray beard, sound asleep. I woke him up.

"Good evening," says I. "Can you tell me where I can find *Allan Quatermain?*"

He didn't get me. He wasn't literary. "Never heard of him," says he.

I heard some one laugh behind me. It was a cool, ripply little laugh, tuned to a little waterfall in the 'cequia. I looked around and saw a girl in a streak of dancing sun that smuggled through the branches.

"S-sh! *Allan Quatermain* escaped—three years ago—across the mountain—and the forest—and the desert—toward Zanzibar! Hush-sh!" She put her finger to her lip and tiptoed across to me. She gave the old geezer a side-look and held her hand up, palm out. "S-sh!" she says again. . . .

Sometimes I dream of going back. I ride along dim old roads that never were, to old houses that couldn't be—great, ramshackle old barracks, doors open and sagging, shutters that swing and squeak over broken windows—dim and dark inside, old moldy pictures on the wall, dust on the tables and chairs and drifted in the fireplace. And I can't remember—quite. So I follow the old road, windin' and windin' through a level, brushy country. There's no tracks turning off, but the road gets dimmer and dimmer, and at last it plays out. So I go on and on to look for ranches I can almost remember, and a little swift river that ought to be somewhere: but the mountains are wrong, and all the gaps are in the wrong places, and everything is changed—except Minnie. She is just the same; she isn't any older; her eyes are sunny; she comes dancing and laughing to meet me through a deep shade. And—this is curious—she brings the sunlight with her, always the warm, clear sunshine rippling about her as she comes. I wasn't expecting her: I try to tell her so—and then I wake up.

I hopped down as she came—the really time, I mean, not the dream. Deacon stretched out his nose, and she pets him. "It is the custom of the valley," she says, "for strangers from the outside world to stay at the—at the palace—until their fate is decided."

She was just a little trick. There was a dimple in her cheek that come and went as she spoke; her eyes were brown, and down in each one lived a little, merry, dancing gold devil—you could see him when she laughed at you. Quaker come up alongside and crowded old Deacon off—he wanted to be petted too. So I pushed his head away, just like he done to Deacon—and then she laughed again. "Got to keep pack-horses in their places," says I.

"They want their dinner," said the girl. "So do you. Come along."

"That's right," said the old geezer, settlin' back for another snooze. "Cow-men, they all stop with her dad—he owns the J. B. You go along with her."

So we walked on down the street; the '*cequia* sung along beside us, Deacon and Quaker looking around, mighty interested, sizing things up.

"Who, which, why, when, where, what, how?" says I. "Where am I? Why is everyone asleep? And why are the mines closed down? Why doesn't no one ever travel the roads? Why hasn't no one ever heard of this place before? Why did the elephant try to scare me back? Why everything?"

So she told me why. "We're waiting for the railroad. It's our sole occupation. That's the answer to all the questions. And now it's your turn, isn't it? Who, where, how? Explain! No wanderer has found his way here since—"

"*Allan Quatermain?*" says I. "For me, Miss—why, I guess I couldn't have stayed away if I'd tried. It was predestined and foreordained that I was comin' here—to wait for the railroad."

"Here's the J. B. house," she said. "Father isn't at home, but Anselmo will show you where to put your horses." She give both of 'em a little pat. "Then come on in. Mother and I will have dinner ready for you."

I turned the horses to an alfalfa stack and went in. Mrs. Briscoe was a nice, motherly old lady, but she acted kinder worn-out and road-weary. After I met old man Briscoe, I knew why. He was a mean old whelp—just naturally cussed. The house was fixed up nice.

That evenin' Minnie sat out on the gallery with me, explainin'. The basin was called the Butterbowl—'member the Butterbowl on Rainbow? I named that myself, after this place. The river was San Lucas; the big range I'd crossed was Black Mountain, and my nice pinky hills was Dream Mountain.

In and around Butterbowl was everything a man could want—grass, lumber-woods, mines, water and soil to grow anything: but it took three days' hard riding in that direction to reach a given point. The early settlers saw that a railroad was bound to tap this country—some time. So they made 'em a town, Central, built them wagon-roads out to the tributary mines and lumber, built orchards and ditches and set down to wait for the whistle. Meantime they raised cattle.

There was one big cattle-company, the J. B., and a lot of little outfits beside. Leastwise, they called it a company, though Minnie's dad, he owned most of it. They hadn't overstocked yet, but they was fixin' to; they hadn't got to stealin' much yet, but they was practicing; and old J. Briscoe allowed the little cow-men was all worthless and not fit company for his daughter: so they had all the makin's of trouble. I thought I'd stay.

In the morning I struck out for my pinky mountains. One of them nice little Southwest spring winds, like we got here, was beating in my face, mighty raw. Once I climbed the mesa, I quit the road and sidled off, so's to split the difference between the one-eyed elephant and the stage-road gap, Holbrook way. I was needin' a place where I wouldn't be in nobody's way, d'yuh see—an' likewise, where nobody'd be in my way. I passed all the cattle, and I passed all the cattle-tracks; I got up on the last bench, level as a billiard-table, right under them pinky mountains: I put in between two of them backbones and run spang onto exactly what I wanted.

I heard the wind ravin' and howlin' up overhead, but in between them two spurs of hill it was still as a Monday meetin'-house. After facing that wind all day, it seemed like a box-seat in Paradise, complimentary. I named it Shelter, right off.

I guess Adam had the best time anybody ever did, namin' things. Ever notice what good names you find in a thin-settled country? That's cause they didn't have no prominent citizens to call things after.

There was a narrow box between the hills for about a quarter, and a big gravel wash. Then we come out in a wide open valley with a big granite fence about two thousand foot high all around it, and I knowed Andrew Jackson Bates had found him a home.

Come to find out afterward, the Butterbowl folks called the place Bottle Basin. That was the shape of it, maybe five miles across from rim-rock to rim-rock, and about six the long way. There was crowfoot, black grama and short, curly, yellow buffalo-grass, and mesquite beans; plenty cedar, juniper and live-oak on the ridges. Put a little fence across the mouth of the bottle, and there I was, snug, my cows fenced in and other people's fenced out. I made camp and went a-prospectin'.

There wasn't any living water, as I knowed before, by there being no fresh cow-tracks, but I could see by the wash that a heap of water come down the draw when it rained. My play was to build tanks and store flood-water—see? By sundown I had it all figured out. Here I was to build a little tank, to hold water for my teams, whilst I was weavin' a big one. Both was to be in a smooth side-draw, where there was first a wide place to hold a world of water, and then a narrow place to make a dam. I was going to put a wing-dam in on the main cañon, and carry flood-water to my tanks in a ditch through a little saddle—so too much heap flood would never break my dams; I was going to make my waste-ways first, make 'em twice as big as they'd ever need to be, and then make 'em bigger. I'd seen dams built before.

It was full moon, that night. I prowled around, a-plannin', proud as a pawn in the king-row. I reckon that was about the happiest one time I ever put in. "Andrew Jackson, I sure made a stake to-morrow," says I. Here I was to build my big dam, and here my spillway; here was to be my corrals, and here my orchard; I began farmin' by breaking in a little flat and edged a little further down every year.

Next day we ambled around looking for water. I followed the dim cow-trails till they got plain, and the plain ones till they got dusty, and we struck a spring, fifteen mile away, where a fellow named Hall held out—give the Bow-and-Arrow brand. Come dinner, I found this was the nearest place for me to haul water from to begin my work. Of course, I didn't tip my hand. Cow-men sure hate to be crowded.

That night I cached my pack and hiked to Holbrook for a surveyor. He ran out my section numbers for me, and made me plots and plans and estimates and specifications. I didn't want 'em: I built my dam by guess and by golly when I got at it; but the law calls for 'em.

Then I wandered over and broke the news gently to old man Hall and asked him if I could borrow some water to haul over to Shelter. He fought his head right smart at first, till he found out what my name was. Then he come to his feed. He'd heard of me. And he judged I'd come in handy to hold the J. B. outfit level. So I got him and his boy Bill to slip down to Globe with me as witnesses when I filed on my claim.

I got a wagon in Globe, a darky named Eph and a span of mules, a Mex boy and a span of big horses, a plow and two scrapers, water-barrels, tools and a tent and such. We took rounders on the Butterbowl and pussy-footed into Shelter unbeknownst.

Hall drawed me over a first load of water on his wagon, for a starter. I set Eph and Esteban to tanking while I broke Deacon and Quaker to the water-wagon. They was dead set against it. It was some comedown from bein' crack cow-horses. I reckon they thought I'd put 'em on the scraper next.

I see they wasn't going to be satisfied, and we hadn't brought much corn up from Globe; so after a few trips I put off down to Central. They was bound to find out about me and Shelter before long, anyway. I dickered for a span of spankin' black mares, Zip and Jezebel, and carried out a load of corn and supplies, with Deacon and Quaker at the tail-gate. They was sure tickled. I knew some one would be curious about me. And sure enough, the next day but one, here comes old John Briscoe, just a-snuffin'. I hadn't never seen him before, but I knowed him right off. He looked like a cartoon of himself.

"What's this? What's all this? What you doing here?" he sizzles.

"Just now I'm a-prizing long, wide, hard, heavy, thick, big rocks out o' my spillway with a crowbar," says I. "And directly I'm going to compound the finest dinner you ever flopped your lip over. Get down and look at your saddle a spell."

"Of all the gall!" says J. B. "We'll fix *your* clock! You'll be glad to get out o' here, quicker than you came—crowdin' yourself in where you ain't wanted. If you're hunting trouble, you've come to the right shop. You'll get it, and you'll get it good!"

Wasn't that a nice crack to make? That's what a man gets himself by going where he's not known.

"Did you ever chance to hear the honored name of Aforesaid Andrew Jackson Bates?" I asked him.

"The pleasure is mine," he says, mighty sneerin'. "I have not. Desperado, I reckon?"

"Worse than that," says I. "A heap worse. I'm a stayer. I've got a positive genius for bad luck—witness them opprobrious syllables, Aforesaid, wished onto me by acclamation of five States and Territories. Fair sir," says I, "you was mentionin' trouble to me. I've had all kinds of trouble a mere single man can have, and most generally got the worst of it; but let me tell you, beloved, none of my victorious and laurel-wreathed antagonists has ever bragged about it any, and that includes the sovereign State of California, the Republic of Mexico, the Espee Railroad, the Diamond-A Cattle Company, Yavapai County, Prescott, Buckey O'Neil and the Arizona House of Reprobates, besides Montana and some few other commonwealths whose memory is now fadin' in the mists that rise down the River of Time. So far, I've had no mix-up with the United States or the Daughters of the Revolution," says I, "but outside o' that, I've met everything in the shape of man or beast that the umpire could furnish and have never yet lowered my arm."

"Trouble?" says I. "Trouble? Before you come talking trouble to me, you'd better read the history of your country. Pending them investigations," says I, "don't you try to run any blazers on me, and likewise smooth your wrinkled front. You may not know it, but you're allowin' yourself to make horrid frowns at me, and I won't have it. I like smilin' faces and cheerful words and happy laughter around me, and I'm goin' to have 'em. I came here seekin' a quiet and peaceful spot to while away the Indian summer of my soul, and if you pester me any, I'm going to do you a great personal injury, forthwith, at once, *ahorita, immediatamente* and now! Declare yourself, Marmaduke Mortimer—a gold chain or a wooden leg?"

J. B. was some impressed by them remarks. He come back at me easy. "But it wouldn't be right for you to turn no cattle loose on this range," says he. "You ain't got no water-right. And you can't get no water by digging—not around here. I've drilled a well five hundred foot, right here in Bottle Basin."

"Shelter," I corrects him.

He went right on! "And this mizzable little tank you're making won't have a drop of water in it three months after the rains. You can't—I mean, it wouldn't be the square thing to turn a herd in the Butterbowl on the strength of that."

"The audience will kindly retain their rompers," says I. "I ain't goin' to turn any cattle loose on your range. This is only my family cistern, to water my horses whilst we collaborate on a big he-tank. I'm goin' to make the desert do that blossom thing; I'm goin' to be a bold yeomanry, my country's pride, and sit under my own vine and fig-tree. I'm going to raise Early Martyr potatoes; I'm going to walk abroad and view the fields where oats, peas, beans and barley grows. You cast your eagle eye down the hollow betwixt them two hills," says I. "Right there, in about ten months or two years, I'm goin' to have me a tame ten-acre lake."

"Huh! There ain't watershed enough, in this little draw," says he.

"Goin' to tap the main draw and lead it through yonder little saddle," I explains to him.

He looks kinder interested. "Why—I believe that would work," says he. "But if you want to farm, why don't you buy a place down on the San Lucas?"

"Me? Shucks, I never could see any good times herdin' with them sleep-walkin' nesters," says I. "Dern a granger, anyhow!"

"Why—why—why, you're going to be one yourself!" says Briscoe.

He had me there. I hadn't thought o' that. It struck me all in a heap.

"Well, not so's you can notice it. I may irritate the soil a little, as a gentlemanly relaxation—but do I look anyways like a splay-footed, sod-hopping, apple-grafting granger? I'm as good a cow-man as ever throwed a loop by moonlight," says I.

"But you said you wouldn't turn no cattle loose on my range," said Briscoe, stuttering.

"Ain't it the truth?" says I. "What's the matter with my range—*m—y, my*? Throw a little fence across that cañon, like a stopper in a bottle—"

I didn't finish, 'cause Briscoe, he was carryin' on something fierce. He was a natural-born hawg, that man was.

I let him rave a spell, till I see that I might as well stop him first as last. "See here, Aloysius," says I, "you're talking pretty brash. I wonder at myself that I ain't bent this crowbar over your old hard head."

He reined his horse around. "Where you goin'?" says I, and I grabbed up a rock. "I'm a patient man," says I, "but if you don't light off that cayuse and stay to dinner, I'm goin' to bounce a pebble off your medulla obligato. It isn't anywise neighborly to go off that way just as dinner's ready; it casts reflections on my cookin'. Welcome little stranger!" I says, as he climbs off. "Welcome to Shelter!"

I tried to rib him up with a jolly whilst I was wrangling chuck. "I know what makes your sorrows grieve you so, Montmorency," says I. "You tot it up that because I've got a pasture I'm goin' to get implicated with your calves. I been all along that road, same as you have—we won't deny it, Epaminondas; but I wouldn't choose any more of the pie. Honesty is the best policy, as who should know better than me? You and the J. B. punchers is welcome to prowl around in here, auditing, any time, and there'll always be a meal's victuals for you and a nice level place to sleep."

But he wouldn't mellow up and he went away dissatisfied. That old man never did like me.

Next time I went to town, old J. B. had me over to the house and offered me five hundred to quit-claim Shelter to him. Seems like he'd set his heart on it, and he couldn't forgive me for him not thinkin' of buildin' a tank there first. That night I met Minnie's cousin

Jane, who was the Central school-ma'am, and old man Duffy, Methodist preacher from St. Johns, and Dee Macfarlane. Dee had sunny hair, the rascal—wavy and sunny. He owned a nice little bunch of cattle, but he didn't 'tend to his business very close, *I* thought. He was settin' around up to Minnie's nearly every time I went near there. That's no way to run cattle. You got to be out amongst 'em.

Well, there come an early rain that year, along in April. That filled my cistern so I got shut of water-hauling. So long as I had a township for pasture, ready-made all but the gate, I thought we'd better fix the gate. So we strung up the wire fence across the box. After that we could turn our work-horses loose at night, instead of hobbling, and they done better. I got another scraper down to Central, and another Mexican—Eusebio. He wasn't much force, not sized up with Eph and Esteban. He had a Candelaria girl in Central. Candy, she worked for Mamma Briscoe. I didn't mind him going down Sundays so much, though he was lonesome to ride with—but he did sing such long-drawn and mournful despair around the camp-fire after supper:

> "*Tal vez, mi amada, en brazos de otro amor,*
> *Duerme y descansa—ay! sin pensar en mi!*"

We began makin' dirt fly on this new dam. Beat all, what a difference it made not havin' to draw water fifteen mile for six horses and a camp. I tied up Deacon or Quaker, turn about, for night-horse. Every morning I was out wranglin' work-stock before day, while the boys rustled breakfast. I did the rest o' the cookin' and all the pot-walloping and blacksmithing. I hauled corn and chuck, and kep' camp in venison, and rustled wood: I jumped in to hold the plow or whatever was needed quick and most, and we inched right along. I hadn't never worked so steady since I was a boy on Staten Island. The plowed dirt smelled good, and the green grass it smelled good, and the chuck tasted good. I felt virtuouser and virtuouser every day. I'd put away childish things: I looked back with pain to them ranikiboo plays I'd hitherto promulgated.

The neighbors took to droppin' in to see me. Nice lot of two-handed punchers, they was—Hall and Billy Hall, Spike and Doc and Squatty Robinson and San Simon—he was a prospector, San Simon was.

J. Briscoe, he mostly flocked by his only, but he come out twice more, raising his offer to fifteen hundred. He sure wanted the Shelter place. Joe Only, the J. B. wagon boss, he happened in pretty frequent, and Chuck Barefoot.

For I began to have other company too. Minnie Briscoe and her cousin Jane, they took to comin' out Saturday nights and staying over Sunday. I got a new tent for 'em, soon as I see they was formin' the habit. I'd go deer-hunting with Minnie at first—or just go browsing around with both of 'em. Jane was an easy keeper, but she wasn't exciting. Sometimes they brought Minnie's ma along for chaperon, sometimes not. It didn't make no difference. Them girls didn't need no chaperon—not much, anyway.

Did I say that the boys had quit visiting each other and made Shelter the reg'lar Sunday headquarters since the girls took to comin' out? Well, they did. It was bound to be that way. So I wasn't obliged to go huntin' with 'em any more. Somehow I wasn't near as glad as I might 'a' been. But I was the host, and also I wasn't much young any more. The play come for me to take a back seat.

Minnie thought there wasn't no place like Shelter, and she kept coaxin' me to sell out to her father. "If you will, I'll get Poppa to let me homestead it," she says, "and I'll have it for my very own. Poppa has used his homestead right. I think you might, Andrew J."

This was about the thirteenth time she'd named it to me. "Why, yes, so I might, but then will I?" says I. "There ain't another place just like this in the whole dinky world, I don't believe. I've done used my homestead right, too. Your little scheme would mean forfeiting my desert claim—and where would Aforesaid A. J. Bates be then, poor thing?"

"You might buy a place," says Minnie, pouting.

"I want to tell you, Miss Minnie," says I, "that there can't no man buy a place—not if it cost him a million dollars—and get so much solid comfort from it as he can where he was the very first man that ever nested there since the world began, and where he has cut every post and built in every stone and set out every tree with his own fair hands. So I go along with Shelter as an encumbrance. If you're dead set to make your home here—take a chance! A bird in the bush is the noblest work of God," says I. "I'm old and I'm stove-up and I'm unlucky, but I'll do my da—— I'll do my best to make it a safe shelter, Minnie," says I.

She flushed all rosy red, and she dropped her eyes, but she shook her head. "I can't," she whispers. "You'd make it a safe shelter, Andy, and maybe it would be better if I could. But I can't."

"Why?" says I. "Don't you like me at all, Minnie, not the least little bit?"

"Oh, I do!" says she. "I do like you, ever so much—but not that way."

"How do you know?" says I.

"I know!" says Minnie.

"Who is it, Minnie? Dee, I reckon?"

"*Don't!* You mustn't!" she says, catchin' her breath short. She let me see her face—my pretty! And there were tears in her eyes. I knowed when she let me see them tears that no matter how much she liked Dee, she might have liked me pretty well too, if the play had come different.

Then she gave me a straight look. "And you don't really want me, Andy—not really! Oh, you think you do—just now! But it's partly because you want to be neighborly, and maybe because you know that I don't have a very good time at home. And you'd always be good and kind to me, I guess. But after a while, you'd be sorry. For there's just two kinds of people in this world," says Minnie. "The kind that thinks a bird in the hand is worth two in the bush— and your kind, Mr. Aforesaid Andrew Jackson Bates! Wherever you are, the soil of that place will be burning your foot-soles. You'll always be wondering what is on the other side of the hill, and you'll always be wondering what is on the other side of the world, and wanting to go see: and you'll always be wearyin' for the bird in the bush!"

"Well, then, don't you grieve your pretty head about me, honey," says I. "I'm old, and I'm tough, and I'll winter through some way. Maybe there's a good deal in what you say. But just you remember Shelter, if ever the world don't use you well. I'll be here, waiting."

"I'll remember," says Minnie. "But don't you put on such a long face. You can't fool me much, Andrew Jackson! You're one-half sorry and disappointed, and the other half is glad you've done your duty and no harm come of it. You'll be good as new in no time, and dreamin' about the bird in the bush. Good-by, and good luck!" she says, and turns her pony's head to town.

"You ain't going to let this make no difference about comin' out, when you feel like it?" says I.

"Oh, no! I'll be out, same as usual—after a little." Her face was kind of smily and teary and cheery all at once, and part mischievous, and kind of poutish too. "I know you only want what's best for me," she threw back over her shoulder, "and that's why I know you don't really-truly like me—that way," she says. "If you did, you wouldn't know you was old or unlucky or anything—and you'd be insisting on havin' your own way, whether 'twas best for me or not!"

I spurred up, but she hit her pony a lick and held up her open hand. So I stopped. "It's too late to insist now, Andy J.—after what I just said," says Minnie, reinin' up. "You go on back to your dam-work that you're so all wrapped up in. And say, Andy—" Her pretty face was all mischief now.

"Orders!" says I, touching my hat.

"Don't let your kind heart coax you to ask Jane! If you do, Andrew Jackson, I sha'n't like it one little bit!" And she was gone.

I think of her a heap, sometimes. . . . Say, it's hell to be old! 'Specially when you're not really a little bit old, inside. I've had a lot of fun; sometimes I think I've had more fun than anyone. But I've missed a heap, too.

Minnie come back, after a few weeks, but it wasn't ever quite the same. She kept Dee or Jane right with her, and she didn't call me Andy J. any more. I was Mr. Bates. So I built dam.

We kep' things rockin' along as per usual, Eph and Esteban and me just a-humpin', and Eusebio trifling along, only a little above the average. Lordie, there's a heap of difference in men! My the'ry is that if a man don't earn more than you give him, no matter how much that is, he ain't worth having around. Half the time Eusebio was plumb in our way.

Along late in September, when it was likely there wouldn't be any more rains, I saw a big storm coming up. "Maybe the last of the season," thinks I. So I called the boys out.

"Vacation!" says I. "We'll just fix our ditch to fill up this hole-in-the-ground and see if she'll hold. The teams is pretty well jaded out. Steve, you and 'Sebio take a week's lay-off—more, if you want it."

"You theenk thees tank not break, Meester Bates?" says Esteban.

"I hope not, Steve, old socks," says I. "For if she goes, we're sure a-going with it. It's no more than the square thing for us to put on our slickers and set on the dam—just as a bet that we been doin' good work."

Well, we done so, and she didn't break. My recipe for perpetratin' dams is to make 'em twice-and-a-half as strong and long and deep and wide and high as there is any use of, 'special the spillway, and then to say a little prayer.

The sun come out warm and pleasant, and we all took a big swim. The Mexican men, they went to rustle their horses so's they could pull their freight after supper, and I set there on the dam, seein' things.

Next mornin' Eph and me slep' till the horses woke us up, beggin' for corn. Eph, he went off to pluck a venison, and I stayed in camp.

I reckon there was where I made a mistake—quittin' work sudden in the middle of the week. If it had been Sunday, now, and folks around, maybe things might 'a' come different. All of a sudden, I felt tired out and old and blue and bald and all-alonesome; and I couldn't get seein' things any more. I couldn't see myself makin' *'cequias* and settin' out fruit-trees; I just knowed that soil wouldn't grow alfalfa; my cows would climb out over them pinnacles; I couldn't think of no decent brand for 'em, and I couldn't think of no name for my cussed lake; and as for rip-rappin' that dam when the water got low, it made me fair sick to think of it.

No sir, all I could do was to study about how sad it would be if anything was to happen to Minnie's little boy-doll. I hadn't a thing against Dee, you understand—square and white a kid as ever rode leather. It just broke my heart to think of that hazardous occupation he was following, and nothing ever goin' wrong. He might fall off a horse, or down a shaft, or in my new lake: a steer might butt him, or somebody might shoot him. There was a new man, Petey Simmons, breakin' bronc's for the J. B.; six or seven feet high, no eyebrows or hair on his face, 'count of having had smallpox—mighty ugly man; I wondered if maybe Peter wouldn't do it. Then Dee might get snake-bit or quick consumption. Railroads, too, they was mighty dangerous. I did wish that railroad would hurry up and come.

Before noon I'd about compromised by havin' Dee run off with Jane. But I see that wouldn't do.

"You're getting morbid, Andy," says I. "I know what's the matter with you. You want to take a little horse-ride."

So I caught up old Quaker and went for a *pasear*—not anywhere particular, you know—just riding the curse off. I felt better right straight. Pretty soon I was singing about how once in the saddle I used to be a gay old bird.

About the middle of the evenin' I was 'way up on a pinnacle, when I saw some one chasing a bunch of cattle in the hills just under me. I took a small peep through my field-glasses.

It was old Squatty Robinson on a blue bronco. He caught a big yearlin' and tied it to a saplin'; then he took in after the bunch and fought 'em on up the draw. I knew what he was up to. He'd drive the mammy-cow off up in the hills three or four miles; then he'd hurry back and adopt that yearlin'.

Quaker was prancing; I began to feel frisky, like I was only a big grown-up boy. Quaker was a flighty, hoity-toity horse, anyway —no fit company for a serious-minded man.

"Andrew Jackson," says I, "this is plumb dishonest, and it ought to be discouraged. Be you goin' to allow such goin's-on, or be you not?"

I went down there. I set that calf loose, and I took the rope that was on her and flung it over a limb, so the noose hung down just about high enough to hang a short man, and I tied the other end around the tree-trunk. Squatty was a short man.

I knowed Squatty would be back soon to drive home his foundling. I hid out to watch him. Just as I got myself spotted, here come a bunch of wild mares up the canon, forty or fifty, and went on up the way Squatty did. They was burnin' the breeze; and behind them, here comes Esteban and Eusebio. That was funny too, because they told me the night before they was goin' to Holbrook. I lay right still.

They come pretty near up to where I was. I had to pinch Quaker's nose to keep him from whinnyin'. They turned out of the cañon opposite me and rode up the hill to a big slick piece of granite below a cliff. They climbed up that afoot, and they hid something in a hole under the cliff. Then they rode back down the cañon.

"I go look-see!" says I, soon as they was out of sight. When I come to the tracks, they was barefoot tracks; yet them horses was fresh shod only yesterday: curious thing! I took away the stones and felt in that hidey-hole. What do you think I found? Two slickers with eye-holes cut in the backs of 'em just below the collar! I tried again and fished out a package. It was little: it had the express-company's seal on it, broken; it had been tied up again. Inside was a bunch of yellow-backs. Them triflin' boys of mine had robbed the stage!

"I'm plumb surprised at Steve," I says. "This ain't honest!" I counted the money. There was twenty-five bills, each for one hundred perfectly good dollars. "Sufferin' Moses!" says I. "I didn't think the stage carried as much as that, all told, in a year." I turned the package over. 'Twas addressed to *J. Briscoe, Central, Arizona.*

"Twenty-five hundred is a heap of cash for the Butterbowl," I thinks. I tucked it away in my shirt-bosom. "Whatever did J. B. want of that much in cold cash? And when did my enterprisin' young friends know so pat when to get busy? And I thought that triflin' Steve was a pretty good *hombre*, dern him. Say! By Jings, I bet that Candy girl of his has been snoopin' through the letters on Poppa Briscoe's desk—and that's how they knew when the money was comin'! They started up them mares to account for themselves if they run onto anybody—and so they didn't see Squatty's trail, or mine, 'cause the mares had done run over 'em. That part is nearly right. But what I don't see, is what J. B. wanted of all that wad."

I was so absorbed I didn't see that same bunch of mares sky-hootin' back down the hill to my horse that I'd left with his bridle-reins dangling. But I was too late. That ornery Quaker up with his tail and threw in with 'em. They went on down to the plain—and I was afoot!

I was pretty sore. I judged Squatty had met them broom-tails and turned 'em as he was coming back. So I got behind a boulder and waited. I didn't want to walk home—not if I could get Squatty's horse.

Squatty come directly. He was real surprised at not finding no yearling, and he said so. When he got down to get his rope, I cut loose a few shots, puffin' up dust between him and his horse. Squatty, he went to the wild bunch.

I kept foggin' away till I saw him come out of the timber two or three hundred yards up and cross a little glade to the main woods. Then I knowed Squatty had gone to waterin' at night.

I climbed his blue bronc'. I turned across toward home, studying up something real severe to say to Steve. But I never got to Shelter. I looked up, and there was that same bunch of mares quartering along in front of me. Some one had headed 'em off again and turned 'em back. They was almost beat out; they was strung along like a snake, rockin' up and down, noses to the ground, like one of them dream-gallops we have, where we don't get any forwarder. Some of 'em could hardly navigate. That old gray fool of a Quaker was hanging on behind. I could see his saddle shine.

I made a circle and fell in beside, sorter headin' 'em toward the stage-road. I closed in, riding easy, took after old Quaker and hurled my twine. The loop drawed up pretty deep on Quaker's shoulders—and just then my blue stumbled, and down we went!

I kep' out from under, but my foot hung in the stirrup. The blue horse scrambled up before I could kick loose; I grabbed for my gun, but it was jarred out where we fell—and away we went, kicking and bucking and squealing, with Andrew J. Bates, Baron Shelter, Lord of the Lake, dragging by one hind leg, on his back or belly as the case might be, grubbing up cactus and soapweed with himself.

One end of the rope bein' fast to my saddle-horn and the other end on Quaker's neck, Blue Beelzebub had to go round and round like a circus-horse doing tricks, hurdling mesquite bushes and the like.

As luck would have it, little Andrew was dragging on the inside. That was what saved him. When Beezy kicked, he missed my face more'n two inches. Old Quaker give a little to keep from chokin', so the little geometrical design I was inscribing with my carcass was a free-hand spiral, like the writing-teacher used to show us to develop the whole-arm movement, only more so.

I kep' trying to climb up my leg far enough to grab that rope, but 'twas only as a matter of principle—I really didn't expect to do it. Then—bang! went a gun. Poor old Beelzebub come down on his side and lay there, with only his legs a-quivering.

I could 'a' had a real lovely time, just layin' still a week or two, but I judged it best not. I got my foot out pretty brisk and rolled over on my hands and knees. Beelzebub was shot right through the brainpan. He was mighty dead.

I boosted myself up by the saddle-horn and cantle and set down on the defunct: I poured the sand out o' my mouth and nose and ears and eyes, and looked round. I was considerable dizzy.

We was right beside the wagon-road: Beelzebub had stumbled, crossing it. Quaker had got some slack and was getting his breath—head hanging down, legs braced. Then I see a man. It was Petey Simmons, the J. B. bronco-buster. His mouth was open; his eyes was buggin' out, and he had a gun in his hand; he sat there on his horse looking at me, and he was whispering to himself. "Well, *I'll* be damned!" he says, "I will be *damned!*"

I looked at Petey a spell, and Petey looked at me. After a bit things steadied down some, and I remembers my manners. "Thank you!" says I.

"Oh, I *will* be damned!" whispers Petey again, as if his soul in them few words he would outpour.

I felt considerable nettled. It didn't seem to me that Petey was showin' the proper sort of spirit.

"Doubtless," says I. "But why so confidential about it? And what makes you think it's interesting to me? If you've fully made up your mind, all right—but *I* don't care, I'll tell you those!"

Petey took off his hat. The sweat was starting on his face. He seemed stunned and grieved and discouraged; he hadn't the joyful look a man ought to wear that had just saved a valuable life. It didn't seem much of a compliment to me.

"Petey, that was a pretty fair shot you made," says I.

"Well, I will—" he began again, but I cut him off short at the pockets.

"Petey, I'll give you just one more chance," says I in a firm yet trembling voice. "You hunt around and pick up my gun and my hat and any pieces of my hide you think can be used again," says I. "And compose your mind good, for if you say any more about your future fate, I'm going to shoot you five times in the middle West. You plumb displease me. But first of all, you look in the road and see if there ain't a lot of fresh tracks headin' for the Holbrook Gap."

He done so and nodded his head.

"I thought as much," says I. "Petey, some one robbed the stage out there this morning—two men named Doe and Roe. Central has done waked up and gone to see how about it."

"Hell's bells!" said Petey in a cracked and horrified voice. "Just the one time it's ever carried any money since Heck was a pup! Curse that black-hearted, liver-lipped, whip-sawin' old J. B., I believe he done it himself!"

"How'd you happen along so appropriate?" says I—wondering to myself how Petey knew there was any money on that stage.

"I been out to your place," says Petey, lickin' his dry lips. "You've gone; greasers gone; nigger gone. Comin' back, I see a saddled horse in a bunch of mares. I tried to cut him out, but they outrun me. So I shacked along on their trail, thinking maybe I'd aidge 'em along toward a corral and find some one to help pen 'em. Next I know, I saw a man clearin' off a place with himself for a three-ring circus. I tore off down here to keep him from being dragged to death—and its *you!* Think of it!" says Petey, exceedin' bitter. "I run hellity-larrup through two miles of dog-holes, sixty miles an hour, hop, skip and jump, till each separate hair on my head stood up like feathers on the fretful concubine—and it's *you!* I'm ha'nted!" says Petey. "That's what it is—I'm ha'nted!"

Any way you look at it, Petey was showin' up mighty ungrateful. He stared at me some more and rode off, muttering, to look for my gun and things.

"Andrew Jackson!" thinks I to myself, "what call has this long, lean, lank son of Satan to show such deep and abiding chagrin because he has been the humble instrument, under Providence, for prolonging your days in the land? Why does he think J. B. had the stage robbed? If he did, wan't it his own money? Who would J. B. be whipsawing by stealing his own money, and why should it stir up Petey's bile? But if so, why? What lot or part did Petey have in that lost and vanished wad?" Here I felt in my shirt-bosom for the money, thinkin' it might have got lost durin' the late exhibition, but it was still there.

"You can't deny it, Mister Bates—you've never been quite reconciled to J. B. sending for that amount of cash. Cash is for people that ain't satisfied with checks. Who ain't satisfied with checks? People that ain't stayin' to have 'em cashed. Pretty big sum, ain't it?

About the price of what? Of erasing somebody? Who ain't satisfied? Petey. How else could Petey earn that much so slick? Erasing who? Hey? Who's J. B. got it in for? Answer: Andrew Jackson Bates, of Naboth's vineyard.

"When did this money come? To-day, September 30th. When did Petey Simmons make his first and only visit to Shelter? To-day, September 30th. Was he displeased at the stage being robbed? He was. Why? Was he pleased at me not staying home? He was not. Why should a gentleman stay at home, if he didn't choose to wish to do so? Was Petey Simmons grateful to have saved a valued life? He was not. Last and most convincing of all, who was it you picked for to be poor Dee Macfarlane's murderer? Petey Simmons!

"Andrew Jackson, you ought to be thankful to J. Doe and R. Roe and Squatty. Only for their thoughtfulness there'd be a singin' soon at Shelter—and you'd be there, but you wouldn't hear it. Petey would just about have killed a J. B. beef beside your cold, unconscious clay, and said he caught you stealin' it. . . . I wonder if Minnie would 'a' believed that?" thinks I.

Of course I didn't think it out in words, like that. I just thought it in thoughts, all at once and good deal clearer. Words is mighty poor, slow tools, and they never did a good job in this world.

That wasn't all I sensed, either. There was impressions, little sidewise glances, things like this: Joe Only was boss; it was his to hire and fire. He didn't hire Petey; old Briscoe hired him. 'Twasn't usual, and 'twasn't liked. Nobody's been real pleasant to Petey. The J. B. boys felt they was pretty adequate to break their own broncos.

All this grand and lofty thinkin' took place simultaneous like a sewing-bee. Petey brought me my things. I cleaned the sand out of my good old gun, shoved her in the scabbard and give her a loving pat. Then I cocks one eye at my noble benefactor.

"Petey," says I, "not to be pryin' into your personal affairs, but was the old man to give you all that twenty-five hundred for expurgatin' me?"

Petey just stared at me, choking the horn of the saddle with both hands. I guess he felt that I was kinder vaccinated against him, after him savin' my life; he doesn't make any break for his gun.

"And you figure that he framed up a fake stage-robbin', to saw off the blame on you?" says I. "So you'd either get rubbed out or scared out?"

"Say, I hadn't thought of that!" says Petey, some startled. He give a pretty accurate description of the old man. He was a real powerful talker. "I'll go kill him right now—the old double-crossin' hypocrite!" he says to wind up.

"Now, now, Petey!" says I, soothin' him. "You don't want to do nothing like that. People would talk. The old man has been dealin' 'em to you from the bottom, I can see that. But I wouldn't kill him, exactly. Say, Petey, if I show you how to get that twenty-five hundred to-night, honest and aboveboard, will you come to Squatty's place by sun-up and give me half?"

"Will I?" says Petey. "I'll give you all of it! But how? How? The money's gone."

"I don't know yet," says I. "You just keep your mind off your thoughts whilst I study a spell."

I unsaddled Quaker and felt in the saddle-bags to see if my fieldglass was broke, and it wasn't.

"First off, Petey," says I, "them bold bandit-chasers are going to be back along here about sundown, ain't they?"

He allowed they was, some of 'em, anyway.

"*Bueno! Pues,*" says I, "they're going to see that dead horse, shot by a master hand. Everyone knows my saddle—and you're going to help me put it on the dead horse, right now."

He done so. It was hard to make the change, but we rolled old Beelzebub into my saddle and cinched it on. Then I put the other outfit on Quaker.

"There!" says I, "What with that and the robbery and Squatty missing too, Central will be one wild and nervous uproar. And who so agitated as J. Briscoe? I grieve to think how scared that man will be!" said I. "Too scared to use any daylight judgment at all. So if you drop in and tell him you had the misfortune to kill me and would like to collect, I reckon he'd give you the wealth without asking for no receipt."

"How in blazes," said Petey, "is he going to give me any money, when the money's gone?"

"I meant, if they happen to find the money anywhere," says I. "If they don't get the money, you don't say anything to J. B. But I think maybe they'll find it. So you trot along and come out there to Squatty's soon as you can. Squatty, he ain't there. We'll divide even—

you for doing the bloody deed and me for concealin' the body," says I. "You tell the old man the play didn't come out just right, as there wasn't any beef-critter handy, and that you've hid out the corpse. Offer to lead him to me, if he holds back. But he won't. I've took a snubbing-postgraduate-course in psychology, Petey," says I, "and I tell you that J. Briscoe will be scared."

Petey took a long look at me. "I believe you are the devil!" he said. He was sweating again. "Lord, I'd like to! But I'll tell you honest, I lost my nerve when I found out whose life I'd saved. A man can't stand but just so much. Suppose the boys suspect me of killing you and find that money on me? They'll put me to bed with a shovel; they'll hang me and old man Briscoe with one rope."

"It ain't likely," says I. "It seems a pity. But I can't take chances of losing my share of that money. I'll fix you out. Is Dee Macfarlane in town?"

Petey nodded, and I dug up my tally-book. I wrote a note to Dee, dating it September 30, six P. M., telling him not to be alarmed at any reports he might hear about me that night, that I was just having a little innocent relaxation after my arjous toils; and for him to tell Minnie—I wasn't going to have my pretty frightened—but on no account to tell anybody else except to save life. "Please return this note to bearer, who doesn't want to be hung," I adds as a postscript. Petey read it, he grinned and started. He turned around and hollered back at me mighty earnest; "Don't you let anything happen to you, Andrew Jackson Bates!"

Me and Quaker terrapinned up the road a stretch, till I come to a rise that I could watch from a long ways off. Here I built up a little stone monument in the road and put that money on top, still in the original package, address-side up. I tacked off east two or three miles, to a bench where I could keep cases on that money with my fieldglass.

After a while the push fell off down the slope, six or eight of the boys loping along in front. I see them stop at my monument. Then I dug it up a draw for Squatty's. Got in about half-past dark, mighty tired. I drove up a bunch of Squatty's saddle-stock with me, and I caught his sorrel Gold Dollar horse. Then I turned Quaker loose with the bunch, opened up a lot of canned stuff and slept a few lines.

About sun-up Petey shook me. "Get up!" he says. "We got to get out of this!"

"Breakfast first," says I.

"Breakfast, nothing!" says Petey. "You come look at the Butterbowl!"

I took one look, and I see Petey was right. The sun was just peepin' over the hills, and the valley looked cool and pleasant. There was bunches of men scurryin' around everywhere, like drunk ants. I guess about the whole he-population was present. The nearest was eight or ten miles.

Some was following Petey's trail, some on mine, but most of 'em was spreadin' out for general results. They got 'em. Every mess of wild horses they scared up stampeded three more batches, and those bands scared more, and all of 'em stampeded every bunch of cattle they passed, and those cattle scared the next lot, and so on—and on—and on: just like politics. 'Twas a stirrin' scene.

My bosom swelled with pride. "Petey," says I, "did you get it?"

"That's what I went after," said Petey. "Here's yours. You keep the odd hundred.

"Let this be a lesson to you, Petey," says I, pretty severe.

"We'd better take to the hills," says Petey.

"We will not," said I, saddlin' the sorrel horse. "I always wished I was a musician, so I could fiddle at a fight. And this is the day when all my dreams come true. You and me, Petey, will go out on the flat." Then I stopped short and slapped my leg. "Chickens!" says I. "Chickens!"

"What's the matter with you now, you old hag?" said Petey, edgin' off.

"Chickens! I never once thought of keepin' chickens at Shelter till this very now! Come on, Petey," says I. "Let's us go play hare and hounds."

Petey came on, but he didn't like it. "You red hellion," says that interesting beast, "I dassent leave you get an inch away from me till all the Butterbowl knows you're alive. Joe Only suspected me and J. B. right off. Otherwise I'd see you rot first. May my right hand cleave to the roof of my mouth if I don't think you're part fiend!"

We had to go a couple of miles toward the man-hunt to get

down out of the hills. They seen us. Then we turned east across the big flat, heading for the big pass, where progress and the railroad was to come in—some time—and the Butterbowl fanned along after us. I reckon the cattle thought it was the Day of Judgment.

We let the boys gain on us, to encourage them—that is, I did. Petey, he was in favor of going on, but I held him back. "I never knowed how popular I was," said I. "Them boys are sure aimin' to avenge the deep damnation of my taking-off. And oh, Petey!" says I, "if you and me could only meet up with J. B. face to face, what a joyful reunion we would have!"

By the time we got in the foothills by the pass, they was pretty close—two of 'em 'way ahead of the others.

"That's Barefoot and Joe Only," says Petey. "They've got the best horses in the works."

And here I got my great surprise. We come out on a ridge above the wagon-road, and there I saw two numbers that wasn't down on my program at all. Right below us, outward bound, was Minnie and Dee, joggin' happily along dead to the world. They'd just climbed out of the San Lucas where the wagon-road quit the Narrows, so missing the glorious and inspirin' panorama being presented on the flats.

I got the idee. Reasonin' from my note that I wasn't dead enough to grieve about, they was makin' the best possible use of the chance the excitement gave 'em.

If so, it was providential; for a little ahead, around a turn, I saw Parson Duffy coming in from St. Johns. I knew his white horses and his little old buckboard.

I called to them, and they jumped their horses apart like I'd thrown a bomb. Then they saw who it was, and they waited.

"Walkin' away to be married, children?" says I. Minnie drooped her head and blushed, and Dee looked foolish. And then I knew that old Andy Jackson was leaving Butterbowl. " 'Cause, if you are," says I, "you'd better get to running."

I waved my hand down the pass. The hardy pursuers were just pouring into the scenery. One look was enough. The eloping party began hittin' the high places. There didn't seem to be any call to tell 'em that wasn't the angry father, but just a few friends desiring to lynch me for causing my own death.

"Easy!" I says. "You needn't ride so fast, for you won't have to ride far. You're both of age, and Parson Duffy is coming, Johnny-on-the-spot, up the road a stretch. If you'd like to be married while you are still in peaceful Butterbowl, Petey and I'll be witnesses, and you can be man and wife before you turn over the divide. Does it go?"

They said it went. We slowed down till we met the preacher. I did the explaining.

"Mr. Duffy," says I, "if you'll turn right around, we'd like to have you perform the marriage ceremony for this young couple, short but binding. You know them; they're of age and otherwise unmarried."

The Parson saw the avengers coming, and there's a twinkle in his eye. "You are in some haste, perhaps?" says he as he turns back.

"Oh, no hurry, no hurry at all; just lope right along," says I, as a couple of bullets whanged over our heads. Then we turned a curve out o' range. And by thunder, that old sport stood up in that rocking old buckboard and married them on the run!

I kissed the bride. "Be a good girl, honey," says I. "Lots of happiness to you both. I'm leaving here for keeps, and I'm giving Shelter to you two for a wedding-present—Mr. Duffy bein' witness. Good luck, Dee!" says I. "Be good to Deacon and Quaker—yes, and to Minnie too. Here's the summit. I'll stay here to check the maddened parent. No, there won't be any violence, Minnie. I'll give you my word. Just moral suasion. I got a heap of influence with the Butterbowl. Good-by!"

"Good-by!" said Dee, and "Good-by, Andy Jackson," said Minnie. "We'll not forget you. If you ever find the bird in the bush—or if you don't—come back to Shelter. It is always yours. We'll look for you. Good-by!"

We waited, sky-lighted on the summit.

The pass opened up wide; across in the east it framed off a big country I'd never seen. Petey and I got off our horses and let 'em puff and blow: the parson fixed up his tally of the marriage for us to sign. I laid one of my blood-money bills in the buckboard seat, for his fee.

"I'm going to stay just long enough for Joe to see us together," Petey snapped at me. "Then you pick one side of the world and I'll take the other."

"All right, Petey," says I. "I'll sorter fade away over into New Mexico. I have always liked that country."

Then the committee of unsafety arrived. Joe Only set his horse up and looked at me a long time, real sad.

"What in the name of the seven deadly sins have you been up to?" says he. "I made sure Simmons had murdered you. Why didn't he?"

"It's a pretty note," I says to him, real peevish and bitter. "When a couple of white, male, free American citizens can't attend a wedding without such a hullabaloo as this!"

"Weddin'!" says Chuck. "Weddin'?"

"Sure—Miss Minnie Briscoe and Mr. Dee Macfarlane. Didn't you get an invite? Petey and I we rode over to be witnesses. Didn't we, Petey?"

"Don't ask me," said Petey. "I have went!" And he did so.

"But what—why—where's Squatty? Who robbed the stage? How'd that money get back?" says Joe.

Outraged citizens was a-burnin' around the bend. I wished I might have been Poppa once more, but I see this was no place for Andrew J. Bates. "You go back, Joe," says I. "You go back and explain to 'em."

Joe Only was much of a man, but he let his voice go up to a screech. "Explain? Explain! What'll I tell 'em?"

"How should I know?" says I, giving him a little push. "Just explain!" And I came away.

XII. No Mean City

As written, to get funds that were sorely needed, this was but two-fifths of the whole Rhodes had in mind to bear the title "Road to Nowhere." This whole story never was completed although Rhodes worked on it, in his head, until the day he died. This published portion has not been reprinted since magazine appearance in the *Saturday Evening Post*, May 17–24, 1919.

There is a technical weakness or six in this story. Chief of these is the long, rambling, introductory background. Yet, this was essential to what Rhodes wished to say once he got his plot started.

This first chapter, too, could be footnoted as thickly as a Ph.D. dissertation to document its facts. Such would bolster the editorial ego and bore the reader beyond endurance. Suffice it to say that, in this one chapter, Rhodes set down the life and death of a New Mexico town, Engle, as and how it happened in life. In this sequence rests the reason why Rhodes, writing of New Mexico, wrote of the American West between the Front Range and the Sierra Nevada crest—it all had happened at Engle, so compressed in time and space that one man could see and be a part of it all.

Let one example of his details stand for the rest, that

where he describes the naming of the sidetracks on the Santa Fe's *Jornada* line. On October 3, 1947, Mr. J. W. Higgins, valuation engineer, Atchison, Topeka, and Santa Fe Railroad, Amarillo, Texas, wrote Mr. C. K. Adams as follows: "Mr. Rhodes' story in the naming of the towns seems to be well founded as we are able to verify the fact that four of the towns—Crocker, Engle, Cutter, and Upham—are the names of engineers in charge of construction at the time." It is worth noting that Morley, whom Rhodes has named his sidetrack Lava, was the famous railroad engineer, W. R. Morley, father of Mrs. Agnes Morley Cleaveland, whose connection with the line is well established.

Rhodes had been absent from New Mexico almost fourteen years when this story was written, which makes his recall of the topography most remarkable. His requiem for vanished days and ways is in this story where he has Teagardner and Cady speak of the submerged Gonzalez Ranch which he had described, unsubmerged, in *Bransford in Arcadia*.

Rhodes took the germ of this story from accounts in eastern newspapers of a German plot to destroy Elephant Butte dam in 1917. Spirited spadework by the Honorable Clinton P. Anderson, United States senator from New Mexico, has failed to unearth any documentation of this plot in official Washington but the story had popular credence at the time.

That Elephant Butte dam was not destroyed, that this fact was common knowledge by the time Rhodes submitted his story for editorial acceptance, would seem to have made a fatal flaw in the suspense angle of his plot. What he had to say in developing the final resolution of this known plot-ending seems to have made the story palatable to the *Satevepost*, both editors and readers.

i

WITH MIRTH AND EXCEEDING JOLLITY seven husky and dusty young men did good work together in a world gay, hoping and altogether delightful. Morley, Pope, Crocker, Engle, Cutter, Upham and Grama—they sought, for a cheerful and hasty young railroad system, the best path between the Mexican hamlets of Albuquerque and El Paso. Peach-embowered, those villages drowsed in two of the great gateways of the world; which fact, had it been told them, would have caused them considerable surprise. The year was 1879. Count back now to 1779, 1679, to 1605.

So long ago was Santa Fé last founded, and so far back those founders followed a path beaten already by centuries of weary feet. After the coming of the Spaniards the path pushed northward a century, eastward a century; to Westport at last; to become thereafter the Santa Fé Trail. You would search vainly for Westport on any map; it is Kansas City now.

The Santa Fe Railroad followed the Santa Fé Trail pretty closely; the most notable change being to drop the accent. Not that surveyors are imitative, but because surveying is an exact science. The old trail followed truly the line of least resistance; its makers left to be settled by later craftsmen details only, the factors of grade, curve and upkeep.

Trail and railroad leave the river valley for the high tableland, to cross the Jornada del Muerto. So is that strip of desert country named from old time—The Journey of the Dead Man.

On the old trail there were cut-offs for wet-weather travel, when water stood in the shallow lakes—cut-offs, that is, for heavy traffic. Wet or dry the stage line ran straight, straight; hauling water for the stage stations from the river, from Bitter Springs, from Del Muerto Springs at Fort McRae. Little Round Mountain was the first station; then a semi-permanent lake, Laguna, the halfway place. Fourteen miles south of Laguna was the only living water on the direct route: Martin's Wells, better known as Aleman, because John Martin was a German. Water was hauled from Aleman to supply Point of Rocks, the fourth and last stage station. But the long caravans of freight wagons traveling together for mutual protection against the Apaches must zigzag for water, aside from the direct route; east to Bitter Springs; west again, seven miles west and down, to Fort McRae; then painfully back to Martin's Wells.

More fortunate, the railroad was to have water pumped up over the mesa from Fort McRae to Laguna, the halfway place. Winter and summer the railway keeps to the cut-offs; hand in hand together, trail and railroad, guide and eager youngster, hold straight for the shining peaks of Dona Ana. Here was a kingdom, long and long ago, "the Kingdom of Dona Ana," of the Lady Ann; here was her capital, close-nestled under these brightest hills. "Happy the state that has no history."

But where the Santa Fé Trail takes ninety miles to cross the desert from Paraje to Fort Selden the Santa Fe Railroad makes it in seventy-five, from San Marcial to Rincon, leaving the river earlier, rejoining it earlier. In each case the railway gets the worst of it in the matter of grades; in each case the change was forced by the all-important consideration of safe bridging. The Río Grande is a sullen and malignant stream, the banks and bed of it are shifting quicksand, trembling, treacherous. Only where the river breaks through mountains may it be safely forded or surely bridged; except at San Marcial.

Eastward from San Marcial is an insignificant hillock, barely to be seen. From this pimply knoll, some time since, poured out a stream of liquid fire and stone, which flooded to varying depths a country half as large as Wales. This lava flow underlies the desert; the deep wells find it. Year by year southwest winds bring to this place certain grains of sea sand from the Pacific beaches, so covering that part of the plain known as the Jornada. The patient chemistry of time binds and blends that sand and fashions it to soil.

Northern bound and limit of the Jornada, the last sluggish dregs of that stupendous flow, cooling almost level with the lip of the crater, make a low swell of black lava, uncovered yet by sand; a swell larger than Delaware, and exactly the shape of a black ink blot. This, too, is being submerged and overblown; even in recorded time sand dunes and struggling sagebrush have made a visible gain.

A westward splash of that ragged black blot of lava sent out in turn a westward spokewise ray which poured a dam of boiling metal across the valley of the Río Grande. Much steam—it is thought—was then generated. The lava cooled, the river promptly cut a channel through; the net result was a safe foundation for a bridge, where a causeway of lava underlies the quicksands of the Río Grande.

If you stand on the observation platform at the last car of your train as you pass that bridge you shall see the black steeps of San Pascual Hill gloom high above you, and dimly sense that you still live in the youth of the unfinished earth—perhaps in the evening or the morning of the third day; you may almost stretch out your hand to touch this late experiment of the great laboratory. But perhaps you are not on the platform of the observation car. You may be inside with the curtains drawn. Playing bridge, probably.

Opposite San Marcial, as our seven surveyors staked out the southern anchorage for that bridge on the steep black side of San Pascual Hill, a benign and elderly giant, chin in hand, sat on a block of lava and observed them with great interest. Elderly, by comparison; the oldest surveyor was thirty, this meditative giant edged toward forty.

Below them the chuck wagon forded the river. The wagon master thoughtfully elected to leave the water where the river's edge was most prepared to be churned to a jelly of quicksand, stalled promptly, jumped from his seat and began with rigorous impartiality to beat his six mules over the head.

The meditative giant laid aside the heavy Sharps rifle across his knees, strolled down to the trouble and threw the wagon master into the river without comment; gave instructions to the mules and brought the chuck wagon out of that. He then directed bed wagon and water wagon to a safer landing. Returning to the hillside for his rifle and saddle horse he led the little cavaran to a sheltered cove half a mile down the river, made camp, unloaded the bed wagon and hauled up driftwood.

"Teagardner," said the giant after supper, his name being demanded for the pay roll by the senior surveyor. "Ben Teagardner. Put me down as extra man if it's all the same to you. I'll sidle over to Fort Craig to-morrow and get you a wagon master. Springtime Morgan, I reckon. And Springtime, he rigged up a tank wagon when he was cuttin' grama hay for Uncle Sam. You'll need that, and his teams. Your one little old water wagon won't nigh do the trick alone. I'll bring along Lew Friend for hunter. He'll keep you in fresh meat, deer and antelope. You just put me down as extra man. I'll fill in right handy. Know the country—been here since 'Sixty-three. Any old pay. I ain't doin' this for the money exactly. I'm a prospector, sort of; and I want to learn a little surveyin' for my own use."

Thus, in all simplicity, Teagardner took over and guided benevolently the destinies of the Santa Fe. The world went very well then.

Those were joyous days. Here was no peril of flood, no endless wrangle for right of way, but a broad sunny plain and a shining straightaway. Small wonder that the young surveying men were elate; and they may be pardoned for what they did. The thing was obvious. Eighty miles across the desert, seven sidetracks, one every ten miles, seven young men, one sidetrack to each young man, and none to molest or make afraid. Who can blame them? They offered Teagardner his pick, as was fitting and proper, but Teagardner smiled and shook his head. Also, at the casting of lots, the senior surveyor drew a sidetrack in the most lunar of earthly landscapes, where the road curved deep through the Malpaís; in English, the Bad Lands, the lava fields. So Morley named his sidetrack, not Morley but Lava. Had Napoleon been godfather he could have done no less without indelicacy. But the other young men drew sites less nightmare-weird than Morley's. Pope, Lava, Crocker, Engle, Cutter, Upham and Grama, these are the stations of the Jornada, even unto this day.

Black-browed Engle was the lucky one. His name town became metropolis and capital of the Jornada. It is true that the youth of Lava was not inglorious, what time Fort Stanton, eastward by two deserts and two great mountain chains, freighted over the great military road through Lava Gap. It is true that at a later day, after ages of dull obscurity, Lava attained a certain importance when De Meir found guano in the throat of the old crater. But the ascendancy of Engle was never truly challenged.

The golden age, the heroic, the pastoral, growth of empire, dark ages, feudal systems, scientific efficiency, Trojan wars and Sabine women, tribute from far places, bitterness of Norman conquest, epic and romance, chivalry and chicane—everything that has ever happened in any place has happened in Engle. Through the mists of dim antiquity, legend and myth cluster about names as loved and bright as Hector or Du Guesclin.

No name of all those shining names may be cited here, though the temptation is great. Engle has a thousand stories; Balzac might have written the Human Comedy without leaving the Jornada.

Construction camps trod on the heels of the survey. The railroad reached El Paso in 'Eighty-one. Engle was marked for greatness from the first; halfway across the desert, Engle was set apart by the glory of two passing tracks; it was here that water was pumped from Fort McRae for the thirsty locomotives. Beyond the river in the Black Range, mining towns sprang up overnight: Hillsboro, Chloride, Fairview, Grafton, Kingston, Hermosa; and Engle was base of supplies to all. Fort McRae was abandoned; Engle was strong enough to keep the gate against the Apaches.

There were two stage lines. Long strings of freight wagons crawled over the low rim of the desert, crowded to the freight depot or loaded direct from the cars. There were two flourishing general stores; saloons, of course; two thriving hotels; an all-night restaurant. And children. Real boys and girls, who rose up in that white tent city, sniffed the pleasant odor of clean resinous new lumber and fared forth to mischief in a world of unfailing sunlight and joy; a world whose chief occupation was target practice.

Civic pride was strong in those children. By cause of those two sidetracks, the pipe line and the water tank, they turned up their collective nose at Lava; they exulted in the metropolitan splendor of the later "Y," built for the convenience of pusher engines which would turn about and go back to San Marcial or to Rincon. Most of all, their pride was centered in the survey stakes marking the branch line that was to run to the Black Range. By that sign they knew the future was secure and that Engle would crowd the map.

Never was childhood such as theirs. Privation? They laughed their scorn—they who had horses and rifles and mountains and miles for playthings. No children were ever happier.

Geronimo's Apaches killed Harve and Sam in 'Eighty-six. They were sixteen years old. One Engle boy died in Amazon country, another in Alaska. This is not their story. But it is sad to know that there is not one left in Engle now who knew that ancient glory—not one of those gay boys and girls or of their children's children. What quite escaped the notice of those proud children—and of their parents—was that the long strings of freight wagons went out laden and returned empty. Oh, yes, a few outgoing cars of ore now and then; one wagon of twenty came loaded back to Engle. Superstition has ever wagged the head at one-way freighting as a bad sign.

The wildcat mining boom collapsed. At Engle the white tent city withered like Jonah's gourd, the frame houses were torn down for the precious lumber. Overnight, all that was left of Engle were the railroad buildings and the huge adobe buildings, gray, sprawling, immovable, which had housed stores, hotels, saloons, mining companies. There was still freighting to the Black Range, but men no longer pummeled each other for precedence at the depot platform; the two stage lines dwindled to one; the one fell from six-horse teams to four. The stores remained, but on the shelves the stock ran low; the vast dining room of the surviving hotel was become an ominous place, given to melancholy echoes. Of the children, seven were left, stunned, bewildered, heartbroken; to them the silent streets were peopled with the ghosts of departed heroes. It is not given to many streets to be haunted within three years of their building.

One of these children, a boy, fourteen and venturous of disposition, diverted himself by painstaking exploration of such mountains as lay within a radius. It befell him that always when he had climbed to a summit where, as he thought, no white man's foot had ever been before, there he found mine monuments and location notices given to sprightly and whimsical names. Always the notices were signed—Ben Teagardner; generally with Pres Lewis as co-locator; sometimes with Abijah K. Witherspoon, Jr., as witness.

The boy became interested. Annoyance gave way to wonder, wonder to admiration. He heard of Pres Lewis only three days away; rode those three days, found Pres Lewis, blacksmith to the Mother Hubbard's Cupboard mine, Mogollon way. Of him the boy made inquiry.

"Yes," said Lewis, "me and old Teagardner rambled about right smart. Teagardner, he's in Peru now; letter from him last Christmas was a year. . . . Mr. Abijah K. Witherspoon, Jr.? Oh, 'Bijah was a ha'nt—like John Doe. 'Bije was Teagardner's witness when Ben was alone. Was that forgery, now, I wonder?" Pres tugged at his silky brown beard as he wondered.

The centuries passed slowly in Engle until '86. Men began to speak of cattle. The railroad built shipping pens. Kim Ki Rogers started the K I M brand in the Caballo foothills; the K Y Company, of Lexington, was formed, and stocked up with a thousand head at Aleman.

The Texans, whose herds had followed up the Pecos and its tributaries, fought the bloody and desperate Lincoln County War because they crowded each other. About '86 they discovered the way across two deserts by way of Lava Gap, Bitter Springs and the Santa Fé Trail to Fort McRae Creek and the Río Grande; so west to the Tonto Basin War. The new-found way could be used only in the rainy season, when the shallow lakes were full. From July to October long slow herds crept over the northern horizon; bedded on the long slope beyond Engle Lake, the old Laguna; passed on over the rim to McRae.

A few, the hardiest, looked at the land, sought out water in the foothills, took root at Engle. The hardiest—of many that lingered for a year or so only the unyielding, the tenacious, the high-hearted, might bear the test of that hard and desolate land. There began the tradition of Engle, a great tradition—to do no less than the utmost. It was a man of another town who has best voiced the heart of Engle: "Don't flinch; don't foul; hit the line hard!"

So the men of Engle went forth, north, east, west and south; each carried afar some part of the meaning of Engle; each in his heart carried the vision of that old gray town as something high, clear and apart, in the desert and the sun, under her turquoise sky.

The old gray town; old in history and in change, grief and joy, mischance and misdeed, in everything that makes for ripeness. And as from Engle, so from a thousand like her, and a thousand. It is by the hands of these wandering men that ideals are blended, to make us a nation purposed and "prepared," equal to either fortune; not a congeries of hostile tribes.

To illustrate: Far in Southern Mexico there is a mining town high in the almost inaccessible mother range, with a single passway to the outer world. Twenty years ago its population was about twenty-four thousand. Of these, seven—not seven thousand, but seven—were Americans; each of the seven had been at some time a citizen of gray Engle. And not one of the seven had lot or part in the coming of the others. It is like the manner of men that the tarrying may have been in part for old time's sake; it is so we are made. But it was chance and the wandering foot and the venturous heart that brought them there.

Of such hard make and breed were the swift-passing generations of Engle; foregoers at heart, children of the road, rolling stones, flouting the acquisition of moss as dullest and most depressing of occupations; taking shape and polish of their thunderous onrush. Disaster? Yes. Fragments, frequently. That is Nature's way of accomplishment. By glacier and avalanche, by earthquake and flood she builds her fatness. Moss-grown stones and sedentary have scornful names for these rolling ones; drifter and wastrel the mildest. Yet it is difficult to think of progress without on-goers, even without first-goers.

So the wandering men fared forth and bore with them some part of that high tradition. A waif word comes back from Guadalajara, from New York, from Château-Thierry—that they are children of Engle yet. Where you have been first-men, there is your abiding city.

The Bar Cross Company came to the Jornada. The Bar Cross bought out the K I M and K Y brands, for a starter. It dug wells, built tanks, pumped water, at Detroit, from the Río Grande; stocked up the Jornada with forty thousand head of Herefords; picked its men by natural selection, best of the best; held to the great tradition of Engle, and bettered it.

The Bar Cross endured fifteen years—fifteen happy centuries. Side by side with it the 7 T X fenced in the Armendaris Grant, forty-five by fifteen, the northwestern corner of the Jornada, running six thousand head; and for them, as for the Bar Cross, the hardships of the desert cut back all but the strongest.

Teagardner returned, rested for a year or two, adopted the Bar Cross outfit in token of approval; was honored by the brevet of Uncle Ben; passed on to Hong-Kong, Java, Sumatra. A Christmas letter came back from him every few years.

Engle was inside the 7 T X fence by a scant mile; the two companies came to a working agreement and both made their headquarters there. "The Holy Roman Empire" was Frank John's name for it. There were dukes and tributary princes in the Caballo Mountains and the San Andres, to west and east; and in the Crown Lands of the 7 T X, far to the southeast in the San Andres, with a separate brand, the Fleur de Lys. The free cities of Paraje and Cantra Recio lay northwest on the river, between the barren mass of Fra Christobal Mountain and the lava fields, their cattle ranging from the river to Lava and Bitter Springs; thirty brands in all, on the Jornada and the bordering hills; jangling at times between themselves, a fierce unit against all outsiders.

The shipping pens grew great. Because there was abundant grass and no farmers with vexatious fences, Engle became the shipping point from the Black Range country in the west, and beyond; from the White Mountain and beyond, the Capitans, the Sacramento, two hundred miles to the east. Those were the golden days. There were children again in Engle—and a school at last. Such a little, little school!

The herds grew great, too great; grass became short; the evil days drew nigh. Men hoped for rain and the drought consumed. Cattle died by the thousand. Cattle companies began to break up, to ship cattle away—to Colorado and California. The Bar Cross was the last to go, after a precarious survival of some years. The Bar Cross herds were shipped out; the fierce vassals clutched at the fragments of empire; and thick darkness fell upon the land. The old gray town fell desolate and lonely; the little pine schoolhouse warped in the sun, the broken door creaked in the wind on rusting hinges. From the brown desert, where grass and grass roots had been trampled out, the blown sand rose to witness against the greed and folly of man—as it rose against Gaza and Ascalon—and drifted high in the silent streets of Engle. Her sons were scattered, her glory was in eclipse.

The stagnant years crawled by at Engle; the sand crept higher against the crumbling adobes. And suddenly a great dream came true and the flood tide of prosperity burst upon the forsaken town.

Three centuries the dream had waited. Be sure that Coronado dreamed it, and Kit Carson, and the builders of the Santa Fe; Uncle Ben Teagardner with the rest. To tame the fierce brown river, to build a new Nile land in the desert, a later Thebaïs. No passer-by, no brown peon so dull as not to see dimly the glory of that dream.

Twelve miles from Engle the Río Grande plunges directly, head on, against the northern knife-sharp edge of Caballo Mountain, recoils from the impact of that furious collision, swerves, passes westward, hugging close to the mountain's western base for the next forty miles. It was doubtless the secret thought of the Río Grande to undermine that mountain, to grind it to dust, and to use that dust for an oyster bed in the Gulf of Mexico. But that project has been postponed for a space by the puny hand of man.

For just at the utmost north of Caballo Mountain stood a black butte, once a volcano. Time and chance and the stupendous chisels of the wind and the sand have wrought the bristling head of an angry elephant, facing the north, startled and startling, sinister, ominous. This was the most heroic statue of all earth.

And just here was the appointed spot to arrest the giant spirit of the Río Grande, to tame and bit that turbulent and angry outlaw and set him to expiate his crimes, serving men and the sons of men. . . . For a space. But—who may doubt it?—in the end the giant dam must be as transitory as the pyramids.

An old, old dream—to turn aside the fury of flood time, to bring the water of life to the acres of ten thousand farms. Men grew old and died, sick with the bitterness of hope deferred. Half a century of waiting and of breaking hearts; then a swift week of years, and the thing was done.

Busy years; a great wagon road from Engle, that clambered and clung and twisted and looped on the gashed hillsides of Mescal Cañon; then a swift spur of railroad, the river turned aside into a man-made channel, an ant army at work in the old river bed, digging down through overlying silt to the foundations laid by Omnipotence. Electric lights made a year-long day. Pneumatic drills channeled trench and tunnel into the living rock, that the concrete might anchor to the everlasting hills, and man's work take hold upon God's.

Six hundred feet above the cañon floor a cable was rigged from cliff to cliff, and wheels to ride that cable; an aërial ferry. A locomotive, caught up in a sling like a child's toy, was hung beneath those dizzy wheels and rode that cobweb to the western bank; other locomotives, cars, steel rails bundled like toothpicks—a railroad complete—to serve the dam from the west side.

From such gigantic detail judge the work: mills that ground mountains to gravel; mixers that stirred them to batter; derrick and pourer and crane. Great lights doubled each year and made it two; the shining dam arose complete, with every safeguard of spillway, sluice and gate; solid concrete, twelve hundred feet long, three hundred feet high, with a walled driveway eighteen feet wide at the top by way of a bridge; substitute for Engle ferry and ford. Engle ferry and ford lie under one hundred and eight feet of water now.

It is thought that problems and difficulties were encountered in building the Engle Dam; in private life we meet such in digging a cellar. Mistakes were made—blunders, perhaps; there was ample waste—unavoidable and other. Huge outcry ensued; blame was lavishly apportioned. Curious; that critics should always be faultfinders. A critic is, by intention and by first meaning, a judge, free to approve; yet praisefinding is a word unaccustomed and awkward to our ears.

One might think that a fact so stupendous and colossal as Engle Dam would be conclusive retort and answer to the critics. But it is generally understood that the critics could have done much better.

The mistakes were corrected, the blunders retrieved, experimental waste made good a thousandfold, the difficulties mastered; the completed work is one with the hills, to serve unborn generations and to inspire greater works of riper years. Yet many a man has reaped unstinted blame in that building; and if any has won praise thereby his name has been successfully concealed. There have been cases like this before; and since.

Now, during the years of that great building Engle town throve mightily, with music of hammer and saw; base for freight and traffic, for building of telephone and telegraph lines, wagon road, the spur of railroad at last. Not one of those children who had so proudly dreamed of a branch line was left in Engle. Indeed, of the few latter-day old-timers who had lingered through the evil days, all except one or two had made haste to secure homes in the fertile valley below the dam, when the beginnings of its building were first assured. It was a new race of men, Baden—Powelled and putteed, who built bank, bungalow and boarding house in Engle redivivus—"the best town in New Mexico by a dam site."

The late-comers were a gay and cheerful pack, youthsome, light-hearted, perhaps something lifted above themselves to have part in the doing of a great deed. Strictly confidential—Uncle Ben Teagardner, oldest of old-timers, warmed to these latest sons of Engle with a guarded and conditioned approval which he kept strictly to the cloistered silence of his thoughts. In his seventy-second year Uncle Ben came back once more to Engle on a personal errand, and incidentally to have a look at the building of Engle Dam.

Engle Dam. It was so known during the building of it; under that name the word of it had reached Uncle Ben in Asia, other men under other skies. The dam was also known, loosely and variously, as the Rio Grande Dam, Elephant Butte Dam. Old habit prevailed; as Engle Dam it was to take its place in encyclopedic pages; Engle was to have her line of history.

Mark now the favor of makers. The compositor, whose heart was in the Polo Grounds with Matty, misread his copy, changed "Engle" into "Eagle." One letter aright, and Engle had been also of the cities of earth, with Aden and with Nome. To the gods it seemed otherwise. Eagle Dam. The Supernatural Year Book for 1910, p. 624.

Protest followed. Government and encyclopedia laid their wise heads together; for "Eagle" substituted "Elephant Butte"; well, indeed, and best, did that grim elephant's head still front the north; not so well since half of that gigantic head is under water.

Elephant Butte Dam reclaims 200,000 acres by first intention, in New Mexico, Texas, Mexico Viejo; more to come, by diversion dams and ditches, and High Level Ditch, still a-building or to be built; most of all as an example, a mark to equal and to overpass. It makes an artificial lake forty miles long, with a shore line of two hundred miles, ragged with gulf and fiord as it seeks a level against the black broken rim of the Jornada or in the black cañons of Fra

Christobal Mountains. The wild ducks carried tidings of the new lake to Carolina swamps and inlets of Yucatan. Enterprising and adventurous ducks came to look-see by prompt thousands; as promptly business men of El Paso, Las Cruces and Albuquerque established a clubhouse near the lakeside—at Cutter. Thus does Nature adjust the balance between her creatures.

Cutter shall have a word. Upstart Cutter, eight miles south of Engle, bored many wells and built recklessly; shared with Engle the riches of the dam-building years. Engle snubbed Cutter, bore herself rather haughtily, secure in her great past.

Cutter built a thirty-thousand-dollar wagon road through Palomas Gap in Caballo Mountain, seized and held the rich Palomas Valley as tributary, and for a space threatened the supremacy of Engle. Engle holds the Black Range trade by way of the road which uses Elephant Butte Dam as a bridge; she holds the upper reaches of the lake, and in the great shipping pens she has an asset not lightly to be matched.

With the completion of the dam both Engle and Cutter dwindled sadly. Jealousy dwindled as well; each readjusted itself to lesser fortunes and set itself to a future smaller but secure.

The year 1914 came; 1915 and the Lusitania; 1916. Engle and Cutter forgot their folly and their pride, drew close together; 1917 came, and the end of unexampled patience. Nashville, New York, Cutter, Boston, Miami and Engle sent forth their sons to war; some to return no more, the dead and deathless.

ii

Clayton's store and Engle Hotel are housed together in an old adobe of fabulous dimensions. As the Humboldt House, in 1882, it had started life as a recumbent skyscraper one story high and twenty long; the accretions of capricious years—ell and annex and afterthought—have changed it to a labyrinth. Clayton owns both establishments; the store, alcoved, cool, wide and dim, serves as lounge and lobby to the hotel, where guest and native mingle with a democratic equality surprising in a country like ours. Witness to-day's company.

To-day was a July day; the rainy season was a week old. In front of the store a saddled horse, a pack-saddled horse and a touring car, huddled sociably together, tails to wind, in a warm driving rain; blazoning forth the democracy within. That democracy numbered six; or seven, if you cared to count Clayton.

The car belonged to Mr. Kinny Apgar, a brisk and debonair man, from that vague, mysterious, far-off world called "the East"; now, and for six months past, clubman of Cutter, mine owner of Fra Christobal. The two horses had arrived during the last burst of rain, their owner, a still dripping boy, seeking refuge in the store. In old days there had seldom been so few as two ponies at the store door. Other times, other manners. That Jack Carpenter, foreman of the Armendaris Cattle Company, had ventured so far afoot—a full two hundred yards from the Broad A headquarters—proved him to be no old-timer. The Armendaris Company ran cattle on the fenced Armendaris Grant, successors to the 7 T X of old time. That the new brand was known as "the Broad A" further explains both the new company and the new foreman. There were two transients, guests of the hotel: a gray-haired patrician, a brown-haired plebeian; last of all, Uncle Ben Teagardner, no transient.

At seventy-two, after twenty-five years of Asia, Teagardner had come back home—to die. So far he had been unsuccessful, and had now postponed the matter to see the end of the great war.

"Only seventeen years old," said Uncle Ben proudly, "and he can open and shut a gate as good as anybody."

"Aw, Uncle Ben!" protested the seventeen-year-old—the dripping boy. "That Bally horse was wild as a hawk. I couldn't put the beef back on him alone."

"No. You had a lead rope and a pack rope, but you couldn't pack two quarters of beef on a bald-faced horse. Of course not."

"I tried to, I tell you, and he dragged me all over the flat. So I rolled the beef up in the tarp and beat it to town. What else could I do? Storm coming up anyhow."

"Ten to one you wouldn't have had no trouble packin' Bally if you had only blindfolded Bally. Or you might have tied Bally's front leg up to the pack saddle and put the beef on Bally. You might have tied Bally's hind leg to Bally's shoulder and put the beef on Bally. If Bally would keep hoppin' round, you could pass a rope round Bally's other hind foot, and pull it out from under Bally, and throw Bally down, and hog-tie Bally, and pack your beef on Bally.

Or you might have thrown your pack on the saddle horse and ridden Bally in. If Bally was too wild to ride you might have broken Bally."

The boy squirmed unhappily. "But I didn't know all these things, Uncle Ben."

"No. You didn't know them and you didn't make 'em up new. Nor yet nine other ways I never heard of. You had a tarp to crawl under till it quit rainin'. You had two horses, two ropes, two quarters of beef, one pack saddle and one head, but you didn't tie the beef on Bally. You lit out for home and mother. Son, I've known boys in this very town, no older'n you, would ha' found some way to tie that beef on Bally, or been there yet. They might have been obliged to put the pack saddle upside down on the beef and put Bally in the pack saddle and pack Bally to the beef, but they'd have brought Bally, and they'd have brought that beef."

" 'There were giants in those days'?" said brisk Apgar.

"Giants," said Teagardner.

"Why is it, then, that you never tell me about them? I am a skillful listener and a notable lover of giants, but I have always failed to get you started. Come now, Mr. Teagardner, we are storm-bound here; oblige us; entertain us with a few chapters of the wondrous tale."

Uncle Ben caressed his long gray beard and regarded his questioner thoughtfully. He saw a man in the ripe vigor of middle age, of medium height, well knit and muscular. Apgar was natty and well-groomed. His eyes were blue and large, his hair was chestnut and wavy; he wore a closely trimmed silken beard of darker chestnut, verging upon auburn. His lip was full and smiling; he kept a fresh and florid coloring of face, despite some months of New Mexico sun. Altogether, Uncle Ben noted, he bore a precise resemblance to King James of Flodden Field, not to be missed by any who had known both men. Nor did the likeness end with face and form. Open-handed, freespoken, Kinny Apgar met the world with a jovial face, hail-fellow-well-met. He was accepted as "good fellow" by Cutter and clubhouse, Engle and Elephant Butte. Uncle Ben, alone, was not quite convinced. Uncle Ben's leisured thought found Apgar's pleasant manners not quite friendly, but a thing lesser and meaner than friendly; affable—almost gracious.

"You see," said Uncle Ben, hesitating, "some of them old-timers are dead. And the rest of 'em—they're alive. I wouldn't just like to tell the ugly stories. And I don't want you to think I was bragging, like you would if I'd tell the other kind."

"Preposterous!" said Apgar. "See here, why don't you come out to the mine and stay with me a while? I wish you would; I would be very glad to have you. I don't suppose you'd care about hunting, at your age. But I'd be glad to get your opinion on my copper-mining proposition. You are experienced in such matters. And when you got better acquainted with me perhaps your shrinking modesty might so far wear off that you could tell me the true story behind some of these wild and highly improbable old tales I hear. It strikes me that we are losing an interesting page of history about you old-timers, and it seems rather a shame."

Uncle Ben shook his head. "There were lively lads here long before my people, and others beyond them. All forgotten; no complaint. And mind you, for any tale I might relate you can go off a hundred mile and find another eyewitness who will tell you the same yarn, only with everything exactly opposite. My good men would be his skunks, and my skunks would be his good men, and he'd believe every word of his yarn, same as I would mine. Liars don't do much harm; it's honest men that get themselves believed."

"You do not take your history very seriously, it would appear," smiled the patrician.

"Who, me? History? Say, mister—take Teddy Cæsar or Woodrow Cromwell or Oliver Roosevelt or Julius Wilson—ask about them from the men who lived in their days. Try it once. You'll find out—just what you're looking for. Also, you'll find out what kind of a jasper your informant is—and maybe a little side light on yourself if you're right quick. History? Ever hear twin brothers explain to the old man how came they fighting? That's history. There! I'm hoggin' all the talk, as usual. I'm done."

"But your talk is very interesting indeed," protested the patrician. "It stimulates thought. We do hear conflicting stories, don't we? Even under oath. And for myself, I only wish I might be of the party when you visit this gentleman's mine." Here he bowed to Apgar. "I'm sure I would enjoy some of your old stories."

"Nothing easier," said the mine owner. "The latchstring is out, and the welcome's on the mat! Apgar is my name."

"And mine is Bowman, sir," said the patrician, grasping Apgar's extended hand. "If I stay here long enough—and if you can persuade your friend to talk—and if he absolutely will not do his talking here—your invitation is accepted with pleasure."

"Oh, excuse me; Mr. Teagardner, Mr. Bowlin. Mr. Bowlin," said Apgar, "is a lifelong friend of mine for the last sixty seconds."

"Bowman," corrected Bowman. "Pleased to meet you, Mr. Teagardner. I would like very much ——"

The door opened and five or six townsmen trooped in, laughing and chattering. Bowman frowned. The rain was a drizzle now, but the day was dark, the clouds were black and heavy; thunder muttered in the far-off hills, dulled by the closing door. The newcomers disposed of themselves, each to his own whim, on chair or counter.

"I would like very much," resumed Bowman, "to hear authentic stories of the wild old days in this country. Though I am by way of being in the cattle business—in fact, I am trying to pull off a deal with Mr. Carpenter, here—I am merely an agent, and neither myself nor my principals—Chicago men—are conversant with the old conditions. What I have heard has excited my curiosity. Of course, in my reading ——" He shrugged his shoulders eloquently. "You know how that is: The temptation of all romancers in this field of fiction is to deal in heroism of the most hyperbolic character. This melodramatic, reckless courage ——"

"Have you no eyes?" demanded Uncle Ben tartly. "That line of talk makes me tired! Do take a look! All the romantic heroes of all the books, all these reckless here-goes-nothing boys you read about, have been discounted and put to shame every day for the last four years! Not one little, lousy, pot-bellied poilu, not one beer-fat Heinie, not one little stunted London cockney but has seen more hell and stood up under it better than all the swashbucklers of all the books put together."

"And that's true too!" said Apgar warmly. "If they can only hold the damned Huns until the Yanks are ready! This last terrible drive! Perhaps I should not say it, but I wish America had never got into this war!"

"I go further than that," said Uncle Ben. "I wish Germany had never got into it."

"It looks bad—bad!" Bowman shook his head sadly. "The cursed boches are terrible fighters—terrible! And their military leadership far outclasses anything on our side.

"Think of the ghastly blunders of the Allies! Or our own, for that matter. Why didn't we get our soldiers over there in time—tell me that, will you?"

"Hey! Come out of it! You're seein' things!" said Teagardner. "Our boys are there in time. They're going over ten thousand a day, and they'll fight like hell. Don't make no mistake. The Allies were all right alone, but when America joined in, right then the outfit changed its name to the Entente Terrible. You keep your shirt on. The Channel ports are enough sight safer'n Berlin is; and no boner the Allies ever pulled was so ghastly as the blunder the Germans made when they started this war. Here, you come back to earth. I wasn't aimin' to start no roughhouse. Just discussin' books."

"Why, so we were, Uncle Ben. I let my feelings run away with me, I guess," apologized Apgar. "The strain and anxiety of the last few weeks have played the mischief with my nerves."

"I was rather hysterical myself," admitted Bowman. "You see, ... I have a boy over there. I can't bear to talk about it. Let's go back to the books. I do not quite get your point, Mr. Teagardner."

"It is hard to tell which has done the most to civilization, the cider press or the printing press," said Uncle Ben, drawling. "Books, some of them, are mighty silly, and they spread a heap of wrong ideas. But they don't spread any wrong ideas about men being brave. Because they can't. Most all men are brave—east, west, north, south or in the middle, Europe, Orup or Irup. If you'll promise not to scream I'll say—the Germans are brave. Brave as hell. Most all men have a heap more courage than brains, any time and any place. Our boys out here were like the rest, no better and no worse. Human nature is the same here and now as always—like the windmills."

"What about the windmills, Uncle Ben?"

"Don't you know that yet? Listen:

To the windmills said the millwheel,
"As the wind wills do you still wheel?"
"Yes, we still wheel as the wind wills,"
To the millwheel said the windmills.

"Eh? How's that? Say that again."

"I never tell that to any man twice. It works itself out—can't come but the one way. It's logical. Like what I'm tellin' you about the brave and bold in books, includin' the Western brave and bold—and them no more and no less than the brave and bold of any old place. Maybe I'm prejudiced. For myself, I've never exactly understood why longitude isn't counted from the meridian of Mesilla. For our old boys, some of the books misdraw 'em, underdraw them and overdraw them; most of 'em made maybe a little mistake about the boys not having no brains at all. But they don't lie about the old-timer's fighting qualities. It can't be did. Look now! Every thirty mile there used to be at least one man who could ride as good as anyone on earth, and at least one man who could shoot as straight and soon as any man on earth. Just so, there was always at least one man who was just as stubborn a fool as any other man, beginning with Horatius at the bridge party and counting both ways. And that is the truth."

"That settles it. You have to come out to the Rocking-Horse and tell me—us," laughed Apgar. "Your statements are too general. We want particulars."

"Rocking-Horse? That the name of your mine? Is it at the old Rocking-Stone? It is? I'll come—some day when I feel peart."

"I'll bring the car any day."

"Never mind your car. I can fork a right gentle horse fourteen or fifteen mile, old as I am. Say, it's been all of thirty-five year since I last saw the Rocking-Stone. Queer freak, isn't it? And they tell me you've built a wagon road up from Crocker and over the divide, and down to the river—the lake, that is—and haul water from there. Why, you might have saved that last road-building job. There's a little spring up in the cliffs, not a mile from the Rocking-Stone. Never found it? I'll be out; I'll show you. It's a mighty little spring, but you haven't a big ore crew—so I hear."

"Come out tomorrow," said Apgar heartily.

It seemed to Uncle Ben that the stranger, Bowman, flashed an impatient glance at Apgar; a glance between frown and scowl. But Uncle Ben was not sure. For some minutes the store had grown dark and darker, though it was midafternoon. Without, the wind had died to an uneasy stillness, broken by slow growling of thunder; pale lightnings flickered through the windows. It was by such trembling flare that Uncle Ben had seen or fancied that brief glance of Bowman's. An arrogant glance; disapproving?—commanding? Why? Uncle Ben stored it away for future consideration.

"Hell, it's gettin' too dark," said Clayton cheerfully. "I'll light up. We're goin' to get a reg'lar old lallapalooza!"

As the lamps were being lit, one after another, the silent plebeian rose from his nail keg and sauntered across the floor. His hands were in his pockets; his gray hat tilted slightly to one side, and the wide brim of it turned sharply up to a bold curve in front. A lean, hard, brown and sinewy plebeian, this; and the careless, springy, unhurried walk of him was like a leopard's. He paused before the mine owner.

"What's the chance for me to get a job at your layout, Mr. Apgar? I'm a miner."

Uncle Ben looked past Apgar to Bowman. Bowman frowned again; an almost imperceptible frown, easy to explain in the case of a man accustomed to deference. The stranger, in gait, pose, eye and tone, bore himself with a carelessness which might well have been termed insolence by the great.

Apgar considered the plebeian attentively.

"Any credentials?"

"Sure-lee!" laughed the stranger. Taking his hands from his pockets he spread them out, palms up. His right forefinger slowly followed and pointed out the calloused places on the fingers of his left hand; his left forefinger performed the same service for his right hand. "Worked six months at my last place—seven years at the one before that." He pulled from his pocket a fat buckskin purse and shook from it a brave music of jingling silver; he flexed his arm and offered a swelling biceps to Apgar's unresponsive fingers; he thrust out a healthy tongue for inspection. "Well?"

"Young man, you pick out a strange way to ingratiate yourself."

"Back up! I'm not trying to ingratiate myself. You must have misunderstood me. I'm not asking a favor; I'm applying for a job. I know my work and I earn my money. If you don't want to trade, say so. I'm showin' you my goods. Take 'em or leave 'em."

"Young man," said Apgar sternly, "why aren't you in the Army?"

"Past the draft age."

"You're a fine American!" broke in Bowman, hotly scornful. "You're a disgrace to the name! Why don't you volunteer?"

"You got a job for me, maybe? You say you deal in cattle. I've done some little cow work. No top-hand, but useful."

"You are insolent, sir!"

"You are an old man, sir." The plebeian turned back and cocked a jaunty eye on the mine owner. "How about it, Apgar? Do I get that job?"

"Young man, Mr. Bowman is right. You are insolent. I repeat his question: Why don't you volunteer?"

"Middle-aged man—I did. They turned me down. My name is Cady, by the way. And I'm not so damn young."

"Physically unfit? You don't look it."

"Morally." Cady's tone was cheerful; his eye was clear and steady. "They wouldn't have me because I've been in the pen. That was the place I stayed seven years."

"Innocent, of course?" sneered Apgar.

"Guilty as hell. Stealing cattle, if you want to know. I've paid the score. So that's all square. Here we go fresh. Just so I don't lose no job by some pure soul narratin' how I been a jailbird, I am to tell that first."

"What!" shouted Bowman. He started up and turned to the hotel keeper a face black with rage. "Have I been eating with a convict?"

"Now, now—no need for it to happen again," observed Cady smoothly. "You keep calm, old gentleman. If you don't want to eat with me—wait till I'm done." Cady turned to the crowd, raising his voice a little. "That goes for everybody. Get me?"

White lightning, unbearable, blinding, flamed at breaking window and bursting door; the floor rocked to the crashing thunder stroke; men leaped, shouted, screamed or cursed; lamps flamed high, went out with a tinkle of falling glass; the scorched and crackling air beat up against the walls and recoiled to a shuddering eddy; all at once, as at a signal, a flood of rushing rain pounded on roof and street, and a great wind came roaring, bellowing in.

And in the first trampling uproar of oaths and shouts a voice shrieked at Uncle Ben's elbow:

"*Mein Gott!*"

It was Apgar.

The crowd rushed to the front door. Carpenter reached it first; his bull voice boomed above the driving rain and the clamor of babbling speech. "Struck the old stage station. Thought it was here, sure. It's burning. Deserted, thank God! Me for home. My wife'll be scared half to death!" He plunged out into the storm.

Two men had stayed behind—Cady and Teagardner. In one of

the alcoves a single unquenched lamp burned wan and smoking.
Two hard-bred men; but in that dim light they looked at each other,
white-faced.

"Now see what you done!" roared Uncle Ben, shouting to be
heard above the downpour.

"Did you hear that?" Cady's eyes went by Uncle Ben, to
Apgar's chair.

"Why, yes," said Uncle Ben. "Now you mention it, seems
as if I did hear something. Thunder, I reckon." He put a hand to
Cady's shoulder, turned him and opened a door into a long corridor.
"Son, you run along to your room or the parlor. You done enough
damage for one day. See you presently."

The old man twisted his beard and looked after Cady with a
perplexed and brooding eye. "If I had a little milk," he said wistfully,
"I'd have a little mush—if I had a little meal!"

iii

The storm broke suddenly, after a furious hour. Patches of pale
sunshine glimmered, checkered the plain, grew warmer, kindled,
spread with incredible swiftness. On the summit of Timber Mountain, on the twin summits of Fra Christobal, thin wisps of cloud
lingered; a few thunderheads banked towering against the north.
The western lacy mist dissolved; one after one the long radiant
ranges rose up, tier on tier, blue and purple, their shining summits
edged with fire against the low sun. Looking eastward to the mountain barriers, Oscuro, San Andres, Organ—their steep slopes, facing
that kindly sun, sparkled and glittered as if their wet rocks had been
all burnished gold; and over all bent a cleanwashed, rejoicing sky,
warm and deep and blue.

Uncle Ben Teagardner came across the plaza. He walked slowly
now, he whose step had been once so swift and sure; turning this
way and that, his old eyes, under gray-tufted and shaggy brows,
were alert for each fresh glory of his bright and beautiful world.
Nor were those old eyes unobservant of practical affairs. On trail
after trail little bands of cattle in single file plodded knowingly to
the northeast; to high uncropped grass, heretofore too far from
water.

Now every water hole would be fresh filled and brimming; the
cattle were in high good humor.

"That derned old scoundrel of a hawse of mine is sure goin' to be hard to find," grumbled Uncle Ben. "Just when I need him, too."

Before the Engle Hotel, his chair tipped back against the adobe wall, sat Cady, reading. The old man bent his steps that way.

"Son," said Uncle Ben, "what are they doing now—kissing or killing? Let's see." He lowered himself painfully into a chair, fitted steel-bowed spectacles to his nose and took the book from Cady's hand. "Oh, that? Salt of the Earth? Why, son, that book's about this very identical country here as ever was—buildin' the big dam and all. But do you find any of all this?" He waved a long slow arm at all this. "Not a hint of it. 'Me and my wife, my son John and his wife—us four and no more.' Take it away!"

"I did notice something about son John and his dad, come to think of it," admitted Cady. "How are the good and great by now? Still scandalized?"

"Not them. They allow to make a point of eatin' supper with you and takin' back them hasty words. I been explainin' to 'em that such a course would show a meek and forgiving spirit, besides being wise and prudent. Son, you talked mighty brash, seems to me, for a man lookin' for a job. Still want to work?"

"Surest thing you know!"

"You're hired. You are now working for me."

"You have now hired a jailbird."

"Suits me."

"Me, too. What do I do?"

"Well, now," said Uncle Ben, "so long as you draw pay from me I calc'late you'll do just what I tell you. First off, I want you should kind of stick round and be company for me. It's been a long time since I've heard any real truthful talk. Got so, nowadays, that when a man happens to tell the plain truth about anything, people think he's witty. Or else they think he's aimin' to insult somebody. Most of the very best people can't tell the difference between an upstanding man and an insolent one. It pleased me to hear you mention the neglected truth that to buy a man's work is transacting business and not a giddy generosity. Engle is right lonesome to me now, since the old boys are all gone—and some way, you seem sort of like an old-timer to me."

The young man stared hard at the mountains; when he spoke

it was with a slight thickening of his voice. "That's queer too. I told you what my name is—Cady. That's no pen name. I was the first boy born in Engle. You named me yourself. Joe Cady."

"The hell you say! Why, how you have grown! Old Matt's boy?" Shake!"

"Yes. Dad died before—my trouble. I remember you, Mr. Teagardner."

"Uncle Ben."

"Uncle Ben, then. It doesn't better things much, Uncle Ben, but I want to tell you how about them cattle. I was nicely brilliant drunk; I was all crosswise with the L S D—English outfit and stingy. I thought at the time it would be right witty and joyous—it being the Fourth of July and all—to Americanize their brand. So I rounds up a dozen or so and did some proof reading—like this."

He took out a pencil and made the brand on the title page of "Salt of the Earth." First he printed L S D. A few added strokes changed the three letters to H 8 $. "There you are: Hate Dollars. Coarse work. Alignment poor. H drops way below the line, and the dollar sign sticks out above. Dead give-away. Seven years. I sort of hated it too. I didn't usually steal cattle much—not so that I'd get caught at it."

Uncle Ben nodded sympathetically. "All over now. You said it —we start fresh from here. I'm with you. Well, well! You and I— why, Joe, we're all that's left of the old days in Engle. Such bein' the case, I'll open up a little project I wouldn't name to anyone else. As a matter of civic pride and betterment, I'm hopin' you'll join me in the movement for a smaller Engle."

"Yes?" Cady's eyes narrowed to pin points. "Yes? A smaller Engle? I'm for it. A—er—recent idea of yours?"

"Yes. Just happened to think of it this afternoon."

A purposed pause followed; steady old eyes met steady young eyes.

"When that lightning struck?"

"Just then."

"And the password will be—in English?"

"English. You got a horse, Joe?"

"In Clayton's corral."

"I reckon, then, you and me had, maybe, better ride out after supper and bring in that beef the kid left, before the coyotes get it. He told me where it was, and I can get his two horses. It will be a chance to have a little talk. Quite a talk. I don't ride as fast as I used to, some way. I got an old stick of a pony, myself, a natural pacer. I can manage a fair gait on him; he's mighty easy. But he's loose on the flat. Get him to-morrow. Think maybe I'll go out to Rocking-Horse and see Apgar's mine."

"Yes. Here he comes now, with Mr. Bowlin."

"Bowman."

"Bowman; yes. Guess supper is about ready."

They rose to go, but Apgar hailed them. "Hi! Wait a minute! We are just going in to dinner."

Joe and Uncle Ben waited. On arrival Bowman's bearing was as stiff and sullen as Apgar's was frank and open.

"A word with you, Mr. Cady—and I speak for Mr. Bowman as well." Bowman bowed. "We wish to express our regret for our hasty utterances this afternoon. We were startled, and that's the fact. Reflection, aided by Uncle Ben's well-grounded counsel, has shown us our mistake. Your candor was as highly creditable as your determination to walk hereafter in honorable ways is praiseworthy. Such a case deserves encouragement; and we freely admit that our reproaches this afternoon were wrong and unjustified."

"That's all right, then," said Joe curtly. "Enough said."

But Apgar continued. "For myself I want to say that the mine has a full crew at present. But should a vacancy occur I will certainly bear you in mind."

"All right," said Cady shortly. But Uncle Ben was less stiff.

"Well said, sir! Handsomely said! Feelin' the same way myself, I have hired Cady for one whirl at least. I have a little prospect out in the Caballo which may develop into something big. But I'm coming out to see you, Apgar—after I show Joe the ropes. How about you, Mr. Bowman? Think you'll make it out to Apgar's diggin's?"

"I fear I shall have to forego that pleasure. I find that my business with Mr. Carpenter is so far forward that a few telegrams may bring it to a head. In any event, I cannot stay long. And I desire by all means to visit your famous dam at Elephant Butte. I am told it is the greatest work of its kind in the world, and the opportunity to see it may not be mine again. Also, if I can find time, I would see the new wagon road through Palomas Gap. The scenery, I am told, is not without a certain rugged grandeur, while the road itself is said to be a notable feat in engineering."

"Yes, indeedy!" chirruped Uncle Ben. "The Gap is worth while." His dreamy eye roved to the sharp outlines of Palomas Gap, coming back to rest speculatively on Mr. Bowman. "Some sightly places on the big lake too," murmured Uncle Ben. "Have you seen our hanging gardens?"

iv

It was not until the third day that Uncle Ben's Sleepycat horse was driven in, though all the Broad A men had been keeping an eye out for him. When found, Sleepycat had been twenty miles away. Still in the pasture, to be sure; but he might have drifted twice that distance and still have been in the pasture.

Saddled and droop-hipped, Sleepycat stood before an open door at the side of the old Bar Cross house; a mahogany-brown horse, broad between the eyes, sleek and plump. He was well on in years, but his sedate and knowing eye retained a hint of former levities and seemed to twinkle with complacent memories.

Sleepycat was fifteen and a half hands high; large for a New Mexican horse. Uncle Ben was no giant now—gaunt, withered and bent; but he was still too heavy for anything in the pony class.

Uncle Ben came out with a canteen, which he hung on the saddle horn; a slicker, which he tied behind the cantle; a rifle scabbard, which he slung under the stirrup leathers, on the off side; and the great-grandfather of all rifles, which he thrust into the scabbard. Long ago, for service rendered, the Bar Cross had transferred to Uncle Ben, in fee simple, one room of these many rooms. And in the locked room that old rifle, an old saddle, an old trunk, with other belongings, had waited for Uncle Ben's return.

Teagardner climbed into the saddle and rode slowly across the plaza. Gay hands waved greetings from open doors as he passed; and the elderly stranger, Bowman, spoke from the hotel porch:

"Give my regards to Apgood, Mr. Teagardner. And good luck to yourself; I'll not be seeing you again. I'm going tomorrow. Good-by!"

"Good-by," said Teagardner.

Beyond the station he turned northward through the morning sun, on a wagon road that kept by the side of the railroad track.

"Don't be too sure you won't see me again," he muttered into his beard. "I think mebbe you will. Apgood? Bowlin? Humph! Queer that both should get the names mixed. . . . Too smart! Them two fellers are sure advertisin' that they're rank strangers to each other. Overplayed the hand. Patriotic too. Dear, yes! . . . Of the two, Bowman is the boss, I reckon. . . . Let me think."

He fell silent, frowning. He passed the cut at One Mile Hill; on the downward slope Sleepycat broke into a shuffling dust-raising pace, and Uncle Ben crooned a low chant under his breath in time to the shuffling feet:

> *If you go to meeting or mill,*
> *Same old Bennie will be with you still—*
> *Bennie!*

At Three Mile he kept to the left, climbing a long slow ridge thrusting out from the southern bastion of Fra Christobal, while the railroad made a wide detour to the right, avoiding that same ridge.

"What do you know about Apgar, old Sleepycat? . . . Too slick and plausible? That's nothing. . . . Never was any good mineral found in the whole derned Christobal mountain? That's nothing. Rich mines been found in country prospected over for years and done given up as N. G. Cripple Creek—Creede. . . . Lonesomest place in New Mexico? Yes, because it's the ugliest place in New Mexico. Only ugly mountain I ever saw or heard tell of. I never liked to go prospecting there, myself. . . . Men workin' for him all strangers? Why shouldn't they be? . . . Gets supplies from the switch at Crocker, where there's no one lives, no section house even, or telegraph office or nothin'—just a passing track? . . . Sensible thing to do. Do it myself if I was mining in Saddle Gap. Saves freighting through this sand from Engle. . . . But his men never come to Engle on Sundays? . . . Now you've said something. . . . Always play-actin'—and sneerin', way down deep, at the ignorant yokels? . . . Always. Clever man, Apgar. And that brand-new lake just beyond him—only ten or twelve miles to drift down the lake to Engle Dam? . . . Not so loud! . . . And, mining that way, he'll have plenty dynamite—this man that talks to God in German? Hush! Sleepycat, you damn old fool, it's up to you and me and Joe Cady. We don't know one blessed thing, but we're goin' to find out."

He came to the top of the ridge; he looked back to the southwest, to where, out of sight beyond the Jornada rim, Engle Dam held back the prisoned waters of the great lake; he looked south to where, beyond the shining mountains, the long, long valley lay below the dam, clustered with homes; his old face hardened to steel.

If you go for to kiss or kill,
Bennie!
If you go for to kiss or kill,
Put your back into wish and will!
Bennie!

At his left the desolate gray cliffs of Fra Christobal hung above him; then the lower hills of Saddle Gap, tumbled and broken, where already he could see the climbing, hairpin curves of Apgar's new wagon road, white with new-cut limestone. Rising beyond Saddle Gap huddled the featureless bulk of Further Christobal, shapeless, treeless and forlorn.

Northward from the ridge where Uncle Ben stood the land dipped down to a white saccaton flat, with Little Round Mountain squatting beyond a gleaming tangent of railroad, and Crocker sidetrack under Round Mountain. A single car was set out on Crocker sidetrack. Beyond the shining tangent, Lava Station, section house and water tank loomed high in the north, far and magnified; the railroad, crossing the white flat, climbed in a long sweeping curve up the low black slope of the Mal Pais to the cut in the first bold rampart of lava that circled Lava Station. Where the railroad left the straightaway for the curve, a wide and shallow valley led away to the northwest, past the tip of Further Christobal, twenty miles away. It was checked with patches of grassland and patches of grassless land, white and glazed; and through this valley, straight and plain, far-seen, ran a broad highway that had once been the Santa Fé Trail. Silent now and forsaken, valley and road, mysterious, promising, beckoning, vanished into the unknown depths beyond Christobal. Uncle Ben felt a pang in his tough old heart; there Paraje once lay, where that old valley fell away to the deeper sunken valley of the Río Grande; Paraje, "the pleasant camping ground." Now Paraje was under forty feet of water, at the bottom of a man-made lake;

and those pleasant faces of long ago—all gone! Uncle Ben raised his bridle hand:

> *If you go to heaven or hell,*
> *Say, "Good morning, and I wish you well!"*

He left the wagon road and turned across the broken country toward Saddle Gap. "I'd sure like to see what old Apgar's got in that freight car at Crocker," he confided to Sleepycat. "But unless you and me miss our guess, these geezers will be keepin' cases on us. We got to be innocent as hell. We want 'em to see where we took all short cuts. That's natural. Us for the roughs!"

> *When you come to Heaven's great gate, Bennie!*
> *When you come to the golden gate,*
> *Make your manners—an' then stand up straight!*
> *Make your manners, and look up and say,*
> *"I've done my work and I want my pay!"*

It was ten o'clock when Uncle Ben came into Apgar's new wagon road from Crocker, where it toiled up a long ridge. Saddle Gap is steep and high, and the road had need for many a double and twist and zigzag to find distance enough so that the grade should not be impossibly steep. It was close upon noon when Uncle Ben came to the divide, and between the steep sides of a rugged defile caught a glimpse of the broad blue lake far below. Engle Dam backs up the water for forty miles upstream, crowding against Christobal Mountains for their entire length.

Once turned down the western slope, the mountains became less bleak. The narrow defile became a twisting cañon, deep and wide; crowned by gray cliffs; it broadened into broken country and a winding pass, with here and there a cedar tree. The pass closed in suddenly and was a cañon again, deeper and wider now, cool and dark, between higher hills and wilder cliffs; plunging down and down in sweeping S shaped curves, gathering mass and momentum at each bend and steep; at a last swirling curve breaking from the cool deeps into a vast sunlit amphitheater, walled about by crest and precipice, with one great gateway to the west, and beyond that gateway, near and low, the long levels of the lake.

At Uncle Ben's right, where the cliffs ended that had made the northern wall of the cañon, the Rocking-Stone loomed high and ominous; a huge granite boulder of indeterminate shape, poised on a pivot like a monstrous top. Uncle Ben's eyes raised instinctively to this sinister and threatening silhouette, clear-cut and sharp against the sky line.

Rocking-Horse camp lay at Uncle Ben's left, on the other saucer slope, a low huddle of buildings at the hill foot, with the mine dump close above. Uncle Ben turned Sleepycat's head that way; two or three men appeared at the door of the long bunk house; one of them called, and Apgar came striding down the trail to meet him.

"Welcome to our city! You waited so long I thought maybe you had changed your mind again."

"Couldn't find my horse."

"You must be pretty tired," said Apgar, turning back. "Where's your man Cady?"

"Well, yes, I am—sorter," admitted Teagardner. "Cady? I done rigged him out with a little old buckboard and sent him out to put a couple of Mex boys to doin' assessment work on my claim. Sent him out the day you left. He's coming right back, though, soon's he gets the *paisanos* organized. I'm expectin' a man to look at the claim next week."

"Baker, come and take care of this horse. Mr. Teagardner, meet Mr. Baker. For the love of Mike, Uncle Ben, what have you got strapped to your saddle—a cannon?"

Uncle Ben crawled painfully from the saddle, straightened his aged joints and pulled the rifle from the scabbard. "That's my old Sharps, Mr. Apgar," he said proudly. "Heft her once."

Apgar took the gun, squinted along the heavy octagonal barrel, balanced it and whistled. "Why, it's a regular Big Bertha! Where'd you get it?"

"Always had it. Nobody ever owned that gun but me. That's what they called a 'Buffalo Gun': 45–120–420."

"Forty-five how much?"

"Forty-five caliber—a hundred and twenty grains of black powder—four hundred and twenty grains of lead. Throws a slug as big as a jackknife; kill a buffalo at a mile. Weighs sixteen pounds; else she'd kick like a mule. Here's the cartridge."

He took from his belt a bottle-necked cartridge. It was nearly five inches long.

"Well," laughed Apgar, "this is a new one on me."

"You'll not see many like this nowadays. Old-fashioned—like me. I left this behind my last trip, but I left her mighty nigh packed in oil. Good shape now as she ever was. Best gun ever made."

Apgar threw back the lever opening the breech mechanism; he looked into the polished spotless barrel. He glanced appreciatively at the front sight, which was of ivory. "It ought to do good shooting, anyway."

"Shoot good? Why Mr. Apgar, you can measure with that gun! When you set the sights at twelve hundred yards, say, why, if you get your meat, then you know it was just twelve hundred yards even. She shoots where you hold her. I'll let you try her."

"But, Uncle Ben, how can you know whether to set your sights for twelve hundred yards or nine hundred yards? I can't distinguish the difference between four hundred yards and three hundred."

Uncle Ben blinked his eyes, took off his sombrero and scratched his head. "Why—I don't know as I can exactly tell you. You—you just sorter know how far it is, I guess."

Apgar laughed again. "Well, come to the cookhouse and we'll have the eats. I'll give you a knockdown to the boys. I've been telling them about you. You'll want to rest up this afternoon. Tomorrow we'll take a look round."

The bunkhouse, with a single room, sixteen feet by forty—the cookhouse, something smaller—the blacksmith shop and the manager's shack, a cubicle with two rooms and office—these gave shelter to the Rocking-Horse force. All were built of rough boards, battened, unpainted, roofed with corrugated iron. There was also a small corral, one side of which was formed by a long shed, shared amicably by baled hay and Apgar's battered car. A long half mile away, on the circling slope of northern hills, Uncle Ben marked roof and door of the buried powder house.

By the cookhouse door stood a water wagon, a galvanized-iron tank on wheels—far different from the clumsy and cumbrous wooden affairs of earlier days. Two hobbled horses grazed on the shaded hillside above the mine.

"I'll hobble my old stick with your saddle ponies, I reckon," said Uncle Ben after dinner. "No use of feeding him your good baled hay. He'll stick round."

"Then we can take a look at the ore as we come back," said Apgar.

"All right. How does your copper mine pan out, anyhow?"

"Why—not very well, just now. The ore looked pretty good for the first fifty feet—almost good enough to ship. Naturally I hoped it would get better as we went down. But it didn't. Just about the same as it was at the grass roots, and the vein no wider; in fact the vein nearly pinched out on us once."

"How deep are you now?"

"Not deep at all. Only a hundred and ten feet or so."

Uncle Ben blinked. "Oh, well, then you're just started. No need to be gettin' discouraged yet."

"Just getting ready to start, you might say. So far, most of our work has been making the wagon road and knocking camp together. That's done now, and we can go on with the development."

"Not a very big gang, I judge?"

"Only eight, besides Billy, the cook, and Kendall, the teamster."

"That's right smart of a road you built, Mr. Apgar, if it is a little straight upandicular in spots.

"Use mules for your teams?"

"Yes, we have a six-mule team. Kendall went for a load of freight yesterday. You saw the tracks, of course. He'll get into camp along about sundown."

"And then someone forks one of your horses and drives your mules down to the lake for water? I see."

Uncle Ben got on his knees, hobbled Sleepycat, and rose up creakingly.

"All right, Mr. Apgar, suh! Lead me to your little old mine. How did you come to locate here anyhow? Stumble on it yourself?"

"Oh, no! Old chap in San Marcial—Springtime Morgan—told me there was some pretty good-looking stuff here. He agreed to show me the place, and I was to give him a hundred if I liked it and wages if I didn't. He got the hundred. Now we'll look at the ore dump and go down the shaft. Then comes the story telling. You don't want to forget that."

"Oh, I suppose so, if you insist. But I tell you right now that's no good way to get a real story. All you get by violence is maybe the skeleton of a story. What you want to do is just let the conversation drift and ooze along, easy and natural. Then, when your man gets strung out and goin' good, you want to act sort of bored, like you had a better story of your own you wanted to tell, and yawn a little, behind your hand, careful. Then you'll get results!"

V

The shots of the day shift were the call to supper, shots of the night shift the summons to rise and shine in the morning. Breakfast over, Banner of the day shift remained behind to help Kendall unload the freight wagon, and afterward to sharpen drills; Green, Dorsey and Case trudged to the shaft, two to work the windlass and one to fill the bucket; while the night shift drifted away to the bunk house. Apgar and Uncle Ben saddled up and drove the mules and the extra horse to the lake.

There was more skillful engineering through that westward break in the circle of hills which fenced Rocking-Stone Valley. This time the road did not follow the deep cañon floor, but kept to a level in a dugaway blasted out along the northern slope. Passing this last barrier it came out on a broad wedge of mesa—a triangle, with the lake for base, sloping gently to the water's edge; below the cañon turned sharply to the left to join the lake long miles southward.

"Except for a strip at the foot of this bench, the shore line of the lake looks like a fever chart along here, where it backs up between the ridges," said Apgar. "And the islands—see them? About a dozen here and there, where there was a bump or a knoll on the submerged ridges. All the way from a hundred yards to a mile from the mainland. There's the biggest one, to the right—the flat-topped one with the cedars on it. There's a big black lava island nearly a mile square, down the river a bit. You can see it after a while."

"Ever go out to explore them?"

"Oh, yes—some of them; in duck-shooting time, and fishing, sometimes. I've got a boat down here. But I'm pretty busy—don't use it much. The boys splash round on Sundays, sometimes, when they go down to swim. Looks different here than it used to in your day, doesn't it?"

"Yes—except that I never was up behind this mountain much," said Uncle Ben. "Not north of here, anyway. I reckon this strip between the river and the Christobals, and from here to Paraje, must ha' been the lonesomest place on the whole world. I made the trip once, and that was enough for me. Far as that goes, I never did hear of anyone else going through here—though I suppose plenty of 'em did. Up and down and repeat—cañons and *barrancas* and mesquite thickets—roughest place I ever see. Too rough to run cattle. Frank Hill run the Heart-Diamond stock from here south for a year or two, I'm told. But that was while I was gone. The old Gonzales settlement was the furthest north in my day. Hello! The road splits here! Where does that right-hand fork go to?"

"That's where we get our wood, up in the ridges to the north," said Apgar carelessly.

Uncle Ben did some swift thinking, of which his wizened old brown face gave no sign. The wood road was as well worn as the water road; yet the camp would use comparatively little wood. Again, there was wood, scattered but plentiful enough, in the open country above Rocking-Stone, halfway from the camp to the summit. Now why would anyone choose to haul wood uphill rather than down?

Aloud he said contemplatively: "Someone will try running cattle in here again some of these days, now there's water everywhere, and the *bosques* all drowned, where cattle used to go wild on us. You'll see! The west slope of the Christobal isn't on the Armendaris grant—know that?"

"Certainly I do. There's an offset here, and the line runs along the crest of Christobal Mountains. But what it was ever laid out that way for—that is what I will never tell you."

"That's easy," said Uncle Ben. "Old Armendaris, he took one look on this side and that was aplenty. 'I gotta draw the line somewhere,' he says to the King of Spain, 'and I draw it right here. Nothing west of the Christobals' he says. 'The United States is a-goin' to start up business in a hundred years or so, maybe,' he says. 'Another hundred years after that, and they'll have this country—and then do you suppose I want to pay taxes on the whole dum Christobal Mountain? Not much!' he says. But about them cattle—look at this! Throw a string of wire fence from the south end of the mountain to the river—and you could make the grant people build half if you built it on the line. Then fence up that box cañon above Rocking-Stone, and somebody'd have a powerful big pasture, cheap, even if it is a mighty rough one. Why don't you tackle it yourself?"

"Me? Oh, I'm no cowman."

"You think it over," urged Uncle Ben, sparkling with enthusiasm. "You done got your wagon road made, and that removes the biggest drawback to a ranch here. Grass, water and fence, a good road to your door ready made—what more do you want? No jungles of cottonwood and mesquite or tornillo for stock to hide out in now, like there used to be. All at the bottom of the lake. And that spring I was tellin' you about—it's up in the pinnacles beyond your powder house—pipe that down and make Rocking-Stone Valley your home ranch—fine! Pity you hadn't known about Squawberry Spring. Might have saved five hundred dollars' worth of wagon road. I'll take you up and show you that spring this afternoon."

"Some other time, if you don't mind," said Apgar. "I've got some letters to write this afternoon. And later, after the night shift wakes up, I'd like to try out that rifle of yours. I want to have Kendall try a few long shots, too. He's a marksman. But he will have to come down here this afternoon to fill up the water wagon."

"Well, you turn that cattle proposition over in your mind," enjoined Teagardner. "That wagon road must ha' cost you four or five thousand perfectly good plunks, all told. And if your mine fizzles on you, that's how you save part of your losings. Start the Rocking-Stone Cattle Company. I'll take a few shares myself."

"I'll think about it," smiled Apgar. "Here we are at the lake. Here's where he drives in to fill up his tanks—rock bottom, you see. And there's my boat, tied to that juniper tree. Pretty good boat for a homemade one, isn't it?"

"It is so. You make it yourself?"

"Dear me, no! I'm no carpenter. One of the men on the night shift made it—Miller, the big fellow. It's pretty large—hard for one man to manage unless he is used to boats. But I figured some of the boys would like to go fishing Sundays."

That target practice was destined never to take place. An hour after Apgar and Uncle Ben returned to camp a buckboard rattled out of Rocking-Stone Cañon; a shackly one-seated buckboard with a shabby top from an old buggy toggled clumsily to the seat for the sake of shade. A big canteen was strapped to the ribs of the buggy top, sharing the shade with a 30–40 rifle; two nose bags and a feed of grain in a gunny sack, for all cargo, were tied by two neck ropes to the iron railing behind the seat; and Joe Cady was the driver.

The team, a pair of spanking buckskins, contrasted oddly with the patched harness and the shabby rig.

Cady brought his pair to a halt at the corral gate.

"Mornin', folks!" he said. "Telegram for you, Uncle Ben. Operator allowed mabbe I'd better carry it out to you. He knowed what was in it, whether it was big medicine or not. So I up and come."

Teagardner opened the brown envelope and scanned the contents swiftly.

"Shucks! I got to go," he said with some vexation. "Wouldn't that jar you?"

He handed the message to Apgar, who read:

> Trinidad, Colorado, July 31, 1918
> Ben Teagardner,
> Engle, New Mexico
> Cannot come Engle this trip. Meet me Albuquerque, Aug. 2.
> A. K. Witherspoon, Jr.

"And this is the first of August! Drat the luck!" cried Uncle Ben. "I bet I never do see that old eel in Engle. He'll be draggin' me back to Colorado with him. You see how it is, Apgar. I've got to quit you."

"Sorry to lose your company, Mr. Teagardner. You'll stay till after dinner, of course. Unhitch your team, Cady. We can spare you water for them from the tank."

"I brought along your mail, Mr. Apgar. Thought you'd want it. And this morning's paper. Here's the headlines: 'Huns in retreat along the whole Front north of the Marne. The Frenchies and the Yanks drive nine miles northeast of Chateau-Thierry, and two north of Fere-en-Tardenois'—crossed the Ourcq River, and captured Sergy and a heap more of them towns. German papers please copy. And there is a movement on foot," said Cady, dropping the tugs, "to provide every German soldier with a Wooden Cross."

"Bully!" said Apgar.

"The treacherous, bloody dogs!" said Uncle Ben as the buckboard crunched slowly up the grade in the box of Rocking-Stone Cañon. Uncle Ben sat with Cady; Sleepycat, at the end of a lead rope, followed behind.

"Apgar tipped his hand, then?"

"Tipped his hand? The damned murderer spread it out, face up, a dozen times. Didn't know where Squawberry Spring is! But old Springtime Morgan brought him here, by his tell. And Springtime wouldn't miss showin' him that spring once in a million chances—not to mention that anybody in the world camping there would find it right away. Son, I've felt it in my bones all the time, and so have you. All the same, it seems monstrous to put it in cold words—but this whole play is an alibi. What they plan is to blow up Engle Dam and drown fifty thousand people. Takin' six months to play it safe—fixin' to be above all suspicion."

"Evidence?" remarked Cady. "I had suspicions aplenty of my own, just by instinct—same as a colt knows his first rattlesnake or a chicken knows a hawk. I'm strong for hunches. A man that won't play his hunch is blind in one eye. All the same, if you've got any facts on hand, trot 'em out."

"The powder house is nigh a mile from camp—just as far away as they could get it and stay in the valley. Something there besides dynamite; TNT, mebbe—or some other high explosive we don't know about. Perhaps that's why they've waited so long—till they could smuggle in the stuff a little at a time—though God only knows where they get it. Dynamite, of course, they can get tol'able easy—for minin'."

"One fact and one good guess. Any more facts?"

"The night shift wasn't asleep when I come, and the night shift didn't sleep much this morning, and the night shift didn't work last night. Set off four or five sticks of loose powder with a little trash on 'em, thinkin' I wouldn't know the difference—and me a miner since I was a boy in Pontypridd! Then the whole delirious shootin'-match—no card playin', throwing horseshoes, singin'; no fun, no joking—quiet and still. Close corporation; no new men to work; none quit in six months; none of 'em ever came down to Engle once. Not natural."

"One big fact and some interestin' observations. Yes?"

"Goin' down to the river," shrilled Uncle Ben wrathfully, "their new road splits. Right-hand prong wanders off into the lonesome north. For wood, says Apgar. No man on earth ever hauled wood up a two-thousand-foot climb without a reason—not with plenty wood up here to haul downhill. Whatever is wrong, that wood road leads to it.

"Another thing—down where they get their water they've got a boat; a first-class little boat that they made themselves. That boat is done finished, but in the tool house at camp, all the carpenter's tools a man would use in making a boat are now missing. Tally?"

"Three perfectly good facts," said Cady respectfully.

"I'm going to use those facts. Watch me! Say, drive slow and stop once in a while. I want time enough to have our talk out. Because I'm going to quit you when we get to the upper end of the box, and go back over the cliffs to see what is doing, while you go on into town. Ten to one they follow us up to watch us. You got that spyglass and grub?"

"Under the seat, everything just as you told me. Better let me take that hill job, Uncle Ben. You're pretty old for climbing and sleeping out."

"Pish! I know these hills like the palm of my hand. I've prospected this country out; I can get back and overlook that camp and never set my foot down except on a rock. You'd leave tracks somewhere. Say, who's bossing this outfit, you or me?"

"You, every time, Uncle Ben. You've got it over me nine ways from the jack. You tell me what to do and I'll do it."

"I got something for you to do presently that will take all your time," said Uncle Ben grimly. "Now to go back to our facts. You haven't forgotten them?"

"Nary a fact."

"These facts, then, force me to think about as follows: They've built a heap bigger boat—or are building it now—with those missing carpenter's tools—up in the lonesome country, where their wood road goes. My guess is the boat is finished and floated off behind one of the islands—the lake's full of islands—to be out of sight, where no man will happen on to it. I guess that they're now loading that boat with dynamite in the nth degree; that they've been waiting for the rains to fill the lake brimful, to do the utmost damage when it breaks; that they are waiting the dark of the moon. Along about with the third, fourth and fifth of August there will be no moon to speak of. I judge they won't wait any for the entirely moonless nights. They must be weary of waiting. I judge that they mean to work their barge down halfway or more the first night, mooring behind the big island below Alamocito—where that big square flat-topped lava butte used to be; that the next night they work her down to the dam, by or before midnight, lower their weighted explosive to the level of the lower sluice gates, wired to an electric battery that'll be adjusted for a time explosion that will blow up the dam just before daybreak. They'll take along the little boat, of course, so they can row back and leave no sign."

"Uncle Ben, you guess like an adding machine," said Cady.

"Another thing—their big barge will be painted black, so the watchman on the dam won't see it. And so the barge will harmonize with the big black lava blocks on the Alamocito Island—where they'll hide her out the night before. And so I won't have any facts left on my hands—for I'll not deceive you; all along I've been constructin' my the'ries to fit the known facts,—now I'm going to fit my last unused fact into my the'ry: Son, in the Rocking-Horse tool house was some several cans of black paint, and no cans of any other color, and no paintbrushes. But there isn't one single tor-plagued thing in that camp painted, black or anything else, inside or out."

"That barge," said Joe promptly, "is painted black. Uncle Ben, why don't we go back and shoot 'em now?"

"For one thing, people would likely be askin' questions. What is a good deal more to the point—I don't want to let them off so easy as all that. Son," said Uncle Ben earnestly, "I'm aimin' to hurt them fellows. They've not done right. There's ten of them, not counting Apgar. At least half of 'em, besides Apgar, will stay behind to make a showin' if somebody should happen to stray into camp—though I reckon nobody ever does, from what they tell me, except them that Apgar drags up here like he did me, so they can bear witness to the innocence of Rocking-Horse. That little boat will nicely hold four; or five, with one at the rudder. Two pairs of oars; they'll figure on making good time coming back here, after the dam is blown up; they can make better time with a steersman. Five to go and five to stay. Joe, if it can be done, we want to manage so any that stay behind will wish hard they'd been the ones that went! I don't just know how yet, but we'll find a way."

"What do I do?" demanded Joe.

"Drive to town. They'll send along a scout to be sure that we really leave. He will see you go and he'll see old Sleepycat tagging along behind. Then they'll proceed to biz—and I'll be up in the cliffs with my spyglass, framing up sorrow for them. You get grub for three days, slip out of Engle to-morrow without exciting any comment, and join me at sundown."

"How'll I get to you without leaving sign?"

"Water leaves no tracks. Clayton keeps a little skiff down where the lake backs up in old Fort McRae Cañon. I'll give you a note to Clayton. You get the key and sidle down to the boat to-morrow. Turn your horse loose and hide your saddle. Row out in the main big lake and paddle along upstream. You know where the old Gonzales place used to be? Well, just east of there is a lava cliff sharp as a knife blade, half a mile long, and high. Only it isn't really a cliff—it's a dike; and it isn't lava, but obsidian. I'll be at the south end of it. By that time I ought to have the proper dope or the makings of it. That's all. Drive on."

A few minutes later, where the road was cut in the southern hillside, Joe stopped his buckboard at the upper end of the box, with the hub against a limestone ledge. He stood up; Uncle Ben raised the cushion, and from the little box under the seat took out a cloth flour sack, partly filled, and his ancient field glass with its leather case and strap. He slipped the strap over his head, picked up his rifle and his canteen, and stepped up to the rocky ledge; Joe handed him the grub sack.

"Hadn't you better take the big canteen, Uncle Ben?"

Teagardner grinned. "I told that baby killer about Squawberry, but I didn't tell him about Hidden Spring. That's up in the cliffs on this side. And the oldest man in the world couldn't tell the smartest one how to find it. That's another reason why you go to town and I don't."

"That old buffalo gun is mighty heavy. Don't you want mine?"

"I'm used to this gun. And you're used to yours. We might need 'em. I've got all the time there is. You drive on! No, wait! One thing more: Apgar & Co. have made a mistake and I may be making another one. We can't always sometimes tell. If anything should happen to me, Joe—don't you forget Brother Bowman! He is mixed up in this or worse. You keep his memory gangrene!"

vi

In the Book of Revelations, where Christobal Mountain is the footnote to a page, the undergraduate may read, among other things, how the earth contracted as it cooled and how the hardened outer crust of it, slow-sinking as it shrank to fit the denser central mass, left occasional surplus feet or miles of needless circumference. Then, where the crust was weak, those surplus feet or miles buckled and crumpled to wrinkles, such as we name Himalaya, Rocky or Andes; buckled and crimped, with arch and dip and fold, with lap and weld and overthrust. Outer miles of surface rock, sedimentary layers, cool and brittle, water-born, heaved up as a trapdoor is raised, bending, cracking, breaking to fold and splintered fault.

Deeper, the fire-born rock, held down by the enormous weight above, without room either to break or melt, yet forced to yield, was crushed together, the seamless rock interpiercing to greater density and a different texture; at the last, incompressible yet still compressed, was squeezed out and upward as paste is squeezed from a tube; was shoved up, irresistible, in dike or boss of granite, syenite, porphyry or gneiss, cleaving or lifting the mass above, shouldering it aside, fusing to living fire at the first touch of air, and stabbing upward in a last flaming thrust to stars and sky.

Christobal Mountain is among the least of these wrinkles. Insignificant and remote, it is yet part of the campus; and here, too, the candidate for a degree may find matter for consideration.

The granite circle which walls Rocking-Stone Valley, when it rose, tiptilted to forty-five degrees the thousand ledges of Rocking-Stone Cañon. It follows that if you start at the upper end of the box cañon of the Rocking-Stone—where Uncle Ben stepped from the buckboard—and loiter down that cañon for three miles, until you reach the granite wedge which holds the mountain from falling over, you will see, in those miles of westing, precisely what you would have seen had you journeyed the like distance straight toward the center of the earth; which may possibly lead you to reflection upon the time used for the slow deposit of even one of these thousand tiptilt ledges, soapstone, sandstone, lime or shale; or the slow ages needed to press it from silt to stone.

On the Jornada, wells have been bored to twelve hundred feet. A hollow bit is used, diamond-pointed; a smooth core, three inches in diameter, is brought up as the drill cuts through rock. If you have a roll call of the various strata in Rocking-Stone Box, you may look at the last core and know surely what the next core will be—pudding-stone, quartzite, lime or flint; and how far before the drill strikes the next stratum—making some allowance for the landslip when the mountain was upended.

Another result is that, starting where Uncle Ben started, climbing as he climbed, you find a mountain of rocky steps, jagged, broken and bare; in outline most like a steep roof would be if the shingles were laid with the butts up; and shedding water just as such a roof would shed it. This mountain is known and shunned as Washboard Hill.

Keeping to the bare rock, Uncle Ben turned back to the west again. He climbed the steep ledge for a dozen yards. Here a fallen block of stone made for him a way to a higher ledge. Edging back, that he might not be in sight from the cañon, he toiled up until he came to a favoring sheltered hollow, where a bush of laurel and a starved and stunted cedar made a screen for him on the very brink of the cañon. Uncle Ben crept into this little basin and laid by his burdens, bestowing the canteen carefully on the shady side of a *sotol*.

Cady, letting the buckskins out now to a long swinging walk, was well over in the open country toward the divide. Already the team grew small in the distance, but the sound of their brisk feet came bell-clear across the still and windless air. They passed from sight into the little defile below the summit. Uncle Ben crawled to the cañon's edge and peered cautiously through the laurel.

While he had been climbing west and up for fifteen minutes the cañon had dropped west and down; so that it was already a respectable precipice over which he looked. Looking down, the cañon seemed incredibly steep as it fell away into the box. But the mountain itself rose stiffly with each westward mile; as the floodway plunged deep and deeper, bristling headlands of the cañon wall, jutting to bold cape and promontory, deep-gulfed by chasmed voids of nothingness between, rose high and higher, cliff on cliff, tier on tier; dimming to beauty beyond the pearl-misted abyss of the outmost gulf, but nearer by, all threatening, bleak and grim.

"Dern my eyes!" muttered Uncle Ben. "Here I've never seen the Grand Cañon yet! How silly of me! Deleted ass!"

He turned his eyes to Saddle Gap. Cady was in the open again, on the last steep pitch. He gained the divide, paused there a breathing space, sky-lined sharply against the blue; he dipped swiftly from sight. Uncle Ben waited.

Stir and clamor in the air, a hollow drumming against the cliffs, a rising wave of sound that shaped to the measured beat of horse hoofs, echoed and tossed from wall to high wall. Far below two midget horsemen crawled to view round a curve in the cañon.

An intervening shoulder hid them, the echoes dwindled to a drone; swelled suddenly as the horsemen came out into the nearer reaches of the cañon. Uncle Ben lay very still. They rode at leisure. They came closer; their faces could be seen—Apgar and Banner.

"This is final," said Teagardner softly. "They might be guilty and not do this, or innocent and not do this; they can't be innocent and do this."

They rode down below him; their words reached his hiding place.

"They've gone on, of course," said Banner. "This is rather useless, you know."

"In a way, yes. Not a chance that anything is wrong. Or only one chance out of all possible chances. We cannot afford to take that one chance. From now on we must omit no precaution. Do you keep a sharp lookout that no tracks turn aside. That old man is capable of anything."

"We will be very wary of that dangerous person." The palpable sneer was as much for Apgar as for Teagardner. "Why, if I may ask, did you find it expedient to entertain a fossil so formidable?"

"The man is Nestor, his influence with the community can hardly be overestimated. His word has almost the force of law. That stiff-necked old fool has always disliked me and distrusted me. Now he has seen for himself; his word will silence any chance of questioning about us. Much more to the purpose, he will make no questioning of his own. It could hardly have fallen out better. I had pressed him to a longer stay; his own affairs called him back. So much for that. For the rest, sir, you grow insubordinate. It is not for you to call my acts into question. You forget yourself, I think."

"This endless wait, wait, wait has been the most tedious business of my life," returned Banner sullenly. "Only two days more—thank God for that!"

"It was necessary. Just as it will be necessary for us to stay on for a while afterward."

"For you, doubtless. You are the owner. But I am merely a blacksmith."

"You are under my orders," said Apgar haughtily.

"Until the job is finished—no longer. Then I move on. I am no enlisted man; nor are you an officer. I find you are too patient and painstaking for my temperament." Banner's voice had been raised in anger. Even so, the fossil's straining ears could hardly hear the last sneering words. Apgar's reply, plainly vehement, was unintelligible; the fossil could only make out a word here and there. They rode on.

Uncle Ben twisted a few small tufted twigs from the dwarfed cedar, squirmed back to his pack, took his field glass from the sheath and masked it with the cedar twigs—lest some chance sparkle or reflection of sunlight on glass should catch a prowling eye—and trained it on Saddle Gap from the rim of his rocky stronghold. When the two horsemen reached the divide Uncle Ben's old eyes watched from behind his Lilliputian rampart.

They shunned the sky line; dismounting, they crept to the crest with a caution second only to Uncle Ben's, and peered over through a spyglass of their own; crawled back, mounted again, and turned back toward Rocking-Stone.

"All safe—the old fossil is gone," croaked the old fossil grimly.

He dropped back into his shelter and buckled his field glasses into their case. He next became suddenly aware that his rocky stronghold, soaking up the sun, was uncommonly warm, and that he was dripping with perspiration. Comforting himself with a mouthful of water from the canteen, he replaced it in the shade, unstoppered, that such faint breeze as stirred might help to keep it cool. Then he lay back and sweltered.

When his enemies passed he crawled to the outpost cedar to listen.

They rode by, wordless and sullen. When they passed out of sight down the cañon Uncle Ben got to his feet with a sigh of relief, arranged his pack, grub sack, canteen and spyglass, picked up his rifle, and set forth for the crest of Washboard Hill.

He climbed in long slow zigzags, and each one took him farther from Rocking-Stone Box, until at last he came out to the southern edge of Washboard Hill. The great long lake spread out below him in full view, inlet and sprawling creek, gulf and bay, deep fiord and dotted islands; the black crater above Fort McRae; the far white-gleaming crest of the dam; the high sharp profile of Caballo Mountain beyond, a spear point thrusting at the dam; the misty winding valley below; in the west the towering bulk of San Mateo, the long panorama of the Black Range, the nearer jagged outline of Cuchillo Negro; in the south, the far blue parapets of Cook's Peak, and Florida Mountain swimming in blue haze.

Teagardner dropped from the edge of Washboard to the southern slope, and there took to a narrow trail-like ledge. It bent to the right and came out in a deep notch; by taking to the hillside he had avoided a long and wasted climb to an abrupt step-off; in fact he followed, on the hillside at least, an old Indian war trail. The Apache on the warpath shunned the broad and easy way and traveled in the most inaccessible and improbable country he could find.

He walked slowly, with frequent rests; but as the afternoon wore on he went no more slowly than at first. He traversed another weary sequence of zigzags; again he left the staircase hill to wind round the southern slope. When first he had followed that old trail it had been lately traversed by savage warriors; it was fresh marked by broken twig and patrin. Far down the steep, Uncle Ben saw monuments of his building—and another's. The Horace Greeley Mine—so long ago!

"Old Pres!" Uncle Ben whispered. His bent shoulders straightened; his faded eyes kindled with a smile for his youth and his dead friend.

He turned into a second gap-tooth notch. He drank sparingly; the canteen was light now. Then he set himself to a third splintered slope, and so came late to the last and highest peak of Washboard Hill, looking down upon Rocking-Stone Valley.

For some time he had kept in toward the right; he was near the edge; close at hand, beyond the cañon, the northern wall heaved up in mighty masonry.

Again he put by his pack; taking his glasses only, again he crawled to the brink, seeking cover behind a prickly pear. This time his caution was needed. A third of a mile away, beyond the mouth of the box cañon and almost on a level with him, a sentinel sat under the Rocking-Stone and kept watch up the cañon.

The old man squirmed back, took up his belongings—heavy belongings now!—and made a wide detour to the south. He found a hazardous way down a shattered limestone cliff to a tumbled and boulder-strewn slope; turned back to the right and came to a southbound cañon heading in a deep pass, gashed between Washboard

Hill and the upshooting granite walls of Rocking-Stone Valley; a steep slope on this side, sheer and inaccessible toward the valley.

New thin soil on the granite, kinder than the tumult of broken stone in the limestone country, was shaggy with shrub and bush, brown mahogany brush or thrifty laurel, with here and there a gnarled scrub oak.

At the head of the pass Uncle Ben came to a thicket of greenery. He leveled his field glass across the dizzy chasm to the watchful sentinel, and then turned to inspect the valley.

Rocking Horse Camp was tiny in the depths. The wagon was gone, the saddle horses were gone; a wisp of smoke from the cook-house was the only sign of life. He turned his glasses toward the western water gap; after a long and patient search he found that which he sought, high on the slopes—a second sentinel, keeping watch toward the lake.

The cook bustled out and carried in an arm load of wood. Uncle Ben waited—and waiting, was suddenly assailed by fears and doubts. Had he taken too much upon himself? Should he have called upon the authorities; warned, at least, the soldiers guarding the dam? "Only two days more?" Yes, two days—but did that mean to the start—or to the finish? What if he had waited too long? Sweat beaded on his forehead, oozed clammy in the palms of his hands. For the first time his stout old heart trembled; for the first time he felt the burden of his years. He brushed the cold sweat from his forehead with his sleeve and waited, sick and shaken.

Not for long. Mule team and wagon came in sight, toiling up through the water gap, two slow horsemen behind. Uncle Ben drew a long breath.

"You cussed old fool!" he growled joyfully. "As if any man alive wouldn't surely wait for moonless nights—only two nights more—for such an enterprise as this! Lost confidence in your thinker, have you? . . . I'm a very old man and a very tired man and an empty one. . . . What's that? Don't you lie to me, Ben! Damn you—you were scared!"

The wagon turned up the road to the powder house; the horse-men came on to camp. Teagarden took up his glasses; his hand shook. The horsemen were Banner and Apgar. With the teamster went the men he had met as Brooks, Miller and Hayes of the quondam night shift, Baker and Case of the day shift. He had identified the nearer sentry as Green. That left Dorsey for the man on guard at the farther outpost. "Humph! They took a heap of pains to pick good English and Irish names, all except Apgar. Dern him! That sounds like a Welsh name, too—though I have no mind of it."

The wagon drew up at the powder-house door. There, greatly to the astonishment of the onlooker, five suitcases were unloaded.

They loaded the wagon with boxes from the powder house— boxes which they handled with great care. Teagardner slipped a long cartridge into the rifle. "Butchers!" His hand was steady now, he cuddled the long rifle to his cheek. But he laid it down reluctantly. "That would let five get away—Apgar with them. But by the living God, if they bring that stuff to camp I'll take no more chances. They all go together!"

Kendall drove down the hill with marked caution. The five men picked up the five suitcases and went into the powder house, reappearing after a little, each bearing a suitcase unrecklessly. They followed the wagon.

Plainly the suitcases were laden with some higher explosive than dynamite, to be carried by man power to the river; or possibly to be taken in Apgar's car.

"Bring it to camp! Bring it to the bunch!" implored Teagardner fervently. "Then, Lord, let thy servant depart in pieces!"

But they did not bring it into camp. The wagon came to the forks of the road and went on toward the lake for several hundred yards. Kendall unhitched and started the mules to camp. The burden bearers followed slowly, deposited the five suitcases gingerly beneath the wagon and turned back to camp. The sun was low over San Mateo Peak; the two sentries came down from their respective aeries.

"That will be all for to-night," quoth Uncle Ben.

He shouldered his load; he followed the downward course of the cañon for a southward mile. A hundred arroyos and little inter- secting cañons had joined it, rushing down from the granite dome behind. At last he turned aside, where the slightest of these cañons came in at right angles to the main course, through a narrow cleft between walls of smooth and polished granite. He followed this pain- fully between walls ever higher and narrowing; his weary feet slipped on the curving glossy floor. He came to a sudden turn, and there, high in the wall above him, a thinnest trickle of water crept from a moss-grown crevice and fell—drip—drip—drip!— into a basin, slightly oval, smooth and symmetrical. Time and that falling water, drop by drop, had hollowed that basin in the living rock. Granite is stubborn—water finds a way.

The old man lay flat on the smooth floor and drank deep from the brimming pool. He sat up and opened his grub sack, finding there jerky, cheese and crackers, and a small sack of ground coffee; the last, with a small tin cup and a tiny bag of salt, packed in a clean and empty tomato can. He dipped up water and washed his hands, holding the cup between his teeth; he poured water on his handkerchief and swabbed his salty face. He sniffed regretfully at the coffee sack, and repacked it, shaking his head. "I do believe I'm tired!" said Uncle Ben.

He made a joyful meal of his three staples; he thumped the granite floor tentatively. "Hard!" he sighed. He made his pack, refilled his canteen and went down the narrow way at a gait between a scuff and a swagger. The rest had stiffened his poor old knees and the good supper had stiffened his brave old heart.

Once in the open he crawled under the next bush to a soft mattress of fresh warm earth, folded his old hat for pillow, tucked the warm sky about his shoulders, and fell luxuriously asleep.

The wan crescent of low late moon rode hour-high when Uncle Ben woke, between two and three the next morning. Uncle Ben was something wan himself—not to mention that he was lame and stiff and sore. But he had open country to cross before he could win to the black cliff of his tryst, and he was very desirous to cross that open before daylight.

He set forth, limping. Yet he made good time, for his way was downward now. He passed the paved rocklands and came to a low country overblown with dune and drift, wind-borne from the endless sand hills beyond the deep-drowned river.

It was heavy walking. Dawn sparkled in the east; there was no time for delay. He pushed on through the deep sand at the narrowest isthmus of it, and came to the cover of little broken hills in the first dim of day.

So far he had borne quartering to the south, bent to cross that long bare finger of sand. He turned lakeward now, due west. Far below, a black ragged line peeped up, irresolute over the down-rushing ridges—a furtive wavering line that made the black crown of his obsidian cliff.

Sun gold blazed on the high crest of San Mateo Peak, flamed swiftly down the tawny sides of it, crept eastward, sluggish, from bench to low bench. But when Teagardner came to his trysting place the cool black shadow of Fra Christobal yet lay dim and darkling on the wide lake, on the long slow ridges behind him, and on the black dike of the trysting cliff.

The low waves murmured along that burnished dike and foamed at its glassy angles. At the southern extremity of it, where a little bay ran in, Uncle Ben built a tiny fire and boiled coffee. His features arranged themselves to joyous expectancy.

Breakfast over, he arranged his bed by folding his hat once more to a pillow and resting his gray head upon it.

"Now if I could be 'sustained and soothed by an unfaltering trust'—or even a lively stock company," said Uncle Ben drowsily, "I might go—to sleep. I think—maybe I—ergh!—will—anyway!"

vii

Joe Cady came early to McRae Inlet, storing his saddle in a neighboring tree top. He stowed his cargo in the little boat and embarked at once. It was not much of a cargo, even for a boat as small as Clayton's; a plump grub sack, a 30–40 rifle, two heavy double blankets, a heavy saddle blanket. But it had been ample cargo for Cady's horse when added to forty pounds of saddle and a hundred and sixty pounds of Cady.

Joe was no great waterman and made but awkward and floundering progress at first. But he took his own time, putting back and head to it.

He came into the main lake just where Engle Ferry had been; so much he knew by reason of the level black headland at his left, supporting McRae Crater. There could be no mistaking that frowning foursquare battlement.

Even in such brief experience Joe had learned to hold his small craft more or less in a general direction, and to maintain a decidedly forward motion. By this time he might have been ranked fairly as a willing seaman.

He turned up the broad lake and pulled sturdily against the slight and almost imperceptible current. Rowing grew easier as the boat moved faster; Joe began to have time to think of what the great dam really meant, and to marvel at so much of new and strange in this old valley.

Once and again he rested his oars to enjoy some new beauty or last surprise of scroll-saw shore or newborn island. A queer feeling came to him as he reflected that he must have been rowing for the last hour over the old round-up ground by Zapato Bottom.

Again, the lake water was clear. Now the water of the Rio Grande had been brown—too thick for batter and too thin for dough. Plainly, the mud had settled. Joe wondered how long it would take for the settlings to fill the entire lake basin, and what provision, if any, had been made at the dam for drawing off the silt. What had Uncle Ben said about deep sluiceways? It would certainly be a hard problem. Another thing—the sand used to blow in and then blow out again; but what blew in now would stay in. Joe looked over the side, and caught his breath. He floated above a still and silent forest, far beneath him in the clear depths. Leafless and bare it stretched far away across the lake floor; at the left he had a glimpse of unforgotten outlines, buried headland and hill—why, this was Alamocito *bosque!* Cady peered long into those deeps, remembering. He straightened up at last, shiversome, and resumed his voyagings.

So far, Cady's attention had been fairly halved between navigation and the practicalities of wonder and delight. But now his thought took up the day's puzzling work. For long he speculated upon the relations and reactions of surmised explosives in connection with problematical sluiceways of unknown depth; he came at last to the sage conclusion that such matters had best be confined to the abstract, and that a practical demonstration was highly undesirable.

So deciding, he turned his head and saw, close on the starboard bow, the shining cliff of his rendezvous.

"Joe, I own up—I was scared! I never was scared so bad in my life. I don't believe anybody else was ever scared so bad, not in the whole world—or had so good a reason."

"You thought we'd waited too long, Uncle Ben?"

"Just that. And when I glimpsed that wagonful of murderers coming back after all—I want to tell you, I felt good! And right then I saw a great light."

The boat was anchored in the little cove under the cliff. Joe and Uncle Ben sat in the shade of a great cedar. A practical observer, noting the coals of the dying fire, the grounds in the empty coffee can, the half loaf of bread, and the half slab of bacon on a flat stone, the scorched and greasy prongs of the two green and fresh-peeled mesquite branches beside the fire, might well have glanced at the earnest noon-high sun and drawn the inference that here were men who had just been eating dinner.

"Joe," said Uncle Ben with conviction, "you and me, we've been a pair of damned fools!"

"Aye, aye, sir!" said Joe—jolly tar that he was—and knuckled his forelock smartly.

"Blind, pig-headed, rattle-brained fools!" said Uncle Ben, encouraged. "We're a disgrace to Engle. We had no right to take chances, like we've been doing. 'Tisn't as if we was young fellows with no families, riskin' nothing but ourselves. No, sir, Joe! I reckon we got more families than any two men in the world!"

Joe nodded a sober assent. "All them below the dam is ours, just now."

"Exactly. We're responsible for all those lives. And here we've been risking and sky-larkin' round like a couple of kids just out of three-cornered pants. Our duty was to make Engle Dam safe and not to be makin' grand-stand plays to amuse the angels. It's only by the mercy of God that them dachshunds didn't beat us to it and blow up Engle Dam."

"But until you actually saw them load the wagon with dynamite yesterday you were only guessing," objected Cady.

"Guessing!" said Teagardner. "Guessing! Commodore, when you take your observations and figure out your latitude and longitude do you 'just guess' that you're maybe somewhere about such-and-such a place?"

"Why—no," said Joe, much impressed by this professional argument. "But wouldn't you kind of hate to kill eleven men on snap judgment and then find out they was innocent?"

"No, I wouldn't! You know I wouldn't. Not when the innocent men are as guilty as them eleven hyenas are. There's about fifty thousand more or less innocent people below that dam, if you like. Don't talk to me!"

"It was a mighty hard thing to believe," said Joe.

"You knew it, but you wouldn't believe it," jeered Teagardner. "Do you believe it now?"

"Sure I do. The choice is not left me."

"Listen to me, then! You remember how I bragged what-all I was going to do to that gang—make a clean sweep and everything? Well, that plan is all changed. Our business is to keep them from dynamiting Engle Dam. We'll row along up to-night and let the curlicues go.

"Still and all, because we've played the fool once is no reason for doing it again. This place where we are now is where we have no right to be. By all good rights we should have got ourselves killed yesterday. Not us! We wanted to do the job with a flourish—make a full clean-up and fix Apgar so he'd have a little time for regret. I did, anyway. Pure self-indulgence!

"But since we are here it would be an added folly not to use the advantage we have gained by taking a foolish risk. It was an unjustifiable risk, but we got away with it. As a result we can slip up there to-night and find that dynamite, and then hide out in easy gunshot. Once we've done that the game will be in our hands; we can shoot into that boatload of dynamite when and whenever we get ready. Once we get that far along we will have a right to wait. It would be a rank shame to have all that powder wasted. We might just as well lay still till we can get enough Huns for a mess."

"I'm with you there," said Joe. "I'd never get over hating it if we couldn't use some of them. And I'll be honest with you. It would always grind me if Head Devil Apgar was to get plumb clear."

"Me too," confessed Uncle Ben.

"I wouldn't want to dynamite Apgar, exactly, either," said Joe. "He deserves to know what's going on, Apgar does."

"Admirable," said Uncle Ben, "I'd be ashamed to tell you even half of all the different surprises I've planned for Apgar. There was one about tying him under the Rocking-Stone and wedging it over on him, right slow. Too bad! That was to induce him to tell who furnished him with all that TNT—or whatever it was that he got. Wish I knew about that. He brought some of it back from those little pleasure trips he was always takin' in his car, I reckon. Don't you forget Bowman, Joe!"

"I've got him logged, sir," said the nautical man.

"Look, Joe! We'll build a compromise about Mr. Apgar. It is not just or fair to suffer the inconvenience of being a fool and at the same time miss all the compensations of it. Am I right? I am.

Then we go up to-night and find that powder boat, real quiet. It is possible that they'll set a guard. Well, I'll have my old gun in my hand. If there's a guard, then you and me and Mister Guard will be done with all our troubles at one and the same time."

"But if there's no guard there, then we'll be free to consider the case of Mr. Kinny Apgar?"

"Exactly. I certainly would like to give Apgar a thrill. Now, listen! Here's what we will do if their powder scow is where I think it is—at the island I told you about, hereinafter referred to as Ship Island. There's where it is, Joe—right at Ship Island. And I'll tell you why. Yesterday afternoon that wagon got back in camp too early to have made two trips to the lake since we left, and too late for just one trip. They had been ferrying the stuff to Ship Island in the little boat—that's what! Not to mention that they wouldn't dare risk mooring the big boat at the mainland. Somebody might come along. Mighty few does, but there's a man once in a while.

"And they wouldn't dare bring the big boat across to be loaded. Men in a little skiff—nobody would think anything of that—fishing or just rowing for fun. Natural enough—never cause a second thought. But a big boat—big as an old-fashioned ferryboat, likely —that would be different. A man would want to know. No, sir, that big boat was never to be seen. So we'll find it at Ship Island. It can't be any other way. Now, half a mile this side of Ship Island, and farther out in the lake, is another little old island no bigger than a brick church, a little knoll all thick with cedar brush for you to hide in. Well, I'll maroon you there, and I'll drop down a ways and go ashore, hide my boat and myself and try to study up frivolities for Apgar.

"Your part will be to keep your gun sights on that dynamite, and to shoot right into the big middle of it under any of the following circumstances: First, if they show any signs of casting loose; second, if they show any signs of suspecting anything amiss—like rowing over toward your island, for instance; third, any time you catch ten of them Germans on Ship Island at once—or nine, or eight; fourth, any time you feel like it.

"In the big meantime if I get Apgar where I want him, I'll fire a shot as a signal. When you hear a shot—shoot! These fellows are busy. They'll have no time for shooting. If they do they'll be making a mistake, for any shot, anywhere, will be your signal. Don't wait.

We'll take no more risks. So long as we're there, unsuspected, we'll give Apgar his chance—till tomorrow night at quitting time. Not another minute. When you see your crowd fixin' to pull ashore for the night, don't you wait any longer. Blow 'em to hell!

"You may have to side 'em, Joe. We don't know how much of that stuff isn't dynamite, and we don't know what else it is. If it should happen to be too much TNT, it might stir up a wave to wash you off, or drop Ship Island on top of you, or upset your own little island—anything. It must be powerful stuff if they figured on smashing Engle Dam with it. But then again they was going to use it as a depth bomb there, I reckon.

"Anyway you size up the contract, you are getting the short end of it, Joe. That is a matter which I would recommend to your particular attention. It may most mighty easy mean curtains for little Joe; but Uncle Ben, he'll be safe ashore."

"It is a sailor's duty," said Joe fervently, "to obey orders if he breaks owners."

Uncle Ben twinkled. "Your watch below, then. I slept all morning. Once we leave here we get no more sleep till our job is done. We've got to make a good job of it, my bold mariner. We want to be a credit to Engle."

"Bos'n," said Uncle Ben, "wake up! It has just struck hell's bells!"

"Eh! What!" Joe came to his feet with a leap. "Anything wrong?"

"Nary. But this might be your last sunset, and I want to tell you it is some sunset! Thought you ought to see it. Take a good big look, and then eat—it's all ready. Action is what I want—action! I haven't been so impatient before since I was a Missouri twelve-year-old and laid awake all night when Dan Rice's Circus was coming to Joplin."

Cady looked at the flaming magnificence in the west, and then turned a slow and speculative eye to the north.

"Uncle Ben, either those fellows up there have gone back to Rocking Horse Camp now, or they haven't. If they stay where their powder is or if they leave a guard there—you and I are done seeing things. Get into the boat. I want to show you one more thing while the sunlight holds out."

"But if they should be looking through a spyglass and see us?" objected Uncle Ben. "Only one chance in a million, of course, but ——"

"They'd see two men in a boat rowing downstream to Elephant Butte. Get into the boat. I'll pass up the coffee. The rest of the stuff we can eat any time. Bring your pack, Uncle Ben."

"I suppose it is too late to quit now," said Uncle Ben doubtfully, as Joe piled their slender outfit in the boat.

"Quit what?" said Joe, pushing off.

"Doing what I ought not to. Because somebody told me to, mostly. Might as well keep it up, I reckon. Man born of woman," said Uncle Ben, "is a queer fish."

Joe pulled out into the lake vigorously for a quarter of a mile. Then he turned downstream and shipped his oars. The boat drifted gently.

"There!" said Joe, and pointed. Uncle Ben looked over the side. A hundred feet beneath them, clear seen through the golden waters, was a long, low, rambling stone house, with other houses, smaller, clustered near by. The doors were open. White trunks and branches of two gigantic cottonwoods, tall and spectral, stood before the big house. Beyond were corrals, outbuildings, fences and long rows of an orchard—long rows fading in the dimness.

"Good God!" said Teagardner. "The old Gonzales place! Back water, Joe! Let me look. They were fine people, Joe. I've had a heap of good times here."

"Me too. They were sure good people."

Teagardner gazed long at that quiet house before he spoke again.

"All lived together—the old man and all his sons. When one of the boys got married they'd build a new house. Some of the daughters stayed here, too, when they married. And grandchildren! This was a fine old nest and mighty fine people!"

"Uncle Ben," said Joe soberly, "this was more like a real home than any place I ever saw. It wasn't everybody just working for himself. They was pulling for the homestead." The light died slowly; the old homestead dimmed and faded.

"They were fine people," said Teagardner again. "Let's go, Joe."

"Downstream?"

"Might as well, while the light holds. When it gets dark we can turn back."

They drifted down; Joe's oars dipped softly and slowly; and Joe sang—because he could not help it—that saddest of all sad songs, La Golondrina:

"Mansión de amor! Celestial Paraíso!
Nací en tu seno y mil diches gocé.
Voy á partir á lejanos regiones,
Do nunca más, nunca más volveré!"

"It wasn't a mansion—it was an old ramshackle stone house," said Uncle Ben. "And it wasn't no celestial paradise, either. But it was a damn sight better thing. It was a home."

New Mexican twilights are brief, surprisingly brief to visitors from colder lands. The velvet dusk rushed down upon them, the stars blazed out.

"Port your hellum! Give him the spurs! Stand by on the weather brace! Ride him, cowboy, you're doing fine! Sta-ay with him! No'th —no'theast by south, three points west!"

"All together, my hearties!"

Bawling these masterly commands in right seamanly spirit, Joe turned the boat's nose to the north and settled down for the long pull.

"Your language is singularly superfluent and technical, captain," said Teagardner gravely. "But you got a damn poor idea of a jolly deep-sea chantey. What you need for a nice clear starry night and an errand like ours is something cheerful, like this:

"The bells of hell go ting-a-ling-a-ling,
For you, but not for me!
I hear them angels sing-a-ling-a-ling,
Their conquering palms I see.
O Death, where is thy sting-a-ling-a-ling?
O Grave, they victor-ree?
The bells of hell go ting-a-ling-a-ling,
For you, but not for me!"

viii

They came to Ship Island in a whispering midnight; they crept along that wavering shore, groping in the shadows, so softly that the little lapping waves made more sound than they; and in the darkest shadow under overhanging trees they found the hidden boat they sought.

They boarded her with infinite caution. Side by side they made a snail-like progress to the farther end, feeling with probing fingers at all they came to—a workbench, barrels, boxes, oars, litter, windlasses and several coils of wire rope.

"Here's the dynamite!" announced Cady in a subdued voice. "There's a mountain of it—I can smell it. This is the time Engle puts one over on Berlin! And there's no watchman. Even if there should be a watchman somewhere up on the island the worst he can do is set off the powder himself and save us the trouble."

"Well, then, why don't you speak up natural? No need of keeping your voice down. Cap Tuttle told me once," said Teagardner complacently, "that a couple of these astronomer chaps figured out the planet Neptune, size, home and habits, before any human eye had ever seen it—just by observing the results of causes and reasoning from hither to hence. I don't see how them astronomers had anything on us. We done discovered a boat that same way. And we got the size and shape mighty near right too. She nearly fits the specifications of an old square-end ferry-boat—so far as here. But, by cripes! My hands report that this end is the queerest rig of a boat they ever felt of. Strike a match, Joe. Let's see what new kind of a devil machine German science has went and gone and rigged up now."

Joe struck a match, and then several more. "Well, I am damned!" he said. "They've made two boats! There's a big one, this one we are on—a smaller one coupled right against it behind, with the dynamite lashed tight—two or three tons of it. Wait, now—let me figure on this, Uncle Ben. If you can study out what you have never seen I ought to be able to get the why and how of what I can see. Let me feel round.

"They've got two big spars running out behind the big boat, clear of the water. The smaller boat is lashed to them two spars; they are to hold up the weight of the dynamite.

"When they get close to the dam they'll anchor—here's a big homemade anchor with three prongs ——"

"It's a grapnel," said Uncle Ben.

"I don't know the name of it, but I know what it's for—it's a grabhook. And I had my hands on a little one back there—good deal smaller, but the same shape. . . . I see! Are there lights on the top of the dam, Uncle Ben?"

"Lights and guards."

"That's it, then," said Cady. "They aim to work their old scow down pretty close to the dam, and anchor there. Then they cut the lashings on the spars, and the little square boat sinks under the weight of the dynamite. They've got valves or plugs, likely, to scuttle her with. They'll hook some of those little wire cables on her first. They know just how deep to let her down; they'll lower her down with them windlasses; the big boat will float her and hold the dynamite just as deep as they want it. Why, Uncle Ben, this will be the biggest depth bomb in the world!"

"Was to be," suggested Uncle Ben.

"Right you are! Was to be! When this craft leaves here she goes as dust! Now, let's see. They'll have the battery wires connected up with the dynamite, and that little anchor—yes, they might have one of those empty barrels for a buoy, or maybe two or three with a little platform in between—they'll fasten their batteries on that, anchor it, set their time mechanism to going and pile into the boat they've towed along to row home in. Then they'll turn the barge loose and let it drift down to the dam, with the dynamite underneath. Or maybe they'll have the anchor cable fixed with a pulley on the barge, so they can let the cable out from the rowboat, and guide the barge just where they want it by rowing one way or the other till they are ready to let the cable slip.

"Or they can tie a knot in the cable to jam in the pulley, if they don't want the barge to drift into the light. Or a traveler. That will be it. When they've let the barge down as near to the light as they dare they'll send a traveler down the cable and jam it in the pulley block. Why, damn their eyes, they've thought of everything! They couldn't have a gas engine to work their old barge; it would be heard. They have to row. They've thought of everything. This is what they've been working on—all these windlasses and contrivances. And they're not ready yet. They've not got their wire ropes attached to their dynamite boat, nor their battery wires hooked up. They'll be here to-morrow. Praise God! I'm sure glad it's my gun that is going to set this stuff off to-morrow!"

"I wish it was my old gun," said Teagardner, half enviously. "It has been a good old gun. Is yet. I half promised Apgar to show him some surprising marksmanship with it too."

"You make a divvy of that grub, take your sack and go ashore to entertain Apgar," said Joe indignantly. "I'm the naval authority of this A. E. F., and don't you forget it. You let me have the spyglass, so I can see what's going on here, and I'll tend to the dynamite part. You look after Apgar and I'll hold down the ten others. I can do easy thinking, as I just showed you—if I've got anything to think about. But I'm noways nimble-minded enough to play with Herr Apgar, if he's the man that planned this job. Let's go hunt my island. We've got nothing more to do here."

"There's your old island," said Teagardner, when they were out in the clear starlight. "But we'd better change our plans again, Joe. Set me ashore and you keep the boat—and keep it about an inch from your hand. You may need it. There's an awful lot of that dynamite and stuff—two or three tons, I reckon. We don't know just what it may do in the way of an amateur tidal wave."

"Say when," said Joe, and changed his course.

"There's Apgar's landing, over here," said Uncle Ben. "Drop down about a quarter, and you'll see a little point. Anywhere beyond that will do me."

Joe doubled the little cape and drove the boat ashore on a shelving bank. Picking up his rifle Uncle Ben stepped out—and immediately reached back for the boat.

"Here, this won't do! Quicksand!" he said. He laid the rifle in the extra oarlocks, clutched the gunwale with both hands, and wrenched his feet loose with a violent effort. Behind each foot as it came free the quicksand closed with a loud sucking.

"Bad stuff!" said Uncle Ben. "Near lost a boot. You scout along up toward the point till you find me a rocky place to land on." He squeezed by Joe into the stern of the boat, so that his weight there would lift the bow out of the sand while Joe backed off.

The rocky place was soon found and Uncle Ben disembarked successfully.

"Well—so long, old-timer," said Joe cheerfully. "I'm off!"

"Good luck, Joe. So long!"

Uncle Ben sat on a boulder for a long time, a very thoughtful old man. From time to time he removed his hat and scratched his head. To vary this proceeding he rubbed the side of his nose vigorously or twisted his beard.

The moon rose, a thin sickle. Then Uncle Ben bestirred himself briskly, as one who has arrived at a decision. He took off his boots, tied them together and strung them round his neck, first stuffing his socks into the boots. He rolled up his overalls, picked up gun and grub sack and stepped gingerly into the water.

He turned up the lake, keeping at the water's edge; he passed Apgar's landing. Fifty yards beyond he came to a little sudden cove no bigger than a hall bedroom, and hardly as wide. Uncle Ben investigated, finding that the little cove, a boulder and a clump of half-grown cedars, made an ideal covert.

It was for something like this that Uncle Ben had been searching. He burrowed under the low branches to a satisfactory lodging place, and stayed there.

Dawn came, and the spreading wild beauty of the lake; the pageant of the sun on San Mateo; the long slow shadow from Fra Christobal, blacker and deeper for the brilliant sunlight all beyond and all about; an enchanted shadow, fresh with an incense not to be forgotten; the slow sun at last.

Long after, a wagon came creaking to the landing; a water wagon, Kendall's, carrying three men besides Kendall: Case, Dorsey and Miller. Close behind followed a car, Apgar's, carrying three men besides Apgar: Banner, Baker and Green.

"Now then, off you go! Green, you bring the boat back and ride up with Kendall," said Apgar. "I'll row out after dinner for a final inspection. You fellows ought to have everything ready by noon, at most; then you can sleep till sundown."

Apgar turned his car and went spinning up the road. Kendall drove into the shallow water, turned the wagon and began pumping into the tank. The six others crowded into the boat and rowed out to Ship Island. An eternity lapsed—almost an hour—before Green rowed back from Ship Island and climbed onto the wagon.

The last sound of that wagon's departure died away. Sometime later a branch of cedar brush came softly down the lake, close to the shore, bobbing gently, drifting with the slow current. It would seem that the current set in to the shore, for the cedar brush drifted against the boat. Had any man been there to see—as there was not—he would have noted that this bobbing cedar brush was not one large branch, but a number of small branches, lately cut by a jackknife and bunched to make a miniature raft; that along the top of that raft, lay a very heavy rifle and a very light flour sack, together with a leather belt holding a few enormous cartridges, and a soft gray hat; and would further have noted that the rifle was held in position by a wrinkled hand.

Had this aroused curiosity—as might have happened—this man who was not there might have looked closer and seen under the cedar branches a withered and wrinkled brown face and a sprightly eye; both appertaining to Uncle Ben Teagardner.

Uncle Ben pushed the rifle into the boat, holding it level, so that it barely cleared the side, and dropped it gently on the thwarts. Belt, hat and flour sack followed. Then he ducked under the boat and came up on the lower side.

Sheltered from any possible watchful eye on Ship Island, Uncle Ben worked up the side of the boat to the bank; he crawled, belly-flat, and unsnapped the boat's chain from a ring at the juniper trees; slowly, cautiously, he pushed the boat into deep water, where the slow current caught it and bore it away, drifting idly, rocking, dancing in the sunlight. The cedar brush followed, gay-bobbing, but fell behind because it was closer inshore, where the current was slower. On that side of the boat farthest from Ship Island Uncle Ben Teagardner floated peacefully, supporting himself with a light hand on an oarlock.

Mr. Kinny Apgar drove his car to the landing place at about half past one. He leaped out briskly. Then he stared and swore. His boat was gone.

Apgar was furious. Cursing Green for carelessness, with a guttural oath quite unlike our kindly, familiar English speech, he set out down the lake shore in search of the derelict. A few hundred yards down he came to a low rocky cape; and here his face cleared, for he saw the runaway boat, safely stranded on the farther side of a little bay beyond. He marched down to the beach, still muttering his wrath.

It was sticky going. A little crust of ground quivered under his foot. He skipped forward lightly; his foot went in over the shoe top. Cursing savagely, he lunged again. His left foot plunged through the crust, calf deep. He tugged to free himself. His right foot broke through.

Thoroughly frightened, Apgar went down on hands and knees.

With a prodigious effort he pulled his right foot free. The quicksand closed with a sucking gurgle. His left foot sank deeper. He threw his body round in an effort to turn back. His foot would not twist. He floundered, heaved and strained; he felt the quicksand quiver and shake under his hands, and rose up shuddering. The crust shook to a jelly under the frantic thrust with which he rose. His right foot broke through. He struggled desperately, sinking deeper with every move.

The quicksand rose above his knees.

He stood a moment, terrified. Round him, in a circle of which he was the center, the crust bent and wrinkled to darting cracks, to fine radiating cracks with connecting arcs—cracks which smoothed instantly and darted out again in another place, like some horrible animated cartoon, flashing always to the same ghastly shape—of a gigantic spider web. Here and there a crack gaped wide to a horrible mouth, square and deep—which quivered an instant, closed with a shuddering gurgle, and left no trace.

Apgar shrieked aloud. He was mid-thigh in the quicksand, he went deeper with every frantic struggle; it was his sinking weight which tensed the yielding crust to that nightmare web, to those awful gaping mouths!

He turned his distorted face toward Ship Island; he fumbled at the revolver at his belt. If he could make them hear—and understand! They could see him. Baker could swim.

"Hello there! You seem to be in trouble!" said a voice behind him.

Apgar's body whirled. Old Man Teagardner, with his long rifle in his hand, came slowly down a sandy ridge through the ragged gap of a mesquite hedge. Apgar screamed; tears of relief came to his eyes as he pushed the revolver back into the scabbard.

"Oh, thank God! Thank God! I'm caught in the quicksands, Teagardner! Help me out! Get the oars and the boat seats. Hurry! Hurry!"

"Oh, don't be so scared," said Teagardner placidly. He moved toward the boat and then stopped, beaming. "You want to hear the war news first. Mighty good! I got it last night. The French have taken Soissons and crossed the Crise River, the entire Marne salient is crushed, the Yanks are hammering north."

"Teagardner! Uncle Ben! Hurry! Help me out!"

"Why?" said Uncle Ben. He sat down on a rock with his long rifle on his knees. "Why?" he repeated unemotionally; and with the flat and colorless tones came to Apgar the stabbing thought which showed him trapped and doomed: Uncle Ben was supposed to be now in Colorado! His terror had forgotten that.

Apgar went white to the lips; his voice broke out in a dreadful scream.

"Almighty God!"

"God, baby killer? This is late to talk of God. Think it over, Apgar!"

"For God's sake, Teagardner!"

The sand rose to his thighs. He was weeping, raving, cursing, begging. Then a new note came to his cracked and straining voice. "Is it money you want? Get me out! You shall have ten thousand—twenty—fifty!"

"Not for all Germany," said Teagardner.

"Then, by God, I'll shoot you now!" Apgar clutched at the forgotten gun.

"That would be very curious." Uncle Ben glanced at him indifferently. "You might try it. Perhaps after you kill me I'll come and pull you out. I don't think you could hit me, but you might as well try it." He looked out across the water. "I'm pretty old. A year or so more or less won't hurt me." He turned his stern eyes back to Apgar and spoke sharply. "Well, baby killer, why don't you shoot?"

Screaming hoarsely Apgar leveled the gun and fired. The bullet struck between Teagardner's feet.

Teagardner held up his hand.

"I thought so," he said, and pointed. "Look!"

Fascinated, without power to disobey, Apgar twisted his head to look.

With a crash of inconceivable thunders Ship Island leaped and shattered in spouting flame, awful lines of red and black against a rocking sky. Apgar fell forward on his hands; his revolver dropped; he struggled up again, stunned and dazed. The crashing air, in thousand-volleyed shocks, came back from San Mateo, from Christobal cliffs.

A giant wave rose from the hissing caldron where that lost island had been. It swept down the lake at incredible speed; the edge of it broke on the rocky cape above—a white crest flung up in the sky, overleaped the cape and flooded the little bay, buried Apgar for one heartbeat's space, and broke to Teagardner's knees where he stood, staring. Receding, it swept the boat away; while on the broad lake the great wave went foaming, roaring by.

The water fell from the little bay in white runnels of froth. Apgar covered his face, moaning.

He was hip deep in the quicksand.

Teagardner stared hard at the little island in the lake, and caught at last a glimpse of a little boat—Joe's boat—tossed in the swirl of crossing waves, and the flashing of white oars in the sun. His heart leaped with joy at that sight.

Teagardner limped up the slope toward the little cape. After a few steps he turned and called back:

"Apgar, you've dropped your gun. You shot at the wrong man. You should have used your bullet on yourself. Well—I'm going now."

Apgar turned wild imploring eyes to him. "You won't leave me here to die like a dog! For God's sake, Teagardner! Have pity, have mercy!"

"The mercy you planned!" said Teagardner.

XIII. The West That Was

Rhodes wrote this essay for *The Photodramatist*, September, 1922, near the close of a personally and financially frustrating three-year stay in Los Angeles, for a magazine aimed primarily at scenarists, writers, and hopeful wordsmiths of the motion picture industry. It was written, ostensibly, to separate the truth from the fictions about the Old West perpetrated by and in Hollywood. It became something else again as Rhodes warmed to his self-appointed task.

Basically, it is a summary of Rhodes' feelings about the fiction of the westward march and its practitioners, as revealing of the man himself as of his opinions. It is, also, the first printed shot in the guerrilla warfare waged by Rhodes against Mencken, Nathan, Lewisohn, Sherwood Anderson, *et al.*, for the rest of his life. Like this appearance, most of his ammunition was expended in obscure publications, but he never faltered in his belief that the code of the frontier and the traditions by which he had been raised were the proper ones.

The thought may occur to sapient readers that Rhodes' taste in classical literature—Dickens, Stevenson, Conrad, Kipling, for examples—was more discriminating than his taste in the fiction contemporary with his own. This same thought has occurred to him who writes this note.

WHEN A REASONABLE MAN says "it is," what he really means is "it seems to me."

It seems to me that no great credit is due the American people because they know so little of the unmatched story of their own country. Kit Carson is as notable a figure as Leif Ericson, and his work staid put. The Retreat of the Ten Thousand Greeks was child's play compared to the Doniphan Expedition—but we are shy of Xenophons. How many Americans know the facts of that high-hearted venturing? Or of Kearney's Road to Empire? Who remembers that Kit Carson was the grandson of Daniel Boone—that so brief a span as three lives went to the changing of a world? Why is not Sam Houston a name as stirring as Francis Drake?

We have kept some faint knowledge of Daniel Boone and Davy Crockett, a blurred memory of the Alamo, a glimpse of Lewis and Clark; we are dimly aware of Frémont; the rest is silence.

The destiny of England has been upon the sea; and England's best have been proud to tell the story of her ships. The history of America is the story of the Pioneer, the greatest building of recorded time—"as has been said before on no better authority." How many books have been well-written on the taking of this half-world? Too few.

There was a time when York State was the West—then the Ohio Valley, Michigan, Missouri, Iowa, Wisconsin. Much has been written of these states—little of their settlement.

"King Noanett" is a splendid story of west-winning when the Connecticut River was the west—of Deerfield, Springfield.

Proceeding, we find "In The Valley," "The Hoosier Schoolmaster," "Huckleberry Finn"—the one American classic; Parkman's Histories; a few admirable stories by Mary Halleck Foote and others; later, Stewart Edward White's stories of the lumberjacks; Webster and Merwin's "Calumet K"—which was the beginning of the era of "business" stories, much despised by those who hate workers and work; an era all unremarked by the High Lord Critics of the day.

But the South? Virginia has been sung, Kentucky has her James Lane Allen; Mary Johnston has written of John Sevier and his friends in early Tennessee. But the settlement of the smiling lands between the long straight rivers falling into the Gulf? Louisiana?

Texas? You who read this—honestly, do you know the history of your country? Have you heard of the State of Franklin? The Cherokee Republic? The State of Van Zandt? Do you know that when Mississippi seceded from the Union, one county seceded from Mississippi, set up an independent government, and made it stick?

The answer is, No! Half of us have huddled along the eastern coast, ankle deep in the Atlantic, our backs to the West, peering across at Europe. Most of the other half have lived and died facing East, eyes on New York and Boston.

The Mississippi, the Missouri—Hamlin Garland, William Allen White, Willa Sibert Cather—three notable and faithful artists, marking the Star of Empire on its westward course, making true chronicle of the cost, in blood and sweat and tears.

Iowa, Kansas, Nebraska, California—these were in the making before the Civil War. We are come now to "the West"—from the Buffalo country to the crest of the Sierra Nevadas—the country settled since 1865. How have our writers dealt with the deeds of our fathers?

They have done well. We find many spirited and truthful books, not a few of them works of art. Wister's "The Virginian" and "Members of the Family," the unforgettable "Red Saunders" stories by Henry Wallace Phillips; Emerson Hough's "Heart's Desire," "The Story of the Cowboy," and his "Covered Wagon" of this year; the New Mexican stories of Charles F. Lummis and his historical studies; Stewart Edward White's "Arizona Nights"; Knibbs, with "Overland Red"; Andy Adams, whose "Log of a Cowboy," with a style as simple as Caesar's, gives an accurate and vivid account of the early days, when cattle were driven up the Long Trail to market; Frank Spearman's stories of the railroaders—"Held For Orders," and "The Nerve of Foley" were about the best short stories ever written in America; B. M. Bower and William MacLeod Raine, Kennett Harris, Lighton with "Billy Fortune," Wason with "Happy Hawkins"—all fascinating, humorous, authentic; Peter B. Kyne, whose best is as good as any best; younger writers, Bechdoldt, Edwin L. Sabin, Jackson Gregory, Dane Coolidge, Hal Evarts, worthily uphold a great tradition.

Some of O. Henry's tales have captured the very essence of the Western spirit—notably "Jimmy Hayes and Muriel"—which shows forth precisely what thing it was which the West contributed to "the American Idea"—now so much despised by the Euramericans. Rupert Hughes and Henry Wallace Phillips collaborated to make one of the best western stories ever written, "Across the Great Divide."

Roosevelt wrote of that country; he voiced the code of the West when he said "Don't flinch—don't foul—hit the line hard." The genius of Agnes C. Laut, more, perhaps, than any other, has grasped the epic spirit of our national story. And the Indian stories of James Willard Schultz, to my mind, are the best literature produced by any living American. Had Ulysses with his own hand set down the record of Troy Town, and his later voyagings, the tale had read like these authentic records of the Blackfeet and their neighbors. The style is simple, direct, forceful, beautiful. One thinks of Bunyan, or the Book of Ruth.

It may be observed that no mention is made of Leatherstocking. My lawyer has forbidden it. Again, I read Zane Grey's "Rainbow Trail" and "Riders of the Purple Sage" with much pleasure. By advice of counsel, I am saying nothing of his later books, especially "To The Last Man"—concerning which nothing shall induce me to make any comment. I will say this, however—counsel or no counsel —that in "The U. P. Trail" Mr. Grey foozled one of the finest opportunities ever missed by any American writer.

California, aside from the gray corner south of Tehachapi and east of the San Bernardino Range, is not of the West, and never has been. California is *chop sui generis*. Therefore, Bret Harte, Frank Norris, "H. H.," Mary Austin, Marah Ellis Ryan, Harry Leon Wilson and their likes are not in this roster. The West ends where rain runs directly into the western sea.

With all these truth-saying books, and with others as good— wouldn't you think Americans might be expected to have a fair mental picture of early Western days? They haven't. To the average American, the West is connected with but one idea.

It is the home of the "Bad Man."

The idea persists that a frontiersman lived with one foot on a brass rail and one hand on a still smoking gun; and that he earned his frugal livelihood by assassination. It is a mistake. What he did was to work. Homicide was never more than a diversion with him. His mind was on his work. He made twelve states and collaborated on three others.

From such books as those mentioned above, the public had a chance to believe that the frontiersmen—cowboys, freighters, miners, railroaders, surveyors, farmers, store-keepers, what-not—were men of many lacks and much undissembled evil-doing, and many wild and unmentionable virtues. But also that they had one characteristic in common—an individuality which verged upon personal identity; an individuality which often amounted to perversity. They did not copy each other, or anyone else. Yet the public has accepted one stereotyped and purely imaginary character as a true picture of all Westerners.

Here are effects; let us inquire into causes. I find

(1) Buffalo Bill's Wild West Shows

(2) Other Wild West Shows

(3) "Wolfville Days"—amusing and picturesque; meant for a joke, a cartoon, a grotesque caricature; accepted as accurate and informing.

(4) The unceasing flood of lurid "Western" novels and stories —written, not at secondhand, but from imitation of a copy of an imitation of some writer who got his dope from what some one had said of what someone else had written on doubtful information from a man of poor memory and few scruples. The Westerner of popular fiction is as false to the fact as the stage Englishman.

These writers show sombrero and gun, chaps and spurs—but they have not a guess about the man who wears them. They do not get even these superficial matters right. The slicker was to wear in the rain; it was taken off during prolonged dry spells; they could understand that, since they wore oilskins themselves, on their native coasts. But the "chaps"? It never penetrated to their darkened minds that chaps were worn as a protection against thorns—cactus, mesquite, tornillo, cat claw, cedar branches—and that in a clear open country, in town or in an aeroplane, the cowboy *took them off!*

Chapparrejos weighed about seven pounds; they were unmercifully hot (in hot countries). We were glad to take them off. And our horses were glad to have us take them off. They carried two hundred pounds, man and saddle; an extra seven pounds was a grievance which caused many estrangements.

(5) The "movies." I hate to say this, for I have many good and sorely-tried friends in the moving-picture business. But, with a

few distinguished exceptions, the moving-picture cowboy can best be described in the inspired words of the poet.

> *Now, there's no such things as the Ginko Tree,*
> *And there never was—though there ought to be:*
> *And 'tis also true, though most absurd,*
> *That there's no such thing as a Wallabye Bird.*

(6) There are also Western books written with splendid artistry by people with all the mental machinery for finding and telling the truth—or some part of it—but which, so far as Westerners are involved, are written in a vacuum. In dealing with the West, they have resolutely ignored history, birth, training, codes, traditions, habits, and aims.

Such books grieve the Old Timer more than the trashy novel; he feels that these people might have done a better job. As samples, take Honoré Willsie's "Still Jim"—a masterpiece save for its blindness as to all meaning of the West—and "The Great Divide" by the late William Vaughan Moody. Here is a good place to state that the one thing the Western man did more than any other one thing was *not* playing poker for a girl. Next in popularity, perhaps, was not branding any lady with a hot iron—either a running iron or a stamp brand. There were few women in the Old West, and the men valued them highly; gambling for women, branding women—such recreations would have been frowned upon. The fact is that the Westerner set women upon a pedestal and rather insisted on keeping them there; often to the serious annoyance of the ladies themselves.

(7) Another factor contributes indirectly towards maintaining the invincible ignorance of the majority in this matter of the Old West. Since a certain date in November, 1918—which date will be supplied on receipt of a stamped and self-addressed envelope—the literary affairs of America have been taken over and guided by "a little group of Syria's thinkers"—Menckens and supermenckens. They announce themselves as The Young Intellectuals.

This group has decreed that a good American story must tell about a Hungarian with adenoids; that the American novel shall deal with the cheerful inward life of a psychopathic case, and shall have a complex in lieu of a plot; and that no book shall be recommended to their readers which did not employ one of three methods. These methods were:

(1) Brilliance with indecency.

(2) Dullness with indecency.

(3) Dullness without indecency.

"*Were*"—not "are." "Vandermarks Folly" and "The Covered Wagon" are turning public attention into more wholesome channels. "You can't fool all of them, all the time."

During the brief and nightmarish hegemony of the Young Intellectuals, they explicitly declared war upon (1) The Puritan, and (2) The Pioneer. Their hatred for America was due—aside from Germany and the liquor business—to what they sneered at as our "Pioneer Culture." Therefore, in their instructions to Women's Clubs, they used one or the other of two set forms for disposal of any Western book:

(1) "Another Western novel."

(2) "I never read Western novels."

Western novels were "romantic," you see. A Romancer is a man who loves something; a Realist is a man who hates something. The Young Intellectuals hated everything American.

Boys and girls, it is no secret that most of you are writing "western" stories. I could give you a bit of valuable advice, but I won't. Punch gave the same advice about matrimony, you remember—but the custom has not been discontinued. Or, I might urge upon you rather to write about the West That Is—dry farming, the building of dams and ditches and roads—a time as interesting as was ever the Old West. But you wouldn't do it. That is not the way the so-called Human Race behaves. Your grandchildren will record the stirring events of today, at second-hand—and will get them all muddled and twisted, of course.

Since you will indubitably write stories of the West That Was, let me at least conjure you to pick your sources with care; and let me urge upon you that to chronicle that magnificent epic is a task worthy of your best effort; of any best.

To that end I would have everyone who would write about the West, everyone who loves the West, to read a recent book by Philip Ashton Rollins, "The Cowboy"; with the subtitle; "His Characteristics, His Equipment, and His Part in the Development of the West." Other books have done justice to the qualities of the cowboy; this is the first to show forth his importance as "an affirmative, constructive factor in the social and political development of the United States."

It is my hope, on a later day, to tell you some particulars about the cowboy and other frontiersmen—sheepherders excepted; how they were made of watch springs and whale-bone and barbed wire; how broad brim and high heel, chaps and spurs, double-cinch or center-fire, the tie-fast men or the "dally," habit and word and deed— had each a logical and compelling reason. Until then, I shall close with one warning. The Cowboy was not other than yourself, except by his hard training. As has been said before, and as I shall say again, "cowboys are just like humans, only bow-legged."

XIV. Aforesaid Bates

Since magazine appearance in *Cosmopolitan*, August, 1928, this story has appeared but once and that in the limited edition collection, *The Little World Waddies* (El Paso, 1946).

The little world of this story, *El Mundo Chico*, is that country enclosed by connecting the communities of Deming, Las Cruces, and Rincon, New Mexico. The titular hero of the story made his first major appearance in "The Bird in the Bush."

Implicit in this story are two major tenets of Rhodes' creed: his hero, actually, is the community—"The Star system never prevailed on the Free Range"—and his villain is the grasping, avaricious power-within-the-law but morally without it.

As one who lived through the conditions that make the plot of this story, the editor makes bold to dub this story the finest depiction of drouth in our literature.

i

"I WOULDN'T MIND going broke so much," said Dick Mason, "but I sure hate to see the cattle die, and me not able to do the first thing to save them." He dipped a finger in spilled beer and traced circles on the table. In shirt sleeves for the heat, they sat in the cool dimness of Jake's Place—Mason, Bull Pepper, Blinker Murphy and Big Jake himself.

"Tough luck," said Murphy. "Losin' 'em fast?"

"Not so many, not yet. But the bulk of 'em are dying by inches. Dyin' on their feet. The strongest can just get out to grass and back. The others eat brush, wood and all. Hardly any rain last year and no snow last winter. Stock in no shape to stand a spring round up, so the yearlin' steers are all on the range yet. If we'd had rain about the Fourth of July, as we most always do, we might maybe 'a' pulled through, losin' the calf crop. But here it's most August, no rain, no grass—not a steer in shape to sell.—and me with a mortgage comin' due right off. Feenish. And I've got a wife and kids now. Other times, when I went broke, it really didn't make no difference. Tham!"

"No, this one's on me," said Jake hastily. "Four beers, Tham."

"We're none of us cattlemen," said Bull Pepper. "And you know us Tripoli fellows never get along too well with your bunch anyway. All the same, we're sorry to see you boys up against it this way."

Lithpin Tham came with the beer. "I gueth all of you won't go under," he said as he slipped the mugs from tray to table. "They thay Charlie Thee ith fixed tho he won't looth many."

"Not him," said Mason sourly. "Charlie See, he had a leased township under fence to fall back on. Good grass, cured on the stem." The door opened and Aforesaid Bates came in, unseen by Mason. "Charlie won't lose much," said Mason. "Why should he? His stuff runs on the open range when every mouthful of grass they took was a mouthful less for ours. Now he turns 'em into his pasture. Grama high as ever it was, cured on the stem. Just like so much good hay. Been nothing to eat it for three years but a few saddle horses. Him and Aforesaid Bates, they're wise birds, they are!"

"What's all this about Aforesaid Bates?" said Bates. "What's the old man been doin' now?" His voice was acid. They turned startled faces toward him.

"You know well enough," said Mason sullenly. "You ran a drift fence across Silver Spring canyon, kept your cattle out on the flat so long as there was a spear of grass, and now you're hogging that saved-up pasture for yourself."

"Well, what are you goin' to do about it?" demanded Bates. He pushed back his hat; his grizzled beard thrust forth in a truculent spike. "Fine specimen you are—backcappin' your own neighbors to town trash!"

"Exception!" cried Bull Pepper sharply, rising to his feet. But Bates ignored him and continued his tirade, with eyes for none but Mason. "Hopper and See and me, we sold out our old stuff last fall. Cut our brands in half, bein' skeery of a drought. And if the rest of you had as much brains as a road lizard, you could have done the same, and not one of you need have lost a cow. But no, you must build up a big brand, you and Hall—hold on to everything. Now the drought hits us and you can't take your medicine. You belly-achin' around because me and Charlie had gumption enough to pro-tect ourselves."

"Say, cool down a little, Andy," said Dick Mason. "You're an old man, and you've been drinking, and I can take a lot from you—but I do wish you'd be reasonable."

"A fat lot I care about what you wish," snarled Bates. "Reason-able! Oh, shucks! Here, three years ago, you was fixed up to the queen's taste—nice likely bunch of cows, good ranch, lots of room, sold your steers for a big price, money in the bank, and what did you do?"

Conjointly with these remarks, Mason tried to rise and Bull Pepper pulled him down. "Don't mind him, Dick—he's half-shot," said Pepper. Simultaneously, different advice reached Mason's other ear. "Beat his fool head off, Mason!" said Murphy. "You lettin' Bates run your business now?" asked Jake.

Meanwhile, Bates answered his own question. "You bought the Rafter N brand, with your steer money as first payment, givin' a mortgage on both brands."

"Now, Andy —"

"Shet up!" said Andy, "I'm talkin'! Brought in six hundred more cattle to eat yourself out—and to eat the rest of us out. Wasn't satisfied with plenty. Couldn't see that dry years was sure to come. To keep reserve grass was half the game. And as if that wasn't enough, next year Harry Hall must follow your lead—and he's mort-gaged up to the hilt, too. Both of you got twice as much stock on the range as you got any right to have. Both goin' broke, and serves you right. But instead of blamin' yourselves, as you would if you was halfway decent, you go whimperin' around, blamin' us that cut our stock in two whilst you was a-doublin' yours!' "

"You goin' to stand for this?" whispered Murphy. Concurrently, Andrew Jackson Aforesaid Bates raised his voice to a bellow. "Ever since you got married, you been narratin' around that you wasn't no gun man." He unbuckled his pistol belt and sent his gun sliding along the floor. "Old man, says you! Stand up, you skunk, and take it!"

Mason sprung up. They met with a thud of heavy blows, give-and-take. Pepper tried to shove between, expostulating. Murphy and Jake dragged him away. "Let 'em fight it out!" snarled Jake.

There was no science. Neither man tried to guard, duck, side-step or avoid a blow in any way. They grunted and puffed, surging this way or that, as one or the other reeled back from a lucky hit. Severe punishment; Mason's nose was spurting blood, and Aforesaid's left eye was closed. Just as Mason felt a chair at his legs, a short arm jab clipped his chin; he toppled backward with a crash of splintered chair. He scrambled up and came back with a rush, head down, both arms swinging. A blow caught Bates squarely on the ear; he went down, rolled over, got to his feet undismayed; they stood toe to toe and slugged savagely. The front door opened, someone shouted, a dozen men rushed into the saloon and bore the combatants apart. Words, questions, answers, defiances—Kendricks and Lispenard dragged Mason through the door, protesting. After some persuasion, Mr. Bates also was led away for repairs by Evans and Early, visiting cowmen from Saragossa; and behind them, delighted Tripoli made animated comment; a pleasing tumult which subsided only at a thoughtful suggestion from the House.

"I been expectin' something like this," said Spinal Maginnis, as they lined up to the bar. "Beer for mine, Tham. Them Little World waddies is sure waspy. I'm s'posed to be representing there for the Diamond A, you know. But they wouldn't let me lift a finger. Said their cattle couldn't stand it to be moved one extra foot, and the Diamond A stuff would have to take their chances with the rest. Reckon they're right, at that. Well, it was funny. See and Johnny Hopper and old Aforesaid was walking stifflegged around Hall and Mason. Red Murray, he was swelled up at Hopper, 'cause Turnabout Spring was dryin' up on him, and he'd bought that from Hopper. And all hands sore at Bud Faulkner, on account of his bunch of mares, them broomtails wearing out the range worse than three times the same amount of cattle. They was sure due for a bust-up. This little fuss was only the beginning, I reckon. Well, here's how!"

"I hope they do get to fightin' amongst themselves," growled Murphy, putting down his glass. "Mighty uppity, overbearin' bunch. They've been runnin' it over Tripoli something fierce. Hope they all go broke. Old man Bates, in particular. He's one all-round thoroughbred this-and-that!"

As Murphy brought out the last crushing word, Bull Pepper, standing next to him, hooked his toe behind Murphy's heel and snapped his left arm smartly so that the edge of his open hand struck fair on Murphy's Adam's apple. Murphy went down, gasping. First he clutched at his throat and then he reached for his gun. Pepper pounced down, caught a foot by heel and toe and wrenched violently. Murphy flopped on his face with a yell, his gun exploded harmlessly. Pepper bent the captive leg up at right angles for greater purchase and rolled his victim this way and that. Murphy yelled with pain; dropping his gun. Pepper kicked the gun aside and pounced again. Stooping, he grabbed a twisting handful, right and left, from bulging fullness of flannel shirt at Murphy's hips; and so, stooping and straddling over the fallen, lurched onward and upward with one smooth and lusty heave. The shirt peeled over Murphy's head, pinioning his arms. Pepper twisted the tails together beyond the clawing arms, dragged his victim to the discarded gun, and spoke his mind.

"I don't agree with you," he said. He lifted up his eyes from that noisy bundle then for a slow survey of his audience. No one seemed contrary minded. He looked down again at his squirming bundle, shook it vigorously, and stepped upon it with a heavy foot. "Be quiet now, or I'll sqush you!" The bundle became quiet, and Pepper spoke to it in a sedate voice, kindly and explanatory. "Now, brother, it's like this. Bates has never been overly pleasant with me. Barely civil. But I think he's a good man for all that, and not what you said. Be that as it may, it is not a nice thing to be glad because any kind of a man is losing his cattle in a drought. No. Anybody got a string?"

Curses and threats came muffled from the bundle. "Did you hear me?" said Pepper sharply. He swooped down and took up

Murphy's gun from the floor. "String is what I want. That silk hand-kerchief of Tham's will do nicely. Give it to Jake, Tham. You, Jake! You come here! You and Murphy both laid hands on me when I wanted to stop this fight. I'm declarin' myself right now. I don't like to be manhandled by any two men on earth. Step careful, Jake—you're walkin' on eggs! Now, you take two half-hitches around Mr. Murphy's shirt-tails with that handkerchief. Pull 'em tight! Pull 'em tight, I said! Do you maybe want me to bend this gun over your haid? That's better. Now, Murphy, get outside and let Tripoli have a look. You and Joe Gandy, you been struttin' around right smart, lately, admirin' yourselves as the local heroes. I don't like it. Peace is what I want—peace and quiet. What's that, Murphy? Shoot me? Not with this gun you won't. This gun is mine."

He laid a large hand to Murphy's back and propelled him through the door.

"You surely aren't tryin' to bust them collar buttons loose, are you? No, no—you wouldn't do that, and me askin' you not to. You go on home, now."

As Pepper turned to cross the plaza, Spinal Maginnis fell in step beside him. "Goin' my way, Mr. Pepper?"

The pacifist stopped short. "I am not," he said with decision. "And I don' know which way you're going, either."

Spinal rubbed his chin, with a meditative eye on the retreating Murphy.

"I don't know that I ever saw a man sacked up before," he said slowly. "Is them tactics your own get-up, or just a habit?"

Mr. Murphy's progress was beginning to excite comment. Men appeared in the deserted plaza, with hard unfeeling laughter. A head peered tentatively from Jake's door. Mr. Pepper frowned. The head disappeared.

The hostility faded from Mr. Pepper's eyes, to be succeeded by an expression of slow puzzlement. He turned to Maginnis and his tones were friendly. "Overlooking any ill-considered peevishness of mine, dear sir and mister—you put your little hand in mine and come along with me."

He led the way to a shaded and solitary bench; he lit a cigarette and surveyed the suddenly populous plaza with a discontented eye; he clasped his knees and contemplated his foot without enthusiasm.

"Well?" said Maginnis at last.

"Not at all," said Pepper. "No, sir. This Dick Mason, he's supposed to have brains, ain't he? And the Aforesaid Andy Jackson Bates, he has the name of being an experienced person? Wise old birds, both of 'em?"

"I've heard rumors to that effect," admitted Maginnis.

"Well, they don't act like it," said Pepper. "Tripoli and the cowmen, they've been all crosswise since Heck was a pup. But Mason, he opens up and lays it all before us. Lookin' for sympathy? I don't guess. Then old man Bates gets on the peck like that, exposin' his most secret thoughts to a cold and callous world. It don't make sense. And that fight they pulled off! I've seen school kids do more damage."

"I didn't see the fight," said Maginnis.

"No, you didn't. You and all these here visiting waddies just happened in opportunely—just in time to stop it." Pepper regarded his companion with cold suspicion. "Eddy Early, Lafe and Cole and you, and this man Evans—that's some several old-timers turnin' up in Tripoli—and not one of you been here before in ten years. I tell you, Mr. Spinal Maginnis, Esquire, horsethief and liar—I've been thinkin'!"

"You mustn't do that, feller," said Spinal anxiously. "You'll strain yourself. You plumb alarm me. You don't act nowise like any town man, anyhow. Not to me."

"I was out of town once," admitted Pepper. "Some years ago, that was."

"Curious," said Spinal. "Once a man has put in some few years tryin' to outguess and outthink pinto ponies and longhorned steers, he ain't fooled much by the cunnin' devices of his fellow humans. But I'm no sheriff or anything like that—so don't you get uneasy in your mind. On the other hand, if you really insist on thinking—Has it got to be a habit with you?"

"Yes. Can't break myself of it. But I won't say a word. Go on with your pranks, whatever they are. But I'm sure sorry for somebody."

"Well, then," said Spinal, "as a favor to me—if them thoughts of yours begin to bother your head, why, when you feel real talkative, just save it up and say it to me, won't you?"

"I'll do that," said Pepper. "You rest easy."

ii

Because the thrusting mesa was high and bare, with no over-looking hills or shelter of trees for attacking Apaches, men built a walled town there, shouldering above the green valley; a station and a resting place on the long road to Chihuahua. England fought France in Spain that year, and so these founders gave to their desert strong-hold the name of Talavera.

When England and France fought Russia in the Crimea, Tala-vera dreaded the Apaches no more, and young trees grew on the high mesa, cherished by far-brought water of a brave new ditch. A generation later the mesa was a riot of far-seen greenery; not Talavera now, but Tripoli, for its threefold citizenship: the farmers, the miner folk from the hills, who built homes there as a protest against the glaring desert, and the prosperous gentry from sweltering San Lucas, the county-seat. These last built spaciously; a summer suburb, highest, farthest from the river, latest and up-to-date. De-traction knew this suburb as Lawville.

Where the highest *acequia* curved and clung to enfold the last possible inch of winnings, the wide windows of Yellowhouse peered through the dark luxurious shade of Yellowhouse Yards. The wind-ing *acequia* made here a frontier; one pace beyond, the golden desert held undisputed sway. Generous and gracious, Yellowhouse Yards; but Pickett Boone had not designed them. They had been made his by due process of law. Pickett Boone was the "slickest" lawyer of San Lucas.

"Wildest game ever pulled off in Tripoli," said Joe Gandy. It was the morning after the sacking up of Blinker Murphy. A warmish morning; Gandy was glad for the cool shadows of Yellowhouse Yards.

"Big money?"

"O man! And the way they played it! Dog-everlasting-gone it, Mr. Boone, I watched 'em raise and tilt one pot till I was dizzy— and when it comes to a showdown, Eddie Early had Big and Little Casino, Cole Ralston had Fifteen-Six, Yancey had Pinochle, and old Aforesaid had High, Low, Jack and the game. Yessir; three of 'em stood pat, and bet their fool heads off; and that old mule of a Spinal

Maginnis saw it through and raked the pot with just two spindlin'
little pair, tens up. I never did see the beat."

Pickett Boone considered leisurely. A film came over his pale
eyes. "And they put the boots to Bates?"

"Stuck him from start to finish. They was all winners except
him and Spinal. About the first peep o' day, Bates pushes back his
chair. 'Thankin' you for your kind attention,' he says, 'This number concludes the evenin's entertainment.' Then he calls for the tab
and gives Jake a check for twenty-eight hundred."

"You seem to be bearing up under the loss pretty well," said
Boone. He eyed his informant reflectively. "You're chief deputy
and willing to be sheriff. But someway you've never made much
of a hit with Bates and the Mundo Chico crowd."

Gandy scowled. "After what Bull Pepper's tender heart made
him do to Murphy, I dasn't say I'm glad old Bates shot his wad. Bull
Pepper here or Bull Pepper there, I'm now declaring myself that
I wish I might ha' grabbed a piece of that. I can't see where it helps
Tripoli any to have all that good dough carried off to Magdalena
and Salamanca and Deming. Jake set in with 'em at first—and set
right out again. Lost more than the kitty totted up to all night.
They sure was hittin' 'em high."

"Well, what's the matter with Lithpin Tham? I've heard Tham
was lucky at cards."

"Some of them visiting brothers must have heard that same
thing," said Joe moodily. "Tham sort of hinted he might try a whirl,
and them three Salamanca guys just dropped their cards and craned
their necks and stared at Tham till it was plumb painful. Tham
blushed. Yes, he did. No, sir, them waddies was all set to skin Bates,
I reckon, and they wasn't wishful for any help a-tall. They looked
real hostile. 'Twasn't any place for a gentleman."

"It is the custom of all banks," said Lawyer Boone reflectively,
"to give out no information concerning their clients. But—" His
voice trailed to silence.

"I got you," said the deputy. "But a lame man can always get
enough wood for a crutch? So you know just about how much
Aforesaid has left—is that it?"

"How little," Boone made the correction with tranquillity.

"I'm thinking the whole Little World bunch is about due to
bust up," said Joe jubilantly.

"He always wanted that Little World country, Pickett Boone did," said Pickett Boone. "Mason's only chance to pay Pickett was to get the Bates to tide him over. Pickett was afraid of that. That's off, after him and Bates beating each other up. To make it sure and safe, Bates blows his roll at poker. Good enough. The banks have loaned money to the cowmen up to the limit, what with the drought and the bottom fallen out of prices. So Mason can't get any more money from any bank. And he can't sell any steers, the shape they're in now. Pickett's got him," said Pickett, with a fine relish. "He'll get Hall too. More than that, he'll get old Bates, himself, if the dry weather holds out."

"But if the drought lasts long enough, don't you stand to lose?" Gandy eyed the money-lender curiously. "As you say yourself, the banks don't think a mortgage on cattle covers the risk when it doesn't rain."

Pickett Boone smiled silkily. "My mortgages cover all risks." Then his lips tightened, his pale eyes were hot with hate, his voice snarled in his throat. "Even if I lose it—I'll break that insolent bunch. Mighty high-headed, they are—but I'll see the lot of 'em cringe yet!"

"They've stuck together, hand-in-glove, till now," said Joe eagerly. "And Mr. Charlie See, with that bunch to back him, he's been cuttin' quite a swath. But they're all crossways and quarrelin' right now—and if the drought keeps up they'll be worse. Once they split," said Joe Gandy, "you and me can get some of our own back."

"Hark!" said Pickett Boone. "Who's coming?"

A clatter of feet, faint and far, then closer, near and clear; a horse's feet, pacing merrily; on the curving driveway Mr. Aforesaid Bates rode under an archway of pecan trees. An ear was swollen, an eye was green and yellow, but Mr. Bates rode jauntily and the uninjured eye was unabashed and benign.

"A fine morning, sir. Get off." said lawyer Boone. "This is an unexpected pleasure."

"The morning is all you claim for it," said Aforesaid Bates, dismounting. "But the pleasure is—all yours. For Andy Bates, it is business that brings him here."

"Say, I'll go," said Gandy.

"Keep your seat, Joe. Stay where you are. Whenever I've got any business that needs hiding I want the neighbors to know all about it. 'It's like this, Mr. Boone, I gave a little party last night and so I thought I might as well come over and sign on the dotted line."

"You thought—what?"

"I want to borrow some money of you. I gotta buy hay and corn and what not, hire a mess of hands and try to pull my cattle through."

"Money," said Pickett Boone austerely, "is tight."

"Oh, don't be professional," said Bates. "And you needn't frown. I get you. Why, I never heard of money that wasn't tight."

"Why don't you go to the bank?"

"The bank wouldn't loan me one measly dollar," said Bates, "and well you know it. If it would only rain, now, it would be different. Too risky. That's just like me. Kindhearted. Sparing you the trouble of saying all this, just to save time. Because I've got to get a wiggle."

"If it is too risky for the banks it is too risky for me."

"Whither," said Bates dreamily, "whither are we drifting? Of course it's risky for you. You know it and I know it. What a lot of fool talk! Think I've been vaccinated with a phonograph needle? You've been yearnin' for my ranch since Heck was a pup. That's another thing we both know. I'm betting you don't get it. Halfway House and the brand, I'll bet, against four thousand with interest, three years 12 per cent. Call it a mortgage, of course, but it's a bet and you know it. I'm gambling with you."

"The security is hardly sufficient," said Boone icily. "I might consider three thousand for, say, two years. Your cattle may all die."

"Right. Move up one girl. If it doesn't rain," said Aforesaid Bates, with high serenity, "those cattle are not worth one thin dime. And if the cattle go I can't pay. Surest thing you know. But the ranch will be right there—and you'll lend me four thousand on that ranch and your chance on any cattle toughing through, and you'll loan it to me for three years, or not at all. No—and I don't make out any note for five thousand and take four thousand, either. You just save your breath, mister. You'll gamble on my terms, or not at all."

"You assume a most unusual attitude for a would-be borrower," observed the lawyer acidly. His eyes were smoldering.

"Yes, and you are a most mighty unusual will-be lender, too. What do you want me to do? Soft-soap you? Tell you a hard-luck story? You've been wanting my scalp, Mister Man. Here's your chance to take it—and you dassent let it pass. I see it in your hard old ugly eye. You want me to borrow this money, you think I can't pay it back, and you think Halfway House is as good as yours, right now. You wouldn't miss the chance for a thousand round hard dollars laid right in your grimy clutch. So all you have to do is offer one more objection—or cough, or raise your eyebrow—and I'm off to sell the ranch to Jastrow. I dare you to wait another minute," said this remarkable borrower, rising. "For I am going—going—"

"Sit down," snapped the lawyer. "I'll make out the mortgage. You are an insolent, bullying, overbearing old man. You'll get your money and I'll get your ranch. Of course, under the circumstances, if you do not keep your day you will hardly expect an extension!"

"Listen to the gipsy's warning," said Mr. Bates earnestly. "You'll never own one square foot of my ranch! Now don't say I didn't tell you. You do all your gloatin' now while the gloatin' is good."

The three rode together to the nearest notary public; the papers were made out and signed; the Aforesaid Bates took his check and departed, whistling. Gandy and Boone paced soberly back to Yellowhouse Yards.

"Mr. Andrew Jackson Aforesaid Bates—the old smart Aleck!" sneered Pickett Boone. "Yah! He's crossed me for ten years and now, by the Lord Harry, I've got him in the bag with Hall and Mason! Patience does it."

Gandy lowered his voice. "We can ease the strain on your patience a little. More ways than one. You know Bates has strung a drift fence across the canyon above Silver Spring? Yes? That's illegal. He's got a right smart of grass in the roughs up there, fenced off so nobody's cattle but his can get to it. If somebody would swear out a complaint, it would be my duty as deputy sheriff to see that fence come down. Then everybody's cattle could get at that fenced grass—"

The lawyer's malicious joy broke out in a startling sound of creaking rusty laughter.

"That would start more trouble, sure! We'll have to make you the next sheriff, Joe. Count on me."

Joe's eyes narrowed. He tapped the lawyer's knee with a strong forefinger: he turned his hand upside down and beckoned with that same finger. "Count *to* me! Cash money, right in my horny hand. Sheriff sounds fine—but you don't have all the say. I've got more ideas, and I need money. Do I get it?"

"If they're good ones."

"They're good and they're cheap. Not too cheap. I name the price. How do I know you'll pay me? Easy. If you don't, I'll tip your game. Sure. That fence now. Uncle Sam's Land Office lets out a roar, old Aforesaid knows it's my duty to take it down. Lovely. D'ye suppose I could make that complaint myself and get away with it? Not much. That old geezer is one salty citizen. And if it comes to his ears that it was you that set up the Land Office—do you see? Oh, you'll pay me a fair price for my brains, Mr. Boone. I'm not losing any sleep about that. We understand each other."

The lawyer peered under drooping lids. "We may safely assume as much," he said gently. "Now those other ideas of yours?"

"What do you think Bates is going to do with that money you lent him? Buy alfalfa with it—cottonseed meal, maybe—that's what. So will the other guys, so far as their money goes—all except Charlie See, with his thirty-six square miles of fenced pasture to fall back on —and Echo Mountain behind that. He doesn't need any hay. Well, you've got plenty money. You go buy up all the alfalfa stacks in the upper end of the valley. You can get it for ten—twelve dollars a ton, if you go about it quietly. Then you soak 'em good. They've got to have it. Farther down the valley, the price will go up to match, once they hear of your antics. Nowhere else to get it, except baled hay shipped in. You know what that costs, and you squeeze 'em accordin'. Same way with work. They'll need teams and teamsters. You run up the price. Them ideas good, hey? Worth good money?"

"They are. You'll get it."

The deputy surveyed his fellow crook with some perplexity. "I swear, I don't see how you do it," he grumbled. "Fifty men hereabouts with more brains in their old boots than you ever had—and they're hustlin' hard to keep alive, while you've got it stacked up in bales."

"I keep money on hand," said the lawyer softly. "Cash money. And when these brainy men need cash money—"

"You needn't finish," said Joe gloomily. "You take advantage of their necessity and pay a thief's price. Funny thing, too. You're on the grab, all right. Money is your god, they say. But you're risking a big loss in your attempt to grab off the Little World range—big risks. And, mister, you're taking long chances when you go up against that Little World bunch—quite aside from money. Get 'em exasperated or annoyed, there isn't one of the lot but is liable to pat you on the head with a post-maul."

The lawyer raised his sullen eyes. "I can pay for my fancies," he said in a small quiet voice. "If it suits my whim to lose money in order to break these birds, I know how to make more. These high-minded gentlemen have been mighty scornful to a certain sly old fox we know of. They owe me for years of insult, spoken and unspoken." He had never looked so much the man as in this sincerity of anger. "Their pride, their brains, their guns!" he cried. "Well, I can buy brains, and I can buy guns, and I'll bring their pride to the dust!"

Gandy threw back his hat and ran his hand through his sandy hair in troubled thought; he eyed his patron with frank and sudden distaste. "My brains, now—they ain't so much. Bates or Charlie See—to go no further—can give me cards and spades. Mason, maybe—I dunno. But I've got just brains enough that you can't hire my gun to go up against that bunch—not even when they're splitting up amongst themselves. You listen to me. Here's a few words that's worth money to hear, and I don't charge you one cent. Listen! *Those . . . birds . . . don't . . . care . . . whether . . . school . . . keeps . . . or . . . not!*—Yessir, my red head is only fair to middlin', but I know that much. Moreover, and in addition thereunto, my dear sir and esteemed employer, those same poor brains enable me to read your mind like coarse print. Yessir. I can and will tell you exactly the very identical thought you now think you think. Bet you money, and leave it to you. You're thinkin' maybe I'll never be sheriff, after all. . . . H'm? . . . No answer. Well, that's goin' to cost you money. That ain't all, either. Just for that, I'm goin' to tell you something I didn't know myself till just now. Oh, you're not the only one who can afford himself luxuries. Listen what I learned." He held his head up and laughed. "That Little World outfit have done me dirt and rubbed it in; and as for me, I am con-siderable of a rascal." He checked himself and wrinkled his brow in some puzzlement. "A scoundrel, maybe; a sorry rascal at best. But never so sorry as when I help a poisonous old spider like you to rig a snare for them hardshells. So the price of ideas has gone up. Doubled."

"Another idea? You'll get your price—if I use it," said the lawyer in the same small, passionless voice.

"What part of your steer crop do you expect to be in shape to sell?" demanded the vendor of ideas.

"Twenty-five per cent. More, if it should rain soon."

"One in four. Your range is better than theirs and your stock in better shape. And you expect to get, for a yearling steer strong enough to stand shipping?"

"Ten dollars. Maybe twelve."

"Here's what you do. There won't be many buyers. You go off somewhere and subsidize you a buyer. Fix him; sell him your bunch, best shape of any around here, for eight dollars or ten. Sell 'em publicly. That will knock the bottom out and put the finishing touches on the Little World people."

"Well, that's splendid," said Boone jubilantly. "That's fine! In reality, I will get my eleven or twelve a head, minus what it costs to fix the buyer."

"Well—not quite," said Gandy. "You really want to figure on paying me enough to keep me contented and happy! What do you care? You can afford to pay for your fancies."

iii

No smoke came from the chimney. Dryford yard was packed and hard, no fresh tracks showed there or in the road from the gate, no answer came to his call. Hens clucked and scratched beneath the apple trees and their broods were plump and vigorous. The door was unlocked. The stove was cold; a thin film of dust spread evenly on shelf and table, chairs and stove.

"Up on the flats, tryin' to save his cows," said Hob. "Thought so. Up against it plenty, cowmen are." Unsaddling, he saw a man on foot coming through the fenced fields to Dryford. Hobby met him at the bars. The newcomer was an ancient Mexican, small and withered and wrinkled, who now doffed a shapeless sombrero with a flourish. "*Buenos dias, caballero!*" he said.

"*Buenos dias, señor.* My name is Hobby Lull, and I'm a friend of Johnny's."

"Oh, *si, si!* I haf hear El Señor Juan spik of you—oh, manee time. Of Garfiel'—no?"

"That's the place. And where's Johnny? Up on the flat?"

"Oh, *si!* Three months ago. You are to come to my little house, plizz, and I weel tell you, while I mek supper. I am to tak care here of for El Señor Johnny, while the young man are gone to help this pipple of Mundo Chico. *Ah, que malo suerte!* Ver' bad luck! for thoss, and they are good pipple—*muy simpatico.* Put the saddle, plizz, and come. Een my house ees milk, eggs, fire, alfalfa for your horse —all theengs. Here is ver' sad—lonlee."

"So Johnny has quit the valley three months ago?" said Hobby on the way.

"Oh, yes! Before that we are to help him cut out the top from all these cottonwoods on the reevir, up beyond the farms. Hees cows they eat the leaf, the little small branch, the mistletoe, the bark. Eeet ees not enough. So we are to breeng slow thoss cows with the small calf—oh, veree slow!—and put heem een our pastures, a few here, a few there—and we old ones, we feed them the alfalfa hay from the stack. The pasture, he ees not enough. But eet ees best that they eat not much of thees green alfalfa, onlee when eet ees ver' es-short."

"Yes, I know. So as not to bloat them. I noticed a mess of cows and calves in the pastures, as I came in. And up on the flat, are their cattle dyin' much?"

"*Pero no, hombre.* Myself, I am old. I do not go—but Zenobio he say no. Some—the old cows, is die—but not so manee. Veree theen, he say, veree poor, but not to die—onlee some."

"I don't understand it," said Hobby. "Drought is a heap worse here than anywhere else. Fifty miles each way, last fall, we had quite some little rain—but not here. Tomorrow, I'll go look see how come."

Tomorrow found Hobby breaking his fast by firelight and well on his way by the first flush of day. He toiled up the deep of the draw and came to the level plain with the sun. Early as he was, another was before him. Far to the south a horseman rode along the rim, heading towards him. Hobby dismounted to wait. This might be Johnny Hopper. But as he drew near Hobby knew the burly chest and bull neck, Pepper of Tripoli, "Bull" Pepper. Garfield was far from Tripoli, but in New Mexico, generally speaking, everyone knew everybody. Hobby sat cross-legged in the sand and looked up; Pepper leaned on the saddlehorn and looked down. "Picnic?"

"Hunting for Hopper, Bates—any of the bunch."

"So'm I. Let's ride. It's going to be a scorcher."

The sun rode high and hot as they came to Halfway House. The plain shimmered white and bare, the grass was gnawed to a stubble of bare roots, the bushes stripped bare; a glare of gray dust was thick about them and billowed heavily under shuffling feet. They rode through a dead and soundless world, the far-off ranges were dwindled and dim, the heat rose quivering in the windless air, and white bones beside the trail told the bitter story of drought.

"Ain't this simply hell?" croaked Pepper. "And where's the cattle? Must be a little grass further out, for I haven't seen one cow yet today. Come to think of it, I didn't see but most mighty few dead ones either—considerin'."

"That's it, I guess. They've hazed 'em all away from here. Hey, by Jove! Not all of 'em! Look there!" Hobby reined in his horse and pointed. Halfway House lay before them, a splotch of greenery at the south horn of Selden Hill; far beyond and high above, up and up again, a blur of red and white moved on the granite ribs of the of the mountain. Far and high; but they saw a twinkling of sun on steel, and a thin tapping came steadily to their ears, echoborne from crowning cliffs; tap—tap—tap, steady and small.

"Axes!" said Pepper. "They're chopping something. I know—*sotol!* Heard about it in Arizona. Chopping *sotol* to feed the cattle. C'me on, cowboy—we're goin' to learn something."

There were no cattle in the water pens. They watered their horses, they rode up the Silver Spring trail, steep and hard. Where once the *sotol* bush had made an army here, their lances shining in the sun, a thousand and ten thousand, the bouldered slope was matted and strewn with the thorn-edged saber-shaped outer leaves of the *sotol*, covering and half-covering those fallen lances.

"Think of that, now! They cleaned off every *sotol* on this hill, like a mowing machine in grass. Fed the fleshy heart to the cows—and chopped off sixteen hundred million outside leaves to get at the hearts." Pepper groaned in sympathy. "Gosh, what a lot of work! They're almost to the top of the mountain, too. If it don't rain pretty quick, they're going to run out of fodder. Here, let's tie our horses and climb up."

"Where I stayed last night," said Hobby, "the old Mexican said the young men were working up here. I see now what they were doing. Reckon there's a axe going in every draw and hill-slope." Turning, twisting, they clambered painfully up the rocky steep and came breathless to the scene of action. The cattle, that once would run on sight, were all too tame now, crowding close upon their sometime enemies in their eagerness for their iron rations; struggling greedily for the last fleshy and succulent leaves. Poor and thin, they were, rough coated, and pot-bellied, but far from feeble; they now regarded the intruders with some impatience, as delaying the proceedings. The axemen were two: Mr. Aforesaid Bates, Mr. Richard Mason. Mr. Bates' ear was still far from normal and the bruise beneath his misused eye was now a sickly green; while Mr. Mason wore a new knob on his jaw, a cut on his chin and a purple bruise across his cheek. Both were in undershirts, and the undershirts were soaked with sweat; both beamed a simple and unaffected welcome to the newcomers.

"Here you are!" said Dick, gaily and extended his axe.

Pepper glowered, his face dark with suspicion. He shook a slow forefinger at them. "Bates, I never was plumb crazy about you. There's times when you act just like you was somebody—and I don't like it. All the same, there's something goin' on that ain't noways fittin' and proper. Friend or no friend, I rode out here to wise you up. And now I've got half a mind to ride back without tellin' you. What do you think you're doin', anyhow?"

"Drawing checks," answered Bates. "Checks on the First Bank of Selden Hill." He waved his hand largely. "Mighty good thing we had a deposit here too."

"You know damn well what I mean. What was the idea of pulling that fake fight, huh?"

"Why, Mr. Pepper!" said Mason in a small, shocked voice. "I do hope you didn't think Andy and me was fightin'? Why, that was just our daily dozen. We been tryin' to bring the cattle up by hand since early in May . . . like this. So we felt like we needed exercise—not to get soft, there in town. Must be you've never seen us when we was really fighting."

"Here, I want to say some talk," said Bull firmly. "That's the trouble with you old men, you want the center of the stage all the time. Information is what I want. Where's your cows and calves?

There's none here. Where's your mares? We didn't see a track. How's Charlie See making it? Where's Johnny Hopper? Who, why, when, where? The Bates eye, the Mason face—how come? Tell it to me."

"I stepped on my face," said Dick Mason. "The rest is a long story."

"We serve two meals a day," said Bates. "Early as we can and late as we can—dodgin' the sun as much as possible. Cows never get enough, but when their ribs begin to crack we stop chopping. Then they go down to drink in the middle of the day, and come back up for supper. Don't have to drive 'em. Just as far as they can hear an axe they totter to it."

"After this," said Mason, "we're never goin' to work cattle that old-fashioned way again—roundups and all that. When we want to take 'em somewhere, we'll call 'em. Maybe we can just tell 'em where to go. That is," he added, "if it ever rains any more."

"And you're feeding little bunches like this all around the mountain?" said Pepper.

"Correct. We brought up two-three wagonloads of axes and Mexicans and grindstones," said Bates. "We tried to give the cattle to the Mexicans and have them pay us wages, but they wouldn't stand for it. Yessir, all along Selden Hill and Checkerboard, for thirty-five miles, you can behold little pastoral scenes like this, any-where there's a hillside of *sotol*. They burn the thorns off prickly-pears, too, and feed them, as they come to 'em. Them old days of rope and spur is done departed. See and Hopper and Red—them nice young fellows with blistered hands and achin' backs—it was right comical. Tell you while we stir up dinner—and that's after we get those dogies fed. No beef. Not a thing fit to kill. Even the deer are tough and stringy. But you first, Mr. Pepper—you was sayin' you was uneasy in your mind, if any. Spill it."

"You and Hopper bought up a lot of alfalfa down in the valley, didn't you?"

"Yes. That was for all of us. Several stacks."

"Well, Pickett Boone he went snoopin' around and found that out. From Serafino how much you paid. Ten dollars. Cash? No. Written contract or word of mouth? Just a promise. Boone says he'll pay more and pay cash. Twelve dollars! No. Thirteen? Fourteen? No, says Serafino, mighty sorrowful—word of a *caballero*. A trade is a trade. Same way at Zenobio's. But old José Maria fell for it, and Boone bought his hay, over your head, at fourteen. Mateo's too. Isn't that a regular greaser trick?"

"I'd call it a regular Pickett Boone trick, myself. Pickett Boone ought to have his adenoids removed," said Mason, with a trace of acrimony. "He reminds me of a rainy day in a goat shed."

"Well, Boone he's fixin' to bleed you proper. He sends out his strikers right and left, and he's contracted for just about all the hay in this end of the valley—cut and uncut. I'll tell a man! All down in black and white. Pickett Boone, he don't trust no Mexican."

Bates sighed. "That's all right, then. Myself, I think them Mexicans are pretty good *gente*. They sure followed instructions. Kept mum as mice, too."

"What!" said Bull Pepper.

"Yes," said Bates. "To feed what cows and calves we got under fence at Dryford, we really wanted some of that hay. What Boone didn't buy, and a couple of loads we hauled up here to my place. But for all the other ranches except mine, it's a heap easier to haul baled hay from Deming on a level road, than to drag uphill through sand from the valley. So we told the Mexicans what not to say, and how. Made a pool. Mexicans furnished the hay and we furnished Boone. The difference between ten a ton and what Boone pays— close on to four hundred tons, be the same more or less—why, we split it even, half to the Mexicans, half to us."

"Give me that axe," said Pepper.

iv

"The time to take care of cattle durin' a drought," said Aforesaid Bates sagely, "is to begin while it is raining hard."

A curving cliff made shelter of deep shade over Silver Spring. Hobby and Mason washed dishes by the dying fire; Bull Pepper sat petulant on a boulder, and lanced delicately under fresh blisters on his hands; Bates sprawled happily against a bed roll, and smoked a cob pipe; luxurious, tranquil and benign.

"We wasn't quite as forehanded as that," said Bates, "but we done pretty well. First off, Charlie See had his big pasture, knee-high in untouched grass, and everybody cussing him. Cuss words is just little noises in the air. They didn't hurt Charlie none—and the grass was there when needed. Then I built a drift fence across the box and kept everything out of what grass there is in the rough country above here. So I had me a pasture of my own. Plenty rocks and cliffs, some grass and right smart of browse. So far, so good. Then last year it didn't rain much, so See and Hopper and me, we shipped off all our old stuff for what we could get. We even went so far as to name it to the other boys that they might do the same." He paused to knock out his pipe.

"Do you know, boys," said Mason, "that old coot has to bring that up, no matter what he's talking about? Every time. Name it to us? I'll say he did. 'Sell off the old cows and low-grades—keep the young vigorous stuff.'—Lord, how many times I've heard that!"

"And did you sell?" asked Hobby.

"No, I didn't. But Bates, he told us so. He admits it."

"Order having been restored," said Bates, "I will proceed. No snow last winter, no grass this spring. It never rains here from March to July, of course; and along about the middle of April we began to get dubious would it rain in July. So we made a pool. Likewise, we took steps, plenty copious. High time, too. Lots of the old ones was dyin' on us even then."

"Just like he told us they would," said Mason, and winked.

Bates ignored the interruption. "First of all, we rounded up all the broomtailed mares—about four hundred all told. Most of 'em was Bud Faulkner's, but none of us was plumb innocent. We chartered Headlight, sobered him up, give him some certified checks and a couple of Mex boys and headed him for Old Mexico with the mares.

"By then the cow stuff was weak and pitiful. We couldn't have even a shadow of a roundup—but we did what was never seen before in open country. We set up a chuck wagon, a water wagon, one hay wagon and two when needful and a wagon to haul calves in— and by gravy, we worked the whole range with wagons. We had two horses apiece, we fed 'em corn, and we fed hay when we had to; and we moved the cows with calves—takin' along any others that was about to lay 'em down. When we came to a bunch, they'd string out. The strongest would walk off, and then we'd ease what was left to the nearest hospital. We made a pool, you understand. Not mine, yours or his. We took care of the stock that needed it most, strays and all. Why, there was some of Picket Boone's stuff out here, and they got exactly the same lay that ours did—no more, no less.

"We tailed 'em up. I'm leavin' out the pitiful part—the starving, staggering and bawling of 'em, and the question their eyes asked of us. Heartbreakin', them eyes of theirs. I reckon they caught on mighty early that we was doin' our damnedest for 'em, and that we was their one and only chance. A lot of 'em died. It was bad.

"We shoved about two hundred of the strongest cows and calves in the roughs above here, in that pasture I fenced off. They've stripped this end bare as a bone now, and moved up to Hospital Springs. We took the very weakest down to the river. Scattered them out with Johnny's Mexican neighbors. And we had to haul baled hay to feed that bunch to keep 'em alive while we moved 'em. But the great heft of 'em, starving stuff, we threw into Charlie See's pasture. Everybody's, anybody's. Charlie didn't have a head of his own in there, except according to their need."

"That was white of Charlie See—it sure was," said Pepper, staring thoughtfully across the sunburned plain below them. "And he was the most obstreperous of the whole objectionable bunch, too. Hmn! I begin to think you fellows make a strong outfit."

"One for all and all for one—that sort of blitherin' junk," said Mason cheerfully. "Men and brothers, fellow citizens, gentlemen and boys—you ought to have seen that work. In two months we didn't rope a cow or trot a horse. We never moved a cow out of a walk, a creeping walk. We never moved a cow one foot in the wrong direction. We moved 'em late in the evenin', on into the night, early in the morning; we spoke to 'em politely and we held sunshades over 'em all day. We never slept, and we ate beans, flies, dust, patent food and salt pork. I ate through four miles of sidemeat and never struck a shoulder or a ham. And concernin' Charlie See's pasture—that you was makin' eyes about, Mr. Pepper—I've heard some loose talk that *if* it rained, and *if* we pulled through, and *if* we was lousy with money three or four years from now, and if we felt good-natured and Charlie had been keepin' in his place in the meantime, and we hadn't changed our minds or got religion, we might do this and that to make it up to Charlie. But," said Mr. Mason loftily, "I don't take no stock in such, myself. Talk's cheap."

"And who was the master mind?" asked Hobby. "Who got this up? You, Uncle Andy?"

"Why, no," said Bates, "I didn't. Charlie See took the lead, naturally, when he threw open his pasture to all hands. We made a pool, I tell you. Combined all our resources. Them that had brains, they put in brains, and those that didn't, they put in what they had. Mason had a mess of old wagons. They come in handy, too. Hopper, he thought of working his Mexican friends for pasture. Hall, he studied up our little speculation in hay; Red thought it would be a bright idea to have Bud Faulkner's mares hie them hence, and Bud, he showed us what an axe would do to *sotol* bush. I'm comin' to that."

"I had some extra harness, too," said Mason meekly. "Coming down to facts, the auditor was my idea, too. That's what I said—auditor. Remember Sam Girdlestone, that was searchin' for oil last year? Well, he come back visiting, and found us in a fix. We put him to work. He keeps track of all costs, and credits us with whatever we put in, cash, credit, work, wagons, or wisdom. We give him a percentage on our losses. He does other little chores—tails up cows, runs the pump and hunts water, chops up a few hundred *sotols* betweentimes. But his main job is posting up the account books—at night while we relax. Likely lad, Sam. Aside from that," said Mr. Mason, "Andy is a pernicious old liar, and well he knows it. Charlie See has got a little sense in his own name—I'll admit that. The rest of us have just enough brains to keep a stiff upper lip, and that lets us out. Andy Bates is the man. We may some of us dig up a bolt or two in a pinch—but old Andy Bates is the man that makes the machine and keeps it oiled. F'rinstance, Henry Hall broke out into prophecy that Boone wouldn't miss nary chance to do us dirt on the alfalfa—but it was Aforesaid that rigged the deadfall accordin'. Bud Faulkner was feeding *sotol*, a head and a half to a cow and a half, in a day and a half. So Bates gets him a pencil and a tally book, ciphers two-three days till his pencil wore to a stub and announces that if so many *sotol* hearts a day—running in size from a big cabbage head up to a big stove—would keep so many cows alive so many days, then several more *sotol* heads would keep several thousand head till it rained, if any. We saw this, after he explained it to us, and we hired all the Mexicans north of a given point. That's the way it went. You tell 'em, Andy. It's a sad story."

"Cows, calves and stretcher cases attended to," said Bates, "we taken a long look. Way out on the desert west of Turnabout, there's tall grass yet. Tall hay—cured on the stem. It's clear away from all water holes but ours, and too far from ours for any but the ablest. We left them huskies be, right where they was. I'll say they was determined characters. Surreptitious and unbeknownst to them, while they'd gone back to grass, we edged the other cattle easy into the hills and began givin' 'em first aid with *sotol*. June, July and now August most gone—and the sun shinin' in the daytime. Tedious. Only when it would cloud up, it would be a heap worse. Look like it was goin' to rain pitchforks—but nary a drop ever dropped. Gentlemen, it has been plumb ree-diculous! We haven't lost many cattle, considerin'. We've kept our stock, we've kept our lips in the position indicated by friend Mason, of Deep Well; and we've kept our sorrows to ourselves."

"Except when desirable to air them?" hinted Pepper. "In Jake's place, for example? With a purpose, perhaps?"

"Except when desirable. But we've lost most of our calf crop, most of next year's calf crop, our credit is all shot, and what cash we have can't be squandered paying old bills—because we need it to buy what we can't get charged. See? And no one knows how long it will take the *sotol* to make a stand again for 'next time'."

"There ain't going to be no next time," said Mason. "Me and Hall is goin' to keep our cattle sold off, like you said. Or was it you that advised against overstocking? I think you did. We got men chopping *sotol* on every hill and men cooking for 'em in every canyon, and another man sharpening axes on a grindstone, men hauling water to the cooks, men hauling hay to the men who haul water to the cooks, and a man hauling axle grease to the men who haul the hay to the men who haul water to the cooks. Three thousand head we're feedin' *sotol* to. Oh, my back, my back!"

"It seems to me," said Bates, "that I did mention somethin' of the kind. That brings the story to date. That's why I wrote to you, Hobby. You haven't been at Garfield long, your credit's good. We want to ease out all the steers that can put one foot in front of another, and get you to wheedle 'em along to Garfield, gradual, place 'em around amongst the Mexican's pastures, where they'll get a little alfalfa, watch 'em that they don't bloat, buy hay for 'em as needed—on jawbone—and get 'em shaped up for late sales, if any. If the drought breaks, we need all the money we can get. If it stays dry, we need all the money there is. That's the lay. If there should happen to be any steer from a brand that isn't mortgaged, you'll have a claim on him to make you safe. Are you game?"

"You know it," said Hob.

"A very fine scheme," said Bull Pepper approvingly. "But like all best-laid plans, it has a weak point. And I don't see why it shouldn't go a-gley as you, Billy bedam please on that one point."

"Yes?" said Aforesaid encouragingly. "Tell it to us."

"I'm the weak point," said Pepper. "I've thought seriously of shooting Red Murray in the back—some dark night, when I'd be perfectly safe, of course. Charlie See, too—worse'n Red. Most obnoxious young squirt I ever see, Charlie is. Hall and Hopper give me the pip, Faulkner sets my teeth on edge. And as for you two, yourselves—if you will excuse me for being personal?"

"Yes, yes—go on!"

"Even for you old geezers, my knees are not calloused from offering up petitions in your behalf."

"Oh, we know all that," said Aforesaid reassuringly. "But how does the application come in?"

"Tripoli, now," urged Pepper. "You have ill-wishers in Tripoli. But no one comes up here even in good seasons. Tripoli thinks you are chousing each other's cattle, cat-and-dogging all over the shop. Tripoli doesn't know of any of these very interesting steps you have taken—not even that you have driven your mares away. Tripoli doesn't dream that you are in a fair way to pull through if unmolested, or you'd sure be molested a-plenty. Just for sample, if Tripoli storekeepers, or San Lucas storekeepers, where you owed big bills—if they owed big money to one of your ill-wishers, and if they received instructions to demand immediate payment—see? Just begin with that, and then let your fancy lead you where you will. Now that you gentlemen have opened up your souls and showed me the works, what's to hinder me from hiking down and giving the show away?"

"You don't understand," said Bates patiently. "If you had been that kind of a man, we wouldn't have said a word. See?"

"I see," said Pepper. "And you haven't made any mistake, either. If my saddle could talk, I'd burn it. I'll be one to help Lull with your steers—and by the Lord Harry, I'll lend you what money I've got to tide you over."

"Why, that's fine, Bull, and we thank you. Glad to have you plod along with the drive, but we won't need any money. Because," said Bates, "I have already—uh—effected a loan. The best is, I've got three years to pay it in. Boone was very kind."

"You old gray wolf. I sensed it, sort of—and yet I could hardly believe it. I sensed it. You gymnasticked around and made Pickett Boone think you and Mason were on the prod; you went through the motions of goin' broke at poker, so you could trick him into lending you money—virtually extendin' Mason's mortgage. For, of course, that's what you got it for. Dear, oh dear! Ho—ho—ho! I hope to be among those present when they hang you!"

"Had to have it," said Aforesaid modestly. "Mason's mortgage is due directly. We aim to pay Hall's mortgage with our steer money, and when mine falls due, maybe someone will pay that. Lots can happen in three years."

"Give me that axe," said Pepper. "I'm working with the Little World now."

Red-faced and sweating, Andy Bates became aware that some-one hailed him from the trail below. He shouldered his axe and zigzagged down the hill.

"That's Joe Gandy," said Bates to Bates. "Gee whiz, I wonder if someone is sueing me already? They have to sue. Can't spare any money now." To the deputy he said, when they met, "Hullo, Joe! What's your will?"

"Sorry, Mr. Bates—but it has been reported to the Land Office that you're fencing in government land, and they wrote up for me to investigate. Made me deputy U. S. marshal pro tem. Sorry—but I have to do my duty."

"Yes, I know," said Bates, without enthusiasm. "That fence, now? I did build a fence, seems like. Let me see now—what did I do with that fence? Oh yes—I know!" His face brightened, he radi-ated cheerfulness. "I took it down again. You ride up and see. You'll find a quarter of a mile still standing across the canyon at Silver Spring. That's on my patented land—so you be damn sure you shut the gate when you go through. Beyond my land, you'll find the fence down, quite a ways anyhow. Wire rolled up and everything. If you find any trees tangled together or rocks piled up, you have my permission to untangle and unpile, if the whim strikes you. Away to your duty with you! I'll wait here till you come back."

With a black look for the old man, Gandy spurred up the trail. It was an hour later when he came back.

"Well?" said Bates, from beneath a stunted cedar.

"The fence is down, as you said—some of it."

"I knew that. What I want to know is, did you shut that gate?"

Gandy's face flamed to the hair-edge. He shook a hand at his tormentor, a threatening index finger extended. "You saved up that grass, turned your cattle in to eat it up, and then took the fence down."

"If such were the case," inquired Bates mildly, "exactly what in the hot hereafter do you propose to do about it? Don't shake your finger at me. I won't have it. Careful, fellow, you'll have a fit if you don't cool off. But you're wrong, all wrong. Somebody told me that fence was illegal, I remember. So I hot-footed up there and yanked her down. You see," said Bates meekly, "I figured some meddlesome skunk would come snoopin' and pryin' around, and I judged it would be best if I beat him to it. That's one of the best things I do—beating 'em to it."

"You insolent old fool!" bawled Gandy. "Have you got a gun?"

Bates stared. "Why, son," he said beamingly, "I wear my gun only when I go in swimming. No need to stand on ceremony with me—not at any time. Be sure I'm awake, and then go ahead."

Gandy pulled himself together with an effort, breathing hard. "You stubborn fool," he said thickly, "if it wasn't for your old gray beard I'd stomp you right into the ground."

Bates smiled benevolently. "Give up the gun idea, have you? That's good. As to the other proposition, it's like this. I got chores on hand, as you see." He waved his hand at the hillside, where fifty cows awaited his return to resume breakfast. "Feedin' my cows. It would hinder me terrible to be stomped into the ground right now. But I'll tell you what I'll do. Either it will rain or it won't. If it don't rain, my poor corpse will be found somewhere beside a *sotol*, still grasping an axe handle in my—in his—I mean, in its cold dead hands. In that case, all bets is off. But if it ever rains, I'm goin' to heave a long sigh, and a strong sigh and a sigh altogether. Then I'm goin' to sleep maybe a month. And then I'm goin' down to Tripoli and shave my old gray beard off. When you meet up with me, and I'm wearin' a slick face, you begin stomping that face, right off. Bear it in mind. Be off on your duties, now. I've got no more time to waste on you. Hump yourself, you redheaded son of Satan, or I'll heave this axe at you."

V

Strained, haggard and grim, August burned to a close in a dumb terror of silence. September, with days unchanging, flaming, intolerable, desperate: last and irretrievable ruin hovered visible over the forlorn and glaring levels. Twice and again clouds banked black against the hills with lightning flash and thunder, only to melt away and leave the parched land to despair. The equinox was near at hand. With no warning, night came down on misery and morning rose in mist. The mist thickened, stirred to slow vague wheelings, vast and doubtful, at the breath of imperceptible winds; halted, hesitated, drifted; trembled at last to a warm thin rain, silent and still and needle-fine. The mist lifted to low clouds, that fine rain grew to a brisk shower, the shower swelled to a steady downpour; earth and beast and man rejoiced together. Black and low and level, clouds banked from hill to hill, the night fell black and vast, and morning broke in bitter storm. All day it held in windy shrieking uproar, failed through the night to a low driving rain, with gusty splashes and lulls between. Then followed two sunless days and starless nights, checkered with shower and slack. The sun-cracked levels soaked and swelled. Runoff started in the hills, dry cañons changed in turn to rivulets, to torrents, to roaring floods, where boulders ground together in a mighty diapason; and all the air was vibrant with the sound of many waters. The springs were filled and choked, trails were gullied and hillside roads were torn. The fifth day saw blue patches of the sky. But the drought was broken; the brave earth put forth blade and shoot and shaft again.

Dim in the central desert lies a rain-made "lake"—so-called. Its life is but brief weeks or months at best; five years in ten it is not filled at all. Because of that, because it is far from living water, because the deepest well, as yet, has found no water here, the grama grasses are still unruined, untouched save in time of heavy rains. Shallow and small, muddy, insignificant, lonely, unbeautiful; in all the world there is no "lake" so poor—and none more loved. You may guess the reason by the name. It was called *Providencia*—three hundred years ago. Smile if you will. But if the cattle have a name for it, surely their meaning is not different from ours.

The starved life of the Little World still held the old tradition of this lonely lake. Everywhere, in long, slow, plodding strings, converging, they toiled heavily through the famished ranges to their poor land of promise and the lake of their hope.

Pickett Boone's steers were in Tripoli pens. Other small herds were held near by on the mesa, where a swift riot of wild pea-vine had grown since the rains begun. Riders from these herds were in to hear of prices. Steers were in sorry shape, buyers were scarce and shy.

John Copeland, steer-buyer, rode out slowly from the pens with Pickett Boone. They halted at a group of conversational cowmen.

"Well, boys, I've sold," said Pickett Boone. He held out his hands palm up, in deprecation. "Ten dollars. Not enough. But what can I do? I can't hold them over—nearly a thousand head."

A murmur of protest ran around the circle of riders. Some were eloquently resentful.

"Sorry, boys," said the buyer. "But we would make more if your stuff shaped so we could pay you fifteen. Your steers are a poor buy at any price. Wait a minute while I settle with Boone." He produced a large flat billbook. "Here's your check, Mr. Boone. Nine thousand, eight hundred dollars. Nine hundred and eighty steers. Correct?"

Boone fingered the check doubtfully. "Why, this is your personal check," he said.

Copeland flipped it over and indicated an endorsement with his thumb. "John Jastrow's signature. You know that—and there's Jastrow, sitting on the fence. 'S all right?"

"Oh, I guess so," said Boone.

"And here's the bill of sale, all made out," said the buyer briskly. "Here's my fountain pen. Sign up and I'll be trading with the others."

A troubled look came to Boone's eyes, but he signed after a moment's hesitation.

"Witnesses," said Copeland. "The line forms on the right. Two of you. Then we'll go over to the other fellows and talk it up together. Thanks. Let's ride."

Boone motioned Copeland to the rear. "Come down as soon as you can," he said in an undertone, "and we'll finish up."

"Huh?" said Copeland blankly.

"Pay me the balance—two dollars a head—and I'll give you my check for five hundred, as we agreed."

"My memory is shockingly poor," said Copeland, and sighed.

Boone turned pale. "Are you going to be a dirty thief and a double-crosser?"

"I wouldn't put it past me," confessed Copeland. "Mine is a low and despicable character. You'd be surprised. But I'm never crooked in the line of my profession. Among gentlemen, I believe, that is called 'the point of honor.' You may have heard of it. If I made any such agreement with you—depend upon it, I took the proposition straight to John Jastrow. I never hold out on a client."

"This is a conspiracy!" said Boone. He trembled with rage and fear.

"Prove it," advised the buyer. "Lope up and tell the boys what you framed up. I've got your bill of sale, witnessed. Go tell 'em!"

"They'd shoot me," said Boone, choking on a sob.

"That is what I think," said Copeland unfeelingly, and rode on.

A shout went up as the buyer overtook the cavalcade. "Here come the West Side boys." The newcomers were Mason and Murray, of the Little World, with young Sam Girdlestone attached.

"Hullo, Dick—Where's your herd? And where's the rest of you?"

"Howdy, boys!" said Mason. "Bates and See, they've gone on downtown. We didn't bring any steers. Prices too low.—So we hear."

"Boone sold at ten dollars," said Bill McCall. "I'll starve before I'll take that."

Mason smiled. "We won't sell, either. Not now. We aim to get more than twelve, by holding on a spell."

Boone turned savagely and reined his horse against Mason's. He dared not let these men guess that he had tried to tamper with the price. Stung for a heavy loss, but afraid to seek redress—here was one in his power, on whom he could safely vent his fury. "Your gang may not sell, but you'll sell, right now. Your time's up in a few days, and I'm going to have my money!"

"Well, you needn't shriek about it." Mason's brow was puckered in thought; he held his lower lip doubled between thumb and finger, and remembered, visibly. "That's so, I do owe you something, don't I? A mortgage? Yes, yes. To be sure. Due about October twentieth? . . . Let me see, maybe I can pay you now. Can't afford to sell at such prices."

"I get twelve dollars," declared McCall stoutly, "or my dogies trudge back home."

"Oh, I'll give you twelve," said the buyer. "Prices have gone up. I just sold that bunch again—them in the pen, for twelve dollars. To Jastrow."

"O-h-h!" A wolf's wail came from Boone's throat.

"How's that?" demanded McCall. "Thought Jastrow bought 'em in the first place?"

"Oh, no. I bought 'em in behalf of a pool."

Mason unrolled a fat wallet. "Here, Mr. Boone, let's see if I've got enough to pay you." He thumbed over checks, counting them. "Here's a lot of assorted checks—Eddy Early, Yancey, Evans—all that poker-playin' bunch. They tot up to twenty-eight hundred all told." He glanced casually at Pickett Boone. That gentleman clung shaking to the saddlehorn, narrowly observed by mystified East Siders. Mason prattled on unheeding, "And old Aforesaid, he gave me a biggish check this morning. Glad you reminded me of it, Mr. Boone."

"You know, Mr. Mason," said Copeland, "you're forgetting your steer money. Here it is. Two dollars a head. Nineteen hundred and sixty dollars. Nice profit. You might better have held out for twelve, Mr. Boone. These Little World people made a pool and bought your steers—and then sold them to Jastrow in ten minutes."

"You come on downtown after a while, Mr. Boone," said Mason. "Bring your little old mortgage and I'll fix you up. Take your time. You're looking poorly."

Sam Girdlestone and Henry Hall were riding down the pleasant street toward supper, when Sam took note of an approaching pedestrian. He had a familiar look, but Sam could not quite place him.

"Who's that, Henry?" said Sam.

Hall reined in, and shouted. "Heavens above! It's Squire Bates, and him shaved slick and clean! Hi, Aforesaid, what's the idea? You gettin' married, or something?" He leaned on the saddlehorn as Bates drew near. "Heavens above, Andy—what in the world has happened to your nose?"

"My nose?" said Bates, puzzled. He glanced down the nose in question, finding it undeniably swollen. He fingered it gingerly. "It does look funny, doesn't it?"

"Look there! What's happened?" cried Sam, in a startled voice. "That man's hurt!"

Bates turned to look. Two men came from the door of Jake's Place, supporting the staggering steps of a third man between them. The third man's arms sprawled and clutched on the escorting shoulders, his knees buckled, his feet dragged, his head drooped down upon his chest, his whole body sagged. Bates held a hand to shield his eyes and peered again. "Why, I do believe it's Joe Gandy!" he declared.

"But what's happened to him, Uncle Andy?" demanded Sam eagerly.

Bates raised clear untroubled eyes to Sam's. "I remember, now," he said. "It was Joe Gandy that hit me on this nose. . . . How it all comes back to me! . . . The Bible says when a man smites you on one cheek to turn the other, so I done that. Then I didn't have any further instructions, so I used my own judgment!"

XV. In Defense of Pat Garrett

The first version of this spirited assault upon the deification of Billy the Kid appeared in *Sunset*, July, 1927. The version here used for the first time is Rhodes 1929 revision of that original for inclusion in his never completed nonfiction book about New Mexico. In view of two recent books, the late Edwin Corle's ostensible novel, *Billy the Kid*, and Frazier Hunt's *The Tragic Days of Billy the Kid*, this defense has the same pertinence that it had in the days of Walter Noble Burns.

Students of the Lincoln County War and professional Billy-the-Kidders can pick minor flaws in Rhodes' statements of fact and undoubtedly will. What is here important is the nature of the man who wrote them.

Rhodes and his father, Colonel Hinman Rhodes, had fought the same faction—the Santa Fé Ring—at the Mescalero Reservation in 1890-92 that *Alias* Bonney had fought in Lincoln County. Rhodes had faced Pat Garrett during the trouble experienced by Oliver Milton Lee over the disappearance of Colonel Albert J. Fountain in the White Sands. Yet, Rhodes could not, would not, let what he regarded as commercial defamation of a brave man and a loyal enemy go unheeded. By Rhodes' definition: "A loyal enemy won't tell any lies about you he doesn't believe himself."

IF YOU HAVE NOT READ *The Saga of Billy the Kid,* by Walter Noble Burns, I hope you do. The book is written with color, fire and charm; the tragic events it chronicles are of surpassing interest. If it were a novel, it would command my unstinted praise. As history, it is misleading.

The facts given, are, *in all essentials,* correct, or as nearly so as is humanly possible. There are inaccuracies and omissions, as is natural; there are harsh judgings of Sheriff Brady on the one side, and of Justice of the Peace Wilson on the other. Both of these men, as I believe, thought that they were doing the right thing under difficult circumstances. Obviously, one of these men must have been wrong. It was a mistake that Mr. Burns, when he was collecting material for this book, did not see Sheriff Brady's son and hear their way of it. John Brady, one of those sons, was elected Sheriff of Lincoln County last fall—and he was elected because Lincoln County thought that *The Saga* gave a raw deal to the murdered Sheriff. To be shot from ambush, in the back and without warning, by four men lying in wait behind an adobe wall—to have the assassins glorified and the victim blamed—that seemed hardly fair. My own idea has always been that whiskey murdered Tunstall; and that whiskey, later, caused the murder of Baker and Morton, themselves the murderers of Tunstall. Again Mr. Burns made his choice—as was his right—between two or twenty versions of the same incident, when such choosing was his only possible course. No one man had ever known the whole truth about the Lincoln County War. But I see no ground for the charge of any willful or conscious mis-statement of facts. My quarrel is with the interpretation of the facts, the twisting of the facts, the emphasis only on such facts as serve a partisan purpose, the swift gliding over facts that would defeat that purpose, the admixture of credible evidence with rumor, surmise, opinion, innuendo, and maudlin sentimentality. It is these things which made the book a skillful bit of special pleading. *The Saga* is no history. It is a movie: Billy the Kid is the hero—and Pat Garrett is the "heavy."

It is my hard task to point out the faults of a book that I admire. A thankless task; the taunt of "sour grapes" is inevitable. Nevertheless, let us hope that my only motive in writing these lines is to protest against the glaring injustice done to the memory of Pat Garrett.

Let us make one point clear beyond the possibility of misunderstanding. As regards the Lincoln County War, my sympathies, without reservation, are with the McSween—Tunstall—Chisum side. I believe, with Mr. Burns, "that Murphy's cause was basically wrong and McSween's basically right: that Murphy was an unscrupulous dictator." I make a small reservation that McSween was a lawyer and that McSween was a man—and thus had two chances to make small mistakes of his own. I believe with Mr. Burns that Tunstall was foully murdered; that the first and greatest guilt of that bloody struggle lies at the doors of Murphy, Riley, Dolan—and their backers. I have lived in that country all my life, and I am now living on Mrs. McSween's old ranch. My friends were all of the McSween party and my enemies were all on the other side. Here is no case of quarreling partisans—so far as Mr. Burns and myself are partisans—and that is pretty far—we are partisans on the same side.

But Mr. Burns was not writing the story of the Lincoln County War. He was writing the life of Billy the Kid; and his enthusiasm carried him away. Billy the Kid was to be the hero and whoever opposed Billy the Kid had to go to the wall. His avowed purpose was to portray Billy the Kid as "the idol of the Southwest." It would be quite as true to portray Hindenburg as the idol of Europe. I have not one word to say to belittle this dead man. It is impossible for his enemies to deny admiration to his courage and daring; it is impossible for his friends to deny that such deeds as the killing of Jimmy Carlyle and of Bernstein were beyond defense or forgiveness. But Billy the Kid has never been the idol of the Southwest. He was the idol of a faction: later, the idol of the muddle-minded. So far as friend and foe are united to make a hero of any one man connected with the Lincoln County War, their praise is for the indomitable Buckshot Roberts, who died at Blazer's Mill: and his story was told by an enemy—a knightly enemy—George Coe.

A word as to the Coes. They have always been known as good men. They were so known even by their enemies, and even during the war. George Coe tried to get Roberts to surrender, but he would not. He thought he would be killed if he surrendered, like Baker and Morton. The Coes would not have allowed him to be injured—even if the others had any desire to kill him, which I doubt. And there were men on the other side as good as Frank and George Coe. This was a war of little mercy: but at the Fritz ranch, when McNab was killed and Saunders wounded, when George Coe's horse was killed and he surrendered—then the victors took Saunders to the hospital at Ft. Stanton and offered Coe no other molestation than to keep him prisoner over night. The next day, Wallace Ollinger turned him loose, even giving him a gun to defend himself if attacked. It is pleasant to remember these things.

The Lincoln County War started with the murder of Tunstall, February 13, 1878. It ended with the fight at Lincoln in July. It began with wrong and outrage, and it was carried on with outrage and wrong—by both sides, but not by all men on both sides. That is the way with wars. *The Saga* records, fairly enough, the murder of Baker, Morton and McClosky, the killing of Dick Brewer and Buckshot Roberts, the ambushing of Brady and Hindman, the killing of Frank McNab; and the final battle, in which Crawford and Beckwith were killed on the Murphy side, Morris, Semora and Romero on the other. These were fighting men, and they were killed. But for the death of McSween, who had tried to check the fighting from the first, an avowed non-combatant and unarmed, there is no other word than murder. And I agree with Mr. Burns that Colonel Dudley's part was the shabbiest chapter of that heart-breaking history.

It is generally thought that the Lincoln County War was a conflict between opposing gangs of desperadoes from Texas. Nothing could be farther from the truth. There were Texans on both sides, but of the principals only John Chisum was from Texas, and he took little part in the war. Tunstall was English, McSween from Prince Edward Island. Murphy, Dolan, Riley—don't ask. (Murphy came from California during the Civil War.) Billy the Kid was born in New York City, Frank Baker came from Syracuse, Morton from Virginia. What is true is this: that, after four months of civil war and eighteen months of anarchy, the men who finally brought the law to the Pecos were, without exception, men from Texas; and all but one from a little town—Tascosa. (You will not find Tascosa on any map.) I, who am not a Texan, may say this with good grace. And it is here that I part company from Mr. Burns. His man-hunters —"Poe was a veteran man-hunter." "Frank Stewart, with a posse of man-trailers in the employ of a cattleman's association." Frederick Bechdolt, writing of the same men, called them "The Law Bringers." I string along with Bechdolt.

This was submitted to Jim East, the only surviving member of the posse that captured Billy the Kid at Tivan Arroyo. His comment is illuminating. He says:

"After all these years I do not believe that the posse were thinking very much about bringing the law to the Pecos. We were common, every day, thirty dollars a month cowboys. We were sent out to recover stolen cattle and to get the thieves, if possible. We got some."

There you have the west. It was all in the day's work. The outlaws got the headlines and the working man got the outlaws. On every ranch you would find some one who would go up against any man in the world, if the affair in hand was part of his proper business.

There was no fighting after the July battle in Lincoln. Murphy died in Santa Fe before McSween was killed. General Lew Wallace became Governor in August. He "made proclamation of amnesty to all who had taken part in the war, except those under indictment for crime, on the understanding that they would lay down their arms." For the most part, the fighting men went back to work gladly enough. From first to last it had been a sorry business. Billy the Kid, Charlie Bowdre, Tom O'Folliard, with five others, declined to quit. They made the deliberate choice to live by the trade of outlawry.

Governor Wallace came to Lincoln and arranged an interview with Billy the Kid. He made a definite offer. If Billy would surrender and stand trial on whatever charges might be brought against him, the Governor made this promise: "If you are convicted, I will pardon you and set you free." The offer was rejected.

On this page (157) Mr. Burns begins the equivocation, the juggling with words and with facts, the reckless appeal to sentimentality, which mars the book from here on. He says:

"Two years later, Billy, in the shadow of the gallows, recalled the Governor's promise of a pardon. But the pardon did not come and his friendship turned to hate."

This is to make mockery of words. That promise was made on the condition that Billy would quit the outlaw's life, surrender and stand trial. Billy refused to quit. In the interval he had been

309

chief of an outlaw band, variously reinforced, that had committed numberless outrages, living by open rapine and plunder. "The subsequent reign of terror Billy the Kid had set up," is the phrase Mr. Burns uses to describe the situation. In the meanwhile Billy had himself murdered two unarmed men. The killing of John Bernstein on August 5 was senseless and unprovoked, without motive or result. I refer you to page 159 of *The Saga*. "Jimmy Carlyle came unarmed, an envoy, under trust." The Kid shot him down; and if you will consult *The Saga* (pages 202–204) you will find that this murder, like the murder of Bernstein, was, as I said before, beyond defense or forgiveness.

In view of these facts, the implied charge—that Governor Wallace made to the Kid a promise which was not kept—is an insult to your intelligence. Governor Wallace was the first sacrifice made by Mr. Burns to his theory that Billy the Kid was a victim hounded to his grave by persecutors.

Because he had fought stubbornly for the better cause; because his courage and determination were indisputable; because he was no fiend incarnate, but only a man hardly circumstanced, desperate and driven, a man who had got off on the wrong foot; because of the intolerable injustice of Colonel Dudley's action at Lincoln; above all, because of his extreme youth, Billy took with him, in the beginnings of his outlawry the good wishes and sympathy of many. Baker and Morton were murdered after they had surrendered under the promise of protection? Well—yes; but they were murderers themselves, richly deserving death. Brady and Hindman were shot from ambush? True; but in war ambush is allowable, even desirable. And this was war, no less.

But Jimmy Carlyle was no murderer, nor was Bernstein at war. The number of Billy's well-wishers fell away. Also, the gang stole cattle from the South and sold in the North, stole from the North and sold in the South. That was a heavy tax on friendship.

Then came the election of Pat Garrett as sheriff of Lincoln, and with it, the appalling discovery that the new sheriff intended to observe his oath of office. Here was a pretty howdy-do.

Reading *The Saga* you will get the impression that Billy got shabby treatment all along the line, that it was inconsiderate of the sheriff to molest him; that it was unsportsmanlike to search for him in his own country, right where he lived, among his devoted adherents; and that it was positively discourteous and unfair that Garrett did not let Billy kill him at the last. That is the impression; but if you will turn back you will find, to your bewilderment, that when Mr. Burns *speaks for himself*—as on pages 288–301 and in the last paragraph of the book—his summing-up gives Garrett, in full measure, all that was ever claimed for him by his friends. How, then, do we get our first impression of the book?

It is because innuendo, insinuation, malice, hatred, rumor and sentimentality have been given space in these pages. It is because the witnesses on Billy's side have been allowed to speak for themselves, with human warmth and passion, so that the book is saturated with their prejudices and their emotions. Nor is this all. Idle gossip, imaginary conversations, reconstructed conversations, are given in full, with the happiest results—and purely synthetic Mexicans are reported in full (page 65), giving forceful expression to the composite voice of rumor. The other side is given in summary only. Not once does any man speak in his own words. Moreover, Mr. Burns has employed lawyer's tricks, cheap and shop-worn, unworthy of him. Let me specify a few of these. There are others.

When Jimmy Carlyle was killed—an envoy, unarmed—he had gone in to confer with Billy the Kid, and Greathouse had volunteered to be a hostage.

Notice, please, that White Oaks had taken no part in the Lincoln County War. This was a private affair between White Oaks and Billy's crowd, stirred up without provocation, by Billy himself—after a few drinks. Says Mr. Burns (page 204):

> . . . Badly wounded, Carlyle struck the ground on his hands and knees and began to crawl away. The Kid's second shot stretched him out on the snow. At once the posse opened a bombardment of the house with their rifles. . . . During the excitement Greathouse escaped. . . . Greathouse showed great wisdom in flight. Carlyle's death inflamed the possemen, who, regarding Greathouse in a measure responsible, would have murdered him doubtless in retaliation.

No man has any right to say that. Since the posse did not kill Greathouse at the moment of Carlyle's murder, it is a contradiction of all human experience to think that they would kill him later, in cold blood. Nor would any sane man have held Greathouse responsible—no, not even if he had killed Greathouse as per agreement. For all Billy knew or cared, he was shooting Greathouse when he shot Carlyle. To hold Greathouse responsible for that shot is to charge that he planned his own death.

After Billy's escape from Lincoln jail, (pages 270–73) George Graham, asleep in Dedrick's barn at White Oaks, heard, by chance, that Billy the Kid was in Ft. Sumner. The next day he told John Poe what he had heard. Poe did not believe it. Like everyone else, he thought Billy had gone to Old Mexico. But he gave Graham a dollar. "Go buy yourself a drink," said Joe. And Mr. Burns says:

"So Billy the Kid was betrayed for a silver dollar."

Graham owed no allegiance to Billy: he had not been trusted: he owed his knowledge to chance. Where there has been no trust, there is no question of betrayal. "Betrayed" is exactly on a par with "man-hunters," and shows a touching confusion of mind.

(Pages 205–206) "Christmas Eve in Ft. Sumner. Good cheer and happiness in the air. . . . Christmas trees hung with gifts and lighted with wax tapers." (Several hundred words of this) . . . "So on this night when all the world was happy, a bare room of the old hospital was filled with heavily armed men."

These armed men were the brutal "man-hunters" coming "on this night when all the world was happy."—The horrid creatures. Only, it wasn't Christmas Eve. It was December 21. Just between ourselves, if it had been Christmas, Fourth of July, Easter and Mother's Day, all rolled into one—what of it?

As I said before, there are more than a few inaccuracies in this book. To point them out would have been easy; this is my own country and these are my people. I have not sought to discredit the book by exploiting little slips, such as are natural for a man to make in good faith. The points are not vital, and it is mighty easy to make small mistakes in writing of a strange country and a vanished generation. But this Christmas Eve thing is just a jury-trap.

Another jury-trap. We see the tears of Charlie Bowdre's wife when Charlie is brought home to her, dead. We hear the screaming and weeping of frantic women when Billy died at Maxwell's Ranch —Does Mr. Burns think there was no grieving for Jimmy Carlyle? That there were no tears when Brady died?

The charges against Pat Garrett's integrity and manhood, his courage and his honor, are not made by Mr. Burns. They are made indirectly, through the words of his chosen witnesses. Mr. Burns himself, in his summing up and final judgment, discredits most of these charges: but his book has given the widest currency to them. These charges are not new. I have been hearing them nearly fifty years. I heard them afresh only yesterday, from a man who insisted to the last that it was most unchivalrous of Garrett that he did not let Billy the Kid kill him. Mr. Burns has reported, most skillfully, all that hate and fear and invincible stupidity has said against Pat Garrett.

(1) Garrett and Billy the Kid were friends—or at least they were on friendly terms.

That is true. Garrett came to Ft. Sumner in January, 1878, just before the Lincoln County War started. He punched cattle for Pete Maxwell for six months, taking no part in the war. After the fall of 1878, Billy made his headquarters in Ft. Sumner, making long business trips to the Panhandle. Between those trips, Billy and Garrett were on friendly terms. I have been friendly with a number of outlaws myself. It is a wise thing to be that way. Besides that—don't be shocked—outlaws are more interesting than in-laws. And they are better house-mates. You and I can afford to be grouchy, if we feel that way. But the outlaw knows the day will come when a few kind words for him will come in handy for his memory; so he is a pleasant man around camp. And—let me whisper—an outlaw is a human being, just like any one else.

No man could have been elected sheriff of Lincoln County who had not been friends with some of the outlaws, on one side or the other. Mr. Burns is hard to please. Sheriff Brady is condemned because, as it is charged, he favored his friends: Sheriff Garrett is damned by the same people because he did not let friendship interfere with his duty. One sheriff or the other should have his good name restored.

(2) Pat Garrett was made sheriff to kill Billy the Kid.

Consider that Pat Garrett *captured* Billy the Kid—and protected him from a mob that wanted to lynch him. You see for yourself that this charge is not true: a charge which no man should repeat. Garrett was greatly pleased that he captured Billy the Kid, and that he did not have to kill him. Also he was pleased that he was not killed himself. After Billy's escape, Garrett was forced to kill or be killed.

(Parenthetically: *all things considered.* I do not think Billy the Kid should have been hanged. Not unless they hanged several hundreds of the others at the same time.)

(3) Garrett was made sheriff to break up Billy the Kid's gang. That is true. He did it. In like manner, we send for the firemen to put out a fire.

(4) Garrett sought Billy relentlessly. Worse than that, Garrett persistently hunted for him where he was—in his own country, where his picked fighting men were at his back, where non-combatants were his friends, who aided him and warned him and who hampered his pursuers. At this time (1880), Lincoln County, with a population of twenty-five hundred, was nearly half as large as Pennsylvania. Garrett searched it. He searched beyond its borders. He found his man. I would call that being a good sheriff.

This charge cannot be denied.

(5) Garrett was afraid of Billy the Kid. See charge (4) above. I know no other answer to make. In fact, I hardly know what they mean who make this charge. There was no rock or ridge or tree but death might lurk behind it for Garrett. The pursued has every advantage over the pursuer, if he wishes to wait in ambush. In one sense, no man ever lived who would not, with reason, fear Billy the Kid, if they were in Garrett's place. In another sense there has been no race, no place and no age which has not produced men fearless enough to keep on with the job—as Garrett did.

It has never occurred to me to think that Billy the Kid was "afraid" of Pat Garrett. Yet here is Billy's own testimony. He was talking to Capt. J. C. Lea; and, as was his cheerful habit, he spoke of Garrett as "the old woman."

"The old woman will get me, some of these days," said Billy. He gave his nose a tweak. "You'll see. I can shoot a heap quicker than she can—and I don't often miss. But the old woman, she never misses."

But Billy kept on his way, none the less. To my notion, the brave man is not the man who does not know fear. He is the man who sees the danger and meets it. If these two were not brave, I have long misused the word. And the best of their respective followers were as brave as the leaders.

If Mr. Burns thinks that he has called no witness to testify for Pat Garrett, he is the more misled. When Billy the Kid surrendered to Pat Garrett at Tivan Arroyo, he showed what he thought of Pat Garrett's integrity and Pat Garrett's word. No oath is needed to make that testimony credible. Billy the Kid had refused to surrender when, with six of his men, he was surrounded at South Spring by a posse of some twenty men under Marion Turner. He had chosen to break through at Lincoln, when he had eleven men against sixty. Four of the party were killed, one left for dead; the others broke through. Outnumbered and surrounded, he had refused to surrender at the Greathouse Ranch. When he surrendered to Garrett, it was because he did not think there was even "one chance in a million" for even one man to break through. No matter what others say, the record shows clearly what Billy the Kid thought of Garrett as a fighting man.

(6) If the last meeting between Garrett and the Kid had been under other circumstances, the Kid would have killed Garrett.

It is quite possible. Or, again, Garrett might have killed the Kid. Or they might both have been killed. This is like arguing that Babe Ruth might have knocked a home run when he struck out.

(7) Pat Garrett killed Billy the Kid unfairly.

I do not know what people mean when they say this. Billy came, at midnight, into the dark room where Garrett sat with Pete Maxwell. He was not lying in ambush for Billy; he was not expecting him; he had come to question Maxwell. He had not wanted even to do that, because he did not expect Maxwell to tell him anything; he came because Poe insisted on it. And then Billy came, gun in hand, on his guard, alarmed at his meeting with strangers on the porch.

"Who are those men outside, Pete?" he said. And then, seeing Garrett, he backed away, saying *"Quien es?"* (Who is it?)

Garrett knew the voice. There was only one thing to do and he did it. He shot Billy through the heart. I cannot imagine any man doing otherwise: I cannot imagine any other thing to do. It is conscious falsehood to say that Garrett should have called on Billy to surrender. No man has ever said that who did not know that with the first word, either Garrett would have been killed or both would have been killed. No man who has said that has ever believed that Billy would have surrendered. The situation was not of Garrett's making; but he met it in the only possible way. *If Billy had killed Garrett, there would have been no question of blame.* It was kill or be killed.

When Billy the Kid, under sentence of death, in chains, and under guard, killed his two guards and made his escape from Lincoln jail, there was grieving for Bell who was well loved. But it never occurred to any man *to blame* Billy for killing Bell, no matter how deeply it was regretted. Billy was one man against the world; it was his life or Bell's; there was no question of blame or praise. The question was—life or death? It was the same question when Pat Garrett answered—with a bullet.

The man who wishes the event to have been otherwise, must, to be consistent, wish that thereafter Billy should have killed the next sheriff, the next, and so on to the present day. It is curious to reflect that Billy the Kid would have been the last man on earth to make for himself the babyish whimperings that have been made for him. He met the death he had expected, the death he had accepted: and he had never complained at the prospect.

In defending Pat Garrett from the malignant stupidity which, all his life long, gave him curses when he should have had honor—in defending him from a hate that will not let him rest in his grave—have I dealt harshly with Billy the Kid? I wonder if you can believe that my deepest feeling for him is pity for his hard fate? Perhaps not. But we can agree on this. He might have killed McKinney and Poe, on Maxwell's porch. He thought they were some of Maxwell's friends, and he did not shoot. He might have killed Garrett at Maxwell's bed, when he saw there a deeper darkness against the dark. He was one man alone against a world of foes; he hesitated, still thinking that this might be Maxwell's friend. Let us be glad for him—who had done so much evil—that his last thought was generous and clean and honorable.

Jungle Lovers

Jungle Lovers

Paul Theroux

HOUGHTON MIFFLIN COMPANY BOSTON

c 10 9 8 7 6 5 4 3 2

Copyright © 1971 by Paul Theroux. All rights reserved.
No part of this work may be reproduced or transmitted in
any form by any means, electronic or mechanical, including
photocopying and recording, or by any information storage or
retrieval system, without permission in writing from the publisher.

ISBN: 0-395-12107-8
Library of Congress Catalog Card Number: 70-144074
Printed in the United States of America

The author is grateful for permission to quote from the following:
"Rimbaud" by W. H. Auden, from *Collected Shorter Poems 1927–*
1957, copyright 1940 and renewed © 1968 by W. H. Auden, pub-
lished by Random House, Inc. "The Greenest Continent" by Wallace
Stevens, from *Opus Posthumous*, published in 1957 by Alfred A.
Knopf, Inc.